LABELS & LACE

YD LA MAR

ACKNOWLEDGMENTS

To my wonderful husband, who never bats an eye when I come up with crazy ideas, but instead just adds to it, making my stories come alive. My children, who tell me every day that they are proud of me.

To my beta readers. You guys are the real MVP. Thank you for sticking with me through the initial phases of my writing journey. All of your feedback has inspired me to better myself and my writing ability. Anita, Alex, Dana, Vicky, Maria, **Terri**, **Tree**, Beth, Shaddy, **Kylie**, Gloria, Sasha, and **everyone** who responded to my beta request in the dark group, and everyone else who beta read, thank you for bouncing ideas with me.

To all my readers, thank you for giving me the chance. I hope I can continue to make you guys proud.

THE FORMATION OF US

LABELS & LACE

THE FORMATION OF US

LABELS & LACE

YD LA MAR

BLURB

Banished from the reservation before the fires even died
down,
my guilt and shadows followed me.
My hands stained in blood, a friendly soul helped me get
back on my feet.
Through the lens of a friend's camera, my eyes catch the
most beautiful woman I've ever seen.
She wasn't the kind of woman who let me admire her from
afar.
Her confidence pulled me in, her strength helped break me
out of my shell.
A slice of heaven I probably didn't deserve.
When the dark stain on my soul rears its ugly head, will she
be strong enough to remain by my side? Or will she leave it
all behind like ashes in the wind?

COURTESY WARNING

This book may contain triggers for some. Triggers include but not limited to: domestic violence, violence, non con/dub con.

*** This book may contain authentic speech used by the different nationalities/ethnicities represented in this book. Some grammar usage was purposely done with broken English to continue to allow the story to flow authentically. ***

NAMES

Matunaagd Big Crow
Atsuko Kobayashi

Mohd Akmal Bin Aqli
Veronica "Vero" Hernandez

Travis Boyd

Miss Megan Miller

Tricia Smith

Alfonso Torres

Mortimer "Morty" Archambault

TRANSLATIONS

¿Qué carajo tu putas creen estas haciendo? : What the fuck do you bitches think you're doing?

Makan : Eat

Na-ahks' : The term for both grandfather and grandmother in Blackfoot

Kristin, ask and you shall receive.
Terri and Tree, without you these characters wouldn't come to life the way they did.

PROLOGUE

I can smell it before I get there. It's a scent that has burned itself into my very soul, accompanied by the feeling of dread in the pit of my stomach. *No.*

The tribe sent me to college to get a further education that would help the Casino. Software engineering was what I chose to go for. It's been over four years. Four years of not being able to watch over my mother when my father gets in these moods.

Our home on the reservation looks like a log cabin. The sight of it is homey, the feel of it is tense. A tension that prickles your spine every time you walk into it.

Walking up to the front now, I see the door is barely hanging on the hinges. *Shit.* My heart is beating out of its chest, a rhythm like war drums, as my mind is running through all the worst-case scenarios. I'm actually hoping that someone tried to rob the house and my parents are out because the other possibility makes my blood run cold. My skull starts to feel tighter and tighter the more my memories flit through my mind.

"Are you fucking cheating on me again, woman? I knew it!" With each syllable that comes out of his mouth, the scent of whiskey becomes stronger and stronger. His words start to slur together at the end.

"No, no... I was out getting some food." The way her voice shakes, the sound of her vulnerability, makes me ball up my fists. When Dad gets like this, I never know what to expect.

"You and your lies! I know you've been whoring around! Always trying to get away from me!" His hands grab at his hair and pull it out in frustration. *"What's wrong with me, huh? Am I not enough for you or something? I see the way the other men look at you!"* His voice raises in octaves with every inhale he takes. I don't even think he realizes his current state. His eyes are blood-shot, his nostrils flaring like a primal beast that's scented its prey.

"It's not like that. I haven't done anything wrong." Her voice is so soft that the sound of the slap against her cheek is sharp and makes my teeth grind. Thwack! I jump in front of my mother and shove him off her, out of instinct. The hairs on the back of my neck standing on edge in challenge. I've had enough of this! How long can my mother be his punching bag?!

I don't see the backhand until it's too late, the sharp pain making me feel like my skin is about to rip off my face. The sting and the warmth of the blood that starts to slowly dribble out the edge of my mouth, a contrast to how cold I feel inside. How can I share blood ties with this beast before me?

"Don't talk back to me. She's mine to discipline. She's only mine. She has no right to whore herself out!" The sound of my mother's sobs sears into my ears like a scar that will never heal. Each hiccup creates a fresh, jagged wound on my soul. I need to protect her.

Running through the front door, my feet grind to a halt at what I find. My heart stutters in an off rhythm, making my chest hurt.

The floor is flooded in crimson. The color is drowning out everything else around me. My mother lies face down like she's resting while my father's open-eyed stoic expression stares at me, almost *accusing* me of not being here to stop his uncontrollable transgressions. Almost as if the beast inside of him took over, and it was *my* fault I wasn't there to challenge him.

The anger I've just only learned to control now spikes to infernal levels. My mind feels tight, my throat is closed, and I can't even roar in anger. I can feel myself bare my teeth and grind down in frustration and pain. It was bound to happen. I knew it. *I knew it!* Why did I let the damn reservation convince me to leave? Damn it all!

Where are they when I need them? Did no one hear the gunshots? There's no other person here to stare into the lifeless eyes that stare back at me...but ME.

I feel like Atlas, with the weight of the world on my shoulders, about to crumble with everything that's thrown at me. My shoulders physically do fall as my knees hit the ground in defeat, slipping on the blood beneath me. Despite the lifeless corpses still within my view, the weight hasn't been removed from my shoulders. I feel betrayed. I feel like a child left out to the elements to die and wither as I watch the downfall of my family lying here in a pool of blood.

The blood that seeps into my pants is cool. How long have they been here like this? The beast within me howls in anguish and refuses to let the reservation take the home I once called mine. The reservation that has brought no saviors to the horrors inside here. No, there will be no more of this. They will remember the pain and suffering they have caused during my absence. The *absence* they created. It will all fall down to their feet, branding them as this moment has branded me.

GUILTY.

My mind is a haze as my body moves through some sort of muscle memory, leading me to the decisions my mind has not yet made. It zones out as I walk back and forth, back and forth, performing movements my mind's eye cannot see.

Dousing my emotions, dousing everything. A send off. My mother to the heavens and my father, the very pits of hell. I almost don't even recognize my own body's movements at this point. Only bits and pieces come back to me as I return to the log cabin one last time.

Standing out in the front, I feel blank. I feel numb...the nothingness of what was left to me. I *am nothing* now. With a flick of my wrist, it is done. The heat on my face brings back only a sliver of sensation to my skin, reminding me of reality, reminding me of the life that still flows through my veins. The glow surrounding me, lighting up what was kept in the dark. *It should have never been kept in the dark.*

As the flames devour the log cabin I once called home with a roar, I turn slowly to walk back to my car and drive towards the exit out of the reservation, never looking back or even glancing at the rear-view mirror.

Who I was is now gone. The betrayal of the reservation is sitting heavy in my heart. It's time I created something new from the ashes of the past.

~

I know I shouldn't be doing this after what happened with my parents. It's been a couple of weeks, but fuck, starting over was harder than I thought. My pride was what carried me over the reservations ground. But now? Where do I go from here? Where the hell do I start?

I ended up at a damn bar of all places, drinking light beer, but enough of it that I'm getting tipsy. Shit, I need to stop while I'm ahead.

My ears pick up on a masculine voice saying, "Bitch, just wait until we get home. Don't fucking give me lip out here if you know what's good for you. Just do as you're told!" Fucking hell, I can't seem to get away from bastards like my father.

I don't know what possesses me, but I follow the couple out of the bar. It's already dark outside, with other drunks hanging around, so my presence is easily hidden.

They must have parked pretty far because we've been walking for a while.

My head snaps to the woman when I see her jerky movements from struggling to run away from her husband towards an alleyway. What the fuck just happened? Fresh thoughts of my mother come back to me and how I never knew if she ever ran or tried to get away. I never knew how hard she fought.

The husband is growling like an enraged beast, with expletives spilling out of his mouth like vomit. *Just like my damn father.*

My eyes are seeing red as I catch up to him and slam him into the wall, the sound of his skull hitting the concrete making me excited to catch my prey. I'm going to make sure he never hurts another person again, especially a woman.

My fists, rage and feeling of missed justice start to inter-mix, creating a heady potion to my senses. I barely feel anything but my fist hitting something solid again and again. My eyes catch a piece of broken glass beside me and with quick movements, I shove the pointy end in and out, left and right. There's something wet and warm on my face, but I don't think I've been crying. I'm too excited and angry to cry. I've cried out all my tears already after my mother was killed. No, Father will never put his hands on her again.

When I finally realize the gentleman isn't making any moves to fight back, my hands slow down and my chest continues to heave in and out until my vision clears up.

The rank smell of the alleyway finally seeping into my nostrils over the metallic smell of blood. Something inside my palms starts to sting and I realize I've been tightly holding onto the shard of glass with a death grip. How did it even get there?

My head lifts up when a shadow looms over me. It looks like a woman, but the drinks I've had are not making me see too clearly. The rage that's leaving my system is not making me see what I should.

"I should be mad, but I'm not." The longer I stare, the more I can see her tear-streaked face with mascara running down the same path, surrounded by a halo of dark brown hair. My mother's face on the floor of our cabin flits through my mind and disappears when the woman places a gentle hand on my shoulder.

"Thank you for saving me. I didn't know how I would be able to get away. I didn't have a way out at all." She comes onto her knees next to me and moves her palm over one of my bloodstained fists, reminding me to let go of the glass.

"I'll tell them there was an altercation with a stranger and he got away. I'll describe him as someone else. Is there anything I can do to help you? You need to get out of here."

I can't believe what I'm hearing. Is this a sign? It has to be. I think...I think I just killed a man. The Queen song runs through my head at that moment, and I almost laugh. What the hell is wrong with me? Has my father's darkness tainted our bloodline? This is exactly why I needed to get away from the reservation. I couldn't be his son. I needed to break away from it all.

How can she help me? I need a damn job. I don't know where to go from here. Only a short time off the reservation and I'm already in a load of shit.

"I need to find work. I need to get on my feet."

"What do you do? I may be able to call up some friends."

I do chuckle then because we're having this damn conversation right by a dead corpse. What the hell is wrong with my life? How does it keep going from shit to shittier?

"Software engineering."

"I might actually be able to help you with that. I know someone who's been looking for more employees. He's not the best guy around, but it's honest work."

1

———————

MATUNAAGD

She keeps calling me over. I know what she wants, and it isn't IT help with her computer modem. She's given me such good reviews that the higher-ups keep putting me with her open cases. Every time I get there it's because of something trivial, for instance not plugging the power cord in.

Pulling up the company car to her neighborhood, I almost feel a sense of dread. It's always like this between us. The sad part about it is, I both enjoy it and hate it to my very core. She wants to brand herself inside of me, that's what she truly hopes to accomplish. Like the taming of the wild mustang, the domestication of a wild wolf. The more I fight, the more she latches on, trying to break me.

The houses in this neighborhood look like the typical suburban town, like the ones you see in Hollywood movies. Surrounded by mostly light-skinned faces, they watch you like a predator just entered their midst. All the homes have well-manicured lawns that almost make you scared of what's on the inside because *nothing* is this perfect. No one is this perfect. Life has thrown enough shit in my face to show me this. The veil of this neighborhood doesn't fool me.

When I pull up the car to her pristine concrete driveway and put the car in park, I throw my head back against the headrest. The firm pressure against my head grounding me. I crack my head left and right, rolling it against the headrest before letting out a loud sigh.

Shit, let's get this over with then.

Grabbing my bag of tools, I straighten my clothes as I walk towards the front door, ready with a false smile.

She opens it before I even have the chance to ring the doorbell. Standing in the doorway wearing a black silk robe with her red hair tied up in a messy knot on top of her head. To a passerby, it would just look like a woman who's comfortable at home. To me, I know the truth. I can see through her tactics.

Miss Miller is a beast on the prowl. A huntress. Or what most people call a cougar.

"What seems to be the problem today, Miss Miller?" We do this song and dance every time. The smile that graces her face makes me want to flinch back but I keep my body standing still until I'm invited in. She has plans. She always does.

She grabs the front of my shirt and pulls me in with all her strength, making sure to shut and lock the front door behind us. I drop my bag onto the ground, knowing that I won't get a word in until she allows me to.

See, Miss Miller has a specific appetite. An appetite to *dominate.*

She drags me into her bedroom, turns me around and

throws me down on my back, quickly taking off my work boots and pants. The adeptness of her fingers is borderline admirable because she does it without taking her sharp green eyes off me; commanding me to submit with a trained look. Miss Miller controls the situation as my mind starts to zone out.

It's been five years since leaving the reservation, though on my bad days it feels like just yesterday.

Driving towards the direction of the city, I'm almost off the reservation grounds when a few of the men stop me. Some of the people nearby have soot on their faces. Everyone around me has a look of grim determination.

I'm numb to it all.

When a crime is committed on the reservation, the tribe handles their own. Not that their decision matters anyway, because I'm getting out of this place one way or another. I no longer wish to be associated with a people that have essentially left my family in a pool of blood long enough for it to cool.

They banished me off the grounds despite still having grandparents there. I turned my back on them as well, head held high, the way they so easily turned their backs on me.

I gulp when Miss Miller climbs over my body to straddle my naked hips, bringing me back to the present. She opens her robe, revealing she's only wearing a corset that covers her waist. I inwardly groan because I hate that she corners me like this, but fuck if I don't sometimes love the shit she does to my dick. The thing has a mind of its own and is a bad judge of character.

She removes the hair tie I have in place, spilling my long black hair onto the sheets beneath us right before she grabs it and tilts my head to the side so she can lick up the cord of my neck, branding me. I shouldn't be letting her do this to me. It freaked me out the first time two years ago, especially because I was a damn virgin. The only short reprieve I got from her was during my month-long vacation from work. I was able to avoid her for another week after that.

I couldn't beat this woman off me with a stick, not that I would. I'm not that kind of guy. Especially after growing up with a father like mine. But some days my fingers itch to throw her body against the wall and watch it slide down with streaks of blood, just to end the misery she puts me in. The guilt over thinking that way sobers me. *I am not my father.*

Her teeth bite down over my right pec almost hard enough to break the skin before she licks it and bites again. I can handle her for the most part, but when she's in a mood like this, I wish I could do more than just 'handle' her.

Closing my eyes, trying to remove my thoughts away from the moment, I hiss in pain when she slaps my dick like she's pissed that it came here to her house like she asked it to.

A few more hard slaps and I'm about to grab her wrist when she swallows my entire dick whole into her warm, wet mouth. Fuck!

Miss Miller is the horniest forty-five-year-old woman I've ever known. It doesn't say much since I've only been with a few girls after she took what didn't belong to her. Women who were willing to fuck me because I seem like a novelty to them. They randomly propositioned me, and I was out of my mind enough to agree. I'm not great with my dating game, but I forcefully put myself out there in hopes of it helping me to remove myself from her clawed grip. But damn if she doesn't weave a tight web around me.

When her mouth starts to suction harder and her nails dig into my balls, I can't help but tense up, making her moan loudly over my straining cock. Her tongue running across the tip of the head, playing with it seductively makes me want to groan, but I swallow it back down. I'm giving her too much already. Right when I think I can't take her abuse on my dick anymore, she removes her mouth with a nip just behind the crown of the head and climbs me like a fucking fallen tree.

She spears herself with my cock and starts to circle her clit with her hands. She never lets me move. She uses me like a damn blow-up doll, a dead piece of flesh with a hard cock. The degradation is what kills me inside each and every time.

She fucks me harder and harder like she's riding a damn bull and soon enough I feel her pussy clenching my dick like it's her mouth all over again. I'm so close, but so far from my climax, it messes with my mind.

My logical brain reminds me how fucked up this whole thing is. When she's done finding pleasure, she fucking leaves me there to clean myself up, not even letting me get my own release. Sometimes when she's not looking, I let my hand quickly stroke myself against the skin of my shaft to release the pressure in the restroom while I'm 'allowed to clean up'.

It seems today is one of those days.

Once the incident that shall not be named is put behind us, I go back to the living room to pick up the bag I dropped on the way in. Today, Miss Miller thought cutting straight through the Cat 5 cable with a fucking knife will bring me to her faster. I sigh as I continue to keep my thoughts to myself, quickly remedying the problem.

I give her my mumbled goodbyes without looking her in the eyes before hightailing it out of there. When my face feels the fresh air outside, I let out another harsh breath. This woman is going to kill me. I need to do something.

When I drive through the quaint suburban town, some of the neighbors who have come out look at me with suspicion.

It doesn't matter if I'm in a company car or not. People who look like me do not usually tread around these parts. Darker skin, long black hair tied back, my cheekbones and dark eyes give away my heritage. The tattoos that peek out don't help out either, I'm sure.

Another sigh of relief comes out of me when I finally exit the town and head back to headquarters.

Walking past a couple of the co-workers, I wave at them with a false smile pretending it's just a normal day and I didn't just have a woman essentially force me into a compromised position.

Is this what I'm going to be doing for the rest of my days? I can't handle any more Miss Millers in this line of work. Thank goodness there's only been one. My soul would be sucked out and leave me just a shell of a person.

"Hey Mat, did you run into any problems with the Miller call?" Shit, if only he knew. Akmal is the only guy I allow to call me Mat, since he's probably my only close friend. Matunaagd: 'He who fights'; some days I still feel like I didn't fight enough to keep my mother alive. Coming back from Miss Miller's house, I feel like I didn't fight enough to keep her away from me.

"Nah, it was an easy fix." Akmal and I have become close since we started working at the company at the same time. He was the friendliest guy there at orientation, making it easy for me to get along with him. He's Malaysian, standing at five-feet-seven inches, his skin only a shade or two lighter than mine. We could almost pass as brothers if it wasn't for my six-feet-two inch height and broader build. In fact, many of our co-workers call him the pocket version of me, much to his dismay, since we're always hanging out together.

"If Tricia were here, you know she would have diverted

the case to someone else. She knows how much you don't like going over there."

"Yeah, thank goodness for small blessings. But she wasn't here today so I had to take care of it."

"It's been pretty slow today for me. You want to go get lunch and get out of here?"

"Yeah, that actually sounds really good." I need more fresh air to get the feeling of Miss Miller out of me.

We both clock out together and Akmal decides he'll drive us down the street today to the sandwich shop we usually frequent, Sammi's Sandwiches.

Sitting on their metal chairs outside, I think about my time working at the company. There really isn't much room for advancement. Morty's been kind enough to take me in after a call made on my behalf. Just Techs is a joke under the guise of a technical support company. We do perform tech support, but I swear there's something shady happening in the background I'm unaware of. To be honest, I really don't care. It's dragging my life and soul down at this point. That thought alone makes me feel like I'm strapped to a damn ball and chain. The thought of being forever trapped in the vicious cycle with Miss Miller makes me want to choke on my own vomit.

"Hey Akmal, have you ever thought about doing something else?"

Akmal is chewing his turkey sandwich thoughtfully before he responds. "I don't know. I guess not. I mean, I have hobbies I do on the side. Why what's up?"

What's up? I feel like my soul wants to roam, but it doesn't have a path or direction. A yearning without a destination. A lone wolf with no actual territory to call his own.

"I don't know man." I truly don't.

Our waitress comes by right as I'm just about to finish up my sandwich, shoving the last bite into my mouth.

"How was it? Was there anything else I can get you?"

I'm just swallowing my last bite when I realize she's staring at me. Is there something on my face? I try to discreetly wipe my mouth with a napkin and look away, hoping to cover the flush on my cheeks. This is pretty awkward. Why is she leaning towards me like that? I can see her just fine where she's standing. Maybe she has a sight problem or something and needs to lean in closer.

"Oh yes, I'd love a dessert to go, please." She's not even hearing Akmal, who's literally talking to her shoulder. She's just staring at me. Sheesh. I think it's time to go.

Scooting my chair back, I get up and put my cash on the table. Akmal, looking put out by her non-response, does the same.

He tries to give her a polite smile on the way out, but she continues to stare at me with a smile of her own and blinks one eyelid. Why is she winking like that? This situation makes me feel a bit strange and uncomfortable. I turn to head back to the car, with Akmal right behind me.

We head back to work and our regional manager, Morty, is informing the team that we'll be getting a new guy tomorrow.

I don't feel anything about it either way. I still don't know what I should be doing with my life, but I can't help but feel like my spirit is being pulled somewhere. Somewhere that's not here at Just Techs.

2

MAT

"Alright guys, gather around. This here is Travis Boyd; he's going to be joining our team as of today. I want you guys to show him the ropes and start taking him out on some of your cases so he can see how you guys do things in the field." Despite his speech, I've never once seen Morty go out or take anyone out in the field since I've started working here. He's always hiding in his office until the day is done. What the hell does he do in there?

"Hey Mat, I was thinking about what we were talking about the other day." Morty's voice is droning on in the background as Akmal speaks in low tones next to me.

"What's that?"

"I've always been into photography. Taking pictures as a hobby and such. I've done some freelance work but maybe I should see if I can do more with it?"

"You're farther than I am. I haven't come up with jack shit. Let me know how it goes, I'll support you, man."

"I'll support you too." I didn't even realize Tricia was standing next to us, listening to our conversation.

"Gentleman and ladies, please pay attention." Akmal and I share a sheepish glance before we stare at Morty, giving him our utmost attention.

"Alright, since you think you don't need to hear this, Travis will be following you today, Aqli." Akmal makes a face at me because he hates it when the boss says his name like that, like he's crap under his shoe.

"Yes, boss." Akmal is right. I need to find ways to use my skillset elsewhere. I need to get out of this company and away from people like Morty.

I was able to avoid Miss Miller today, thanks to Tricia handling the calls coming in. The thought of that woman puts me on pins and needles, which only adds to the way I feel about this job. The day went by smoothly without that extra case to handle.

Driving home, I feel a sense of relief wash over me. Walking through the front door of my apartment, a calm settles over my entire being. *Home sweet home.* Located on the lower level, not too far from the city, the apartment is big enough for a guy like me.

Two bedrooms, a kitchen and a bathroom. Nice and simple. Thinking of the bathroom, I start stripping down out of my uniform and tossing the clothes into the dirty hamper before stepping inside for a hot shower. The cool tile beneath my feet reinvigorates me. My hair's grown out halfway down my back, the feeling of the ends sliding against my skin. I can't seem to bring myself to cut it just yet. Am I holding onto a past that I should let go of? Thoughts of my parents drift back into my mind, and much too soon, the images are tainted in a red haze.

I punch the tile wall with a *thwack*, the throbbing in my knuckles grounding me back into the present. I'm tired of the way they still haunt me; the way my guilt still shrouds me. My hand grabs the soap, ignoring the sting, and starts to lather my upper body across the scattering of multiple colorful tattoos I've collected over time. Wanting the pain of the needle to numb the ones on the inside when it washes over me like a tidal wave.

It's probably about that time again, the time to get fresh ink. As I continue to lather and wash my hair, I start to wonder if I should just cut it all off and start over, really let the past go. *I should.*

The warmth of the shower leaves me too quickly once I'm done and toss on some boxers and shorts. Being a bachelor means I have a lot of pre-made meals in the fridge, but it suits me just fine.

Plopping myself down on the chair by my kitchen table, I open up my laptop that's been sitting there. Deciding to unwind with a little gaming, I open up the chat server while I eat my reheated meal. Chewing a few bites, I realize this is not one of my favorite Hungry Man microwave meals. I'll have to remember to never buy it again.

Akmal is already online with a few of the other guys we've grown to know from teaming up in the game. I don't even remember how I came up with my screenname tinfoil-hat, but I just stuck with it. Akmal's screen name still makes me chuckle no matter how many times I've seen it. His ode to wishing he was taller.

Shaquille.oatmeal : Hey, I got this photography gig next month at a car show.

PaniniHead : @ ima.robot, are you logging into play tonight?

Tinfoilhat : Sweet, I bet you'll kill it.

Avocadorable : Congrats!

Shaquille.oatmeal : I'm so nervous, man. I've never shot such a big crowd or event before, mostly individual or family portraits. My hands are getting sweaty just thinking about it.

Ima.robot : Yeah, let me finish up my food and I'll login real quick.

Tinfoilhat : I'm sure you'll be fine. You got talent, that's why they requested you.

Avocadorable : He's right, you'll do great.

Shaquille.oatmeal : Yeah, I guess you're right.

We continue the night chatting about stupid stuff and play some first-person shooter games until the crew starts disconnecting to end their night one at a time. It's the best way to unwind at the end of the day. Some nights we switch it up with other MMO games.

Shutting off my laptop, I walk myself to bed to lay down. The softness of the comforter envelops me in coolness before absorbing the warmth from my skin. Running my hand through my hair, I decide I *will* cut it to change things up. My hand runs across my chest and I think of what other kind of artwork I should get. Both of my pecs are completely covered, as well as one full sleeve on my left and three-quarter sleeve on my right.

My right hand grazes across my abs, and I can feel my dick twitching in response. I guess I could cover this area. My mind starts to wander as my hand reaches inside my shorts to grab my semi-hard dick and starts slowly stroking.

Shit, don't think about Miss Miller. Don't think about

Miss Miller. My dick starts to soften at the mental image of her face, and I have to physically shake my head and think of something else. The shadow of a woman enters my mind. I'd want her smaller than me. I'd want her to be the opposite of me in general because I can barely deal with myself on normal days. I can't see her face, but I can see her body just fine. The contrast of her skin against mine makes a heady potion for me. Like a forbidden flower that I crave to pluck and sully.

She's sensual. Her long black tresses flowing over her delicate shoulders make me want to run my hands through it to see if it's really as silky as it looks.

My dick starts to harden as my mind plays images of the mysterious woman disrobing, her dark perky nipples making my mouth water. Each breast is just more than a handful. Gripping my cock harder, I continue the slow and steady rhythm I have going as my mind reveals her soft pink lips slightly parting.

My mind is running through all the different scenarios we would have together. Her face is still shrouded in dark-ness, but her smile, my god, her smile lights up my fucking life. It feeds my soul with something addictive. Her full lips making promises I'm only given a glimpse to. A man like me doesn't deserve it, but fuck if I don't want to steal it.

I visualize her in a swimsuit; I visualize her in office wear with her creamy breasts overflowing and spilling out her unbuttoned white top that does nothing to hide the red bra she has underneath. She bites her bottom lip gently with her teeth and she begs so sweetly with just a look. Each scenario my mind pictures with her, is a scenario with me dominating her. The yearning to cover her with my body, to control everything that's happening between us. The magic that I have to weave for her to be under my spell.

And she would love me being selfish, taking everything from her.

When my illusion woman bends over a desk and spreads her round ass cheeks to offer herself to me, my sack tightens. My other hand roughly brings down my shorts, exposing my cock to the air as I pull back the skin of my dick with a firm grip and cum all over my abs with a groan. It takes a moment for me to slow my breathing and come back down to reality.

Damn, now I got to clean up again.

3

—————

MAT

My muscles burn with every stride I take. The pounding of my feet on the pavement, the heat rising up from what the sun has baked all day. On the days my demons take over too much of my mind, I run. As swift as the wolves in the forest, I hope to outrun the memories and feelings of guilt that drown me when I'm in too deep. I need to get lost in the motion, the wind in my face, the smell of earth around me.

My chosen path is a decent sized park nearby. Sweat drips down my face, almost making it to my eye, and I wipe it off with the back of my forearm. It glides as it mixes with the sweat that's already accumulated there as well. It's a good seventy-seven degrees Fahrenheit today, but the brutal pace I'm setting for myself is making me sweat buckets. Taking off my shirt, I wipe my whole head down and tuck it in the back pocket of my shorts.

Just two more rounds. My calves and thighs are burning, but I need the pain. I need to ground myself back to the present, back to sanity.

Finishing up my run at the far end of the park, the walk back to the apartment is my cooldown. I only brought one bottle of water with me, so I had to pace my drinking. Three quarters for the run and a quarter for the end. Finishing it off while I stand in front of my building, I go to toss the bottle in the trash can when I hear a gasp from behind me.

Turning around, one of the older ladies in my apartment building is shielding the eyes of what looks to be her teenage granddaughter. I feel my face flush as I mumble an apology before grabbing my shirt from the back and putting it back on. I'm sure she's offended by the tattoos on my back and wouldn't want her granddaughter to get ideas.

I leave the scene as quickly as I can, walking towards my apartment door. Sticking my keys into the lock, I hear something behind me. Turning to see what it is, I see a young woman who looks to be in her mid-twenties. She has a weird expression on her face.

"Is everything okay?"

She clears her throat and her voice sounds a little shaky. Maybe there's something going around?

"Um, yes. Sorry about that. I was just walking to my apartment and got distracted. You must be one of my neighbors?"

There's been an empty apartment a couple of doors down. She must be the one moving in since I don't recognize her.

"Yeah, I live in 145. You must be moving into 149? It's been empty for a while." She giggles and starts to twirl her brown hair. I'm still trying to figure out what she's laughing about when she responds.

"Yea, that's me. 149. I'm Emily, by the way."

"Mat." There's an awkward silence that follows, and I think I'm wearing out my hello, so I try to make a quick getaway.

"I need to, uh, hit the showers. It was nice meeting you." Not waiting for her to answer, I shut the door right after I walk inside. I'm not great with these pleasantries and I'm sweaty as hell. She was probably clearing her throat because I smell funky.

Stripping out of wet clothes is disgusting, but the ice-cold shower is just what I need after a hard run, like the one I just finished. Feels good to get clean and cool down. I probably shouldn't wash my hair this often, but it was sweat drenched as well. Quickly finishing up, I get out and grab the towel on the shower door.

Not bothering to put on any clothes yet, I walk around the apartment to help air dry my hair. I really should start cooking instead of eating these microwave meals, to be honest. It probably affects my workouts. Akmal and I have a guys' night tonight on my couch to catch some old Star Wars movies on the flat screen. We've both seen it already, but we still enjoy kicking it and drinking a couple of light beers.

Walking back to my bathroom, I braid my hair in front of the mirror. Staring at the empty expanse on my abs, I'm glad I made that appointment at the tattoo shop. Getting dressed in a loose t-shirt and jeans, I grab the images I printed off this morning from the printer tray.

Exiting the door, I don't see Emily or any of the other neighbors on my way to the apartment parking lot. The tattoo shop is about a twenty-minute drive from my home. Letting down the front windows of the car, I bask in the cool breeze that comes in on the drive there.

The ink shop is pretty empty today when I walk in. Good,

the less people the better. I'm not the greatest in big and boisterous crowds. This shop is known for groups of rowdy drunk kids coming through a time or two since it's located not too far from a local college.

"Hey! Good to see you again. What are we going to be getting done today?"

"Hey, Chris! I'm thinking about something to cover the expanse of my stomach."

"Alright. Do you have a picture in mind already or do you need me to sketch something up?"

"Nah, I know exactly what I have in mind." I proceed to tell him the details and show him some of the images I printed off Pinterest this morning.

He takes a few moments to trace the picture for a stencil as I hang out in the lobby and set up my playlist on my phone.

Once he's done, Chris calls me to the back and preps his station as one of his co-workers takes over the front desk. Laying back, I make sure to put on my earphones as Chris gets to work. The sound of Zakk Wylde's voice and guitar drifts into my ear as I almost doze off, listening to Black Label Society. The sting of the needle against my skin creates an ache I enjoy, one I sometimes find myself craving more of.

My mind drifts back to Miss Miller and my mood sours. Is it her? Has she tainted me mentally that I now need this pain to feel something pleasurable? I can't even call what she gives me pleasurable when it's all said and done. The feeling of her against my skin lingers after the act, making me want to scrub my skin raw with stone. The humiliation and the degradation makes me want to claw my eyes out.

I must be tensing up because Chris taps me a few times, reminding me to relax. Chris is my go-to tattoo artist. He's great at what he does and he's efficient. Thanks to Miss

Miller, my pain threshold is higher than it ever was. Chris and I agreed to power through an eight-hour session today, finishing it up at the next appointment.

He taps me again in a different pattern, letting me know we're done and I bring myself to the mirror. The majority of it is there. A Native American wolf baring his teeth in challenge with a crow overhead, his wingspan opened wide and traveling along under my pecs. I decided to go with just black ink to signify the past, the death, and rebirth.

"Hey, thanks, man. I'll see you at the next appointment."

"Yeah, see you next month." I slide him a hundred dollar bill as a tip before turning to leave his station.

Exiting the doors, I walk towards my Honda Civic sedan. My stomach stings a bit when I reach forward to start the ignition but I revel in the burn. I hope Akmal doesn't expect me to walk him to the door tonight after I sit my ass on the couch with a nice ice-cold beer.

The drive home felt longer than the drive there, probably because my mind kept thinking about the stinging from my sitting position. Once I got out of the car after parking, I let out a breath. Not really paying attention to my surroundings and moving on muscle memory to my door, I hear someone clear their throat behind me a few times as I'm inserting my key.

Turning around, I see Emily and she looks straight into my eyes. She must have something to say.

"Is everything okay?"

"Yea, I just wanted to say hi. You know, since we're crossing paths and all." Her laugh sounds a little strange, but maybe that's how she normally laughs and I just don't know it. I mean, I've just met the girl.

"Oh, okay. Well, hi."

She laughs again before saying hi once more and I'm

saved from any further awkward conversation when Akmal walks up behind me and slaps me on the back in greeting.

"What's up, man? I take it your appointment went well?" Akmal's got a small six-pack of beer in his hand as I open the door and let us in. I nod my head to him and tip my head up to Emily for a goodbye before I shut the door and lock it. What a weird woman. Maybe she's lonely and doesn't have anyone to talk to. I think there's an animal shelter not too far away from here. Maybe she needs to get a dog or something.

Akmal automatically puts the cold ones in the fridge. He comes over so often, I don't have to tell him to make himself at home. Grabbing a beer, I head to the couch and relax, kicking off my boots.

Akmal does the same and we're browsing Netflix, seeing what new releases pop up. Akmal usually only chugs down two drinks max because of his culture, or so he's told me. He's not even supposed to be drinking at all but he's a little bit of a rule-breaker in his family. He's informed me that in Malaysia, they are much stricter and since he's not there, he's much laxer about it.

We ended up deciding on a Marvel remake instead of Star Wars and keep the volume at a medium. We tend to do our talking during the movie anyway since we can't talk as much as we would like at work without people eavesdropping on our conversation.

"How's your family doing?"

Akmal gulps his drink before letting out a burp to the side. "Ah, they're alright. Same, same. Two of my sisters are still living with my parents, of course. My middle sister is going to university now, so she spends most of her time there and has a little house near campus to make attending her classes easier. My parents are still bugging me about finding a woman to marry so they can have a million grand-kids to spoil."

I chuckle because I've met his parents a few times. Despite how friendly they are, they scare me. I've cut back my visits because every time I'm over there, they try to get me to marry their oldest daughter. It's nerve-wracking. I'm not good with big crowds and conversation to begin with, but I don't want them to think I don't appreciate their hospitality.

"Mat! Come in, Come in. Akmal, you don't visit us enough." The friendliness of Akmal's family threw me for a loop the first time I met them. Now it's become more anticipated. Once we both enter, Akmal's mother looks behind us and frowns.

"Akmal, why didn't you bring anyone, huh? You need to find someone so I can have grandchildren while I'm still alive." I stifle a laugh as Akmal groans through her tirade. It's the same conversation every time we see her.

His parents start pushing both of us towards the floor to join in on their lunch. The house smells amazing. Akmal's sisters are already sitting around with different plates of chicken and fish in front of them. They all give me a smile and giggle as they wave. Despite having been here with Akmal more than once, I still feel awkward when his mother shoves me to sit by the girls.

"Makan. Makan. You guys look like you're starving. There's plenty to eat la. We will make sure you leave here full and give you some to take home." I'm practically rolling out of here when we're done with our visits with how much food they shove at us.

Malaysians eat with their hands, so I sit myself down and cross my legs to join in on their family meal. I've seen them cup their hands when they gather rice, so I try to mimic them when I eat. Akmal's mother has placed me by her oldest daughter again and I inwardly groan. She's a lovely and very friendly woman and all but...

"Mat, doesn't Hasanah look lovely today. You know she is of marriageable age and we already love you like a son. You guys would make beautiful grandbabies for us." Akmal's mother is sitting right by me as she tells me this, looking between her oldest daughter and myself like she's already planning the wedding cere-mony. I can hear Akmal choking on his food, and his mother sends him a stern look.

Like every visit, I send a prayer under my breath that I survive this lunch without getting engaged to one of Akmal's sisters.

"Laugh it up, Mat. Why do you think I'd rather come over to your place so often? It's like walking to the guillotine every time I go home with their constant questioning and pestering about if I'm seeing anybody. I'm almost afraid to bring any girl I'm interested in around because they'll be planning the wedding before our arrival behind our backs."

"Hey man, at least you're surrounded by a family that loves and cares about you. Even if it seems like they care a little bit too much."

"Yeah, you're right. I shouldn't complain. But man, they can be a pain."

We both laugh and continue watching superheroes kick ass and save the world. Akmal knows about my past and never brings it up. That's why he's a good friend and an easy-going person I don't mind hanging out with.

4

———

MAT

S he cuffed me to the bedpost like a damn sacrifice. I'm glad I heal quickly because Miss Miller's eyes lit up when she saw my new tattoo. The little black switch she brought out of her closet makes me groan in dread on the inside because it means she's feeling feisty today from her excitement. Damn this job and damn this woman for always figuring out ways to sabotage her stuff to call in for service, always asking for me. It doesn't help that I actually perform my job to fix the issue, therefore no one at headquarters ever sees her cases as anything but what they are: cases to be solved and closed.

I should change that somehow. *Thwak!* The sting of her whipping me takes me out of my thoughts for just a second. I should really figure out a way to either offload her cases to someone or figure out a way to blacklist her from our company. I wonder if Akmal can help me brainstorm the latter. *Thwak!* Shit, I think she whipped my obliques. That shit stings a little worse than the last one, making a hiss escape between my teeth. Her smile is feral now and her eyes are dilating. She loves getting a reaction out of me since I work hard to not give her one.

Miss Miller isn't bad on the eyes. She's a full-figured, confident redhead. What hot-blooded male would say no to her?

Me. *I'm* that hot-blooded male that would say no. The only problem is that I was trapped in her web of lies and manipulation before I even realized no would be an option. I was naive and she took advantage of it. Took advantage of the fact that I don't like hurting women. Now I'm in so deep, some days that light at the end of the tunnel seems so hopeless.

I don't know what's going on in that mind of hers as she uncuffs my hands and forces them on her hips as she positions her pussy above my face. Do guys actually get pleasure out of being treated this way? Like a damn dog? She slaps my face when she notices me zoning out and I start to lap at her lower lips the way she's taught me. She starts to moan, grabbing my hair by the fistful as she rubs herself all over my face unabashedly.

"Fuck yes, just like that. Eat my pussy, lick it clean." I swear this woman is going to scar me for all women for the rest of my days.

Flicking my tongue on her clit, hoping to make her cum quickly so all this crap can be over with, her grip on my hair starts to get tighter, signifying her climax approaching. *Fuck, hurry up woman.*

Her body starts to shake a little as her pussy clenches over my tongue when I spear her one last time to push her over the edge. She squirts on my face like I'm a fucking toilet seat and I can't do a damn thing about it. She doesn't squirt often, but when she does she tends to be a little nicer to me for the rest of the time I'm here.

"Fuck...yes… you like that don't you. You like me dirtying you up with my juices. You're such a good boy." She loves petting me like I'm her puppy. I need her to get off my face.

My thoughts must be transmitting clearly from the last time I fixed her modem because she does just that, gets off my face and falls to her side on the bed in an unattractive heap.

I quickly get up and go hop in her shower before getting back into my work clothes. I need to get out of this stifling house. After what feels like a five-minute shower, I come out to see she's back in robe again, hair all mussed up from all the messing around we did… rather, all the messing around she forced me into. My cock is only semi hard and I'm glad for it because I don't want her anywhere near it today.

I don't even have the energy to say anything to her as I fix her 'IT issue' and run out of the house as fast as I can without looking like a crazy person to her neighbors.

Only when I shut the driver's side door do I breathe a deep sigh of relief before quickly starting the ignition and backing out of the driveway.

The neighbors I drive by all give me a disgusted look, since the screeching of the company car tires are probably leaving tread marks on their pristine roads. Well, screw them. I never liked their neighborhood, anyway. Too many bad memories thanks to a particular client.

When I make it back to the main building, I park the car in the designated employee lot and lean my head back to rub my scalp. Miss Miller almost ripped my hair out this time as she came on my face. My follicles still feel tender as I continue to massage my head in slow circles.

A knock on the driver's side window makes me jump. Akmal is pointing his finger down to tell me to roll down the window. I do and Akmal is giving me a critical once over.

"You alright, man?" Shit, if only he knew. Akmal only knows that I hate going over there and that she doesn't treat me right, but not about the details.

"Fuck, I can't take Miss Miller's cases anymore. We need to do something. Tricia can't be there to save me every day."

Akmal stands back as I roll the windows back up before exiting the car and leaning against the driver's side door.

With one hand on his hip and the other under his chin, Akmal and I both stand next to each other in silence as we try to come up with a plan.

Akmal surprises me when, a few minutes later, he snaps his fingers.

"Fuck, I got it! You need to buddy up with Travis on the next Miller case."

"Why the hell would I want to buddy up with a rookie? How is that going to help me?"

"Listen to me, man. I've only buddied up with that guy a few times and his need for attention and recognition is annoying as hell. Who better to give it to him than Miss Miller, eh?"

My eyes widen at his idea. Shit. It just might work.

"Shit, Akmal. This is exactly why you're my bro. Fuck yeah." We slap our palms together and bump each other's shoulders. I have to hold on to him since he almost topples over, but we're both laughing as we walk into the glass double doors.

"Hey guys!"

"Tricia? Aren't you off today?" She's dressed in normal clothes, so I don't know what she's doing here. I wouldn't want to hang around this place during my off-duty hours.

"I, uh, needed to talk to Morty about something. Since I was kind of in the neighborhood anyway, you know…"

"..okay. Well, I guess we'll see you tomorrow at work."

Morty walks out of the restroom at that very moment, still fixing his pants by lifting it up over his gut. He looks surprised to see Tricia here, too.

"Tricia, you're on schedule for tomorrow."

Tricia lets out a weird laugh and starts to say something to Morty. But I don't hear it since Akmal and I are both already walking away to the break room. We don't usually eat here, but we do sit down for brainstorming on where we should take our lunch if we have to.

"Hey guys! Wait up!" Akmal is still holding open the door as we both turn to see Tricia jogging towards us.

"You guys want to go get lunch or something?" She's staring at me when she asks this and I look back at Akmal. He shrugs, indicating he doesn't care whether or not she comes.

"Yeah, that's cool. We usually hit up Sammi's nearby. Akmal, you up for sandwiches?"

"I'm up for anything I can fill my stomach with. I'm starvin' like Marvin."

I chuckle. Well, that's settled then.

"Who's up for driving?"

"That would be me. You drove last time." Tricia smiles at me as all three of us walk back to the employee parking lot towards my car.

Opening up the passenger door for her, Tricia sits in the front passenger seat as Akmal crawls into the back.

We pick the same table outside when we get there, grabbing an extra chair from the nearby table for our extra person. Seems we also get the same waitress as well.

"Hey boys, what'll you have? The usual?" Her smile falls

off her face when she sees the other guest that's joined us today. Suddenly there's a tension in the air and I can't understand what it's stemming from. Both Akmal and I are looking at each other discreetly with scared looks on our faces. How do you diffuse something when you don't even know what's wrong to begin with?

Tricia sends a strained smile at the waitress as she gives her her order, and the waitress sends a strained smile back. Sheesh. Women are so hard to understand. Maybe they know each other?

We all eat in relative silence after our food is brought out. The strangest thing happens when the waitress brings our bill. She places it in front of Tricia and that weird tension comes back. I grab the bill when the waitress turns around and toss down enough to cover our food and a tip so we can leave before she returns again. I don't understand women, but I don't think I can sit through another session of whatever it is that's going on.

5

ATSUKO

"**A**tsuko, are you going to make it to the vintage car show next weekend? I heard there's going to be a lot showing up on the fairgrounds this year."

"Of course! I actually scheduled a photoshoot with a free-lance photographer. He was offering a good deal. Figured I should update my portfolio." Hopefully, this guy won't be as creepy as the last one I hired for the air show.

"Yeah? I need to do that too. I'll accompany you, maybe I'll hire him too if he's good." Veronica, Vero, is currently reapplying her Cherry Bomb red lipstick on her lips, pressing them together and making a pop sound in front of a mirror sitting on the makeup counter.

With her round ass sticking out and wriggling, more than a handful of guys have taken steps backward to do a double take. Vero has the best ass around, so I don't blame them at all. When an older silver fox starts to loosen his collar from afar watching her apply another coat of lipstick, I slap her ass, making her jump up and turn to look at me with a sparkle in her eye. She slaps my ass back, and I can hear the gentleman groan under all our laughter.

Vero and I have been best friends for the past fifteen years. We met one day at a classic car convention while photographers were asking us to pose for pictures for one of their calendar shoots. We hit it off like we were born sisters and with our mutual dark hair and light skin shade, you probably would think so as well if it wasn't for the difference in our nationalities. Where I am of Japanese American descent, Vero is Hispanic.

"What was that for?" Her words sound like she's mad, but her inability to hold back her smile tells me otherwise.

"You know what that was for. Shaking your ass like that. You're going to cause an accident near my workspace! Ain't nobody got time for that!" We both laugh because it's true, and she knows it. The makeup counter needs to be kept pristine to attract the customers. I work for commission for my day job and having Vero here on her days off to hang out helps a lot because she's a bombshell and her makeup game is on point. She always looks like she just stepped off the pages of a pinup magazine. It's our go to look when we're off work, tackling the world like we're double trouble. We're almost the same size, allowing us to swap clothes back and forth.

It's about time to change shifts with the next girl and I was able to make a few good sales today, thanks to Vero. Women would come by asking what product she used and she would tell them the names of all the ones I sold, despite not even wearing them on her face. She always has my back like that.

Bending over to grab my bag on the ground, a large warm hand covers my ass cheek over my pencil skirt with a caress.

His other hand starts to travel from my waist to my abs over my top before his familiar voice carries to my ear.

"Shit, babe, you can't bend over like that in front of the public. I might end up in jail again."

Alfonso and I are on and off. Standing at about five-feet-nine inches, Alfonso's got the bad boy look down to a T because that's exactly what he is. To be honest, he isn't my man besides seeking each other now and again for mutual benefits, but he sure likes to act like he is whenever he's around. Always metaphorically pissing all over the place to stake his claim just because we tumble in bed together a time or two when I'm horny enough.

Come to think of it, I didn't even know he knew my schedule.

"Why are you here Alfonso?"

"Why you gotta be like that, huh? Can't I just come see my girl?" Now that I'm turned around facing him, his hands continue to take liberties at my lower back. I don't love it and I don't hate it. But I really don't want him to think this is something more than what it just is.

"Your girl? I'm not your girl. You're going to need to take your hands off me since I didn't give you permission to touch me." My eyes scan his five o'clock shadow across his jaw.

"I love that mouth of yours. You want to go back to my place?" He doesn't have a place last I remember. Alfonso's tendency to be in and out of jail makes it hard for him to have anything of his own.

"You mean take her back to Joaquín's house? Don't you get embarrassed banging my girl at some other guy's house? She deserves better than that." Vero is glaring at Alfonso with the corner of her lip curled up, because she *really* doesn't like him. She also knows that a girl has needs and Alfonso is the easiest catch when I need some D. Despite her five-feet-five stature, Vero's nature is to never back down from much when she's got her hackles up.

"Why don't you just shut the…" He shuts his own mouth up when he sees the daggers I'm starting to glare at him. I'll admit it, Alfonso can be a little uncouth. Who am I kidding? He can be a damn heathen sometimes. It used to get me going when we first hooked up. Now it gets downright annoying, especially when he's shooting that stuff at my girl.

"Baby, don't look at me like that. You know me. Sometimes my mouth goes before my mind does. Come on baby, I've missed you." He tries to grab onto my waist but I side step him just far enough away from his reach.

"You need to go Alfonso. I'm off work and I want to go home."

"Yeah, you need to go. Don't worry, I'll take care of Atsuko real good if she's got an itch she needs to scratch." Vero begins to caress my tits right in front of him. This crazy girl, that's why I love her.

Alfonso looks pissed because he's a possessive motherfucker, but he's not my man, and he knows it. When I feel her fingers start to pinch my nipples through my shirt and bralette, I squeak and slap her hand. We both laugh and hear a groan from somewhere nearby. Alfonso goes off stomping and growling on his way towards who I assume is the guy that groaned.

Vero and I take that moment to slip out from the vicinity, making our escape. Our laugh bubbles out of us all the way out to the parking lot like we're a bunch of teenage schoolgirls despite me being thirty five and Vero being thirty three.

"You need to shake that fool off. Alfonso is trouble. That boy is like a bomb about to blow every time he's around you."

"I know, I know. I've tried! He's like a stray dog, though. You give him a little and he keeps sniffing back for more."

We start separating ways towards our respective cars but continue our conversation anyway, with louder voices.

"Then stop giving it to him! Buy a million dildos if you have to, but do not take him back. Shit, if the itch still can't get scratched, you got me!" The sound of a loud crash nearby makes us both turn our heads just in time to see a teenage boy crash to the ground from tripping on the metal trash can. That's what he gets for eavesdropping.

"Mouths and fingers can only do so much you know?"

"Maybe what you need is a permanent boo. But that will never happen with Alfonso sniffing around."

"Can you please stop making sense? It pisses me off."

My keys are already in my driver's door before I hear Vero yell, "No it doesn't. That's why you love me. That, and because you love my tongue game!"

A few guys leaving their cars start choking on their drink but we pay them no mind. Vero and I wave as I get into my Toyota Camry and start the ignition. Vero's right. Maybe I need a permanent man, one that doesn't just want me for what's between my legs. I hate the dating scene. Since hooking up with Alfonso a few years ago, I never dipped my foot back in. Turning out of the parking lot and onto the street, I tell myself that maybe there aren't any good guys left out there.

6

MAT

Tricia is off today. I volunteered to take Travis on my next call, which happens to be to Miss Miller's house. The plan is set in motion. I need to shake this woman off me. My soul can't take it. I should feel bad about what I'm doing. I really should.

"Man, I hope she's hot. Wouldn't mind some eye candy while we do work, right my man?" Right.

"She's one of our regulars. She's not too well versed in...technology and usually calls in trouble pretty frequently. They're usually easy jobs. If you want, you can go do this one solo."

"Yeah, I'm down for that. I don't need all this training Morty has me going through. I've done IT before; I know what I'm doing." And so the trap is set. This kid's cocky enough to jump on any opportunity to show off his skills.

"Alright, I hear you. Yeah, let's do it then. You take this

one on your own and I'll be in the car doing paperwork until you're done."

"Fuck, it's about time." I hope she eats you alive.

Driving through Miss Miller's neighborhood, Travis whistles.

"This place is fucking loaded with money. I bet it's loaded with desperate housewives too, you know what I mean?" His unnecessary lifting of his eyebrows irks me. How did this cocky bastard even get the job, or keep one, for that matter?

This time when I pull up to her driveway, I don't feel the same sense of dread I usually do. I'm actually laughing on the inside, but my face is calm on the outside.

"Are you sure about this? I can always go in with you just in case."

"Nah! I got this. Come on, man, I'm not that stupid. I know what I'm doing. You just sit back and I'll be out in a few, I guarantee it." Do you now?

"Alright, alright." I watch as he gets out of the passenger side with his tool bag. The confident swagger he has going as he walks up to her door. I know the moment she opens it because his mouth falls open and throat starts bobbing. A flash of a hand and she's pulled him in. The sound of the slammed front door making me breathe a sigh of relief.

Guess I'll be taking an impromptu break in the car. Taking my cell phone out of my pocket, I open up my browser. I've been to Miss Miller's house enough to know her network password, not that she cares one bit.

The last page comes up and there's a blue classic car right at the top, the kind of blue that was common in the fifties. Some are fire engine red, others have flame paint jobs. All of the cars are well taken care of with a shine that catches your eye no matter how old the model is.

Akmal sent me the link to the convention coming up

where he will be doing a photoshoot with some of the pinup girls. I'll be off that day, but I don't know if I'm going to go. It doesn't seem like my scene. Plus, there will be way too many people there.

Glancing at the clock on the top left of my screen, it's only been ten minutes since the door slammed. I don't hear any screaming, so I keep on scrolling.

I wonder how my grandparents are doing on the reservation. I think about them every now and again, but I'm too much of a coward to contact them after I was banished off the land. Are they disappointed in me? Ashamed? Have they disowned me by now since I've turned my back on our people and left without another backward glance?

Shaking the depressing thoughts out of my head, I think about my time working for Just Techs. I wonder if Morty even knows what goes on with these calls. I wonder if I'm the only one with a Miss Miller problem or if this is a common occurrence for the other guys? Nah, judging by their bored expressions when they come back from the field, it's probably just my bad luck.

Quickly getting bored, I do actually start catching up on paperwork. Once I'm all caught up, I tap my phone screen to check the time. Travis has been in there for about thirty minutes. Maybe it's time I check up on him.

Getting out of the car, I walk up to Miss Miller's front door and press my ear against it before knocking. I can't hear a damn thing, so I knock and turn the door handle. Seems Miss Miller must have been in a hurry because the door was unlocked.

The moment I'm halfway to her bedroom is the moment I hear, "You're a dirty little boy aren't you. And you fucking love everything I do to you."

Hopefully I didn't scar the poor kid for life.

When I walk closer to the bedroom doorway, I actually take a step back from the sight before me. Miss Miller is butt naked in heels, one of which is currently being pressed down onto Travis's balls as he lays there on his back on the ground with a damn smile on his face.

Walking lightly back towards the front door, I hear, "Suck my toes. Mmmmm, just like that. You're so dirty, just the way I like them."

With that, I make sure to close the door as lightly as I can so her attention doesn't turn to me. I should feel like a bastard, but I don't. That smile on Travis's face tells me he's right where he wants to be.

Another fifteen minutes later, a freshly washed Travis comes back to the car, opening up the passenger door.

"Holy shitballs. Is this what you guys do every day?"

"I don't know about the other guys, but Miss Miller is a regular. If you want, you can take her cases when they open up. She seems to have taken a liking to you."

"Hell yeah, I'd love to. That woman might break my dick off one of these days, but what a way to go." He laughs like he couldn't care less, and then winces when he moves a certain way. Thank fuck, because I could not care less that he's saddled with her. Things are starting to look up for me already.

7

ATSUKO

*V*ero and I decided to try out one of those dating apps that have become popular. She didn't want me to feel alone on this new journey and being the best friend she is, she hopped on the bandwagon without a hitch.

"Some of these guys look like they're using photos from their high school days. Come on, look at this guy! Age thirty-eight, but he looks like he's twenty? I don't believe it." Her finger swipes left as she continues to browse through the different pictures. Vero is a free bird like I am, another reason why we get along. We don't necessarily go out looking for men, men are usually in abundance around us, especially at car shows. I love dick just as much as the next girl, but when I have an available one a phone call away, I haven't really been looking.

"Some of these guys look like they have yellow fever." We

both laugh because some of these guys do look like complete creeps.

We're hanging out at our apartment, in my bedroom. Our bodies are laid out haphazardly with some of our limbs hanging off the sides of the full sized mattress.

"My finger is going to get a cramp from all this swipe left shit." Vero dramatically groans as she drops her hands down to her sides from their upward position since she's lying on her back, her luscious locks spread all over the white sheets. I bump my shoulder against her but kind of miss since I'm lying on my stomach, still holding my phone between my hands. This crap is getting warm too. How long have we been doing this?

"Come on, you can't give up that fast. What if the right guy is the next one, huh?" Vero blows out a raspberry and turns her phone back on, lifting it over her head again at my suggestion.

We both stare at her screen. The next guy looks like a total creep who still lives in his mother's basement. Vero slaps me on the ass, and we both laugh uncontrollably on my bed, making it bounce. Damn, this dating stuff is hard. Or maybe we've just both been out of the game too long.

"This is exactly why I always end up back with Alfonso. What the hell am I supposed to do when I have an itch? Dating takes too damn long and if you jump the guy's bones on the first date, he will automatically think you're a slut, you know?"

"Alfonso is bad news, and you know it. That boy is on you like a man on crack. Addicted with no hope of recovery. With his history that can get dangerous."

"I know. I know." I groan because dammit, *I know,* but I don't know how to shake him off. But damn if his dick doesn't scratch that itch. My toys can only do so much! This is the curse of a woman who knows her body well. At thirty five, I have no shame for the cravings that come to me. I love my sexuality, I love that I love sex. It's finding the right partner, one that isn't a danger to you and your sanity and might snap at any minute. But maybe that's Alfonso's allure. The bad boy.

But that bad boy is also a loser, hanging out in his buddies' homes with nothing of his own. Ugh!

"Why are you groaning over there like that? Don't you dare consider that fool! His dick is not that great! Come on Atsuko!"

"I know what you're saying, but I don't want to just be jumping from dick to dick either, you know? It doesn't make it any better."

Covering my face with my forearms, I lie on my back and contemplate my sex life. Do I get a bigger dildo? What? What can I do? Toys really are not the same versus the real thing. The relief is so temporary. Maybe I just need a main man. A straight up constant boo to call my own, to ravish whenever the need comes up. Just thinking about it makes me scissor my legs. A big 'ol dick, constantly at my beck and call, one that knows how to work my body the way I like it.

"You don't have to jump from dick to dick when you have me."

Soft hands run up my knees to my thighs, gently pushing them apart. My body relaxes into the touch as the fingers grip the waistband of my cotton shorts, dragging both it and my panties down my legs in the slowest of motions. The cool air of the room caresses my hips and junction between my legs, making an enticing contrast to the atmosphere in the room that's starting to charge up with sexual tension. I can feel the goosebumps rise up on the surface of my exposed skin.

My breathing is still calm but slowly becoming deeper and deeper. My arms are still over my face, the restriction of one of my senses making all my other senses heightened. I love guessing what's next, lost in the darkness.

Once I'm naked from my waist down, the hands come back with a soft caress from my ankles to my mid thighs. Not so gently, the hands force my legs open wide and I submit to their command. I feel the light brush of her hair on my inner thigh before the heat of her mouth and tongue swirling on my clit. A tease with the tip, a tease with the flat of her tongue. Vero tortures me by pushing my sensitive bud with too much pleasure and then too little.

The room starts to feel stifling, my hunger growing with every movement she makes over my pleasure zone.

My hips start a slow dance, pushing itself towards her mouth, silently begging for more while still trying to remain submissive. When she covers my opening with her soft lips, her tongue darts out aggressively, invading my wet pussy with the muscle, making me moan. In and out, in and out with a flick of her tongue upwards. I widen my legs for her to get closer and deeper, making her moan against me; the sound vibrating against my lower lips increases the sensation that's already heightened.

She starts making out with my pussy like it's my mouth and slowly moves her lips over my clit again. The feel of one finger, then two enter me as her mouth and lips continue their attention on my clit and make my hips start to thrust against her even more. I feel like I'm going to combust into flames but I hold back my sounds, letting her take the lead, letting her tell me how fast she wants this to go.

It starts to feel better and better, my body chasing something that's so close and so far away at the same time. When

Vero starts to flick my clit and sucks it hard, inserting a third finger at the same time, my body explodes and I swear I see stars behind my closed eyelids. She moans and continues to suck on my clit hard, almost to the point of pain. I love it. Her fingers never letting up on their thrusting against my pulsating pussy, her lips making way for teeth to join the party makes my aftershocks climb even higher instead of die down. *Fuck.*

Removing her fingers, her tongue travels down to my pussy and her nose grazes my clit every now and again as she licks up all my juices, making me squirm. I can feel some of it trail down to my back hole, making me clench my ass and pussy around Vero's tongue.

I feel her shuffling, the bed moving with her as she removes her mouth from me. Taking my arms away from my face, I watch as Vero crawls up my body, slowly removing her own clothes in the process. All that's left is her panties as she grabs one of her breasts and feeds her nipple into my mouth. My arms go around her, pulling her in closer so I can get a bigger mouthful of her beautiful tits in my face. Doing the same thing she did to my clit, I suck hard, twirl her nipple with the end of my tongue and nip at it in different patterns. Vero loves having her C cup breasts played with. So do I, but I'm too horny for her right now to think of me. I'm desperate to make her feel good, for her to use me for her pleasure.

She grabs my hair and pulls it back hard, making her nipple pop out of my mouth right before she shoves my face to her other breast, commanding me to satisfy her craving for breast play. I happily comply. The more I suck her nipple, the more I knead her other breast with my hands, the more she loosens her grip on my hair. She moans and bites her bottom lip, revealing just how much she's enjoying what I'm doing to her. I am too and I can feel myself get even wetter than I already am.

Her breathing is picking up and I love that I'm doing that to her. It makes me feel powerful.

"I need you to eat my pussy. Now." Her nipple pops out of my mouth as she quickly lifts her torso up and my inner nympho is purring in satisfaction, watching her nipples both glisten and look angry red from my kisses.

The room feels hotter and hotter, the air thick with sex, especially with both our bodies sliding against each other. She starts to climb again until she's sitting right over my face, her cotton panties sticking to her pussy from how aroused she's become.

Grabbing her ass with one hand and pulling the bottom of the panties aside with the other, I start to dip my tongue into her wetness. She tastes so fucking good, it's making me hot and horny all over again.

She leans back and tweaks my nipple hard, making me moan into her pussy. She's like this. She gets feisty when she's not getting what she wants from me. It's her signal that I need to up my game.

Grabbing her ass with both of my hands, I make her shove her pussy even lower on my face. My tongue continues to thrust into her, my lips and teeth nipping at her lower lips and clit every so often. One of my hands caresses her ass and squeezes it hard before it travels low enough to stick a finger inside her back entrance. Some of her juices have already traveled down, making it easy for me to rub it there. She tightens and then relaxes her hole enough for me to thrust my finger inside as she groans. She's getting wetter by the minute and the moment I tease her ass and add another finger, she cries out in pleasure and starts grinding hard on my face and tongue. I love how shameless Vero is with her body. She knows she's hot. She knows she's edible, and it turns me on. Her confidence only boosts mine, that's why we're best friends and roommates.

She continues to ride my face and tongue despite my fingers having been removed from her ass. When her body starts to go limp, she rolls to the side of me, onto her back, trying to catch her breath.

Getting up to clean my hands in the adjoining bathroom, I come back with a toy and lie right back next to Vero. She smiles and there's a wicked glint in her eye.

"You are such a slut. You can never get enough. I either feel bad or good for the man that catches you, Atsuko." We both laugh like psychos. Vero is the only person I allow to call me that. She knows I'm not a slut, I just love sex.

With the dildo in my right hand, I start to tease my lips and clit with the head a few times to lube it up before pushing it in me. I moan, my lips and insides still overly sensitized by what Vero put me through. The stretch makes me even hornier, making it glide in and out, in and out.

Vero rolls over and pulls my tank top down, exposing my left breast to her waiting mouth. She pinches my clit while she sucks, like she's waiting for milk to flow if I had any. Just the thought of that taboo makes my pussy clench around the girth of the toy. This is the difference. Vero scratches the itch only a little with her fingers in my pussy, but my pussy always knows the difference between what it really wants: a big dick inside to fill me to the brim.

My hand thrusts the dildo in tune with her sucks, and soon enough I let out a strangled moan when my climax hits me for the second time tonight, even harder than the first. When the beat of my heart starts a steady decline, I let out a satisfied sigh. My body feels lax. It feels somewhat satiated for the time being.

I watch with hooded eyes as Vero takes the dildo out of my pussy and starts to lick it up seductively in front of me.

"Ugh, stop! You know what it does to me."

Her tongue swirls around the crown of the toy and she laughs, falling back down on the bed beside me.

"Do you think I'll find someone who can keep up with me?"

"I don't know, Atsuko. But you'll never know until you try."

She's fucking right. She's always fucking right.

8

MAT

I don't know what happened, but Miss Miller started asking for me again. Travis has been to her house for the past few days and it seems he's already worn out his welcome. How can this be? I thought they were doing good together? How did this fool mess up a thing like that?

"Hey! Are you going to Miss Miller's house? Let me tag along."

"Who are you supposed to be buddied up with right now?"

"Bradley, but he wouldn't mind." I don't trust this guy and anything that comes out of his mouth.

"Yo Bradley!"

"What's up?"

"You don't mind Travis buddying up with me on this case?"

"Shit. Take him." Seems like Travis is wearing out his welcome in more places than one.

"I got you. I'm going to take him on my next one."

Bradley nods without even turning around. He doesn't care where Travis ends up. They must have butted heads about something for Bradley to act that way. He usually gets along with everyone.

"Sweet!" Travis is rubbing his hands together like a kid that just won a candy prize.

When we reach Miss Miller's house, I decide to try my luck and get out with Travis. I need to understand where it went wrong, why she's decided to request me again when she has a willing victim right here.

Travis looks like he's going to jump out of his skin with how his steps are bouncing the closer we get to her door.

The air shifts as she opens the door to greet us in her signature black robe and hair bun. The smile she shoots at me is lecherous, dying down when she turns to see that I'm not alone. Damn, this guy really messed up somehow.

"Well, come in, boys." Am I really doing this? Maybe she won't do anything with both of us here.

"Don't mind if I do." Travis is already walking past the doorway as Miss Miller continues to stand there, looking me up and down. It makes me feel like spiders are crawling all over my skin, but I try to give her a smile anyway, being on the job and all.

When I enter her living room, the sound of the door shutting and lock engaging makes me close my eyes and take a gulp. When I open them back up, Travis is already halfway stripped out of his clothes. My god, does he have no shame in how desperate he looks right now?

My eyes widen when he gets onto his hands and knees, butt naked and starts crawling to her. A smile creeps up on her face and her attention is off me, thank heavens. She opens up her robe just as Travis reaches her and shoves his face between her legs.

Quickly, I check out the IT problem, fix it and start plastering myself against the walls away from them. Maybe the shadows will help make me invisible as Miss Miller throws her head back and moans the more Travis licks her.

My hands are reaching out for the front door lock when Miss Miller gasps, making my eyes shoot to her position. My heart slams into my chest, thinking I got caught when in reality Travis's hands are kneading her ass, making her widen her stance against his face.

Quickly and quietly unlocking the door, I escape and close it back before anyone realizes I'm gone. The sounds of her moans silenced by the seal of the door.

Wiping the sweat off my forehead, I rush back into the work vehicle and shut the door for some security, making sure to lock it. Leaning my forehead against the steering wheel for a moment, I let my heart rate come back to normal before taking out my phone and relaxing for my impromptu break.

It seems I haven't changed the page on my phone's internet browser because when I open up the app, the classic cars are there again. I decide to text Akmal and see how he's coming along with preparing for that photoshoot since it's scheduled for this coming weekend.

Me: Hey! Are you ready for the photo session this weekend?

Akmal: Yeah! I'm still kind of nervous. You down to go with me in case I need some assistance?

Me: Man, I don't do well with crowds. I'm not the most sociable person.

Akmal: I'm not either! You can just be my backup IT guy

in case my laptop jacks up while I'm shooting photos. Heck, or just stand in a corner so I don't feel alone.

Me: I don't know.

Akmal: There will be HOT girls there. Like smoking. You shouldn't miss an opportunity like this.

I don't know how Akmal does it. His culture doesn't even let him have any sexual touches or relations before marriage, yet he's going to go do a photoshoot with a bunch of attractive women walking around wearing who knows what. I wouldn't be surprised if he ends up in the hospital for a bad case of blue balls after this gig.

Me: That's true. But I suck at talking to girls too.

Akmal: Who said you need to talk? Just stand there, man. One of them is bound to come up to us to ask for a photo at least.

Me: LOL

Glancing at the time on my phone, Travis has been gone for thirty minutes. The sound of the door makes me turn my head to look out the driver's side window. Speak of the devil. He's kind of limping but looks relatively unharmed.

He slowly sits himself on the passenger side and winces when he reaches for the door to close it. Well, he knew what he was getting into.

"All good?"

"Yup." Alright then. Starting up the car and backing up, the drive back is a quiet one.

9

ATSUKO

*V*ero's on duty today behind the bar at the local Cuban restaurant, Havana Palace. It's not too posh, so I come to hang out with her when I'm off and the manager doesn't mind during the slow times. Both of us have our day jobs, but our hope is we get picked up for a contract through modeling that we wouldn't need our day jobs anymore.

Vero and I have done a few magazine shoots but getting picked up for something like a pinup clothing line would be a nice and steady income.

"What are you going to wear to the convention, Vero? Can I borrow your red pumps?"

"Of course, chica, take whatever you need. I think I'm going to wear the black wriggle dress so I can showcase my ass-sets, you know?" We both chuckle at that because Vero's got some good assets indeed, the perfect hourglass shape in a dress like that.

Maybe we should go as twinsies. "Alright, I'm going to grab the wriggle skirt jumper and a white top. Your red pumps will help the outfit pop."

"Don't forget to wear a red bra so we can see a peek. I bet it would look hot on the photoshoot." That's a damn good idea.

Taking a sip out of my water on the counter, we watch as the customers come in and out. It's still a little early to be drinking, so Vero has lots of time on her hands. Leaning over the counter to whisper to me, I can see her cleavage almost spilling out her button top.

"Maybe you'll find some good D there. Lots to choose from. Then you can finally kick Alfonso to the curb."

"We shall have to see." I'm not too fond of the idea of jumping on some random cock. What if it's not even good? This is why I always find myself going back to Alfonso time and time again. He knows my body. What is wrong with me?

"Hello ladies. How are you today?" I take another long sip of water from my straw before turning to the right to see who's talking.

It's a handsome guy, looks like he's in his mid-twenties. A five o'clock shadow graces his face, contrasting nicely to his smooth, wavy brown locks. He's looking from me to Vero and back to me, trying to decide who to hit on. Since Vero's tits are currently on display, he decides to face her fully. I couldn't care less, but this is exactly why I'm kind of scared to venture away from what I know. This guy looks like a five pump chump.

What if a guy only pretends to want me because of what's on the outside? I know that's the point of a hook-up, but I can't help but feel weird about it. At least with Alfonso, we've known each other for so long, I know it's not just for what's between my legs. Hence why he always tries to 'get back together' and make me 'his girl'. It was good while it lasted between us but he continues to have no prospects. I love myself too much to settle for that.

I must have been musing in my own mind for a while because Vero and the gentleman have already disappeared somewhere. Hopefully, she keeps it down so the manager doesn't come out to check on what's going on.

What kind of man *do* I want? I've been riding the solo train for so long, I never really took the time to think about it. Being in my mid-thirties, I guess I should. Where does one even start? How do you know you're not setting your standards too high or too low? Alfonso's got one thing going for him besides his cock, he's a one track minded, devoted guy. He does teeter on dangerous territory when he's under the influence, which is usually when I avoid him.

I wish things could be simple, like a notification that pops up in our mind when our soul mate walks by. Is that too much to ask?

I'm just about done with my water when the gentleman from before walks past me quickly and winks at Vero who is still fixing her hair and top. Trying to suppress my smirk, I look down into my cup to gather myself. My my. That was a quickie.

"How was it?"

"Eh, good enough for a quickie. I mean, he's a little young. He rams really hard and deep, I'll give him that." I swear this girl and her descriptions. She doesn't even keep it to a whisper in case anyone else walks by. I'm just glad she's smart enough to always use protection.

"Well, I'm going to head back home to message the

photographer again one last time to make sure everything is a go. I'll see you there later?"

"Yup! Stay safe on the way home." We kiss each other on the cheek before I head out the door.

MAT

Fuck, Travis has got to be doing something wrong because Miss Miller is requesting me *again*. Why can't I shake this woman off? Isn't a willing dick good enough?

We pull up into her driveway and I'm actually getting a little ticked off this time around. Both Travis and I get out of the work vehicle and walk towards her front door. I re-knot the bun on my new undercut. It was a celebration haircut when I thought I got rid of Miss Miller forever. Seems my celebration was done a little too early.

She doesn't open the door when we get there this time, so I actually have to knock. My fists may be a bit heavy-handed with how I'm feeling. She opens up on the second knock, my fist still hanging in the air. Her smile is a different one. I can't decipher it just yet, but I'm on edge anyway because this is Miss Miller we're talking about. She's got a lot of tricks up her sleeve.

"Miss Miller, very lovely to see you again." Travis is trying to smooth talk on his way in, but she hasn't shifted her eyes to him yet. They're tracking me like I'm prey, and my fight or flight is starting to make me antsy under my skin.

The days I was able to shove Travis in her direction was a taste of freedom I got used to. Now I don't want to give it up.

"Miss Miller." I nod my head and say no more, hoping

she'll just tell me what the problem is, the reason for the call this time.

"I seem to have lost my cable. Help a lady out and maybe crawl back there to see if it slipped somewhere out of my reach?" Tricky, tricky fox. She wants me on my hands and knees, in a vulnerable position below her.

"Travis, can you check that out?" I never take my eyes off hers either as I give Travis the command. You can't take your eyes off a predator that's issuing a challenge. Seems we're at a small stalemate because Miss Miller bites her bottom lip, trying to think of another way to make me do what she wants.

Is that a crack in her control? It's making me feel things, but by the look of it, it's making her feel things too...things I don't want her to feel about me.

Travis takes that moment to crawl back out, still on his knees, towards Miss Miller as he hands her the wire she tried to hide. He's rubbing on her thighs, but she hasn't taken her eyes off me yet. She needs to just take what's offered to her on a platter and leave me the hell alone because I'm getting kind of tired of it.

Crossing my arms over my chest, I can feel my face frown at her determined look. What is it about me that makes her chase me so? I'm nothing. Just another male. She can have anyone else.

Travis is noticing the tension between us and decides to stand up in front of her, grabbing her face with both of his hands and forcing a kiss on her. Good. It's the moment I make my move and exit the front door.

ATSUKO

$\mathcal{I}$t's the morning of the car convention. Vero and I have been primping in front of the full-length mirror for a hot minute. I decided on the classic Hollywood waves in my hair while Vero is sporting some victory rolls.

We match with our dark hair and our similar choice of dark attire, but my red pumps help make me stand out. We both have our fire engine red lips on. The corset inside our outfits is cinched to create the perfect smooth hourglass and tight waist.

"Let's take the Camry, it's more comfortable than your clunker."

"Shut up ho, that clunker gets me to and from work." We laugh because it's on its last leg.

"Yeah, for now. And you don't have any triple A insurance for a breakdown."

"Chica, you're supposed to be my triple A." *Pffttt.* What if I can't get off work? This is why we take on photoshoots for extra side cash. Building up a good portfolio helps with getting gigs. Vero's family is very close, but she doesn't like asking them for anything since moving out. Trying to keep the independent woman thing going. Her parents are proud of her anytime they talk to her on the phone, always inviting us over for some homemade meals.

After placing her cat eye sunglasses on, she slaps my ass, making me squeak. She can't keep her hands off me. We walk out together and the cat calls start. There are some bachelors that live in our apartment complex but their fratboy lifestyle is such a turn off.

Putting my own retro sunglasses on, we ignore the neighbors and gracefully get into the camry and drive out of the neighborhood.

Vero bends over towards the console and puts on some Imelda May. Her voice and beat fill the car and it gets us in a relaxed mood. The trip to the convention is about a thirty-minute drive. The weather feels wonderful, so we put our windows down while we cruise and take our time watching the scenery go by. The scarfs on our heads help to keep our hair from going nuts before we can even arrive at our destination. The breeze caresses my cheeks like a lover's palm.

The closer we get, the more the parking lot looks full, the smell of vintage car exhaust filling the air. It's a nostalgic scent. These fairgrounds usually host the county fair during certain times. It's the perfect size for a car convention, allowing all the classic cars to have space between each other. Finding a good spot, we pull in and throw the car in park. Stepping out with grace, one extended foot after another. These shoes make our legs look a mile long and we know it. The way the fabric clings to our curves, molding against us like a second skin.

Seems the men and their show cars are the ones arriving first. Some are accompanied by their women, but most are not. Most have their eyes trained on our legs as we swing our hips like we're walking down the catwalk.

The first building we enter holds some of the old model A and T Fords. Their paint is glossy enough to use as a mirror. Some of the older men enjoy these, smiling and winking at us as we walk by. I smile and Vero is blowing kisses randomly.

Exiting the building through the back, we come upon the muscle cars. These get our girly bits going. The age range of the owners is more our speed. Some of these silver foxes with their slick back hair and long beards can make a woman internally combust. One of them is blowing a kiss my way and I blush, fanning my face to cool it down. Some of the guys are younger and full of tattoos, their arms bulging against their button-down shirts as they cross them when we walk by.

Vero laughs at some of the men trying to get our attention, just soaking it up, as we continue walking around the cars until we see some of the lingering men on the side with their DSLR cameras and different lenses. The freelance photographer I'm supposed to meet up with named Mohd Akmal around this area.

We slow our steps and stare for a minute. There are about five guys here and only one guy kind of looks like a Mohd Akmal, but I don't want to make assumptions.

The five-inch heels put me at about just shy of six feet tall. A very friendly-looking man with light facial hair who is standing at least five inches shorter than me walks forward from the group. He bows in greeting, and I find myself smiling. This is different in a nice way. His eyes are never lecherous or going over our assets as he introduces himself as my photographer. I have a good feeling about him already.

"Hello ladies. Where would you like to start, Miss Kobayashi? Did you have a particular location in mind already?" Look at this guy, so polite. His Nikon is hanging off his neck and a messenger bag is slung behind him. Very cute in a nerdy type way. You just want to put him in your pocket. Vero seems to agree because she's trying to get his attention by canting her hips to the side a bit, but he seems to be immune to her charms and her bountiful breasts.

"I think we walked by a fifties Packard Clipper on the way here. How about we start there?" He looks clueless despite still having the friendliest smile on his face. Trying to stifle my laugh, Vero and I lead the way.

"He's so adorable. He wouldn't even look at me when I was bending over, did you see that? I can't believe they still make them like this." Uh oh, looks like Vero's got her eyes on this one.

I slap her arm to make her tone down her voice. "Girl, you are so bad. Leave that poor man alone. If you distract him, he might mess up my photoshoot." We both giggle because Vero is unstoppable when she's got her mind set on something.

After a brief conversation with the car owner who looks like he could double for Vero's dad, the photoshoot starts. Simple poses like leaning my hip back and leg up to bending over the hood. Vero even photobombed some of them, the bitch. We laughed it off since Mohd Akmal was being so kind about it all. Vero is preening like a peacock every time he looks her way, only to deflate when his gaze doesn't linger.

He must be a strong-willed person to not notice someone

as beautiful as Vero. That or maybe he bats for the other team. That would make more sense.

A few more shots in front of muscle cars, a few with me laying on my back on top of the back trunk with my legs pointed towards the sky. I'm feeling pumped up because this guy seems to really have a good eye for this. He even let Vero sneak in a few professional ones with me with a smile. *Maybe he doesn't bat for the other team after all.*

"Alright ladies, I actually asked one of the car owners if we could borrow his Plymouth Barracuda. I think that's what he said."

Oh, this sounds *fabulous*. That's a hot car.

"He parked it in one of the smaller buildings on the lot. Let's head over there and out of the sun, shall we? My buddy is supposed to meet up with me to help me with the computer in case anything goes awry. My personal IT guy."

Our heels click on the ground at a steady pace as we follow the photographer to the designated location. It's much cooler inside the building from the shade it provides. Good, because I think I'm starting to glow a bit from the sweat.

Akmal is putting his messenger bag on a table that is sitting to the side while Vero and I cool down by the car, fanning our faces with our hands. A large and very tall figure walks in and goes directly behind the table to help the photographer set up his computer. His complexion is similar to Akmal's, perhaps a few shades darker but his high cheek-bones, thick eyebrows over his very dark eyes, and strong nose are what sets him apart from his nationality. There's very light stubble on his face, shadowing the angles of his lower features. His undercut and hair bun only further high-lights his cheekbones, making him look quite attractive.

He hasn't looked our way yet. These guys are a different

breed than what we're used to. It's refreshing and strange all at once.

My eyes continue to track his movements, watching the way his shirt would stretch across his firm chest when he reaches for something on the floor from another bag. How can a simple t-shirt and jeans look so filled out on a person? His shirt is still loose enough to make a woman curious as to what other artwork lies beneath.

Akmal is still figuring something out with the buttons on his Nikon in my periphery, but my eyes have never left the vicinity of the newcomer. I can hear Vero trying to talk to the photographer, distracting him from what he needs to do. The IT guy brings his eyes up once and catches mine. It feels like time slows as we both stare at each other for however brief a period it is before he casts his eyes back down.

A shy one. I'm intrigued.

"Alright ladies, let's just do a few shots and we'll be good for today."

I position my ass leaning against the Barracuda, making sure to stick out my chest while my hands drift down to my cleavage right above the bow on my top. My head is tilted back and I'm thinking of orgasms as my lips lightly part.

Click click click click.

The shutter speed on the lens clicks in rapid succession with every slight move I make to change position. Getting into the driver's side of the Barracuda, I bring my legs up over the steering wheel, making sure to cross them and point my toes while staring out the front window right at the IT guy. His eyes don't give away any hint of what's going on in his mind as he stares right back at me from behind the laptop's monitor. No smile, no hint of anything on his face.

I can feel my pussy clenching at the thought of this little game we're playing. The subtlety of it all. He's proving to be a challenge and I like it. My lips lift into a coy smile, showing him that I see exactly what he's doing. Staring at me when he thinks no one is looking.

Click click click click.

"Alright! These look great! I'm going to have Mat download the digital images, making the raw preview available for you soon. I will message you once the photos are touched up and ready for your portfolio. Thank you so very much again for your time."

I can hear Vero gushing over some of the pictures he's showing her on the viewscreen behind the camera while I slowly bring my legs back down to the floorboards of the car. Stepping one heel out and then the next, bringing my body out of the driver's side. My ass shuts the door with a loud metallic thud, making Mat's eyes drift to mine for only a second.

I'm thinking about what it would feel like to run my hands through Mat's luscious black hair when I hear a voice I didn't want to hear today.

"Atsuko, what the fuck? I've been looking everywhere for you!" His words are running into each other a bit. This isn't good.

"What are you doing here Alfonso?" This is starting to get a little annoying and creepy how easily he can track me down. He doesn't even have a damn car. Did he take the bus all the way here...like that? Or did Joaquín drop him off?

"No one invited you to this shoot, Alfonso." The tension in the air is starting to amp up when my BFF starts to lift her lip at my ex. She really doesn't like him.

The closer Alfonso gets to me, the more he smells like he's had a few drinks prior to finding me. That's never a good sign. He already has no filter as it is when he's sober.

The corner of my eye catches Mat quietly stand up,

staring at the scene from his table. The photographer has started to back up towards his laptop at the same time Vero is starting to place half of her body in front of me.

"Get the fuck out of my way, Vero. Ain't nobody here for you." Yeah, he's slurring a bit. His speech is a little bit slower.

"I'll get out of the way when I feel like it, fool. You need to back the fuck up yourself."

"Alfonso, you need to get it in your head that we're not together. We haven't been for years. You need to go, please, before you make a scene." Hopefully, by keeping a calm voice, he remains calm as well.

"Go? Make a scene? I'm not leaving you here with two men and this chick."

"Excuse me?" Vero's attitude is starting to seep into her voice.

There he goes, metaphorically pissing all over the place again to mark territory. I need to stop feeding him scraps because he's not letting go. This is my fault.

"Is there a problem here? I think I heard the lady say she wanted you to go." A deep voice I don't recognize gets closer.

Alfonso is snarling as he turns around to face Mat, who stands at least half a foot taller than him with a much broader build, despite trying to hide it behind his loose t-shirt.

"You need to stay out of our fucking business. I'm talking to my girl."

"I'm not your girl." Let's just clarify that again.

I don't know what Alfonso was going to do or say to that when suddenly Mat grabs him by the throat before he can turn to me and slams him onto the ground. My heart is beating rapidly, both of fear and excitement. Wow. Mat is one strong mofo.

Vero and I both take a step back, watching what happens next.

Mat's voice hasn't changed one bit from his calm demeanor.

"I'm not going to tell you again. You smell of whiskey and it gets on my nerves. I'm going to ask you to leave."

Mat literally picks Alfonso back up by the scruff of his shirt and tosses him towards the doorway to the building. Wow.

Our eyes clash one more time when he turns around before Mat turns back to the laptop to pack things up like nothing happened. How can he be so calm right now? In fact, Akmal doesn't look that worked up either.

"Well, thank you again, ladies. Miss Kobayashi, I will make sure to message you with the raw images and finished product as quickly as possible. Would you like us to walk you back to your vehicle?" Wow, still so professional.

That was very nice of him to offer, but my eyes haven't left Mat's back. He hasn't turned around, but I thought I saw his shoulder stiffening a little bit with the question. Interesting.

"Yes, I think we would like that very much, thank you." I think I would like to know more about this IT tech of his.

"Fuck yeah, I don't want to run into that fool again." She's right, I don't either. Not when he's like this.

Akmal tucks his laptop back into his messenger bag and walks to the right of Vero, while Mat silently walks to the left of me, making sure us girls are in the middle. My heel gets caught on something at the threshold of the entrance, and my hand automatically shoots out to Mat's bicep to prevent me from falling. *My god, his arms are firm.*

When I lift my head to look at him, I can see just how dark his eyes are. Secrets that are buried within the shadows of his face. His eyes look like they're tracking my jaw and then the slope of my neck, making my face heat up. Guys hit on me all the time, but it never feels like this... with just a look, Mat makes me feel a little speechless. I didn't realize that his arm is also around my waist while my hand is still on his bicep.

We both clear our throats as we detach and catch up with Vero and Akmal.

11

MAT

I'm not sure what happened to be quite honest. One minute, I'm minding my own business trying to make sure the first session of photos are uploaded correctly to the right folders in Akmal's laptop, the next the smell of hard liquor burns my nose bringing back memories that makes my body tense up.

From the sound of their conversation, Alfonso must be her ex. *Her.* The beauty whose body looks like it was molded to replicate the gods. Her friend is practically molded the same but there's something about *her.*

I didn't pay her much attention in the beginning until our eyes kept connecting. Like a magnetism that draws me, calling me to look when I have no reason to, only to find her looking at me as well.

Getting rid of the ex was easy. I probably have at least fifty pounds on him. The smell wafting from his mouth makes my mind go into a slight haze, my fist wanting to meet his face. Since his exit was a smooth one, I was able to control the rage that was starting to simmer and boil into something. Especially since I saw how she reacted to him. She didn't want him there and it doesn't look like this is the first time he's been around her in this state.

Akmal was smart enough to offer to escort the ladies to their car. Females as delicate as these would be easy victims to anyone else who had too much to drink at this car show. When Miss Kobayashi, though I could have sworn I heard the guy call her something else, trips into me, my body starts to buzz from the contact.

Still kind of high from the adrenaline at throwing out her ex, my senses are heightened.

It felt like time stood still as we both locked eyes again. She looks as delicate as a flower with curves made for a man's touch. Any man would be lucky to have a woman look at them the way she seems to be looking at me now. I feel like a bastard for being privy to steal the glance she's giving me, like she's trying to wait out for something. What she's waiting for, I have no clue.

My hand can still feel the remnants of her warmth long after I remove it from the small of her waist. I'm not good with these kinds of interactions. I'm not sure what constitutes as pleasantries and what is too much. The good thing is, once Akmal and I escort them to their cars all that's required are simple goodbyes.

So why do I feel like I missed an opportunity for something? Once the ladies are in their car and drive away, Akmal and I slowly walk to the other side of the parking lot.

"These pictures are going to be amazing. Not only were the ladies gorgeous, they really knew how to work their bodies in all the right angles. It's not their first time in front of a camera, that's for sure."

"I didn't catch their names?"

"Oh, the Asian girl was Atsuko Kobayashi and I kept hearing her call her friend Vero."

Atsuko. Her name sounds almost as delicate as she does. How does hair even cascade in waves like that? Like a soft waterfall that falls past the beautiful slope of her shoulder.

"What do you have going for you tonight?"

"Nothing. It's my day off. That's why I decided to come to help out."

"You want to help me with the touch ups on the pictures? It will make the work go faster. I want to set a good precedent for my freelance work with efficiency. Maybe Vero can be my next client. She's got hips and ass for days, the perfect hourglass." So did Atsuko. They were almost like twin goddesses in their skin tight dresses and high heels making their legs look even longer.

What would it be like to have that softness against me? Miss Miller's face mentally takes over and my lips lift in disgust. I need to figure out a way to purge that woman from my system.

Following Akmal's car back to his place, we set up the laptop and camera to transfer the rest of the photoshoot. Sitting back in one of his office chairs, my eyes take in every detail of every single picture that uploads.

The close up headshots Akmal was able to take showcases the delicate freckles that kiss her face. The fullness of her red lips is a stark contrast to the color of her skin. She reminds me of a damn flower petal, delicate and smooth. Her long black lashes against her makeup and the hooded look she has on her face as she gazes out the car window straight into mine. It makes my dick twitch watching that look on her face without actually being a creep while doing it. I didn't want to make things awkward by staring when we were there, but now I can stare my fill.

"These photos are amazing, I don't think there will be much need for any touch ups."

Akmal scoots his chair towards the table and places his chin in one of his hands.

"I think you're right. These girls are a real beauty all on their own." A few photos of both the girls pop up and the way they bend over the car would bring any man to their knees to worship them.

"Damn. Vero is stunning isn't she?" Akmal's voice comes out in almost a whisper next to me. I knew he couldn't be immune to her, cultural dictations be damned. The poor fool isn't even allowed to touch himself.

My eyes are still glued to Atsuko on every single picture that uploads into the computer. "Yeah, she really is." Unlike Akmal, I will most likely be touching myself tonight to these images.

"Alright, I'm going to put this in a network folder and grab the other laptop so we can both work on it at the same time. I'll take one batch and you take the other. Try to leave it as natural as possible and don't be afraid to ask me any questions if you have any. You've used photoshop before, right?"

"Yeah, I've messed with it here and there with gaming images. I'm sure I'll pick up on what you need me to do."

With that settled, we both start to work. Akmal must have a million shots of her. He told me to pick only a handful of good ones to work on. This is going to be hard when she looks beautiful in all of them.

We've been going at it for the past hour when Akmal excuses himself to the restroom. I don't know what comes over me but I shoot a couple off to my email so I can continue to stare at her in the comfort of my home. The moment I hit send, is the moment a message pops up from Akmal's photography website.

It's not my fault the window opens up all the way, showing me what's written.

A. Kobayashi : Thank you so much again for today, I really enjoyed the session. Cannot wait to see the final product.

   MAB. Alqi : _

Do I dare? Akmal is still in the restroom and I'm burning with a strange desire to speak with her again. She doesn't even know it's me though. Does that still count as me speaking with her?

MAB. Alqi : It was great working with you as well.

The next message comes back quickly.

A. Kobayashi : It was also nice meeting your IT guy. Matt, was it?

My heart is kind of beating irregularly at this mention of me. Is she really asking about me? How would Akmal respond to that? I don't have to think about it when he comes waltzing back in, bending down to my screen to see what's going on.

"Oh good, she enjoyed working with me. Here, scoot over and I'll shoot off a message to her."

I quietly switch chairs and watch as he types.

MAB. Alqi : Yeah! He's my go to guy. You are correct, his name is Mat and he is currently assisting me with the photoshoot so that I can quickly return the finished product to you. Would you like a copy of some of the raw images now?

A. **Kobayashi** : Thank you so much, but that won't be necessary. I trust you will do amazing things with the finished product. My friend Vero wanted to know when your next available time slot would be?

Akmal has a big goofy smile on his face when he turns to me. Looks like he's got a crush on the Latin goddess.

"Dude! Her friend Vero wants to book a photoshoot with me. What luck! If I need you, would you be available? I'll make sure to do it on one of your days off."

"Is...her friend going to be there."

"Oh, shit. I don't know. I should ask."

MAB. Alqi : That sounds great. I will have to get back to you once I look at my calendar. Will you be accompanying your friend the way she did with your shoot?

A. **Kobayashi** : Most likely. We usually do come in a pair. How about we meet up to talk in person when you finish with the shoot from today?

"She wants to meet in person to schedule her friend's shoot. You got to come with me. I'm not good being with so many women at a table by myself."

"What are you talking about? Your family is huge. You're surrounded by women all the time. I know for a damn fact you guys have huge parties."

"Yeah, but that's different. They're family. These are hot girls. And from what I gather, hot single girls. Come on man, you got to come with me so I don't make a fool out of myself."

It wasn't like I was going to argue but I didn't want to look that desperate right away despite my heart rate kind of kicking up at possibly seeing Atsuko again.

"I don't know… I'm not good with social situations either. You know me."

"That's why we both need to be there! To buffer each other when it gets awkward. Come on man, do it for me yeah?"

Giving him a moment of silence so he thinks I'm deliberating it in my head, I take a deep breath and nod in agreement.

Akmal throws a fist up in the air. "Yes! This is almost like a double date, even though it's just to schedule a photoshoot."

Now that he mentions it, it is like a double date isn't it? I've never been on a date. My nerves are starting to get the best of me. Shit, what if I fuck this up?

Akmal's fingers are already flying over the keyboard.

MAB. Alqi : That sounds great. We will most likely have the edits done by the end of this week. When would you like to meet up? And where?

It takes a good minute or two before she responds and I'm almost assuming she's bailing on us before it even starts. That would just be our luck.

A. Kobayashi : Sorry about that. I had to work it out with Vero. How does this Saturday sound? There's a nice sandwich shop right across the street from the park. Do you know which one I'm talking about?

We both look at each other. I can feel the hairs on my

arms lift up. She's talking about Sammi's? What are the odds? Is this a sign?

MAB. Alqi : Yea, we know exactly where that is. Sounds good. See you on Saturday.

Akmal is about to close the chat window to his website when one last message pops up.

A. Kobayashi : Tell Mat thank you for today.

I can feel a smile on my lips and it's the strangest thing. It reminds me that I probably don't smile as much as I should since my cheeks ache a little from how big I'm smiling now. I like that she's thinking of me. Granted she's probably not thinking of me the way I'm thinking of her. Shit, I'm going to have to jack off tonight.

We work for another couple of hours before calling it a night. Akmal walks me to my car and waves me off when I start pulling out of the parking lot.

Driving back to my apartment in the dark, I can still clearly see Atsuko's face and body in my mind's eye. I walk to the front door and living room in a daze, unsure of how I managed to shower and lay down on my bed when I don't remember anything but her face and the way she moved those hooded eyes in my direction behind the car's front windshield.

Shit, I don't think my dick is getting any rest tonight with her running around my head.

12

MAT

The week went by quickly. Maybe because I've been anticipating Saturday. Tricia was able to divert Miss Miller's calls when she was on duty. When she wasn't, I told Morty that Travis was good to do solo trips in the field. He gave me a funny look but agreed. I never did find out what the issue was between those two. But he's still going over there so it must not be that big of an issue for her.

A whole week without Miss Miller and I'm already feeling like a new person. Travis hasn't complained one bit, so I don't feel bad about it.

"Are you ready for tomorrow?"

"Yeah, are you?"

"I'm excited and nervous. I hope she likes how the photos came out. I really hope Vero wants to work with me."

Akmal's been mentioning Vero's name more and more

the closer we get to Saturday. I think the crush he has on her is starting to grow. I don't blame him. She's beautiful.

Just not as beautiful as Atsuko. Damn, just thinking about her name makes my dick twitch.

"Hey what are you boys talking about? What's happening tomorrow?"

"Nothing. Just stuff with my side gig."

"Oh" Tricia looks at me and all I can do is shrug. You can never have a decent conversation in this place without someone nearby listening. Both Akmal and I don't like people in our business. We like to keep our lives simple and drama free.

When Tricia gets tired of us keeping our mouths shut, she walks away. Good. Not before another person comes towards us.

"Fuck, thank you for passing your cases to me man. I love this job." Travis is out of his damn mind because no one likes working here, except for apparently him. I hope he gets his fill of that woman.

The rest of the day goes by smoothly without any other interruptions and Akmal and I say our goodbyes despite most likely talking to each other later tonight.

When I get home, my mind starts to overthink things and I start to think of all the possible ways tomorrow's meeting can go bad. I shouldn't think this way, but I can't help it. Good things don't normally come my way, not without an obstacle. Hasn't my past taught me that? And anything involving Atsuko seems too good to be true.

She's probably not even interested in me that way and I'm just in over my head about stuff. Yeah, that's it. I log into the game chat and continue on with my nightly routine chatting with Akmal as usual without another thought about anything happening between a woman as beautiful as Atsuko and myself.

∼

We decided to carpool on Saturday, since Akmal is all jittery about this date. Is it a date? It's basically a business meeting more like it.

We sit at our usual table outside of Sammi's. Our regular waitress is on duty today as well. The girls aren't here yet, so both Akmal and I only order water for the time being. Akmal tells me that he's been getting some inquiries since the car show. He was smart enough to hand out some business cards while he was waiting for the girls.

"You know, I might be able to do it. I might be able to do photography full time. I wonder where the girls are. What time is it?"

"You're going to have to chill, man." Akmal's knees are bouncing a little bit under the table, but it occasionally vibrates my glass.

"I just really want this freelance photography to do well, you know? It can be a solid full time job if it does. I can finally quit working under Morty." For some reason, Morty never got along with Akmal. Some days I think it's because he's jealous that Akmal knows more than he does and feels threatened by the potential of losing his position to him. With Akmal's friendly demeanor, he could probably run that company with better morale.

"I believe in you, man. You do good work, even a blind man can see it."

I feel a shift in my soul and it makes me look up. There at the far end of the street are two dark and beautiful angels coming our way. Is it possible that she's gotten even more beautiful since the last time I saw her?

Her dress is simple and flares out, swishing with her every step. The light colored little sweater she has over it only highlights her dark silky hair. Something is different but I can't put my finger on it.

I hit Akmal in the arm with the back of my hand and we both stand up before the girls can reach us. My hands are in the pockets of my jeans and the closer she gets, the more I feel like I don't deserve to be in her presence. She practically fucking glows.

"Hey! I'm so excited to see what you have for me!" Has her voice always been this soothing? My eyes never leave hers and when the girls finally reach our table, I realize what's different. She's much shorter than I remember. I glance down at her feet and she laughs, making my eyes shoot back to hers. There's a sparkle when she laughs and it draws me in. Am I smiling?

"I'm sure you've noticed. We're not in heels today." My arms itch to touch her but I can't. How can a guy like me touch an angel?

"Damn, I'm starving. Have you guys ordered yet?"

"Not yet. Here, let me get that for you."

Akmal and Vero's voices sound close but far at the same time. I can't seem to pull my eyes away from Atsuko's. The delicate shape of her face, the freckles I've memorized, the slope of her neck. Shit, am I staring? I'm acting like a creep even though I've stared at her pictures in my email all damn night.

Clearing my throat, I pull out a chair for her as she lowers herself to the seat. There's a small smile on her lips and I can't help but stare at how the edges of her lips tip up.

I can feel the heat on my face as I tear my gaze away and get back to my own seat next to Akmal.

The waitress comes out and takes our orders, quickly retreating back inside once Akmal starts to set up his laptop on the edge of the table.

"I've already sent you a copy of everything I'm about to show you to your email. If there are any problems opening them up, please let me know."

The girls are occupied for a short time, going through the gallery of pictures and I take a few moments to sneak in some more looks at Atsuko's side profile as I tip my glass of water up for a drink. Why am I so thirsty all of a sudden?

At this angle, I can see how the soft skin of her neck continues down to the hint of cleavage that peeks out from the top of her dress. I can feel my face heating up at the potential of being caught checking out her breasts. What the hell is wrong with me? But who could blame a guy? I'm only a man who has been placed in the presence of the most beautiful creature he's ever seen.

My eyes are staring at a particular freckle that sits near her collarbone when I hear a soft feminine throat clearing. It's so soft, I almost miss it. Atsuko is looking right at me, biting her bottom lip and my dick twitches in response. Swallowing down a groan by taking another sip of water, I turn my head to the side and hope she forgives my transgressions. I really suck at this social stuff.

Now that my eyes aren't on hers, my mind wanders to what Akmal mentioned earlier. He really could probably do freelance photography as a full time job. Where does that leave me? I'll be losing one of the only good things about that stupid IT job. What's holding me back? What other reason do I have to stay? I mean, I can do IT anywhere. Is it just the comfort zone of having been with this company for so long?

That shouldn't be a good reason to stay because the place doesn't allow me to grow. Who the hell wants to work for Morty for the rest of their life?

"What are you thinking about so hard over there?" Her voice is like a siren's call, I don't have control over myself as I slowly turn her way. The soft smile on her face does something to my insides and it makes me feel nervous.

"Just work related stuff. Nothing important." Hopefully, my mumble was clear enough to understand. I'm saved from any more awkward conversation when our waitress places our food on the table.

Akmal and I eat in relative silence as Vero talks about ideas for her scheduled photo session. When the waitress comes by with the bill, I quickly grab it and throw down enough cash to cover all four of us and then some.

"Thank you, Mat." The sound of my name on her lips makes my dick strain against my jeans and I almost physically grimace when I tell her it's not a problem.

Akmal and I walk the girls back to their car. We learned that they are roommates, so they both came in the same vehicle. Akmal opens the passenger door for Vero and she gives him a bright smile making him take a subtle step back. I'm not sure what else I should be doing besides opening the door, so I stand there, waiting for her to get in.

She doesn't. Instead, she bites her bottom lip, distracting my thoughts again as she pulls me towards her by my front pockets. *Hot damn.* I almost stumble into her if it wasn't for my other arm shooting out to the top of her car because I didn't see it coming. She gets on her little tippy toes and my heart almost beats out of my chest. I bend down her way so she doesn't have to stretch so much. Her lips divert from my cheek and her breath caresses my ear with her message.

"Call me."

I'm stunned in place as she gets into the driver's side and closes the door with a *thump*. Akmal comes to stand by me and we both watch the girls drive away.

"Holy shit."

"Yeah."

"What was that about? I could almost feel the electricity in the air between you guys." I can say the same for him, though he was stepping away from her.

"I don't know. She told me to call her. I don't even have her number…" I go to stick my hands in my pockets again and feel something in my right front pocket. Grabbing it, I see that it's a slip of paper with her number on it.

"Shooo! You got her number now!"

That I do. I can feel my face smiling again as I stare at the beautiful script on the piece of paper.

13

MAT

$\mathcal{M}$y hands are clammy and I'm rubbing them against my jean-clad thighs. I don't know if I can do this. I shouldn't do this.

"Just do it, man!" Akmal's legs are bouncing next to me as we both stare at the ripped sheet of paper on my coffee table like it's an artifact in a museum of wonders.

"I don't know what to say."

"Hell, I don't either but you need to call her. She told you to."

"What do *you* usually say?"

"Hell if I know, I've never been on a date before." Look at us fools. The blind leading the blind. This isn't helping one bit. What if she didn't mean it? What if this was all an accident? What am I saying? She said to call her. I just don't know what to call her about. How do people do this kind of stuff all the time?

Bringing up my browser on my cell phone, I start typing.

"Are you calling her? Wait, are you putting it on speaker phone or something? What are you doing?"

"No, I'm googling how to ask a girl out on a date. I don't know how to do this shit."

"Oh, good idea. What does it say?"

We both lean in and start reading the different links about how to ask a girl out. After about fifteen minutes, I don't feel any less nervous but I think I got the gist of it. Alright, the websites say to keep it simple. Be prepared for rejection. Shit, that makes my stomach churn. But she gave me her number right? I really hope it wasn't a mistake.

We both lean back and I take a deep breath. Okay. Here we go.

My hands are shaking and I misdial the wrong number a couple of times. It's a good thing Akmal was next to me to let me know it was the wrong number.

When the right number starts ringing, I try to stabilize the phone next to my ear. My head feels hot and she hasn't even picked up yet. Does the number of rings before she picks up signify something?

When the sound of her hello comes on, my heart stops. Fuck, I can't do this.

On the second hello, I finally get the courage to take my head out of my ass and respond.

"Hey, it's Mat." Smooth, real smooth.

Her voice is almost a purr and it does something to me. "Hey Mat, I'm so glad you called."

I'm grimacing and Akmal is slapping my shoulder in a show of support.

"Yeah? Me too. Um. What are you doing next weekend?" This is it. This is it.

"Nothing, nothing at all."

My voice is shaking but I need to power through.

"You want to go out next Saturday?"

"Oh Mat, I thought you'd never ask. I'd love to go anywhere with you." Shit, my stomach drops because I didn't think it would get this far. I didn't plan on where to take her.

I cover the microphone with my other hand and frantically whisper to Akmal for some help. "Shit, where should I take her?"

Being the buddy he is, his fingers fly across the screen of his phone. When he's done looking for whatever it is he's looking for, he lifts it up so I can see.

"Mat, are you still there?"

"Yeah, sorry about that. Um, how about the uh…" Covering the microphone with my hand again, I glare at Akmal mouthing to him 'what the hell kind of place is that?'

"Shit, it sounded good. Just a burger joint, you know? Keep it simple, right?"

"How about I pick you up and surprise you." I'm too embarrassed to say the name Big Burger. Hopefully, she'll say yes.

She chuckles and it's the most feminine sound. "Sounds good. I like surprises. So, what time will you be picking me up?"

Damn, how many details go into dating? I'm sweating bullets. I turn to Akmal and mouth to him about a time. He's scrambling on his phone to google a good time to date. We're both sweating bullets.

"Mat, you are too cute. How about you swing by my place around seven. I'll text you my address. Vero wants you to tell Akmal she says hi."

Shit, she knew this whole time. I'm embarrassed but relieved she still wants to do this with me.

I try to chuckle like I didn't just get caught with my

buddy stumbling over this dating thing. "Alright, sounds good. I'll be there to pick you up at seven."

"Goodbye Mat."

"Bye." My shaky finger manages to end the call. I toss my phone onto the table and put my face in my hands, running them through my hair. That was the most nerve wrecking thing I've ever experienced in my twenty nine years of life.

"Shit, you did it!" Akmal is howling and celebrating for me. I'm still waiting for my heart to come back down to earth. I can hear my phone ping with a message. It must be Atsuko sending me her address.

"She told me to tell you that Vero says hi."

Akmal chokes on his next howl and I have to slap him on the back a few times to settle him.

"Damn. I should have gotten her number. Then we could have done another double date, you know?"

That would have been much easier. But it isn't the case, and the date is already set.

"I need to keep her away from my family when they come by. They'll take one look at her and start making wedding plans and thinking of baby names." I chuckle at that because I can see it happening easily. Though judging by the way he acts around her, I don't think he'll be able to keep her away that long.

Once the nerves pass, I think about the job situation again.

"Akmal, what can a guy like me do with my skills? I don't want to be at the company forever. Once you leave, and you know you will, where does that leave me?"

"Sometimes, you just have to take a leap of faith. Comfort zones are known to be dangerous territory because they can blind you. What do you want to do?"

"I don't know, I guess I've never thought about it. I just

work and go home."

"You know, I wouldn't mind having someone I trust to help me with this new photography endeavor."

"Yeah? But what do you need my skills for?"

"My website isn't the greatest. How about you come on as my Web Developer and Tech Manager."

I'm laughing because who the hell am I managing? There's only one guy in the company - Akmal.

"I'm serious Mat. After passing my business card around at the car show, I've picked up at least ten more shoots. We can do this. I can probably squeeze in even more jobs if I knew I had you at my back, so I can just concentrate on the camera work."

I am liking this idea more and more. There's a freedom in it, a freedom I never knew I needed.

"Shit, Akmal. We really doing this?"

"Yes, man! Why not? We're not getting any younger. No time like the present. We can even change the company name if you want. I'm not that big yet."

"Nah, you don't have to do all that. But yeah, I'm in. When were you planning on quitting with Morty?"

At the mention of his name, Akmal makes a disgusted noise.

"Shit, as soon as possible. I got some money in savings that will float me until I get both feet on the ground. How about you?"

"I've been doing nothing but working and going home. I have a good cushion in my savings as well."

"Let's do this then."

Fuck yes. I get up to grab the calendar off my kitchen wall and bring it back to the coffee table. We both stare at the dates and start deciding when we should put in our two-week notice.

14

MAT

*D*id I think I was nervous when I called her? Shit, it doesn't compare to what I feel right now as I pull up near her apartment. I'm really doing this. I'm going on a date with Atsuko.

Akmal tried to help me out with what to wear, but in the end we were so clueless that I just went with whatever was clean and within hand's reach.

I smooth down my button shirt when I get out of the car and try not to trip on my way to her front door. My knuckles hit the wood softly as I clear my throat in preparation for a smooth greeting. I read somewhere that showing up with flowers was a good thing, I'm just praying my fists don't clutch the stems too tightly and damage them.

I'm about to knock again when the door opens and her smell reaches my nose. It's something soft, subtle and slightly floral making you want to lean in to take a good whiff. I shouldn't though because that would be creepy, right?

When did my eyes close? I open them to find her absolutely glowing in front of me with her hair in a ponytail with a curl on top of her head reminiscent of the fifties. She's in heels again, making her closer to my height. The eyeliner she has on only emphasizes her beautiful brown eyes. She doesn't even look like she has much makeup on and it only showcases her natural beauty even more. Her dress clings to her curves in all the right places and is smoking hot red.

Her voice is purring again, the way it always does when she talks to me. Does she sound like this to everyone she talks to?

"Mat, you brought me flowers." I was starting to question myself about the decision until her beautiful lips pull up into a smile and she takes the bouquet from my hand to bring to her delicate nose.

"I've never had anyone bring me flowers before." Her smile is now blinding and I almost forget my voice for a second as I stare at how it transforms her face.

"Then we should remedy that."

"Yowza! Mat, you clean up well. Is Akmal around?" Why would Akmal be around if I'm just here for my date?

"Ignore Vero, she can't stop talking about him. You might as well tell him to call her."

"He doesn't have her number."

"Vero, you didn't even give him your number. Make sure you get on that." Her eyes never leave mine as she hands Vero her flowers, steps out and closes the door behind her, not waiting for her friend's response.

We start walking towards the car when I see some of her male neighbors peek out their door to look at her. Irrational anger flares up and I'm feeling kind of possessive as my hand covers the small of her back to make her walk in front of me blocking her perfect ass from their sights.

I caught her first. They shouldn't be looking at what's mine.

She chuckles at something as her hips continue to sway with her walk to the car. Opening up the passenger side door, I watch as she gracefully slides inside, one long leg after another. Holy shit, how did I get so lucky?

Trying not to slam the door, I run to the other side to get in as fast as I can.

The burger joint is already programmed into my phone's GPS in case I don't remember how to get there. Akmal and I did a few dry runs just in case, so I don't think I'll need to turn it on.

When we pull up to the parking lot, I'm having second thoughts again. She's dressed much too pretty for a place like this. It looks like a small diner.

"I love Big Burger! How did you know?" I refrain from wiping the sweat off my forehead because this could have gone so many different ways. I'm glad it wasn't a bust.

"Just a lucky guess."

"Vero and I come to this place all the time. I love the vintage atmosphere."

I have no idea what the atmosphere is like since I've never stepped foot in this place before. Opening the front glass door for her, I immediately see what she means. It's like a throwback diner with its black and white tile floors and retro decor. There's even a colorful jukebox in the corner.

Sliding into one of the empty booths, we place our orders to the nice waitress who comes up to our table. This is the moment Akmal and I have been training for. We've been practicing with each other on how to do small talk. I'm feeling confident. I think I can get through this date unscathed.

"Mat, just relax. I won't bite unless you want me to." Everything I've practiced and learned has gone up in smoke with that sentence. What the hell do you say to that?

She chuckles as I cast my gaze down at the table, trying to figure out how to steer the conversation back to more comfortable ground.

"So what are your interests?" There. That should get us back on track.

Her smile makes me blush and lose my train of thought for a second.

"I'm interested in you, Mat." Okay, Akmal and I have never anticipated this response.

"I'm interested in you as well." That's good, right?

"I'm glad." I'm saved by the waitress when she starts putting our plates onto the table.

We eat in relative silence. The food here is actually pretty damn good. I'm kind of glad Akmal chose it now.

"I need to use the ladies room." I nod my head as I wipe my mouth after taking my last bite out of the burger.

I notice the guy at the table behind us look her way and I glare at him until he notices me. He does and quickly averts his gaze back to his meal. Damn, is this going to be a regular occurrence? I know she's fucking beautiful, but keeping the other wolves from sniffing after her is starting to look like a job in itself. My gut tells me she's more than worth it. Maybe it wasn't a good idea to let her go to the restroom alone. An irrational fear and anger courses through me at the thought of some other guy cornering her at the restroom and taking advantage of her. Men can be damn animals when it comes to what they want to chase.

I toss a few bills down and quickly get up to go find her.

There's a few guys lingering and it doesn't look like there's a line to the restroom. *I knew it.*

Being one of the tallest guys here, I shove my way inside the small hallway until the door to the ladies room opens up revealing my woman, safe and sound. She's still looking down at her little purse and I take the opportunity to glare at every fucker here, throwing in a snarl to the guys who glare right back at me. I'm about to punch the guy to the left of me for taking so long to bring his gaze up to mine when I feel Atsuko run into my chest.

My hands automatically go around her body to steady her but my eyes are still sending daggers into this fucker's head. He's just lucky my hands are occupied right now. He finally sees me and scampers off. Damn straight.

"Oh, sorry. I didn't see you there, Mat. Have you been waiting here this whole time I was gone?"

My brain is telling me to remove my hands now that she's fine and safe, but my hands are refusing to listen. They're transmitting that this is exactly where they belong.

"Just making sure you were alright."

She laughs and I can feel that shit hit me in the chest. I should be the only guy to hear her laugh like that. It's a dangerous sound. There are too many men around here waiting to pounce.

"Why wouldn't I be?" Fucking hell, does she not have eyes?

"Because you're fucking beautiful and men are animals." The words slip out of my mouth before my brain is quick enough to filter it and she gasps. *Shit.*

"Are you an animal, Mat?" Are her eyes hooded? What the hell is happening here? My cheeks feel like they're flaming with embarrassment at my behavior.

I clear my throat and finally make my hands do as they

are told, leading her out of the diner and back into the passenger seat of my car.

The feel of her body still tingles on my palms when I get into the driver side and place them on the steering wheel and gear shift.

"What else do you have in store for us today?" Why does her voice always sound like that? It makes my dick harden when I should be concentrating on the road and not crash.

"I was thinking of a walk at the park. It's a nice day today and fresh air is always good for one's soul."

"My god, you are real, aren't you?" I'm not sure if this is a good thing or bad thing. Does she not like the idea?

"I mean, we could do something else…"

Her hand on my thigh stops my mouth from continuing. I have to try hard to concentrate on breathing and not how close her fingers are to my dick.

"I'd love to take a walk with you at the park, Mat." I let out a long breath and continue to drive us safely to our next destination.

The research I did last night told me the weather would be in the seventies today. Perfect for a quick stroll. Honestly, I only thought of it because I have no fucking other idea about what to do. But I didn't want the date to end after our meal. I just wanted more time with Atsuko. The movies seemed like a bad idea because I wouldn't be able to really be with her if we're just sitting there in the dark, staring at a screen.

I felt a little too selfish for that, so a walk in the park it is.

After strolling for about a few minutes, Atsuko's hand slips into mine. The softness of her skin makes me think of how soft it would feel like holding onto my cock. Shit, I need to think unsexy thoughts before I won't be able to walk at all. That wouldn't go well.

I clear my throat and attempt again to start a conversation. That's what people do on dates, right?

"Have you lived in this area long?"

"Yeah, my parents live a couple of towns over. I left the house when I was twenty-one and never looked back. My parents are pretty independent free spirits. They didn't mind. In fact, they probably celebrated and are out partying all the time now that they're empty nesters."

"Does that mean you're an only child?"

"Oh no, I have a couple of brothers. One of them joined the military and the other is working in a different city. I don't know what he does, I just know he's doing fine living the bachelor life. I'm the baby of the family, the last to leave. We text now and again to see if the other is still alive but that's about it."

"Oh."

Not one to usually talk about my past, I try to keep the conversation about her by thinking of some more questions, but she beats me to it.

"So, do you work with Akmal full time? He said you were his personal IT guy?"

"Uh, yeah, I work with Akmal. But our normal day job is with a technical support company. It's how we met. He's the best guy I know."

"How nice. You guys seem close. Like Vero and myself. We've been friends for over a decade."

"How about you, do you model full time?"

Her laugh is beautiful.

"I wish. It would be much easier. No, as of right now, I work a makeup counter for commission. It's amazing how much money women are willing to spend on makeup. You would be surprised by the amount I bring in on a good week.

Vero helps with that by hanging out when she can to boost sales with her beautiful face."

"She's not as beautiful as you."

Her eyes sparkle and her smile grows wide. She's really stunning when she smiles. I'm glad my slip of tongue didn't put my foot in my mouth. She squeezes our joined hands and takes my arm as we continue our leisurely walk around the park grounds.

15

MAT

The walk ended way too soon. The entire date ended way too soon. We're at her front door and I'm not sure what I'm supposed to do. The sites I looked up a few days ago left me conflicted on whether or not I should give her a kiss at the door. To be honest, I've never kissed anyone before and the thought alone makes my palms sweat. Miss Miller has fucked me, the women who propositioned me have fucked me. But the simple thought of kissing makes me feel like I'm about to fall to my death.

I don't know how long I stand there contemplating whether dying is worth it when Atsuko grabs the front of my shirt bringing me down and places her mouth on mine. The softness of her lips is a contrast against the strong grasp she still has on my shirt. I don't know what I'm doing but I'm lost in her touch, in her smell.

My mouth starts to pick up on her patterns quickly and

soon enough a feminine sigh escapes as our tongues start to tentatively explore each other. Shit, this is almost better than sex. Who knew kissing could be this intense? Her hands leave my shirt and start to caress my face making me groan. I haven't shaved in a few days, hopefully she's not put off by my scruff.

The door behind us opens up but it doesn't stop the tongue dance we have going. I'm consumed by Atsuko's presence - fucking drowning. My mouth is getting more desperate for her by the minute, never getting enough of what she's giving me.

"I'll...uh..see you guys later. Atsuko, I'll be back tomorrow chica." I think I hear Vero leave the apartment but I'm not too sure because Atsuko grabs my shirt again and drags me into her home without taking her lips or tongue off mine, shutting the door by slamming me against it. *Holy shit.*

I make a sound of complaint when she removes her lips from mine, the sight of her smeared lipstick doing something to my insides. My cock is starting to hurt with how much it's straining behind my pants. Hours of jacking off yesterday hasn't helped me one bit.

My eyes zone in on her hand as she slowly drags the side zipper down on her dress. My hands are on the same page despite my brain being fixated on the way the bright red fabric slides to the floor revealing her beautiful naked breasts and red lace panties.

I probably broke some of the buttons in an effort to rip off my button shirt to get naked as fast as I can. I just need to feel her skin against me. I need it like my next breath.

She removes her hair tie and her dark hair cascades down like a fucking Hollywood movie. I growl under my breath and I start to take steps towards her. There's a glint in her eye as she starts to take steps back, stepping out of her heels along the way. Her eyes are raking across the expanse of my chest, arms and back to my face.

There's something inside overtaking my senses. Something primal. The farther she gets from me the more I growl in frustration because I can't smell her as much as I crave to. I need her scent on me and all over me. I'm somehow out of my pants and stalking towards her in just my boxers when I find us in a room that smells strongly of her. Her bedroom.

She turns around and looks at me over her shoulder, fuck if I don't feel my cock leak at the sight. Ever so slowly she pushes her lace panties down her legs without bending her knees whatsoever. *My god.*

When she starts crawling onto the bed, I snap and pounce on her. I've never been aggressive when it comes to sex but this girl right here does something to me. She makes me want something so fucking badly that I can't control myself.

Covering her body with mine, I flatten her onto the mattress as I rub my face all over those delicate slopes of her shoulders that have haunted my damn dreams since the first time I've seen them at the car show. My hands are greedy and they can't decide where they want to go or where they want to linger. So they're caressing everything they can reach. She's just as soft as I thought. Like a damn flower petal that a man like me shouldn't be allowed to touch and taint. Something that should have been beyond my reach.

When her ass comes up a little and grazes my erection, I hiss and kiss the shell of her ear.

"Fuck, the things you do to me."

Her breathing is deeper, a little faster.

"What do I do to you, Mat?"

"Everything. You take over my senses. I can't think straight. I can't close my eyes without seeing you."

Our lips crash again despite our awkward position while

one of my hands pushes down my boxers and the other runs through her silky hair, the strands sliding through my fingertips. I'm heating up, about to internally combust every time her tongue swipes mine. The overall temperature of the room is rising. I'm slowly getting drunk off the smell of her.

Something comes over me, making my hand grip her hair firmly, tugging her onto her back. My mouth can't get enough of her taste as I kiss, nip and suck her jaw down to her neck. *Fuck.* That little freckle by her collarbone is taunting me and so I take my time to suck even harder in retaliation to it. She grabs one of my hands and places it on her exposed breast, pushing it down, letting me know what she needs.

They're so soft, she's so damn warm. All the hours in the day wouldn't be enough for me to have my fill of her. My mouth travels lower and I envelop one of her dark nipples into my mouth like a starving man. Thoughts of my mystery girl during my lonely nights flit through my mind. Atsuko is a million times better than anything my imagination can come up with. The taste and feel of the real thing is like fucking heaven.

Not wanting her other breast to be lonely, I trail my tongue across her chest to the other nipple. If her moans and grip in my hair is anything to go by, I think I'm on the right track. My dick is telling me to hurry with the way it's forcing my hips to push against her leg. *Down boy.* I need more of a taste. I don't want this over just yet. I wonder if she tastes just as amazing between her legs? There's only one way to find out.

Peppering kisses down her belly, the smell of her arousal makes me want to cum on the fucking sheets right here. This has got to be the most beautiful pussy I have ever seen. She's nice and trim, allowing me to see her labia pinkened and puffed out. Her clit is beautiful and engorged, peeking out of its hood like it's calling me out to play. It's glistening and it makes my mouth water in anticipation of her taste. The moment my tongue touches her wetness between her folds is the moment my inner beast takes over. Licking, nipping, lapping and teasing. All those years of abuse from Miss Miller taught me how to treat a woman's pussy like a temple of worship.

"Oh my fucking god."

Nah, it's just me. Mat. And I'm fucking hungry for this. I can't stop because she tastes fucking incredible. The stiffening of her clit makes my tongue play with her even harder, kissing and teasing it like it's her mouth I'm making love to. Her body's responses only make me hotter; what she's giving me is making me feel powerful. I'm used to my dick being tortured in wait though, so she's going to have to suffer through her own form of torture with my mouth.

When her legs tighten around my head, I open my eyes to watch the look on her face. Both of her hands are squeezing and plucking at her nipples, her beautiful mouth parting as she cries out in pleasure. It's a sight I will forever sear into my memory. My tongue spears into her wet pussy as my thumb takes over where my mouth left off on her clit. I need her to give me everything she has, I deserve that reward. I've been good.

She does reward me as she rides the waves of her orgasm on my tongue, thrusting her pussy against my face in time with my tongue thrusting into her opening. My other arm pushes her legs wider in case she tries to push me off. That's not fucking happening. When the gyrations of her hips die down, I'm feeling a little put out that she only had one orgasm and so my tongue starts to thrust into her again and again a little harder. I can feel her pussy pulsating against the muscle.

"Oh my god, I can't take it. It's too much." Fuck that. She's going to take it because I need her to cum again. I fucking need it. It's for me.

Changing tactics, my mouth switches places with my hand. My fingers slowly enter her as my tongue plays with her swollen bud, nipping and sucking every now and again. Much too soon, she orgasms once more and I have to quickly maneuver my tongue in her so I can taste all of her before it escapes. It's fucking delicious and I groan against her lower lips.

Her body becomes more lax as I continue to clean up everything she's given me. My dick feels like it's going to explode with just a graze of the wind. I'm grimacing but it's a good pain. I love that I can make her feel this way, make her feel worshiped because she needs to be. She's mine to worship.

Climbing up her body, our mouths crash again and it makes me hot with how unabashedly she tastes herself on my lips. Her delicate hands graze across my chest and run down my abs making me tense up in anticipation of its destination.

She gasps into my mouth when her fingers graze across the head of my cock, making it jump in her hand like a damn pet waiting for its command. Ripping her lips from mine she looks down and gasps again.

"Holy shit. A reverse prince albert."

I've become addicted to her kisses and this little break is already killing me. She shouldn't create an addict if she isn't ready for the repercussions. Grabbing her neck, I tilt it back up where it belongs, slamming my mouth on hers with my tongue at the ready to invade her space.

Who is this man? It's me, but it's not. I've never seen this part of me before. Atsuko has opened something I don't think I will be able to close. The way she submits to everything so easily, it's a complete contradiction to every woman I've ever been with. It makes me greedy to find out everything she's willing to do.

My own fucking fantasy come to life.

The skin of my shaft is rubbing against her pussy lips back and forth, the head of my cock grazing her clit every so often. We're both breathing hard as we continue to devour each other's mouths.

"Please. Please, I need your cock in me." Has a request ever sounded so sweet? I've never once had a woman say please like she does. I can get used to this.

"Do you? Why is that?" My kisses travel to the slope of her neck again as my hips continue its torturous slide against her wet core.

"Because I feel so empty without you." Shit, it's like she's speaking to my soul. Now that I know what it's like to have her, I feel so empty just thinking about what it would be like to not have her.

Pulling my hips back, I plunge into her as deep as I can fucking go. I want to reach the depths of her soul the way she's already buried herself deep into mine. This is it. This is where I belong. This is the place my soul has been restless to find.

Atsuko's arms go around me tightly as I start to ram into her because I can't fucking help it. She feels too damn good. I don't understand why it's so different with her.

Every time it feels like I'm about to cum, I slow my hips down because I don't ever want it to end. She whimpers beneath me but I pay it no mind because I've been good. I deserve this. She brought me into her home, invited me inside of her. Just thinking about her begging me makes my dick even harder.

I don't know when my hair tie came off but my hair is falling into my eyes, slapping it every time I slap my hips against hers. The entire room smells like sex, only adding to the intoxication of the moment.

"I love the way you feel inside of me."

Shit, another thing I didn't know I was missing out on. A woman's breathless bedroom voice, whispering sweet nothings into my ear.

"I need to feel you cum inside of me. I'm on the pill."

When her tongue glides across my chest, my pounding becomes frantic. She's right. I need to feel myself cum inside of her too. This instinct to mark her as mine.

Her cries are becoming louder and louder the harder I pound into her. My abs and balls tense up, and it feels like I've been struck with electricity as I cum what feels like gallons inside of her pussy. Shouldn't masturbation reduce the amount? It feels like I've been through a long and rough dry season when it's not the case at all. The combination of our juices makes us glide against each other as the intensity of the orgasm slowly dies down. I don't want to pull out of her though, I don't want to sever the connection just yet.

Grabbing her face again in both of my hands, I place my lips gently on hers. She's my first kiss, the only person I ever want kissing me. Our mouths aren't as frantic as it started, but it's still just as sweet. My heart feels full, like the void has finally been filled to the brim and is now almost overflowing.

She tastes like fucking home.

16

ATSUKO

I've never been so worn out from sex before. I didn't even realize we fell asleep with tangled limbs until the sun came up and shone on my face waking me up. He smells of male musk and sex. This entire room does, and it makes me fucking horny. Turning my head to look at his face, he's got one arm over his eyes and the other hanging off the bed with his legs open. His decency is only covered by the corner of the sheet.

Perfect.

Slowly crawling so as to not shake the bed, I make my way south. He's beautiful to look at. The tan of his skin, the way his muscles stretch and play against the artwork across his body. The wolf on his abdomen looks like he's snarling at me but I can snarl right back.

I'll make you howl in a minute, pup.

My hands grab the corner of the sheet and slowly pull it

off him like a private strip tease, revealing his defined abs and dusting of hair that points straight to the promised land.

His dick is already hard, tenting the fabric but it still does nothing to stop the small gasp that comes out of my mouth. How did I take this monster in me last night? The sun casts at just the right angle, glinting against the small curved bar on top of his penis. He's uncircumcised but the bar is small enough to fit under his foreskin, only giving a peek of what's beneath at the very head of his cock. My mouth is already watering at the memory of how it feels inside of me. I wonder what it feels like in my mouth?

Mat stirs a little, his arm still over his face, but doesn't wake up. He must be a deep sleeper. *Good.* I store that fact in the back of my mind for future reference as my hands lightly slide across his upper thighs. He has some firm quad muscles, it's impressive. No wonder his stamina's so high.

I can't take it anymore as I watch his cock twitch when I touch it with my fingers. It's like it wants to be petted but doesn't know how to ask.

That's okay boo, I got you. *Come to mama.*

I tease the firm crown of his head slowly with the tip of my tongue, running it along the underside and running it across the adornment. It makes me hot to know he's got this secret hidden away from view. Just thinking about other women knowing this about him makes me fired up with a tinge of jealousy and possessiveness.

My emotions burn with intensity as I take his entire head into my mouth, making sure my teeth don't get caught with the balls of his piercing. My tongue dances along the shaft as I take him in deeper and deeper.

His cock stretches my mouth in the most delicious way. His size matches the size of him all over. He's a big guy, but perfect for me.

The length of him almost makes me gag, but I love it. I love everything about it. My mind is imagining him fucking my face and it makes my pussy weep. Up and down, up and down, my tongue swirling on every pass around the crown of his head. He's so big, my mouth is salivating and it drips down his shaft as well as my chin, making the movement slide even more.

On one of the downward passes, I make my throat swallow, eliciting a moan from his lips. I'm getting into it, anticipating the finish when I feel a large warm hand behind my head. It only rests there, not doing anything more, making me a little frustrated at the fact. I need him wanting, I need him craving me with the same intensity in which I'm craving him. *I want to make him lose control.*

On one of the upward passes I remove my mouth from him and start licking his shaft like it's fucking melting ice cream. Nipping down the underside of his shaft all the way down, my tongue teases his ball sack, watching it tighten up with my ministrations.

Well look at that, a reaction. I love it.

My hand takes over stroking his cock where my mouth left off as I transfer my concentration to this new area. Slowly but surely sucking his sack into my mouth, my hand squeezes the crown of his cock on an upward pass. A hiss escapes him and it amps up my efforts. Moving his balls in my mouth a few times, I remove myself and return to the main attraction, his wondrous cock.

When his hand comes over the back of my head again, I moan, sending vibrations down his length, finally making him grip my hair. *Yes, just like that. I love it.*

Removing my mouth with a pop, my tongue teases his slit seductively, licking off his precum, as I open my eyes to look straight into his hooded ones. He's moved his arm to his forehead just far enough for his eyes to see everything I'm doing to him.

"I want you to fuck my face, Mat. Fuck it like you mean it."

I don't give him time to deliberate what he wants to do because I start sucking like a girl on a mission. A mission to make him give me my reward in my mouth.

My mouth is getting tired, but I don't let up. No, I need him to cum in my mouth. I need it so badly. My inner ho is crying for it.

It seems like a while before Mat gets brave enough to do what I say, and I swear I can feel my pussy clench in response, trying to grab onto empty space. *My god. I'm so fucking horny*. His hips are starting to thrust, making me gag every now and again. He's still holding back, still being too nice. But we'll get him there soon enough.

When his cock starts expanding in girth, I know I'm in the home stretch. My hand starts to fondle his balls and I give him one really good suck on the way down his shaft. The warmth of his cum shooting in my mouth does something to me. It makes me feel proud. It makes me feel like a good little girl getting her reward.

"Shit."

I take everything he has to give me, and it is a fucking lot. It starts to spill out the side of my lips despite the speed at which I'm trying to swallow. When his dick stops pulsating, and a guttural groan echoes around me, I slowly remove him from my mouth and lick the side of my lips while staring into his dark eyes. I love the way he looks when he just wakes up. I want to see it every day. I want to wake him up like this every day, worshiping his dick like he deserves.

My eyes glance back down to my hand that's still slowly stroking, and I'm surprised at what I see. He's still hard. My lady bits are getting excited at the possibilities of what this might mean for me. Could it be?

Mat's strong arms grab me and throw me onto the bed face down, lifting my hips up. His warmth comes up behind me, and he nuzzles the back of my neck. He enters me in the slowest of motions, torturing my already sensitive pussy in the best of ways. I'm so wet that he just glides in and out leisurely, as his lips kiss a trail across my shoulder blade.

"You're so fucking beautiful it hurts, Atsuko."

The stuff that comes out of his mouth just can't be real.

His dick starts to increase in speed and my ass starts to back up in time with it. I want him. I want him so bad. My pussy is starting to clench and the bitch loves the big dick it's clenching around.

The wet sound of our bodies slapping is doing something to me.

Thump thump thump.

"Keep that shit down, I'm trying to sleep!"

His masculine chuckle against my spine sends shivers down my body straight to my core. I love the way he feels so comfortable with me right now. Like he's a whole different person from the man I met the first time. *I did that.*

His hand suddenly pushes my neck from behind, shoving my face into the mattress every time his thrust becomes harder and harder. Despite the muffled message from the other side of the wall, my cries start to become louder and louder every time he buries himself in me to the hilt.

His speed picks up like he's a fucking beast, the pleasure teetering onto the point of delicious pain from the friction until he groans again and buries himself one last time. I can literally feel his cock pulsating inside of me and it's empowering. A goddess's potion.

He keeps my hips up as the hand that was behind my

neck travels to the front of me right onto my clit. The man plays me like an instrument, slowly rocking his softening cock inside of me until a climax takes over and I see stars behind my eyelids. *Holy shit.* I've never felt so satiated like this, ever.

Mat might just be the man to kill me through sex... but what a way to go.

17

MAT

"I take it that the date went well?" Akmal has a goofy expression on his face, and you know what? I probably do too. I feel like I'm on fucking cloud nine.

My sack feels lighter, that's for sure. Atsuko is just as insatiable as I am. Who knew? Thinking about anyone else knowing that fact about her makes me feel uneasy. I really need to rein in my temper around her.

"I've never seen you late to work ever. You barely made it with like a minute to spare."

"Well, I made it. I had to take care of my girl. Vero kicked us out because she couldn't sleep, so she spent Sunday with me."

"Shooo! From one date to spending the night? Damn man, I'm going to need you to give me some pointers."

"Shit, I have no fucking idea what I'm doing. It just feels

like once we start, we can't keep our hands off each other." I want my hands on her right now.

"Life goals, man." Akmal looks like he really is contemplating his life at the moment. How did my life turn around like this? One day I'm just an IT guy helping a buddy out, the next I'm in a whirlwind of a relationship.

I have no regrets. It's the best thing that's happened to my life so far.

"Boys, quit messing around. We got calls lining up." Tricia's voice brings me out of my Sunday reverie and I start grabbing my tools before heading out to the designated work vehicle. I wonder if she made it to work alright.

"Shit, I only wish I was so lucky." I am a lucky bastard, aren't I?

"I forgot to tell you, Vero wants your number. She mentioned it before I took Atsuko out. Sorry, it slipped my mind all weekend."

Akmal is throwing punches in the air and bouncing on his feet causing the other employees to look at us. I'm laughing because I really don't give a rat's ass about this place anymore. Akmal and I both are going to put in our two-week notice soon.

"Akmal, you got this order." Tricia hands him the written telephone order and then turns to me, the octaves of her voice getting a little lower. "Hey you, Miss Miller is requesting you again."

My day just went sour.

"Pass her to Travis. He's familiar with her cases." Tricia's face has an expression I can't read but it disappears quickly so I pay it no mind. I'm still feeling the high of last weekend.

"Travis! You got an order!" Without taking her eyes off me, she hands me the work order that's under Miss Miller's case without another word.

Good. Now my day is looking up again. Atsuko is good for me. I'm feeling on top of the world.

I handle the morning's caseload pretty quickly and soon enough, it's lunch time. Akmal is just putting his tools away when I hear Tricia speaking to someone behind me.

"We're about to close for lunch break, you'll have to come back later."

"Oh, I was hoping to catch Mat. He hasn't left yet, has he?" I know that voice anywhere. It's been whispering in my ear in the heat of the moment.

"Does he know you?" I've never heard Tricia sound like *that* before. It's kind of ticking me off, how she's speaking to my girl.

Walking back towards the direction of the front desk quickly before anything else happens, Atsuko's eyes and face lights up when she sees me. It feels like my heart is being squeezed. Damn, a man can get used to that kind of welcome.

"Hey, beautiful." I don't have any more words to give her because my mind is on one track right now, to touch her as fast as possible.

I do just that when I reach her, placing my arms behind the small of her back and bending her back to kiss the lips I've been missing all day.

"Give them some privacy Tricia." I don't know what she's doing and I don't care. My entire being is zoned in on this woman in my arms. *My woman.*

Atsuko moans a little as our tongues tangle, her hands running through my hair, probably losing my hair tie again. Shit, I can feel my dick stirring and trying to home in on her hot center.

Using what strength I have, I pull my mouth from hers and caress her delicate nose with my own.

"Have lunch with me." Her smile is blinding no matter how many times I've been privileged to see it and it makes my heart stutter.

"Of course. I missed you." Her hooded eyes make me want to eat *her* for lunch.

"Good because I missed you too." I should just leash her to my side. Would that be too much?

"Uh.. should I do lunch solo then?" I can barely register Akmal's voice as I continue to stare into her eyes.

"Hell no, you're not. Excuse me chica, I'm going to have to ask you to stop staring at my BFF with her man. It's kind of rude. Akmal, you're not bailing on me, are you?"

"I … uh, I didn't even know you were here."

"That's because you forgot to ask me for my number. I came to make sure you never forget it again."

"Holy shit." I chuckle as I hear Akmal's voice under his breath.

"So, who's driving?" I can already see Vero dragging Akmal out the front door in my periphery as I give Atsuko another kiss on the lips.

"Tricia, we'll be back in an hour." Clearing my throat, I straighten my woman back up without removing my hands from her.

I don't hear what she mumbles as Atsuko and I leave right behind Akmal and Vero.

We eat at Sammi's, and with the addition of Vero, conversations go a little smoother. For me and Akmal anyway. Vero can talk anyone's ear off.

"So Mat, where are you from?"

"Uh.. originally Montana. I was living on one of the reservations." It's been a while since I stepped foot in that state. I drove as far as my car would take me after leaving.

Atsuko's face brightens at that tidbit. I really don't like

talking about my past. I don't want her to know of the dark stain that's on my soul. Surprisingly, she isn't pushing for more.

"Oh, I see. So does that mean you have a tribe? Is that what they call it? I'm sorry if I'm prying." Vero doesn't look sorry at all, but she also doesn't look like she means anything malicious by her statement. I can't blame her curiosity, at least she has the decency to ask and not assume.

"Blackfoot Indian."

"Does that mean you have an Indian name?" Atsuko's question is soft, probably to let me know that I don't have to answer if I don't want to. When she's like this, I want to do whatever she wants.

"Matunaagd Big Crow. But Mat is fine." A smile creeps up on her lips but Atsuko doesn't say anything else. There's a calm about her that I enjoy. My soul feeds on it, always wanting to be around her so that it can rub off on me.

"Does your name mean anything?" It's my turn to ask her. I find myself falling deep into her eyes. It feels like no one exists at this moment but her, here, now.

"My parents are second-generation Japanese American. From what I've been told, Atsuko means honest and sincere while my last name Kobayashi means small forest." I take in everything she tells me like it's gold. Small forest, huh? Is this where my soul was longing to roam? This can't be a coincidence, can it?

"Akmal…" Vero's voice is practically purring like a kitten towards him. She is not shy about showing her interest at all. That's one thing I noticed about these two women. They are full of life and confidence.

"What does your name mean?" She puts her hand on her chin and leans in closer while Akmal subtly leans a little farther back in his chair.

I stifle a laugh when he tries to clear his throat and keep a friendly smile on his face before he answers her. Vero has a really strong energy and it can be overwhelming to be around.

"Blessed clever son of an intelligent mind. Or something like that."

"Ohh… clever and intelligent. Just the way I like them. Perfect, really."

Her finger touches his thigh and Akmal almost falls off his chair. The girls laugh and Akmal gives us all a sheepish look when he straightens back up and takes a big sip of his water. This poor guy's got it bad and he can't do a thing about it.

18

MAT

*A*kmal and I put in our two-week notice at the same time. Morty was dumbfounded when he saw us come into his office together, but it serves him right. He's always thinking everything under his control is going fine and dandy when in reality, not many of us are happy with the way things are. A great leader makes a big difference, and Morty is always hiding himself away in his office leaving the peons to pick up all the slack. Some days I wonder if I'm really the only one with a Miss Miller problem.

It's only been a month since the car show, but all the time Atsuko and I have been spending together never seems to be enough. My craving for her is only getting stronger and stronger, making me question whether my obsession with her is even healthy.

Akmal and Vero still haven't gone on an actual date yet, but she's been coming by the job often to eat lunch with him.

Akmal is a harder guy to catch despite how friendly he is. He's not used to all the attention and Vero kind of scares him with her personality. I'm kind of scared for him myself. His culture also doesn't let him get too close to a woman before marriage, let alone touch them in more than a friendly manner. Vero's got her hands full if she wants to catch Akmal.

Atsuko has been spending half her weeks with me at my place and it kills me every time she goes back to her apartment. I shouldn't be this greedy, I should appreciate whatever she gives me but damn if I don't want to just lock her up in my bedroom and throw away the key.

Every time I walk her to her front door, her male neighbors are always hanging around. It's like they know her schedule and fucking hang out in packs waiting for my female to return to her damn den. I try to get a handle on my rage by signing up for an MMA gym to get some of my aggression out on the heavy bags.

But today is not going to be one of my best days.

Atsuko is just about to insert her key into her door when the hairs on the back of my neck rise. The sound of male voices are getting louder and louder and my head is starting to feel tight, making my teeth grind. They sound drunk and rowdy. I hate rowdy crowds.

My girl shouldn't be subject to living next to this shit.

"Hey, baby! Haven't seen you around in a while. Where have you been giving tail? I want some of that."

My mind is in a red haze and I can't see anything but his neck and eyes as they start to become bloodshot from my hands squeezing tighter and tighter. I don't even know how I ended up on top of him, pushing his skull into the ground in time with my choking the life out of him. Hands and limbs are trying to pull me off which only makes me angrier.

Releasing one of my hands, I elbow the face behind me before I start pummeling this fucker's nose in so he can stop sniffing around my girl. The impact of my knuckles and the sound of the crunch makes me smile as I continue to throw blow after blow. My fists start to slip with the blood that's starting to seep out.

This fucker has been after my girl every single time I bring her back to her apartment. All these stupid frat boys and their drinking parties, hanging out like stray dogs sniffing up the wrong fucking female. *My female.*

The smell of hard liquor burning my nostrils starts to flash my mind back to the past and my body goes on autopilot. Male grunts, the sound of flesh hitting walls, the tinkling of broken glass, the shattering of broken bottles, the metallic smell mixing in with the alcohol. It all becomes a blur.

It only feels like a second in time but I know it's been longer. I'm standing over a pile of bodies that are moaning and rolling on the ground. Some blood is splattered in areas, some faces are unrecognizable and smeared in crimson.

When the red haze slowly lifts from my mind's eye, I take a few steps back causing the broken glass under my boots to crunch. My breath is heaving, the blood flow in my veins making me feel hot all over. There's tension in my shoulder muscles and I still feel the adrenaline coursing through me.

When none of the boys on the ground speak anything coherent, I slowly turn my gaze behind me. Atsuko's eyes are wide. There's fear but there's also concern in her gaze. Shit, what did I do?

"You are your father's son. We share the same blood. So don't look at me like you're better than me because you aren't. Just wait and see, boy."

No, I'm not my father. I'll never be him. My inner

demons are trying to lie to me again, trying to play their tricks on my mind.

I can feel my teeth grind down again when the sting and throb starts to register in my fists and elbows. Fuck, I can't believe I lost control like that. In front of Atsuko of all people. What must she think of me?

"...I..." I fucked things up, didn't I?

Atsuko walks towards me slowly like I'm an injured animal about to make a break for it. To be honest, that's exactly how I feel and it's exactly what I'm contemplating.

When her hands cradle my face in her warmth, my eyes close in resignation knowing what's coming. It was heaven while it lasted but a man like me never deserved her. A man like me never deserved to even have that little slice of heaven I was given.

~

ATSUKO

What just happened?

I knew these guys were going to get their asses handed to them one of these days. Cocky young guys always do, or else they never learn. It's a good thing I blocked Alfonso's number because he would have been trouble too.

I just didn't think it would be my sweet Mat to do it. I never knew he had this side of him. He's never given me any indication of anything other than being a shy and genuine person when he's around me.

When his body straightened up to his full height and the tension in his shoulders started stiffening, was the moment I knew something was going to happen. Something big. I would never be able to hold him back even on my best day. Mat is a big guy even though he never throws it around.

But today. Today was the day I saw a beast emerge from its cage. It was like watching a train wreck in slow motion except everything happened so damn fast. All I saw were bodies being thrown, limbs moving and the sound of Mat rearranging the poor boy's face.

I should be appalled.

Alfonso has this temper.

I should be upset.

But Alfonso is never in the right when he goes ballistic. He's usually the instigator of problems.

I shouldn't be so turned on with all the blood he's shedding in my name.

Mat's body is all lethal grace even when he's erupting in fury. A controlled chaos.

And I've had all that potential power and energy down on his knees between my legs, worshiping me like I'm the most delicate thing he's ever had privy to hold.

My poor baby has so many facets to him, depths I haven't seen and it just draws the curious pussycat in me even more. Cradling his face between my hands, I can't help but feel my heart break with the look of resignation I see there. What's going on in that mind of his?

"Mat."

His eyes are still closed, worry lines appearing on his forehead and I can feel a sense of sorrow radiating off him in waves.

"Mat, look at me please."

I can tell he's fighting with himself about something. There's an internal battle I'm not invited to. My eyes are glued to the way his dark lashes fan across his high cheekbones, memorizing the slopes of his features. Mat sighs and finally opens his eyes, his dark irises staring into my soul with a question I'm not sure I understand.

The groans on the ground remind me that we're still outside of my apartment.

I give him a soft kiss on the lips before grasping his hand in mine and leading him inside, making sure to lock the door behind us.

19

ATSUKO

*L*eading Mat to our small couch, I urge him to sit down while I go find the first aid kit. He doesn't look like he took too much damage versus the other guys, but it's still good to give him a once over anyway. The good thing about Vero being my roommate is that we're both pretty organized. Things are quickly and easily found.

When I return from the restroom, Mat has his head in his hands, elbows on his knees. My heart hurts all over again at the sight before me. I've never seen him look so defeated.

Slowly getting on my knees before him, I put my hand on his shoulder and place the first aid kit on the floor beside me. His knuckles are bleeding but it doesn't look to be bothering him one bit. His breathing is slow and even, the muscles of his forearms flexing every now and again. He isn't moving besides that and I'm starting to get worried. Taking a chance,

I slowly get to my feet and wrap my arms around him in a hug despite him continuing to sit leaning forward.

"Mat, baby. It's okay. I'm here. I'm not going anywhere, alright?"

He groans and turns his body to bury his face in my chest, arms wrapping tightly around me like he's afraid I'll leave him, as I sit my butt down onto the couch beside him.

"I don't deserve you. You must hate me." I can barely hear his whispers since he's essentially talking to the top of my breasts but I slowly rub his back until I start to feel some of the tension leave his body.

The room is quiet except for the sound of our mutual breathing. I was able to maneuver my body so that at least half of me is lying down on the couch with Mat right on top of me, still holding onto me for comfort. *My poor baby.*

With my head on the armrest of the couch, I start to just spew out the first thing off the top of my head.

"You know, I didn't grow up in the best of neighborhoods. One of the girls on my street, who had it out for me, was following me from work while I was walking home."

My hands continue to caress his back in slow patterns as Mat starts to settle into the crook of my neck, his warm breath fanning my cleavage. I take a deep breath through my nose, taking in the unique smell of Mat. *My man.* There's a hint of copper today, probably from the blood.

"I knew what she was up to, so I took a detour. She followed me of course, because she thought she had me. About a house or two from my destination, I ran. She tried to take me down but I turned around just in time to throw the first punch, knocking her to her ass. Vero came barreling out of her house and we were both ready for her to get back up." I chuckle as I remember my BFF and I together. It was before any of us had a car. You can try to take the girl off the streets, but you can't truly take the streets out of the girl. It becomes a part of you, a dark splotch inside of you that can never really be washed away. We are the sum of all of our parts.

"She tried of course, but we took her down. She never followed me home again. Seems she had it out for me because the guy she liked was hanging out around the coffee shop I worked at too often."

I kiss the top of Mat's head and run my hands through his hair.

"There will always be outside forces that work against us, even if we try our best to mind our business and just live our life."

I caress his exposed cheek and urge him to come closer to my face, which he complies. Our kiss is slow, steady, a reaffirmation perhaps. Our tongues enter each other's mouths like a lover's embrace, our lips keeping it soft and subtle like we're making love through our kiss alone.

Making him pull away from our kiss with my hands on his cheeks, I look deeply into his eyes watching to see if the sorrow is still there. He watches me back just as intently, panting lightly through his parted lips.

"I see you, Mat." My eyes roam his face from his brows, to his dark eyes, to his clean shaven face today, to his strong nose and back to his full lips. My fingers move his escaped locks of hair from his eye and caress his ear. "You're all I see."

His kisses become desperate and needy. They're searching for something, and I don't know what it is. I only hope that I can give him what he needs from me. I feel like I'm drowning in his transferred emotions when he pulls away from me ever so slightly, both of our lips parted only millimeters away from each other, the warmth of our breaths still close enough to mingle between us.

"I don't understand why you would even want to be with

someone like me, let alone after today. I don't deserve you, and yet it feels like my heart is being ripped out of my chest at just the thought of being without you." Despite his jarring words, his lips start to travel down towards my cleavage. One of his hands roughly pulls down my shirt and bra, exposing my breast to his warm mouth. Mat is a master at worshiping every part of me. He's wrong. I probably don't deserve someone like him.

Suddenly, our hands are clawing at one another, trying to rip each other's clothes off as fast as we can. Once we're able to get the essential pieces off, Mat's already slamming his hard dick home with one of my legs over his shoulder making him feel even deeper than before. Mat is a man who knows how to work what God has blessed him with. But it's really the passion behind everything he does that takes sex to a whole other level.

The sound of the door opening almost doesn't register amidst the grunts and cries we're making on the couch. We're both drowning in each other, chasing that elusive cliff, wanting to free dive off it together.

"What the fuck happened out there?...oh..."

We don't hear from Vero again until Mat purges all his frustrations out on my pussy a few more times that night.

2O

*A*tsuko and I have become closer since that day I lost my control. I don't know how she does it, but she calms me. I'm not a perfect man by any means, God knows I don't come from perfect stock either. Hopefully, she never has to find out about my past misdeeds, the stain on my soul. She's the bright light to my darkness. Shit, I don't deserve her but I can't fucking let her go.

I was able to convince her to stay at my place at least four days out of the seven. I'll take anything she'll give me. Honestly, I need to start figuring out how to make her permanently move in without seeming like a creep.

When she's not around, my dick is getting abused by my hand constantly and it still isn't enough. It's nowhere close to being the same when I'm buried inside of her warmth, being held in her arms. How can such a small person bring me happily to my knees?

"Mat, what's going on man?"

"I'm trying to figure out how to keep Atsuko at my house permanently."

Akmal laughs like it's the funniest shit ever, when I'm fucking serious as hell.

"Nah man, I'm not laughing at you. I'm laughing because you look fucking serious as all get out. You guys are intense. Has she mentioned anything about it?"

"I mean, she's at my place half the week anyway. What difference does it make if she stays the whole week...and just never goes back? I can take her to work, do whatever she wants me to do."

"I guess it really isn't that different. What does Vero think about that? I mean, they're best friends and all."

"She never crossed my mind. Maybe I'll just keep myself between her legs until she can't say no. Eat her out until she doesn't want to go home."

"I mean, that sounds like it could work. I wouldn't know, since I've never done it. But it sounds legit."

I'm contemplating when to put this plan into action when the sound of a voice I have been avoiding floats into the air of the building. *It can't be.*

"There you are. Why haven't you been taking my cases? I've been requesting for you for what feels like over a month and a half."

Miss Miller is standing at the front desk, staring at me. I almost don't recognize her because I've only ever seen her with a robe and hair bun and not normal street clothes. Where the hell is Tricia? I know for damn sure she's on today, I saw her this morning.

"Akmal, where is Travis?"

"Shit, let me go look for him."

"Miss Miller, I'm going to have to ask you to take a seat while I find someone who can help you."

The front door opens but I can't remove my eyes from her because she's that damn predator that takes anything as a challenge. I can't back down from this one. Not now. It's been too good, I knew something was bound to happen sooner or later.

I hear Akmal talking to who I hope is Travis in one of the rooms nearby.

"No, I'm not going to have a seat because I want you to come back to my house, to me. I want things to go back to the way they were. I miss you. I miss you between my legs."

"What. The. Fuck. Did. You. Say?" Shit, the person who came in was Atsuko. She was so quiet during her entrance, I didn't even know if it was a woman or man who entered.

"Excuse me little girl, I'm trying to have a conversation with my man right now. You're going to have to just wait your turn."

"The fuck? I think you are mistaken *ma'am,* because you are talking to *my* man right now who is about to go on his lunch break with *me.*"

"Oh honey, he's just toying with you. I'll always be his one and only. His *first* and only." Shit. I don't know why my words are stuck in my throat. I feel like punching something, but I'm still on duty with a few more hours of my day to go.

Miss Miller leans towards Atsuko and I'm already walking around the counter to stop this nonsense she's spewing.

"He always comes back home to mama, with his head between my legs. If you think I'm lying, let me tell you that that piercing on his dick was for *me.*"

Atsuko's fist collides into Miss Miller's face with a loud *thwack* before I can make it in time, landing the poor woman on the floor. I can see Travis from the corner of my eye, seeing to her sprawled body and sobs as I grab Atsuko by the waist and lift her off the floor to prevent her from dealing out any more damage than necessary. Atsuko is seething in silence, but her face is contorted in utter rage. She's kicking, trying to jump out of my arms, and I'm surprised I'm able to bring her safely out of the building through the back entrance by the employee parking lot.

When I place her feet back down on the ground, she's throwing punches at my chest. What the fuck did I do?

"Were you seeing her behind my back? She took your virginity, right? That's what she was fucking saying? Are you still hung up on her because she was your first?"

She's out of her fucking mind. Miss Miller is nothing to me. Nothing but an evil ball and chain that refuses to let me leave and live my life in peace. My mind is racing with everything I want to say but my mouth can't catch on to what I should say first. I must look like a dying fish with my mouth opening and closing without actually talking.

"I knew it was too good to be true. You were too good to be true...to want just me. What does she have that I don't, Mat? Is there something I'm missing? Am I not enough for you?"

Watching her eyes tear up makes me snarl and growl into the air. Fuck, I suck at this shit. The anger inside of me, the humiliation, the suddenness of it all is making me tongue tied, and I'm fucking it up even more by not saying the right things to fix it.

"It's not what it fucking looks like."

"Yeah? What does it look like to you Mat? Because to me..." She's crying. The tears she was holding back are falling down her face and I feel like a fucking piece of shit for causing it. I want to claw my eyes out so I don't have to watch her tortured expression before me. Am I as bad as my father? Is my blood that tainted in darkness that I end up hurting my woman like this? I feel like everything is going out of fucking control with each tear that falls down her precious face.

She's losing her voice through her sobs and hiccups. "...Because to me, I don't know Mat. But it fucking hurts. It *hurts* so fucking much." She covers her face in her hands and runs away from me. Like that, I feel worse than a piece of shit. I feel like nothing. I did that to her. She should never have to cry because of me.

Fuck!

The sound of her car screeching away makes me feel like acid is burning beneath my skin. I can't catch my breath, what the fuck do I do? How do I fix this? I'm not cut out for this relationship shit and I should have known it was going to end up this way. I never deserved her.

My body squats down and my head is in my hands. I feel like pulling my damn hair out as I growl once more towards the ground beneath me.

"Shit, what happened?" Akmal's voice is barely registering. All I can hear is the woosh and roar of my heartbeat next to my ears. My head feels like it's stuffed with cotton. My heart. Fuck, my heart feels like it's been ground under a large boot, singed by fire and smeared back into the Earth as ash.

ATSUKO

My heart hurts. It feels like it's been shattered into a million pieces. The way it scrapes my insides even though there are no physical wounds.

I don't know what to believe because, I know Mat feels deeply for me. But what that woman said slithers into my mind like poison, infecting anything I believe, everything I thought I believed. I know it shouldn't let it, but it does.

"I'll always be his one and only. His first and only."

It echoes in my mind like a damn chant, beating me down a little piece at a time when I *know* I'm not stupid enough to believe it...but it still fucking hurts to hear it. My insecurities and doubts start to overtake my mind like vines on a deserted building.

Mat didn't say anything at all. What does it mean? Does he agree? Was he just trying to let me down easy? After all we've been through together? Was it all just one-sided? Was I the only one feeling the deep connection between us? Was it only for the sex? He should have said that up front if that was the case, and this wouldn't hurt so bad.

It never hurt this much the first time Alfonso and I broke up. But then again, I've never felt this deeply about someone before.

I never told him...but I was falling in love with Mat. Heart, mind and soul.

The way that woman spoke of Mat's cock like she's been so intimate with it for so damn long - It speared me, ripping out my heart to watch it die a slow death.

Was what she said true? He's been with me almost every day since we've been together. *Almost.* What does he do on those other days? Does he run back to her?

She came to his place of work. Does he go back to her while on duty? Is that how they met? Again, where does that leave me? Who am I? Am I the side piece?

...Is this why he always says he doesn't deserve me? Was he admitting to something and I just wasn't smart enough to catch the clues?

Just thinking about it makes my chest ache. These tears won't stop falling and I can't even speak straight to explain to Vero what happened.

I should be too old for this, shouldn't I? Isn't this what teenagers do? I can't fucking help it. I can't stop the way I feel. Mat was my reason for waking up, what made me smile before I went to sleep. I was thinking about maybe bringing up the idea of us living together when I walked into that shit show yesterday - just to watch it all burn down into ashes. All it took was one kindle, one flame to tear everything my heart has built up.

I'm in Vero's arms and she's rocking me, giving me tender kisses on the forehead as we both sit here on my bed. I feel so pathetic. Damn my heart for loving a man like Mat.

"Okay, try to catch your breath chica. I'm not sure I'm getting the story right." That makes me sob even harder and hiccup into her chest because dammit, it feels like it just happened a minute ago even though it's already the next morning. My words catch in my throat, unable to relay how my heart was torn again. Shaking my head side to side, my forehead scraping against her shirt roughly - I just can't. My eyes burn too damn much, these stupid hiccups wont let me talk straight or gather my thoughts corrrectly.

"It's okay. It's okay."

She took a few days off work, calling into my job as well, to be here with me while I wallow in my self pity party. Because really, isn't that what this is?

My body slinks down to the side on my bed and Vero comes with me, still holding me from behind for comfort. I must have fallen asleep because when I open up my swollen eyes, my room is dark and Vero is nowhere to be seen. With no motivation to even move, I just close my eyes again hoping for the darkness to consume me quickly so I don't have to feel anything anymore.

VERO

What the fuck happened? I've never seen Atsuko like this. She's has a trail of men left in her wake trying to catch any scraps she might give out. She's the one usually dolling out heartache, not receiving it - She's never cried like someone just fucking died right in front of her. I hope no one died. I don't *think* anyone died.

I'm sitting in front of her closed bedroom door sitting on the ground with my head back, listening to her breathing slow back down, letting me know she went back to sleep. My heart aches in echo to hers from listening to her own heartache seeping out of her very pores. Closing my eyes all I can see is her puffed out eyes and pain - I feel so damn help-less! I feel like punching someone but I don't know who I should punch! She hasn't eaten anything all day, only taking small sips of water since I've been leaving random bottles in her room. Her hiccuping sobs were making my chest hurt. Holding back my own tears for her was hard because I didn't want to add to it. I wanted to be strong for her.

Slowly getting to my feet, I stretch out my kinks and go to the living room to get my phone. Sitting my tired ass on the couch, my fingers start flying across the keyboard.

Vero : what the fuck happened between Mat and Atsuko yesterday?

Akmal : I'm not really sure. One of our clients showed up out of the blue.

Vero: what the hell does that have to do with anything?

Akmal : It's a long story.

Fuck this shit. Someone needs to tell me *something* because Atsuko's story was so fragmented, nothing made any damn sense.

Dialing his number, I put the phone to my ear. Fucker better pick up if he knows what's good for him.

"...Hello."

I'm whisper-yelling through the phone's microphone, not wanting to wake Atsuko. "Akmal! Tell me what happened, right now! I don't know how to help Atsuko if I don't know the full story."

"...I..I'm not sure myself."

"Tell me what you *do* know. You know more than I do because you were at least there."

I listen intently to everything Akmal is telling me. My heart is breaking for Atsuko all over again because I can see where she's coming from. The question remains with what happened between the two love birds in the back parking lot though. According to Akmal, Mat was already reverted into a shell of despair and rage by the time he arrived on the scene and Atsuko was already long gone.

2 2

MAT

*T*here was at least a week left on the two weeks notice we put in. But I couldn't go back to work after the crap show with Miss Miller. That sorry excuse for an IT company is a dark stain on my mind.

I couldn't go back to my place either, too many memories of her. My bedroom alone smells like her, making the cavern in my chest open even wider. Life isn't the same. Home isn't where my heart is anymore. My heart drove away as I felt myself crumble into dust.

Akmal was nice enough to let me crash at his place. This is going to be his last day with Morty, because he said he only stuck around to be with me anyway. *Fuck that place.*

I don't know what kind of company I'm going to be for him, feeling like a shell of myself. I don't have any motivation to do anything but wallow in the sorrow that's consuming me. All this time alone is dangerous for my mind because not only do I constantly have thoughts of what could have been with Atsuko, my failures, thoughts of the past start creeping up again. Like it was just waiting for a chance to eat at my soul when I'm in a weakened state. And I feel fucking weak right now.

Have I eaten today? Fuck, I need to punch something.

Getting off Akmal's couch, I grab the duffel bag I took from my place and change into workout gear. The movements of my body slow as I walk out of Akmal's home and lock the door behind me. The drive to the gym is a quiet one, the music in the car doing nothing to calm me, instead only sounding like TV static in the background no matter how many times I change songs.

When I get to the gym, there's already a small handful of guys there. I pay them no mind as I walk towards the item that's going to receive all of my frustrations. *Thwack thwack.* From the side, the front, more shoulder power. What frustration I came in with has now increased tenfold. *Thwack Thwack Thwack Thwack.* I'm sweating like a beast, my wet hair slapping my face as I continue to pound into the heavy bag in front of me. Sometimes I imagine it being Miss Miller's face because I would never hurt a woman in real life. But in my anger and rage, this red heavy bag makes me think of Miss Miller's red hair. My knuckles are starting to get sore but it doesn't stop me at all. The clinking of the chains that hold the heavy bag up is turning into a melody that slowly soothes my hurt soul.

With a snarl and growl, I throw my last few punches with as much force as I can, making the heavy bag swing in a wide arc. Grabbing my hair, I turn and feel like ripping it out again but hold myself back. FUCK! I'm in public, and I probably already look like a raging beast about to blow a gasket and devour the crowd already here. A few of the people are looking at me discreetly from their workouts, but no one dares to say anything.

Grabbing the towel from the back pocket of my shorts, I wipe off my face and contemplate my life. All the shit I've gone through thus far...just to be in *more* shit? In *more* of a mess? This can't possibly be my destiny. What was I put on this earth for? Everything good in my life gets taken away. It's worse when I'm given a taste of how good it can be. I fucking laugh like a lunatic. Matunaagd: *He who fights*. Big Crow: *aren't crows a symbol of death anyway?* I must have always been destined to forever fight something until the day I die.

This must be part of the torture, right? It wouldn't hurt so bad if I didn't have a taste at all. I should probably just give up on finding anyone. No one compares to Atsuko anyway. There's no woman in the world that would live up to what I now know - of what it could have been between us. A slice of heaven down here in this hell we call life.

After showering, I walk out of the gym towards my car, my thoughts still morose. The heavy bag was only a temporary fix.

My mind for some reason drifts to the men in Atsuko's building and to Atsuko's ex. Fucking hell. They're probably chomping at the bit already when they realize I'm not coming around. I'm pissed all over again but more so about the fact that I now have no right to beat them to the ground. I should fucking do it anyway to make myself feel better.

"Mat? Is that you?" I'm still brooding over the many ways I can kill a man and get away with it before I realize I recognize the feminine voice.

"Tricia? What are you doing here?"

"...I, uh, I just signed up. What are the odds we'd have the same gym, right?"

"I guess."

There's an awkward silence between us and I'm getting agitated because my mind hasn't come up with ways to stay out of a hypothetical jail yet after I kill every male that sniffs around Atsuko.

"Hey, I heard about what happened the other day."

What happened? She makes it sound like a mere incident report instead of the crashing and decimation of my whole fucking world.

"You know, if you ever need anything. I'm here for you. Even if it's just...to work out frustrations." What the hell is she talking about? I was just working out my frustrations on the heavy bag, not like it fucking helped any. I don't know her reasons for signing up for this particular gym and I really don't care.

"Yeah."

I start walking to my car again, my mind still full of morbid thoughts, when the feeling of someone's hands on my bicep stops me.

"I'm down for a quickie if you need it. As friends, of course. Just trying to help a friend out. I mean, you're a guy and I'm a girl. I can help you scratch an itch if you need it." She bites her bottom lip and it reminds me of Atsuko. The way her eyes would get hooded and her lips would part when my head is between her legs, worshiping her for hours. I fucking miss her even more and my heart is hurting all over again at my loss, the wound ripping open like it's the first time. Trying to think of anything else to balm the hurt, I think of everything that happened that day.

"Where were you that day, Tricia? I could have sworn you

were on duty. But when Miss Miller came by, you were nowhere to be seen. How the hell did Miss Miller know to come in at that time anyway? She never comes in."

Something crosses her features. The adrenaline from my workout hasn't gone down all the way yet and so my senses are still heightened. What the hell was that? A sick feeling enters my gut and my mind is quickly starting to piece something together.

But it doesn't make any sense. Does it? Why would she?

"Where were you, Tricia?" I'm not one to be this way. To be out of control with my temper. But losing Atsuko did something to me. It unleashed a beast, and the beast just sniffed a trail of deceit.

"I..I must have been in the restroom or something."

"Then how did you know about what happened? I never came back to work and Akmal isn't a talker when it comes to my business. You handle the calls, so how would Miss Miller know that I've been purposely avoiding her?" I mean, Miss Miller could have taken a good guess but something is just not sitting right.

I'm looking at all of Tricia's features with suspicion, when I see her face change from innocent to angry. What the fuck is happening right now?

"You were fucking mine. I saw you before that Asian bitch ever did, you know that? I was handling Miss Miller, figuring out how to permanently get her away from you, and what do I have to show for all my hard work? Losing you to someone who slid in when the opportunity arose. An opportunity I created, because I always had your back, Mat!"

Come again? Am I in the fucking Twilight Zone right now? The way she's raising her voice at me is triggering something inside and it's pissing me off. What the fuck did *I* do? Trying to calm my nerves, I take a deep breath in and out before I speak.

"Tricia, I have no idea what you are talking about. I appreciate everything you did for me with Miss Miller. Travis was handling things on his end as well."

"Travis? Ha! That fucker is lucky he hasn't been written up. Miss Miller has been sending in complaint cards on him and it was *me* who kept trashing them so the arrangement could continue. I mean, I don't blame the old woman. I've been trying to get a piece of you too but you are just too damn hard headed to see it."

I must have not eaten enough today because nothing is making any damn sense. My head must not be hearing things correctly, my brain synapses aren't firing right.

"I have no idea what the fuck you are talking about, Tricia. I never sensed any interest from you, besides being friendly at work."

"And this is exactly why there is a trail of hearts behind you, Mat. You're too fucking perfect." She takes an exaggerated deep breath. "Let's just stop fighting, alright. Come on, let's go back to my car and I'll suck your cock. Would you like that? I'll make you feel good and help you forget all the crap that's happened."

How in the world did we get from redirecting client cases to her asking to suck my dick?

"I don't think that's a good idea, Tricia. Sorry, but it's going to be a no."

Trying to escape this beyond awkward situation, I take quick strides to my vehicle. I'm about to unlock my car when Tricia turns me and slams me into the driver's side door. *What the hell?* My eyes widen when she lowers herself and starts fumbling with the buttons of my pants. I have to force her hands and body away from me with a firm grip on both of her wrists.

"Tricia, I said no."

"I heard what Miss Miller said about your cock, Mat. I want that pierced dick in my mouth, please!" *What the hell?* That means Tricia *was* standing in that office the entire time the shit show happened...and *let it* happen.

Wait.

"Fucking hell, Tricia? Did you set that shit up?" Tell me it isn't so. Fuck.

"If I say, yes will you let me go down on you? Fuck, Mat. I don't know how else I can tell you how much I want to be with you. It's always been you. That girl got in the way. I had to end it. I had to, you have to see that I did it for *us*."

This girl is out of her fucking mind. If I was the person I was before meeting Atsuko, I might have fallen for this shit. But Atsuko has helped me break out of the shell Miss Miller has forced me in. I don't want to go back to that pathetic person. Not with Miss Miller, not with Tricia who seems to want to be the next Miss Miller v2.0.

"I'm going to say this nicely, and ask that you leave me the hell alone, Tricia. I don't work there anymore, I don't work with *you* anymore. Please move on. There are plenty of men who would jump at the chance with what you're offering."

"Mat, please! I don't want anyone else. I only want you, can't you see that? I've loved you since the moment you started in the company. You just never saw me. But you see me now and I'm ready. Take me however you want me. I'll do anything you ask, I promise. You want it up the ass? Take it right here, right now. I don't fucking care who walks by."

I can't handle this shit. I don't want to hurt her but at the same time, I want to fucking strangle her for putting my relationship on the line for her own selfish needs. Fuck!

I still have both of her wrists in my grip. With a last minute decision, I shove her body off me letting her land on her ass on the ground, and slip into the driver's side door, making sure to push the lock button before I start the ignition.

23

MAT

"You're joking with me right now, right? Tricia?"

"I tell you no fucking lie, Akmal. All these women are going out of their damn minds. I must have a target on me or something." I groan as I lay my head on the back of the couch.

"Damn, I'm glad today was my last day at work. That place is a hot mess. I honestly thought Morty was screwing her."

Both our faces scrunch up in disgust at that visual.

One good thing about the Tricia debacle, is that it gave me the kick in the ass I needed. This whole shit show was set up. I was set up.

How do I fix it? What do I do to get my woman back? Does she even want me back after everything that came out of Miss Miller's mouth?

Sitting on Akmal's couch, I lean forward and put my head

in my hands, tugging at my hair as I try to think of a solution.

"Shit, maybe you just need to get your head away from this for a minute. I've got a shoot coming up. It's a car show next week a few cities away from here."

My ears perk up at that. Atsuko might be there, right? "What kind of car show?"

"Another vintage one. And yes, Vero is bringing Atsuko so she can take her mind off things." Akmal's got a smile on his face. They set this up for us. Fuck, this is it. This is my opportunity.

"Fuck yes."

The rest of our talk consists of what we need to bring and the time we need to be there. I need to get Atsuko back, at all costs. She's everything I live for, the only thing I've ever wanted this badly. I can't let meddling people fuck it up for us. Our relationship was never destined to die and be left in ashes.

The day of the car show starts early. Akmal didn't change any of his equipment or anything, and I guess that last time I came with him, I was late into the shoot as well. It doesn't matter, since I couldn't really sleep that well the night before. All I could think about was seeing her again. I'm nervous and anxious, a weird combination. I want to see her so bad, I really hope Vero was able to drag her out here. *Please let her be there.*

We parked nearby in the designated lot. Akmal is checking the settings on his Nikon.

"Who's the client?"

"A vintage car owner. But he gave me the go ahead to use any of the willing models at the convention around his car."

"Has Vero texted you today, yet?"

Fuck, I feel like a damn schoolboy waiting for news about whether she read my note passed in class.

My eyes are scanning all the car isles and corners for her as we walk towards one of the enclosed buildings, but there's way too much going on to see anyone clearly.

The shoot goes by without a hitch, and Akmal was able to pass more business cards around. He's damn good with his camera. All you can hear is the clicks and rapid shutter speed as he changes position every now and then. A crowd is starting to gather and Pinup girls are lined up to get a picture with the '59 Cadillac. None of them are Vero or Atsuko though, not from what I can see. My mind is wondering where they are, and if any of these car guys are sniffing around them. It makes my blood boil because I know damn well they are. How could they not? She's fucking beautiful.

"Thank you ladies! You've been a great help. I will make sure to send everyone a copy. Please, don't forget to write down your email on this list."

Almost in eerie unison, the ladies around us say, "Yes, Akmal". The giggles are getting on my nerves because I can't hear Vero's or Atsuko's voices if they're nearby.

"*The fuck?*" Shit, Vero was here this whole time? "*¿Qué carajo tu putas creen estas haciendo?* What the fuck do you bitches think you're doing? Alright chicas move along!"

Being taller than most of the crowd, I turn towards the voice to see Atsuko looking drop fucking dead gorgeous. My gut is churning at the thought of all the guys she walked by, looking like that. I'm almost snarling at the thought of them getting a whiff of her beautiful scent and following her around.

Her pants are so fucking tight, it's showing too much of her delectable ass and hips. The legs of her pants barely reach her calves, leading to what looks like six inch heels. Her top is just as tight, showcasing her tiny waist, only held on by a slip of fabric that crosses and goes around the back of her neck. The front part dipping so low, her cleavage is on show. My head feels tight again, and I think I'm grinding my teeth because I can see our client basically panting like a dog beside her.

I need to reel this anger in because we can't lose customers before we even get them. But I can feel the red haze starting to creep in from the side of my vision.

I push my way through the crowd and they part for me, making an opening straight to my woman. Fuck, she looks even more beautiful than I remember. Her eyes land on mine and so many emotions are flitting through them.

It feels like everything around us disappears as I try to slow down my heart, standing in front of this angel.

"Atsuko…"

Her eyes widen and I swear they're starting to tear up. Fuck!

"Please, just…"

"Just what, Mat? Let you stomp all over my heart again? Because… I.."

I can't stand this shit. I can't stand this canyon between us. I lean into her because I can't help it. It's like our gravities are aligned, pulling us closer and closer together. Her six inch heels put her close to my height today. Stepping out of my comfort zone, I lean in but she turns her head to the side last minute, landing my lips next to her ear. I take whatever I can get. I'm just glad she hasn't run away from me.

My hand comes up to gently hold her neck, pressing her

face against mine. I need to feel her against me, I don't care how.

"I'm sorry. I'm sorry for ever making you doubt me. Just please...come back to me." My voice is breaking but I don't fucking care. I just need her to come back to me and make things right again. I can feel and hear her breath hitch. I'm not sure if it's a good thing or bad thing. Fuck, if there's a higher power out there, please let her hear my plea.

Suddenly, she pulls from my grasp, turns and starts to walk away, swaying her hips like I didn't just bare my fucking soul to her. Vero is not with her, which means she's still with Akmal. I can't let Atsuko walk into a crowd without some sort of protection.

I follow her. I stalk her from afar. I stare daggers into any male that even tries to look her way. I just need to wait her out, wait until she comes to her senses and see that we can't be apart anymore. She has to know right? Know that we're too tied together by this point. I'm fucking mated for life...with her.

Following her through the car show crowd, she doesn't slow down. She also doesn't look anywhere but ahead and it makes my chest constrict. When her arms cross over her chest, my hands itch to pull her into my embrace, but I can't. I'm fucking this up. I don't know what I'm doing. She's the only real relationship I've ever had and she's always been out of my league. I've known this. I've fucking known this!

The smell of hard liquor reaches my nose and my senses go on high alert. It's never good in a crowd of beautiful women like this. It's never good with *my* beautiful woman open to attacks. I'm increasing my speed, trying to catch up with her, when I see a male who looks like her fucking ex get to her.

Shit, I'm seeing red.

I run, and start pushing and shoving people out of my way when I have him in my sights. The grunts and complaints fade away into the distance, until my ears hone in on his voice.

"Atsuko, I could fucking eat you right now. Shit baby, my dick misses you." *Fucking hell.*

Everything is a blur again when I end up tackling him to the ground, knocking some bystanders down near us. The crowd opens up quickly around us, and some feminine screams can be heard. My fists are out of my control, the squeeze of his neck between my palms soothing the rage within me. When I start slamming his head against the concrete ground, other hands are pulling at me, only making me do it harder.

My height and weight would make it hard for anyone to remove me when I'm in the zone. And I'm fucking in the zone now.

"She's fucking mine. Mine!" Am I snarling? More hands are pulling at me, but I use my weight to pull right back. I move my head next to his ear to make sure he can hear me clearly over the crowd's roar. "If I ever smell you near her again, you'll regret the day you put a fucking bottle to your lips because you won't have a fucking head left. I will fucking kill you. Atsuko is mine, make sure you remember it."

I don't get to say the rest of what's on my mind, because I'm finally pulled off the fucker in a snarling rage by a few of the bigger men in the crowd. When my vision clears enough, I look around and Atsuko is nowhere in sight. Fuck, I lost her again. I'm howling like a pained wolf inside as my head feels like it's about to explode in frustration and regret. I stomp away outside of the building to get some much needed air before I lose my damn mind.

24

MAT

Have I gone crazy? I've been following Atsuko to her job and back, just to make sure she makes it okay, of course. I've been camping outside of her apartment, making sure none of her male neighbors take advantage of her.

When she's grocery shopping, I'm about an aisle away, watching every movement she makes, remembering what it feels like to have those delicate arms wrapped around me when she picks up random items to place in her cart. Watching her hips sway seductively in her dress, as she pushes the cart from aisle to aisle. Glaring at all the men who look a little too damn long for my liking.

Akmal had to remind me to shave the other day, because I'm losing track of time with the shit I'm doing. I'm creeping and stalking. I know it. I've gone off the deep end. But there's nothing else for me but her. My mind is fragmented when I come back to Akmal's home, just to pace around like a caged animal thinking of what I might be missing because I'm not there with her. What if some guy is following her home right now? What if one of her stupid neighbors sneak into her window? What if I'm not there in time to save her from something? What if she needs me and I'm not there to make her feel safe?

Akmal convinced me to go out to eat with him since I'm missing meals when I'm left to my own devices. He tells me I need some new scenery. I need to get my mind off my task. The photography business is booming, and I've done all my duties within a few short hours of concentration. It's really because I'm in a hurry to get back to watching Atsuko.

Watching her at the makeup counter. Watching her talk to Vero. Watching her leave her car to walk to her front door. How can she not be suffering from withdrawals like I am? I'm going crazy every waking minute I'm without her.

"Mat! Are you listening to me?"

Shit. I'm not. I've been moving my food around my dish for the past however long we've been sitting here at this table. I can smell how good the food is, but my stomach doesn't really care for it. I don't have an appetite with all the burdens I have on my shoulders right now.

"You've got it bad, man."

I groan and put my head in my hands on the table. He doesn't understand. I don't have it bad. She's the *only thing* I've ever had. The only thing worthy of holding onto. What is my life without her in it?

Akmal finishes his plate, and I manage to get a handful of bites in before we pay our bill, and start walking towards the front door to exit the restaurant. The cool outside air lets me breathe again, knowing I'm that much closer to being able to watch Atsuko once more.

A feminine gasp escapes near me and I hear, "Mat…"

I really don't feel like talking to anyone right now because it will eat up the limited time I have, but I turn around anyway. There, right outside the front doors of the restaurant, is a woman I wish I never met.

Miss Miller is in a red dress, standing stunned, looking at me with eyes full of desire. It makes me full of rage because it's mostly her fault I'm in this damn predicament. The reason I lost half of my fucking soul, living in this hell on earth.

Akmal is quiet near me. He only knows snippets of what I've told him. He really doesn't know the whole story of what went on between Miss Miller and I.

"I've missed you, Mat. You can always come home whenever you want…"

I snap. It must have been the last straw, and I wasn't prepared for the explosion.

"Get it through your thick skull Miss Miller. I was never yours to begin with. You stole something precious from me once and then you dare to do it again. Never again. NEVER AGAIN! Stay the fuck away from me. There was never an us and there will never be an us. You've made me a shell of myself. Stole half of my fucking soul like the she-demon you are. I hope you rot alone in your home with that fact. I'm done with you. Leave me. The fuck. Alone."

I leave her there with her mouth hanging open, because I need to get Atsuko back, and nothing is going to stand in my way.

I can hear Akmal running to catch up behind me as I continue to just stare ahead. We make it back to our vehicle without another word spoken between us.

ATSUKO

I shouldn't be here. Vero still talks to Akmal and I couldn't stay away when he feels so close but so far. Sometimes, I just miss him so badly, I pick up tidbits about where he'll be from Vero's phone conversations with Akmal and just follow him a bit. Does that make me crazy? I mean, I'm not stalking him. I just want to know how he's doing without me. Does he miss me as much as I miss him? I know the exact times he logs online to his game chat servers. Vero's been playing online to try and get closer to Akmal, and I use that fact to my advantage.

I followed him once to the gym just to watch him for a short while, but the way his muscles moved under his sweat just made me go out of my mind with want and regret. I stopped following him to the gym, but continued to follow him to other places.

Gosh, what thirty five year old woman follows her previous lover around? I've gone fucking insane. He makes me insane. When he whispered into my ear at the car convention...my heart skipped a beat. I couldn't take it. I couldn't take wanting him that badly and knowing he's the one that holds my broken heart in his hands. He's the only one that could literally kill me.

It sounded too good to be true.

"...Just please come back to me."

I wanted to so badly but it would show him how weak I am, wouldn't it? He would take advantage of that fact and hang it over my head. I can't go through another heartbreak. I'm barely hanging on as it is. When he started beating

Alfonso, my soul couldn't help but be drawn to him again, to his darkness, to his sorrow.

But I couldn't put my weakness in front of me like that, especially in that big of a crowd. I was too scared, and like a coward I ran and didn't look back, until Vero texted me to ask where I was.

And now I'm here. Like a creep, spying on him having lunch with Akmal at a restaurant in town. How pathetic am I?

It's not even like I'm sitting in my car from afar discreetly. I miss his smell. I just wanted to be close enough to smell him.

I'm in regular clothes, not in my usual vintage style. My hair is in a messy bun and I have sunglasses on. He wouldn't be able to pick me out from the crowd. Oh, but I was close enough to hear everything he said to that woman who made me believe there was something going on.

My heart was breaking for him. My heart was breaking for us.

I've never heard him speak to a female that way. The passion in which he delivered his speech left no room for error. He made it known that there was never anything between them. Have I been in the wrong this whole time? It doesn't erase the very real hurt I felt that day, the hurt I still feel because I knew he's always been too good to be true.

I felt no sympathy for the woman. A young gentleman came in quickly to swoop her up. Oh, she was a sobbing mess. But she deserved it because *she* left *me* in a sobbing mess. She seemed to know that guy, since she clung to him quickly like they've already been intimate. I think I heard her call him Travis.

My poor Mat. How do we fix this? How do we make it

past what life has thrown at us? I'm so embarrassed for even being here to witness what happened, but I'm glad I was anyway. I think it gave me the courage to kick myself in the ass, to do something instead of just following him around like a psychotic ex-girlfriend. Quickly walking back towards my car, my mind starts to formulate a plan. It has to work because there's no other alternative. I can't bear for it to not work.

MAT

*J*still haven't gone back to my apartment since the Miss Miller debacle. I'm probably wearing out my welcome at Akmal's bachelor pad, but he hasn't said anything to me. We were able to finish up with editing all of the client's photoshoots and send out emails to the appropriate people. Both of us combined are a quick and efficient team, and business really is booming, uplifting both our spirits.

We're gaming tonight with the usual crew. Akmal has two laptops and an extra headphone set. I don't even know what we're playing, but I'm assuming it's an MMORPG when we boot up the game. He's been texting on and off while playing, I'm not even sure how he can concentrate on the games. Who am I to judge? I can barely concentrate on the day to day with thoughts of Atsuko consuming my every waking thought.

Someone messages me and my eyes do a quick glance

down on the screen before my concentration goes back to the dungeon we're trying to complete. We have a good number of people on our team tonight, enough to beat it without too many casualties.

Bellanova and I have been speaking sporadically through some of our time gaming together when she joined our small guild a short while back. I think it's a girl, but who knows these days. It's been random pleasantries. Easier for me to do when I'm behind a screen.

I must have been a little drunk one night because I started spewing to her a little bit about my woman troubles. My mind was probably thinking that it wanted another woman's perspective on the matter. I shouldn't have been drinking to that extent at all, knowing what I know about my father and his habits. But it was hard dulling the ache in my chest. The gym has become such a short lived, temporary fix. At least being at Akmal's place means I can stay out of trouble and my hands won't be coated in red.

Bellanova : You should just tell her that it's not over. Tell her what she needs to hear.

    Tinfoilhat : how the hell am I supposed to do that? She's avoiding me.

    Bellanova : Don't lie to me. I'm sure you haven't kept your distance.

    Tinfoilhat : you got me there. I might be creeping a little. It's only because I can't help it. I don't know what to say though.

    Bellanova : Tell her the truth. Tell her and make her understand that you're not going anywhere. Maybe she just needs that reassurance that what you guys had is real.

    Tinfoilhat : it was fucking real. I'm just not good with words.

Bellanova : So show her a different way. You know her best. What would make her respond?

My character almost gets killed when thoughts of fucking Atsuko come to my mind. My dick twitches and it's practically howling at me for keeping it away from what it wants. Is it really that easy? What if she fucking calls the cops on me? My mind thinks back to the conversation I had with Akmal that fateful day.

"I mean, she's at my place half the week anyway. What difference does it make if she stays the whole week...and just never goes back? I can take her to work, do whatever she wants me to do."

"I guess it really isn't that different. What does Vero think about that? I mean, they're best friends and all."

"She never crossed my mind. Maybe I'll just keep myself between her legs until she can't say no. Eat her out until she doesn't want to go home."

"I mean, that sounds like it could work. I wouldn't know, since I've never done it. But it sounds legit."

Didn't I say I was going to worship her until she decided to stay with me? Will she even be receptive to me at this point? I'm too drunk for this shit right now. I let my character die, and decide to not respawn. Letting Akmal know that I'm done for the night, I go to his spare bedroom and sleep the buzz off before I do something I might regret.

The conversation from last night still lingers in my mind. Nothing else from that night is clear, nothing but that damn conversation. I'm sitting here in my car, rubbing the scruff on my face, waiting for Atsuko to come home from work. What the hell is wrong with me? Am I really doing this?

No time to think, because there she is in all her angelic glory, gliding out of her car towards her apartment door.

My instincts kick in and I leave my car, catching up with her path. The males in the hallway see me coming and quickly retreat back into their apartments. Good. I don't want to be distracted from the mission today.

I stay a short distance behind her, waiting just around the shadows of the corner of the hallway that leads to her apartment. This is exactly why she needs someone to watch over her. Look at how easily I'm hiding. When Atsuko puts her key into her doorknob and opens it up, I quickly push myself inside behind her and shut the door with my back to it, locking us both inside.

Her eyes widen as she looks at me. She doesn't say a thing. I've memorized Vero's schedule by now, and I know for a fact Atsuko is alone. My eyes scan her beautiful features, the slope of her delicate neck, and the way her chest is heaving from her breathing getting deeper. The air in the room is starting to become stifling, but it's now or never. I have to man up, and not let my nerves get the best of me, even though I feel like someone just ripped out my intestines and tied it around my throat.

"Atsuko, please, just listen to what I have to say." My voice is barely above a cracked whisper, but I got it out there.

I can see her throat take a swallow and it makes me think of the days when she's had my dick down her throat doing that. Now I'm nervous and horny. Fuck, stick to the mission.

"What do you want, Mat?"

"I want...to explain myself."

"Does this mean there's been things you've been hiding from me that need explaining?"

"No, I mean, maybe? It's not what it looks like, I promise you. Please, believe me."

"Why should I?"

Shit. Shit. Shit.

I'm down on my fucking knees because she's fucking worth it. She's worth any humiliation she wants to put me through. I've been through worse. She's fucking worth everything.

Her eyes widen and I'm not sure if that's a good thing.

"Miss Miller is a nightmare from a past I've let go of. Yes, she was my first. But no, it was never freely given. I was young and naive. Easily manipulated. But I assure you it's over now. I promise you, I never touched her after you came into my life."

"Mat…"

I start to strip out of my clothes, imagining I'm peeling my skin off so I can bare my soul to her, bare everything to her. I'm down to my damn boxers on my knees in front of her. What the fuck is wrong with me? God, *please let this work.*

"What are you doing?" She looks scared. *No no no.* I need her to stay on the same page with me, not skitter away.

"I'm begging you to take me back, Atsuko. I can't live without you. I can't fucking eat or breathe without you. It's been a living hell. I'm no good at this shit. It's only ever been you."

"Mat..I.."

Fuck, she's going to rip my heart right out of my damn chest with these kinds of responses. I sit back on my ankles almost in defeat but I can't fail, not when I've come this far. Might as well jump off that metaphorical cliff now.

"Say you'll take me back. I'll do anything. *Any fucking*

thing. My soul has been ripped in two since the day you walked out of my life."

She gasps and my eyes lift from the floor to her face. I don't know what she's thinking. I don't know what that look means. All of this is out of my league, but I have nothing else to lose. I've already lost everything important to me.

She slowly puts her bag down onto the couch and says my name, while she makes her finger do the come hither motion. Is this it? Did I do it right? Am I being a good boy? My dick is telling me to follow the command we're being given.

I'm crawling towards her on my knees when she cradles my face between her hands, the way she used to do. My eyes close, because I'm truly terrified at what she might say to me. I'm afraid to watch her eviscerate what's left of me.

When her lips kiss each of my eyelids, it feels like a kick to the damn chest. How can such a soft small touch affect me like this. Is this good? Does this mean I'm doing good? She's not saying anything.

When her lips touch mine, I explode into action. I don't know what comes over me as I devour her mouth like a man on the verge of death, about to get his last wish before he's sent to the electric chair. The most amazing thing? She responds with just as much fervor.

I'm on my feet now and I'm lifting her body in my arms as she wraps her legs around me. The feeling of her surrounding me, settles my fucking soul. I can literally feel the two pieces being soldered back together by fire.

Our mouths haven't stopped their assault on each other as I make my way to her bedroom from memory. Laying her gently down on her sheets, I look into her eyes, searching to see if what I'm assuming is real. This means we're back together, right? Everything is okay between us? I'm afraid to ask it out loud in case it jinxes the moment.

"Mat."

"Yes?"

"I'm going to need you to do something for me." *Anything. Just say it.* "I'm going to need you to prove to me that I can trust you." This is it, isn't it? My test. The test. Shit, what if I fail?

"Whatever it takes, Atsuko. I'll do anything you ask of me." Shit, please let me be able to do anything you ask of me. My heart is pounding out of my damn chest waiting for her response. She's killing me with this pause.

When the corners of her lips tilt up ever so slightly into a smile, I feel fear and elation all at once. She pulls me into her space by the back of my neck until we're nose to nose.

"I'm going to need you to dominate me." *Fucking hell.*

My hand goes around her delicate neck and squeezes, as my mouth starts to plunder hers, my tongue seeking entrance to what was forbidden from me for so damn long. She moans into my mouth and my hand squeezes even more. When the second moan gets swallowed in our kiss between our breaths, my hand starts to rip her clothes off frantically. I need her like I need the air to breathe. She is my fucking air. I have so much I need to make up for. There's been so much lost time between us.

When she's naked and fully displayed before me, I pin her arms over her head by the wrists, making her magnificent breasts jut out towards me. My mouth waters even before my lips make it to her nipples. My tongue swirls around her dusky areolas, biting and teasing, and sucking each nipple until her whimpers turn into screams. My cock is straining to come out and play, but not yet. No, I need this for me. I need this to reassure me she will always be mine. I need to mark her.

When both of her breasts are glistening and peaked, my hands remove themselves from her wrists slowly, caressing the length of her arms and sides until they reach below her hips. Pushing both of her legs towards her shoulders, I lick her from her back entrance to the hood of her clit. When my tongue gets that first taste of her arousal, my vision becomes tunneled and I start to eat her pussy with abandon. Her lower lips are puffy and weeping, probably crying for me the way my cock's been howling for her. Her half ass pleas and cries for me to stop goes through one ear out the other as I make her cum again and ride the waves of her orgasm on my tongue. I've missed this. I've missed her taste, that's uniquely her. My body heat is starting to rise up, the room smelling of sex.

Thoughts of Miss Miller and fucking Tricia flit through my mind, making me angry with what they put us through. I let Atsuko's leg rest on my shoulders, as my teeth start to bite, and my tongue comes in to soothe the pain I bring to her pussy lips and clit. Each pass of my tongue across the hood stiffens it up, making it easy for me to suck it into my mouth and tease it. Tricia and her stupid propositions. My finger slides into her hot core, thrusting a few times before bringing her wetness down to her ass and entering there. Creating extra friction with the flat of my tongue against her clit, I can feel her wetness increasing down to my fingers, increasing the lubrication for her back entrance. I've never heard her moan like this, it fuels me. When her third climax peaks and dies off, I flip her over onto her stomach and slam my dick home. Fuck, *home*. The self-imposed banishment is finally done, and I can't help but fuck her hard into the mattress with the rage I felt when she left me there in broken pieces.

I don't want to cum like this, though. It's too easy, too quick. Her pussy would easily milk the life out of me if I let her, and there will be other times for that.

Pulling out quickly, I flip her onto her back, making her head hang off the edge of the bed, right before I shove my dick down her throat. My feet are planted on the floor as I roughly thrust into her. Her gags, and inadvertent throat swallowing, almost make me finish my task too quickly. I play with her nipples that are once again jutting out towards the ceiling, and start to pinch and pluck, the way I've seen her do to herself. Her whimpers and screams around my cock make me groan and slam my fucking balls into her face even more. She never complains, she never pushes me away.

Is this what she's been waiting for all this time? Was this the key to keeping her?

Memories of her telling me to fuck her face come back to me and I do just that. I fuck her like I'm pissed, because I am, but not with her, but the situation with Miss Miller and the fact that Atsuko wasn't my first when she should have been.

I can feel my sack and abs tightening, I shouldn't be doing it this hard to the girl I fucking love, but this is what she wanted. Slamming into her throat a few more times I let go and let my climax consume me, pumping my cum down her throat. I can see her throat swallowing from this angle, see some of it leaking out of the corner of her mouth and it makes me groan in satisfaction. There's a primal need in me to mark her, make her smell like me. When I no longer feel my dick pulsating, I slowly remove it from her mouth. Her intake of air makes me feel good that I was almost able to choke her the way she wanted to be. I'm only doing what she's asking of me.

"Oh my fucking god."

Dropping to my knees in front of her, I kiss her just like that, while she's lying there upside down. I can taste my release on her but fuck if it doesn't make me hard for her again. When we're both almost out of breath, I pick her up and rearrange her back on the bed the correct way before spooning behind her, making sure my arms hold her tightly against me in case she changes her mind. I wouldn't be able to survive it if she left me a second time.

26

MAT

J'm up way too early, the sun is barely cresting the skies through her window. My fears from last night continue to play over and over again. I still don't feel like we've solidified things. She's squirming subtly and scissoring her legs, but I don't think she's awake yet. My hands have already traveled south, rubbing circles on her clit, and rubbing the wetness that has already accumulated. Last night wasn't enough. It was just to get our frustrations out.

Sliding my dick home slowly, she moans into the pillow, and I start moving in and out of her in a sluggish rhythm. My fingers have left her clit and are now traveling to her puckered asshole from behind, right against my shaft penetrating her slick pussy lips. I kiss the delicate slope of her shoulder before me, licking a wet trail over any freckle I catch. I need to fill every hole, make sure she never has a need for anyone else. All she needs is me. I'll be whatever she wants me to be, as long as she stays by my side.

"Mat…"

I miss the sound of my name on her lips like a whisper. Slowly removing myself from her wet pussy, I gradually push into her other hole. She's already relaxed from my previous ministrations with my fingers. Atsuko starts to push her ass back towards me, letting me know how desperately she wants it. The moment the head of my cock breaches her back entrance, is the moment I let out a sigh.

What was once slow is now starting to become a frantic and brutal pace, a chase to the finish line. If the sounds she's making with her mouth is anything to go by, she loves getting it this hard from behind as well. My hands grab her hips roughly so I can get better leverage to pull her back against me, as my hips continue to surge forward and soon enough, my dick is shooting all of its load into her. We stay connected like that for a long moment, my hands caressing the beautiful curve of her spine, before she peeks at me over that delicate shoulder of hers with a small shy smile.

We both stumble out of bed, and head to the shower to clean up. The room becomes steamy for more reasons than one, as our hands discover each other all over again with the added lubrication of water sliding between our skin.

We shower each other until the water runs cold.

Putting on some boxers I must have left at her place, I quietly watch Atsuko sitting across her breakfast table from me, dressed in my shirt. We're eating breakfast in no rush, as we just stare at each other without a word being spoken.

What is going on in her mind? Has she decided to take me back? That's what this is, right? Getting back together? I can't describe what we did together other than explosive makeup sex. But my fear of saying the wrong thing to break this spell is keeping me slowly crunching on this cereal.

Her eyes become hooded and my dick starts to respond, but I still don't say anything. I've taken that first leap of faith and jumped over that metaphorical cliff. The ball is now in her court now with how she wants to play this.

She's eating a small bowl of cereal as well. I've never seen a woman look so fucking desirable eating a damn bowl of cereal, in a wrinkled shirt, with her hair going every which way. But here she is, in the flesh. Fuck, she's real and she's mine...right? She *is* mine. I'm going to make sure she knows it every day so she never doubts me ever again. How do I do that? What do guys usually do in these situations? I can't call Akmal, he's still a damn virgin and can barely hold himself together when he's around Vero.

How does one legally mark a woman as his? My synapses start firing on over time when I come up with the perfect solution.

Taking one last bite, I get up to grab her empty bowl, and go wash the dishes. She startles me a moment when her arms come across my abs from behind in an embrace. Her warmth suffuses confidence in me. This is exactly why I need her.

Once the dishes are done and I dry my hands, I turn around to hug her back. Without her sexy shoes on, Atsuko only stands to my chest, which is perfect for me. My nose grazes the top of her hair, letting me inhale the floral scent of her shampoo. Taking another deep inhale, I mumble into it.

"Atsuko, move in with me."

She lifts her head from my chest and stares directly into

my eyes. There's a pause, my heart is jumping, but I need to listen intently to her response.

"You're asking me to move in...with my boyfriend?" Yes, that's exactly it. And fuck yes, that means we're definitely back together.

"Yes. I want to wake up to your scent, I want to go to sleep holding onto the girl of my dreams in my arms. I can't stand being apart from you, it was a living hell that I don't want to visit ever again."

She tucks her head back into my chest, and I don't know what that means.

I can feel her soft lips against my skin when she says, "I'd love to." She's going to kill me with these long drawn out silent moments.

My heart lets out a sigh of relief and then starts jumping again, because I forgot I haven't been home in a really long time and it probably smells like something died there.

27

ATSUKO

his place was not as I remembered it. It literally looked like someone died, and it's been left to rot. There's dust everywhere and it looks a bit ransacked, like someone left in a hurry. *My poor baby.*

But having stalked Mat, I know he's been staying at Akmal's place, which probably was the best for him to maintain his sanity. Because I would definitely go insane living in this alone. We both cleaned up what we could, but it was such a slow and go. The job was much bigger than we anticipated, and in the end, had to call in reinforcements: Vero and Akmal. Akmal also has a huge family full of sisters, who knew? They came in after him like a tidal wave, sweeping and cleaning up everything like a super maid service.

They all seem to know and love Mat like a brother. It was nice seeing it, especially after Mat and I started bonding even more over talk of our past, while we were cleaning together.

My heart goes out for his parents and for the fact that he's never returned to the reservation to see his grandparents. I can't even imagine what that would be like. He must have felt so alone. I'm really glad he ended up with a friend like Akmal. What about his grandparents though? Have they ever reached out to him, I wonder? Maybe I can help change that.

Akmal's sisters left hours ago, and as a 're-homecoming' gift of sorts, Akmal got Mat a new computer so that he would have one fully dedicated for work only. That was very nice of him. Vero has work in the morning, so she kisses me goodbye on the lips. She whispers in my ear that she's so happy to see me happy again, and my heart swells. This is why she's my BFF.

When she walks towards the door, I see the boys with wide eyes looking between us and stifle a laugh. That's right, they don't know how close we are.

"Akmal, are you coming or what? Three's a crowd, baby boy."

"Alright."

When they both leave, I grab some drinks for us as we set up a video game for tonight. Mat actually looks really excited to share this with me, he's so damn cute. We're sitting on the floor with our backs to the couch, laptops on our thighs. The game starts to load and our characters are dropped in.

Bellanova : So how did it go?

Tinfoilhat : I've never been happier. I got my woman back.

Bellanova : I knew you could do it.

Tinfoilhat : I just wanted to thank you for pushing me. Shit, and for the alcohol making me tipsy enough to tell you about the crap in the first place.

Bellanova : you are too cute.

Tinfoilhat : LOL. Look, I'm going to be really blunt here. I'm going to have to ask you to refrain from saying stuff like that even if it's through chat. I am happily in love with my woman. I don't want anything to mess up what I worked so hard to get back.

My heart stops for a second in my chest. I turn to look over at Mat who looks like he has the most severe expression on his face. So serious. He's lifting his beer to his mouth when my heart makes me blurt out, "You love me?"

Mat chokes and almost spits out his drink towards his laptop. I slap him on the back a few times and grab him a towel since the drink dribbled down the front of his shirt instead. I'm peppering kisses on the side of his face, as he continues to blot his wet stain. This man of mine.

"What? Where did that come from?"

I smile and try my best to stifle the giggle that wants to come out. Does it make me a bad person? I don't care, I have my man back.

I whisper into his ear, "You are too cute."

The look on his face is priceless. I can literally see the cogwheels clicking slowly, like they're rusted, and then faster like they just got oiled.

"Wait…"

I grab his face before he can ask anything else, and plant a kiss on his lips. Pulling away only slightly, so our lips are still barely touching, I whisper, "I love you too."

He slams his lips back on mine and devours my mouth until I'm breathless. The laptops having been scattered somewhere, we end up sprawled on the ground with Mat on top of me. His hard chest rubs against my breasts, making my nipples tingle, since I don't have a bra on. My legs automatically wrap around his waist, a comfort position I'm coming to find. I almost forgot what I had asked him when his lips travel across my cheeks and to the shell of my left ear.

"You've had my heart in your hands from the first day I met you. I love you Atsuko, don't you ever doubt that."

He made sure I never doubted it again, right there, on the floor of his apartment.

28

ATSUKO

*V*ero and I are starting to pack some boxes for my move into Mat's place. I feel bittersweet about it, because I love Vero. She's my girl.

"How are things going with you and Akmal?"

"Girl, that boy is like a one way mirror sometimes. He does not understand flirting whatsoever. I bet if I was butt naked and bending over, he'd be so polite as to get a sheet to help cover me in case I lost my clothes somewhere. I almost wonder if he's asexual, but I mean look at the cutie. He can't be, can he?"

We both laugh out loud at that, because it's beyond true. Mat is only halfway as bad, but Akmal is a whole different breed. It must be because he's Malay, they have a whole different set of rules, I'm assuming. But I've seen the way he looks at Vero when she's not looking. He's definitely interested.

We pack up half of my stuff and start labeling the boxes. This is going to be a process, but that's okay because this is a step Mat and I need to take. We're both too addicted to each other, too afraid of outside forces coming in between us again. We place the boxes in the trunk of my Camry. Vero steps into the front passenger seat and I start the ignition.

Mat's neighborhood is nice and quiet, right by a cozy little park. No frat boys like our side - I mean, Vero's side. I do worry about her being alone, though. What if she needs help, who will be there for her if she doesn't get to her phone on time?

We're already moving some of the boxes out of the trunk when I tell myself that Vero is a full grown woman, who grew up in the same neighborhood I did. She's got this. I have to trust that she's got this, or else my mind would go nuts with worry over her.

A young blond almost runs into Vero and the big box in her arms. "Yow, watch where you're going chica, I almost dropped this stuff."

"Oh, I'm sorry." She's looking between Vero and I with some sharp eyes. There's something I don't like about her already, and I don't even know who she is. "It looks like you guys are moving in? I didn't know there was an empty apartment on this floor?"

"This foxy mama behind me is moving in with her man, because he can't get enough of what she does to him." This girl. I would slap her ass if my arms weren't holding a big box myself. Vero turns to me and winks before she continues to walk, and I follow right behind her to insert the key to Mat's door.

"I'm sorry, are you sure you have the right door?" What is up with this girl? I have the damn key, right here.

"What's your name again? I don't think I caught it on the way in."

"Oh, uh, Emily. I live a couple doors down."

"Ah.. well nice to meet you Emily. I'm Atsuko. If you don't mind, I need to hurry and put my stuff away, so I can be ready to fuck Mat's brains out when he gets home from work. My man's got a strong appetite, you see."

Vero is laughing at this point as she follows me inside. Emily's jaw is still on the floor.

"Shit, you got that right. That's why I had to kick her ass out. They were keeping me up all night."

We slam the door on her face and continue to place the boxes in their designated areas, before heading back out for the rest of the boxes in the trunk.

"Damn girl, you got your hands full with that one. I mean, I think the problem is that he doesn't know how good he looks, you know? It also makes him damn endearing. Take Akmal for instance, did you see that crowd of girls at the car show? I thought I was about to take off my stilettos and earrings for that shit. It's a good thing he's fucking oblivious and innocent."

I'm grunting and laughing because my arms are sore, but we have one more set of boxes to bring in. Vero is crazy over Akmal. I have no idea how this shit is going to work because that boy literally has a neon sign over his head that says 'virgin'. Every girl around him can see it, and every girl around him wants to be the one to corrupt his innocence. Him being so damn friendly doesn't help his case whatsoever, it only makes them chase him harder.

I pity the girl who stands in Vero's way, because that broad can be a stubborn and vicious one when she has her sights set on something. And she really wants him.

We're laughing about Vero's failed flirting attempts with Akmal on the way to the car and back when I get a chill down my spine. Before we even get the chance to close the front door, someone shoves us inside.

I drop the box in my hands and I hear Vero do the same before she cusses under her breath.

Alfonso is standing there like a madman, and he smells very strongly of hard liquor with fading bruises on his face. This isn't good. I've since blocked his number when I went on that date with Mat the first time. I've been living blissfully without his drama. How did he know where to find me?

"Atsuko, you fucking bitch. How could you cheat on me?" *What the hell?*

"Get your head out of your ass Alfonso. You guys are NOT together."

"Bitch, you don't think I know it's YOU who's been keeping my girl from me! I know you fuck her and talk behind my back. You're the meddling cunt that made her break up with me. It's always you, Vero!"

I scream when Alfonso throws a punch right at Vero's face, knocking her to the ground. What the hell is happening?

Grabbing the closest thing I can get my hands on, I throw a lamp at Alfonso's head before turning around and running. But he's faster than me for some reason, even though he's drunk. My body hits the carpeted flooring when he tackles me, sending pain up my elbows. Turning my body around, I'm kicking and screaming, throwing punches where I can and scratching his face. But he's got more weight on me, easily subduing me after he comes to his senses from the wound I put on his face. I can feel the bulge between his legs pressing against me. He loves the fight I'm putting up, it's turning him on and it's freaking me the fuck out.

I scream bloody murder and turn my face left and right when he tries to come in for a kiss. He has my wrists pinned down on either side of my head but my legs are still kicking like a she demon. This is not happening right now! I won't let it! I think I knee him in the balls, but it must be his drunken state because it doesn't deter him like I think it would. One of his hands starts tugging on my shirt and my mind is telling me this is it. He's going to rape me right here on the floor.

The door slams open with a loud bang when I scream again, and suddenly, Alfonso's body is lifted off me right before I start to sob. This asshole! How did it come to this? Shit, where's Vero?

I'm turning and crawling around looking for her, when I see Akmal by her side, cradling her as she rubs her face into his chest.

The sound of flesh hitting flesh, and a growl I've come to recognize, makes me get to my feet and turn around just in time to see Mat turning into a beast intent on murdering Alfonso. I'm not sure if I should stop him, or let him proceed with his plans. Alfonso has been a thorn on my side, this was bound to happen. Was it my fault? Did I let it go so far that he would choose this path? A glint of something metal and Alfonso is landing cuts on Mat with a pocketknife. Oh no!

Mat continues like there aren't bleeding streaks of red in random locations. I can't take my eyes away from them. Watching Mat's muscles reminds me of a predator taking down it's kill. The skill and dance to his body's movements are magnificent. Something only found in nature, but before I can get lost in this ballet, my mind slaps me back to reality with the fact that if Mat kills Alfonso, he would be sent to jail.

There's blood spurting from Alfonso's nose and cheek

before I decide to run towards Mat and grab his bicep. When he turns, the look on his face is feral. A wild animal operating on instincts, performing what it does best. Mat has a darkness in him that he has to try hard to restrain. Especially knowing what I know now, I need to stop him before he does something he will regret.

"Mat, baby, he's not fighting back. It's done. Come back to me." His arm and shoulder is still vibrating with energy, just barely restrained from the momentum of another swing. I take the risk of cradling his face in my hands, and staring into the eyes of a natural born predator.

"Come back to me."

I kiss his snarling lips and it takes a while before he drops Alfonso's unconscious body like a heap of trash onto the floor. He's shaking throughout the kiss, and his arms are hugging me a little too tightly but I understand his fears. I was afraid too. It was a close call.

"That fucking asshole! I knew he was off his fucking rocker. You should have fucking killed him Mat!" Vero is going ballistic, about to jump at his unconscious body and kick the shit out of him if it wasn't for Akmal holding her back firmly. She's right though. She's always right. I should have never led him on that long.

"I'm so sorry, Mat." My eyes are tearing up with everything that's happened. It's Mat who starts to caress my cheeks with his palms, lovingly placing his forehead on mine, breathing me in the same way I'm breathing him in.

"Never be sorry, Atsuko. I'm more than willing to leave a trail of dead bodies for you, but it would keep me away from the woman I love. Thank you for stopping me, because... I wouldn't have stopped."

My lips crash onto his as his arms come around my waist

and lift me up. I can hear Vero talking on the phone, while my tongue seeks reaffirmation from Mat's mouth, about everything that's happened today.

"Yeah, fuck, I want to report a break in and attempted rape. I'm pretty sure this fucker is on probation too."

29

MAT

The police removed that piece of trash from our home. I need to call in a carpet service to replace the bloodstained ones in our living room. This is exactly why I need to have Atsuko near me. It reminds me that Vero is still very much on her own, next to those drunken frat boys.

"Vero, are you going to be alright living on your own next to those rowdy frat boys?"

"Wait, you live next to a bunch of drunken college men?"

"Yeah. It's not like you ever asked. Plus they usually stay on their side and I stay on mine."

Akmal looks aggravated, but schools his expression pretty quickly. I feel you man. I felt the same way about my girl.

"You're not living there anymore. What if some other lunatic comes in and none of us are around? We were just lucky that we wrapped up work quickly and came back to see you guys. Nah, you're coming to stay with me Vero. I have an extra room. It's safer."

"Oh, is that so? Extra room, huh? I do need you to nurse my injury. Would you be my male nurse, Akmal?" I don't know how their relationship can even work with Akmal's culture cockblocking them. In fact, I don't even think he's supposed to have a female in the same house if they're not married.

After clearing his throat, Akmal looks a little uneasy. "Yes. It's a temporary solution but I'm not having you go back to live around a bunch of drunken men. What kind of guy would that make me?"

"Oh, I'd love to find out, Akmal."

"I'm telling you right now, what kind of man I am. You're *not* going back, you're staying with me."

Atsuko and I remain quiet as we watch the show in front of us. It's like watching a tidal wave hit sand. These two are polar opposites.

I rub my nose into Atsuko's hair, making her bring her attention back to me. "Did you get everything you needed from the apartment?"

"I still have a few more boxes to pack up."

"I'll go with you. We might as well bring these two along in case Akmal rethinks his temporary solution. I don't think his family would approve of his suggestion if they ever found out."

"I figured. Not many people approve of Vero, she can be a bit much."

The rest of the move went quickly. Seeing the proof of all the males around Vero helped to solidify Akmal's decision. Good. He needs to grab onto her if he's serious about her. Maybe I should take my own advice. Would moving in be enough? Is it enough to make her understand she's mine in all ways? I put a GPS tracker on her phone when she wasn't looking. I need to know where she is at all times, in case I do need to handle something with Akmal and the business.

Akmal and Vero left not too long after dinner before the sun went down. Atsuko and I are lying on the couch, her on top of me, watching mindless television. Dinner was an amazing affair. Who knew home cooked meals tasted so different from ones that comes in a box? Is this what I have to look forward to each day? *I'm a lucky bastard.* Atsuko was most kind enough to be my nurse for some of my superficial wounds. I didn't even feel them when I was pummelling her ex. All I could think about was removing the threat to my female.

My hands are running over her amazing ass covered by one of my shirts, grinding her pussy into my growing erection. She hums against my chest but doesn't reciprocate. It kind of makes me hornier that she's trying to avoid me.

Lifting her up higher, I bring her shirt up and place one of her breasts in my mouth. She stops avoiding me now as her hands run through my hair, light moans escaping her breath. She pushes off me to toss her shirt aside and my eyes are glued to the junction of her thighs. She wasn't wearing panties this entire fucking time. Without having to prompt her, she crawls up my body, and sits over my face. Damn this woman. Happily licking what's offered to me, she starts to grind her pussy into my face more and more. My hands squeeze her ass, forcing her to sit on my face even more as my tongue continues to spear her wet pussy. When her orgasm comes crashing, she cries out in pleasure, and slowly slides back down my body until her face is between my own legs. I've never had a woman worship my dick like she does, and it's the most intoxicating thing. What's even more intoxicating is the fact that she loves the way I dominate her in this position. She makes me confident in myself, the exact opposite of what any other woman has made me feel.

When her mouth swallows my dick, I grab the back of her hair and start thrusting slowly until I can't anymore. When she moans, I can feel the vibration all the way down to my fucking sack and it tips me over the edge, making me climax into her mouth. The feeling of her greedily sucking my cock makes me growl, but she loves it. I hope she never plans to leave me again because this is fucking heaven.

When she crawls back up, I take her mouth in mine, while my slow brain finally comes to the conclusion of what I need to do. I'm lost and drunk in her mouth making love to mine, our tongues tasting each other. When I pull back to catch my breath, I whisper against her lips, "Marry me."

There's a pause between us and she doesn't answer. I kiss her again to further convince her, in case she even considered saying no to me.

Flipping her onto her back on the couch, I dive between her legs and use all the skills I have to make her give me the answer I want to hear. Shit, what if I'm moving too fast? What if she says no? I shove my tongue deeply inside of her, tasting everything she has to give. Her legs start to close in around my ears when I almost miss it.

"Yes, Mat. Oh my fucking god. I'll marry you. Shit, don't stop."

Doubling my efforts and using my fingers to thrust into her, I listen to her scream in ecstasy as I bring her to another climax.

EPILOGUE

*I*t took a bit, but with the help of Akmal and his computer skills in addition to my snooping around Mat's stuff when he's not home, we were able to track down his grandparents. They are still living on the Blackfoot reservation in Montana.

It's been a really long time since he's contacted them, and after talking to them on the phone, I found out why. Mat had only just opened up about what happened with his parents, but he never told me he was banished. I never knew he carried all this guilt and weight on his shoulders. He's only mentioned his grandparents briefly during conversations, but I could tell that he missed them, and I'm sure they're wondering how he's doing as well. He's family after all.

I couldn't arrange a visit to the reservation knowing what I know now, so I had to ask them to come and visit us. I hope they're well enough. My mind keeps imagining this poor decrepit old couple trying to drive across a few state lines. I could have asked Mat to do a road trip with me to meet them halfway, but he would be suspicious and I'm not sure how he would receive me going behind his back about this.

My gut tells me I'm doing the right thing. I really *hope* I'm doing the right thing. Mat shouldn't have to be alone without family.

They called about five hours ago during one of their pit stops. I'm getting kind of nervous. I've been busy in the kitchen, making all sorts of meals, even though I don't even know what kind of stuff they like. The whole apartment smells like a restaurant at this point. It's probably going to seep into all the curtains and furniture.

Akmal texted and told me he would try to hold Mat over with work until it was close to time. Looking at the clock over the stove, it looks like he should be home soon. I might have a little time on my hands.

The sound of a key being inserted into the doorknob makes me snap my head that way. He wasn't scheduled back for another thirty minutes.

"Hey, beautiful. Wow, it smells amazing. What's all this? Am I missing an important date for something?"

Greeting him with a hug and kiss on my tip toes, I watch as Mat's face lights into a smile. He really is handsome when he smiles, though every time I try to take a selfie with him, he never does.

Closing the door and locking it behind him, Mat walks me backward with his arms still around me and continues to rain kisses on my face, making me giggle, when there's a knock at the door. *Oh my goodness, this is it. I think it's them. Stay calm, stay calm.*

"Are you expecting someone?" Uh oh, he doesn't look happy. Oh man, I hope I did the right thing.

When Mat opens the door, he stands stock still. I'm getting more nervous by the second when no one says anything. Is it someone else at the door?

"Na-ahks'. What are you doing here?" My heart is swelling even though I don't recognize the first word he said. But it must be them, surely.

"Matunaagd." I can't tell if they sound happy or sad. Even on the phone, Mat's grandparents sounded the same. Mat's body is moving. It looks like they're shaking hands. That's a good sign, right?

"Come in, come in. You must have had a long journey. How did you know where to find me?" Is his voice croaking with emotion too? My poor baby. He's been missing his grandparents even though he doesn't say it out loud.

When Mat turns his broad shoulder to give them room to enter, I see two very sturdy looking elderly individuals step in. His grandmother has a full head of white hair braided back and has the friendliest smile on her face. His grandfather's hair is peppered and tied back, his face clean-shaven with a smile that makes his eyes crinkle in the cutest of ways. I can see a lot of Mat's features in him, they must be his grandparents from his father's side to have genes that strong.

My eyes tear up for his reunion, and I give them both big hugs and usher them to the table where the meals are spread out, waiting to be consumed.

As his grandparents sit down, Mat comes up behind me with a big hug, putting his face close to my ear.

"Did you do this?" I nod my head and turn to hug him back, tightly.

"Thank you Atsuko. This means so much to me."

"Anything for you." Releasing him before I can tear up, I turn to Mat's grandparents with a big welcoming smile.

"So who's hungry?"

~

"You guys are what?!"

"We're engaged!"

"Holy shitballs!" Vero and I are screaming at the news. It's been a few days since Mat's grandparent's departure, and Mat is currently over at Akmal's place for another couple of hours to work on a small family portrait session they recently had.

"Ugh! I'm so jealous of you, Atsuko! But you fucking deserve it. He's great for you. You guys are great together. Now if only I can just get Akmal to even look at me." She's so dramatic. That boy is definitely interested in her. I saw the way he was bristling when he was around the frat boys near her apartment.

"You're crazy, Akmal looks at you all the time when he thinks you're not."

"That is fucking nuts because I have tried to get him to come to my room in so many ways without success. I'm even walking around in a tank and panties all over his place. That boy is a damn saint! It makes me so fucking horny!" She says panties but for all I know she's walking around in a damn thong in front of that poor guy. I really am surprised he hasn't jumped her by now.

"You have your toys, right?"

"I do! But it's not the same!" Vero is utterly whining by this point. I've never seen her this frustrated. But she usually can pick up a quickie at work, I wonder if she still is?

"Are you getting anything at work? You know, to relieve your stress?"

"Atsuko! I can't do that to Akmal. I don't want him to see me that way. I haven't had dick since I started chasing that fucker. And he's making it so hard for me, my pussy is in tears and weeping every time he's around me!" She's groaning as she lays her head back on the armrest of the couch. Poor thing. She's already playing with her tits as we speak. She's so damn frustrated.

Any other time, I would have helped her but now that Mat and I are getting married, I don't think he would be able to handle it. He's a pretty possessive guy, something I love about him. The conversation we had about my relationship with Vero was an interesting one, to say the least. My pussy throbs just thinking about it.

"So...you and Vero?"

We're sitting on the floor in the apartment again. He looks a little scared, like Vero might be competition. It's interesting that I find Mat's jealousy and possessiveness quite endearing versus Alfonso's.

Is this what love does to you? Makes you see everything in a whole new light?

"Me and Vero? We're best friends and yes, we do help each other scratch itches sometimes. But I haven't had an itch since you came into my life. You more than satisfy all my needs."

"...so she's tasted your pussy?"

I can feel my eyes becoming hooded, because Mat is trying to get at something. I just know it. Whatever it is, the low timbre of his voice is turning me on right now.

His hands peel back my cotton shorts quickly, removing the panties with them making me gasp. He's become more and more aggressive since we've been together.

I love it.

His lips touch my inner thigh and my legs fall open to make room for his broad shoulders.

"You know this pussy is mine, right? No more girl time down here. I'm not going to tell you again."

My breath hitches because it sounds like a damn challenge. I can't help but rise up to his bait.

"Why's that? What happens when I'm a bad girl?" Why is my voice so breathy right now? I moan when Mat uses the flat of his tongue to lick my swollen lips all the way up to the hood of my clit, sucking it into his lips, while he stares at me with his dark eyes.

A few more sucks and a few more licks, Mat undresses quickly before finishing me, leaving me a hot and bothered mess. His dick is hard and angry looking, and it's pointing right at me accusingly. The precum glistening against his piercing and head is making my mouth water. But the look on Mat's face says he has something in store for me.

He crawls between my legs and pushes my chest down until I'm on my back. His hand is going towards his cock.

Thwack thwack!

Oh. My. God.

Thwack!

Mat dick slaps me hard, making my hips jump right before he leans in and starts to rub his shaft against my wet labia folds, poking the head of his cock against my clit. I'm breathing heavily, and my mind is still reeling over the fact that Mat dick slapped me when I feel him bite into the crook of my neck right before he slams home inside of me.

"Sorry babe, I can't help you. And I'm going to have to ask you to refrain from touching yourself around here. Don't pull me into that! I'm engaged with Mat!"

She's pinching her nipples through her shirt a few more times before she groans and stops her ministrations.

"Fuck, you're right. I'll stop. I'll stop."

Her eyes are closed and suddenly she pops up into sitting, scaring the shit out of me. "What if I get him drunk and blow his mind? He wouldn't be able to say no to me then, right?"

I'm laughing. This girl. "How do you come up with this stuff?"

"It's not me! It's my pussy! She's telling me what to do. She's lonely, and she wants Akmal badly. He has got to be the most off limits man I've ever met. It only makes me want him more!" This poor girl. She is suffering. I don't know how to help her.

The door opens, surprising us. The boys are home early.

"Hey beautiful. We finished early and wanted to get back. Did you two have fun?"

"Yeah, I'm glad you're here." I jump into his arms and he catches me with ease. Our welcome home kiss is starting to get a little heated and I can hear Vero groaning behind us. Oops.

"Sorry, Vero." What kind of a friend am I? Vero literally has the female version of blue balls as we speak.

"It's alright Chica. Come on Akmal, let's go home."

"Er...Yeah, we'll catch you guys later."

AKMAL

This woman drives me nuts. My dick is going to stain every single pair of pants I own. My culture dictates that I can't even whack off. How can a woman be this damn sexy? I'm trying my best to remain calm and polite, but it's getting harder and harder the more I'm around her. Ironic because it's not the only thing getting harder the more I'm around her. Feels like my dick is going to fall off with how stiff it's been without any relief.

When I drive her home, I think of the fact that I probably shouldn't even be doing this. What if my family finds out?

Shit, what if one of my sisters decides to come by? But I couldn't leave her at her apartment all alone, basically surrounded by a bunch of men who would jump at the chance to be with her. I want a chance at her before anyone else. I saw her first.

How do I fix this? How do I fix this and not go against my culture? There's really only one way I can touch her, but I don't know if I should. She'll probably think I'm crazy.

My thoughts are running a mile a minute as we get out of the car and start walking toward our door. *Our.* We're basically together, aren't we? Isn't this how the regular folk do it? Damn, the way her ass sways when she walks in front of me is hypnotizing. I don't say any of these things because I'm trying to be a damn gentleman, but it's getting really difficult.

"Akmal, do you want to watch a movie with me?" *I want to do so much with you, if only you knew.*

"Yeah, what do you feel like watching?"

"Whatever you want. I'll go grab us some drinks." It's a bit early for drinks but I'll do whatever she wants. She's taking over my every waking thought. Her scent is making me desperate to sit near her. She smells like something light and airy with a hint of sweetness.

We start watching Star Wars Episode 1 and three quarters into the movie, I'm feeling a little drunk. Damn, how many bottles has she handed me? Every time our fingers brush, I feel electricity zap, and it travels right down to my dick. I just wanted to be able to sneak these little touches, again and again, when she thrust the bottles my way. Does that make me pathetic or what?

I must have been fading in and out because I can feel the soft cushions of the couch beneath me. When did I lay my body down? Opening my eyes, the room starts to warp a little. Damn, this isn't good. How the hell am I going to get to my room?

A warm body is on top of me, my slightly drunk addled mind thought it was a blanket for some reason. But blankets don't moan and rub themselves on you, do they? Shit. We shouldn't be doing this. I'm not supposed to be doing this. *She feels so hot between her legs.* It feels like she's rubbing herself on my shin.

"Vero?" My voice is croaking from what she's doing to me, and from me being scared of the position I found myself in.

"Shh...let me take care of you. It looks angry." Wait, what?

Shit shit shit. When did my pants get undone? I can feel her warm breath across my rock hard dick and I'm swallowing a gulp down my throat because I want to push her off and I want to keep her there at the same time. *What do I do? What do I do? Is it getting hotter in here?*

My mind is processing too slowly, because I'm still trying to figure out how I got in this position to begin with, when something hot and wet envelops the head of my dick making me almost jump out of my skin. Holy hell, is this what I've been missing out on? *My god, this can't be real.*

Her tongue. My fucking god, *her tongue.* She's doing some sort of witchcraft down there. I can't take my eyes off her, I'm under her damn spell. The room warps a little bit every now and again, but the sight of Vero's head bobbing up and down on my shaft keeps me somewhat focused. How can something feel this good? If a mouth feels *this* good, what would a pussy feel like? *Shit, stop thinking like that. Control yourself.* The light from the TV is casting fascinating shadows on her face as the credits roll up in my periphery. Trying to think random thoughts still doesn't stop my abs from tensing up with each suck she performs on her way up my shaft.

When her hand starts to fondle my sack, I explode into her mouth with a loud groan and jerk of my hips. Shit, should I have done that? What the hell did I just do? Fuck. But I can't stop. It feels so damn good. That was the biggest orgasm of my damn twenty eight years of life. Which doesn't say much really.

The way her mouth suctions on my cock as it continues to shoot out jets of cum, almost sobers me. Damn, look at how beautiful she is. She loves it, *I think*. I mean, she's moaning on my cock as she does it. It must mean she likes it? My mind is starting to clear and the situation at hand is starting to rear its ugly head at me. We've gone too far. Beyond too far. There's only one way to fix this. But how will she receive it?

Vero gives my dick one last sultry lick right over my slit, making me groan again before she climbs over me and brings her body down flush with mine. I love the way she feels on top of me.

My hands slowly, ever so slowly, touch her cheeks. I'm scared, I've never done this before. This is all so new to me. But if it has to happen, I wouldn't want it with anyone else but Vero. My hands become more confident, and firmly cradle her face in front of me. She's so fucking soft, the most beautiful woman I've ever seen. She's a hurricane that came into my peaceful existence, knocking me to my damn knees. I thought I was strong before I met her, but what just happened between us proved me wrong. She destroys any control I thought I had.

"Hi." Her breathy voice, in combination with her stunning smile, pushes me over the edge. I have to do this.

"Will you be my wife?" It almost feels like my heart doesn't beat again until I see her smile widen even more.

"Damn, if all it took was a blowjob to make you see me, I

would have done it sooner. Fuck it. Why not? Hell yea, I'll be your wife."

She kisses me before I can stop her and tell her that we need to refrain from anything else before marriage.

But like she says, fuck it. Just one kiss wouldn't hurt. We're getting married anyway, right?

A beta reader had mentioned wanting more of an interaction between the grandparents and Mat during their reunion. After consulting my person on the traits she noticed in her husband and grandfather who is Blackfoot, I was informed that the men in her life are very stoic. Hands-on attention is not given as freely as some Americans.

So why did the story have to end like *this*? Why not some sort of build-up like with the other two main characters? Or maybe even a dreaded cliffhanger?

The person I was consulting on Akmal's culture informed me that if Vero even thought of leaving the guy hanging, he would probably avoid her like the plague and hide at his parent's house. It was an interesting move I had to make in order for the two side characters to be ABLE to move forward together (and I really wanted them to have a book!).

Another question that was brought up was why would Vero disregard/disrespect Akmal's culture with that move of getting him drunk? My answer is because all those times they "hung out" at lunch were more of Vero talking his head off and the poor guy just nodding his head and smiling in order to be polite. Remember, he is good when it comes to professional conversation, but not when it comes to relationships and girls. He is allowed to date, but no touching of *that sort* until marriage.

Now that the stage is set for a wedding ceremony (Akmal's mother is probably already setting it up before Vero even gets there) can you imagine loud mouth, overconfident Vero having to restrain her inner self when the wedding happens? I was informed that this would actually be a WHOLE DAY affair. She would have to refrain from cursing as well.

I hope you guys are excited to see what book 2 has in store for us all! These characters take over my story as I write. Even I don't know what's going to happen next!

BONUS CHAPTERS

MORTY

Watching the security feed, I see Tricia sneaking into the employee file cabinet again. She does this every so often, when no one's in the front. Zooming in the other day, I found that she's been sneaking into only one file in particular: Matunaagd Big Crow.

Her delicate fingers flip through the pages for only a few seconds before she places everything back where they belong. My mind is already conjuring up things I want to do to her. I'm not a bad man, I'm truly not. I've left the family business behind me, this IT company being good and honest work. But I'm tired of sitting in my office with my bottle of lotion, thinking of those creamy fingers and what they would feel like around my cock. At forty-eight now, I think it's time I live my life and grab it by the horns before I get any older.

When Tricia came in on her day off, my heart skipped a beat. Those big blue eyes stared into mine when she said she was here to see me. In reality, she just wanted to use me as a distraction before she dropped off one of the papers she stole from Matunaagd's file.

Tsk Tsk. Naughty, naughty girl.

It's time I teach my girl a lesson. I haven't had to teach anyone a lesson in a very long while.

"Tricia, in my office please."

She jumps at the sound of my voice, as she closes one of the filing cabinets. It's the work order cabinet, luckily for her. How fun would it be to catch her red-handed? My hands are already itching to smack that little ass of hers.

Tricia is a beautiful woman, with tits that are just a handful and an ass that's perfect to punish. Her creamy white skin is just begging for marks. Damn, I can barely walk straight with my dick this hard. Adjusting the belt on my pants, I hope she doesn't notice, as we both walk back into my office.

"Shut the door." Her eyes grow wide, and it makes my dick leak. Sitting back in my chair behind my mahogany desk, I steeple my fingers and stare at her. She's a young one, I believe her file puts her at twenty-three. She's the best receptionist I've had, working under me since the tender age of eighteen. I should have claimed her then. But alas, I wanted to be a better man after leaving the past behind. I guess I couldn't leave it all behind after all.

"I-i-is everything okay? Did I do something wrong?" Oh, Tricia, I do love the sound of your voice this way. Teasing her, I remain quiet as I continue to stare.

She starts to cross her arms over her chest, pushing her perky little breast up for my viewing pleasure.

"Please, I need this job. Please don't fire me." How lovely she begs.

"Is there a reason you would think, you need to be fired

for?" My eyebrow quirks up. Let's see what the little minx has to say.

Her mouth opens and closes without a sound, making me think of things to stick into it. Might as well, time is a wasting. Most of the employees have already gone home. Tricia usually stays behind to finish up paperwork, and I'm usually the last to leave, making sure to lock up.

"Tricia."

"I-I didn't mean anything by it! I swear! I was just - just."

"Enough!"

"Please! Please, Morty, I need this job!"

"It doesn't seem that way with the things you've been doing. You know I see everything through the cameras."

Her eyes are as big as saucers as she shuts her mouth, and clasps her hands in front of her like she's praying. Oh, I'll make you pray. I'll make you pray and beg for my cock every day.

Getting up from my chair, I round my desk to the front side and lean back with my arms crossed over my chest. I find I miss watching young women squirm in front of me.

"How badly do you need this job, Miss Smith?"

"Please, Morty!"

"On your knees and crawl to me."

Her mouth opens again in a cute O, but she does what she's told without having to be told twice. We're off to a good start.

Yes, little kitty. We're going to have lots of fun together.

❧

TRAVIS

Miss Miller's work case finally popped up today. She hasn't called anything in for the past week. I was starting to get antsy, about to pop into her house even without a work order. After the situation in front of the restaurant, she's been avoiding me. I don't know why.

What is it about our relationship that makes her push me away? Am I not submissive enough? Isn't that what she wants? Just thinking about the way she uses her foot to rub my balls makes my sack tighten.

I need her. I crave her like I crave my next breath. She's every man's dream. She better not have traded me in for someone else because I will kill that fucker. Miss Miller is mine from the moment I licked that cunt of hers.

Tricia hands me the work order and I'm out the front doors before she can even say a word to me. Get ready Miss Miller, I'm coming.

The drive to her house gets my blood pumping. The anticipation giving me a slight high. I'm going to give her the best dick of her life so she'll never think to reject me again. I'm going to make her fucking understand she belongs to me.

Pulling up to her driveway, I quickly throw the company car into park and jump out. Knocking on her door a few times, I adjust my pants to give my erection some form of comfort. The air in front of me is displaced when she swings the door inwards, opening it, revealing to me her luscious body under her black silk robe. Her eyes widen. Was she expecting someone else? Fuck, that makes me pissed. It should only be me seeing her like this. Mat's never coming back.

I step in before she can tell me no, shutting the door and locking it from memory.

Her eyes tell me she's unsure. Why? What happened to that confident woman I met the first time? What happened to that fire? Was it because of Mat's rejection? But how can one guy do this much damage? It didn't seem like he was into what they had together.

"Miss Miller."

Her eyes sharpen at my address. There she is. There's my vixen.

"Travis, I wasn't expecting you. I think a rat ate one of my cables. If you can just replace it and go, we'll be good."

"Why are you trying to get rid of me so quickly?"

"I'm not. I called the company for a quick fix. I have things to do today."

"Things like what? Are you seeing someone else? Is this what this is about?"

"What does it matter to you? What if I am?" Oh, there's a fire in her eye now. She's being a brat.

Dropping my work bag onto the floor, I take a step forward. Miss Miller takes a step back. Oh, this is a first. What's happening here? Is my presence affecting her?

"Just fix the problem, Travis. I'll sign your work order and you can go."

"I'm not going anywhere until you fucking understand that you are mine. I don't share well. Not after having a taste of what's now mine."

I can hear a little intake of air, even though her expression hasn't changed. She's good at putting up a front. But I'm not leaving this house until she understands her place with me. I've played her games. I've let her control her environment to make her happy. But talking about going to another man? That's where I draw the line.

Playtime is over.

She's trying to stand her ground with a defiant look on

her face. It makes my cock twitch. Oh, we'll see how long she can hold that face when I'm done with her. I'm not letting her go. I'm never letting her go. She's *mine.*

When we're chest to chest, I look deep into her green eyes. Miss Miller only stands to my shoulders, so my head is bent down while hers is tilted up.

My hands run up her arms, stopping to cradle her neck and jaw between my palms.

"Travis, I just need you to fix the problem and go."

I slam my mouth on hers and force my tongue into her mouth. She fights for only a second and then melts into me. *I knew it.* She's afraid to give up control, that's why she tries so hard to be a bitch even though I enjoy that shit.

But only from her.

I walk her backward until we hit a wall. My hands are opening her robe and squeezing her luscious breasts.

Before I'd like, she shoves me off her and glares at me. Oh, we're playing that are we?

My hand shoots out to her neck and making her open her mouth to me again. When our lips tangle, she pushes me just far enough to slap me in the face. Fuck.

Bending at the knee, I toss her over my shoulder as she growls and kicks. Slapping her ass to settle her down, I throw her onto her bed and start stripping out of my work clothes. Every time she scrambles to get off the bed, I slap her pussy. *Thwack!* When she turns over to get away, I slap her ass. *Thwack!*

"You fucker! How dare you!"

Once I'm naked, I push her legs apart and settle myself in between. Holding her still by the neck again, my mouth swallows whatever else she wants to say to me. I don't miss the little moan that escapes her mouth when I start to grind against her hot pussy lips. She fucking loves it, judging by how wet she's getting, she's just afraid to ask for it. She's afraid to let go. What's made her so afraid?

My lips travel from her mouth down to her neck without removing my grip. The taste of her is intoxicating. She whispers my name like it's a plea.

Sucking on her pale skin, I make sure to leave my mark on her in case she forgets she belongs to me when I leave again. She moans as her pussy pushes against me, gliding against my shaft. *That's it, baby.*

Letting go of her neck, I suck and nip at her tits until they're marked up to my liking. Her hands are in my hair tugging hard but it doesn't stop me from what I need to do. I need to make sure she feels me all over her body even after I leave.

Going lower, I push her legs as far as they will go and then maybe a little more. When she cries out, my head dips and my tongue spears her between her puffy pussy lips. They're so pink and precious, her clit peeking out wanting attention too. My fingers spear her when my tongue starts to play with her clit, sucking it enough to elicit a cry of both pain and pleasure. Her fingers in my hair, that was once pushing me away, are now pulling me closer, her sharp nails digging into my scalp telling me just how much it's affecting her resolve.

Two fingers turn into three and her legs have stopped fighting to close back up. The feel of her starting to tighten around my fingers makes me take them out before she can crest that peek. My mouth moving in where my fingers left off. Licking, sucking, and finally nipping at her swollen lips, I continue the assault until her cries make my dick weep.

Crawling away from her and getting back on my feet in front of the bed, I grab her arms and put her on her knees in front of me.

I thought she'd put up more of a fight, but apparently, this is exactly what she needs. Shoving my cock against her lips, she looks up at me with what I can only describe as adoration in her eyes. She loves this shit. I fucking knew it. It makes my chest hurt, looking at how well she submits. All she needed was a strong hand. I can be that for her. I'm all she'll ever need.

She's sucking my cock with enthusiasm and it makes my abs tighten. Fuck, how is she so good with this when she barely gives head when she's playing dominatrix? My hands go into her hair softly for a minute, until my grip starts to tighten, right before I start fucking her face.

When I feel her tongue swirling around the head of my cock and her throat swallow when her face is against my groin, my balls telling me I'm about to shoot my load.

Pushing her head so my cock is down her throat, I cum and feel her swallow every pulse I give her. *That's a good girl.* She's too fucking good at this. This isn't the first time she's submitted.

When my sack empties, I pull her off me and throw her back on the bed before our lips crash again.

Between our tongues dancing and my teeth nipping her lower lip, I whisper, "You belong to me Megan, don't you ever forget it. If I find another man sniffing around what's mine, you're going to pay for it...and you're going to love it."

PLAYLIST

Queen - Bohemian Rhapsody
The Dresden Dolls - Coin Operated Boy
Imelda May - Mayhem
Imelda May - Tribal
Black Label Society - Bleed For Me
Peggy Lee - Fever
Postmodern Jukebox - Seven Nation Army
Christina Aguilera - Trouble
Imelda May - Pulling the Rug
Big Bad Voodoo Daddy - Maddest Kind of Love
Lavay Smith & Her Red Hot Skillet Lickers - Oo Papa Doo
Christina Aguilera - Ain't No Other Man

THE CONCEPTION OF US

LABELS & LACE

THE CONCEPTION OF US

LABELS & LACE

YD LA MAR

BLURB

How did a 28 year old virgin like myself catch a woman
like her?
From the first time I saw her behind the camera lens, I knew
she was out of my league.
Every man's fantasies come to life, I couldn't get her out of
my mind.
Out of all the guys she could have, she chose me, the nerdy
Malay guy.
I'm so nervous about bringing her to meet my family, my
palms are sweating.
What if they're too much for her?
What if I'm not enough for her?
What if she decides she can't handle the fact that we can't do
anything before marriage?

Catching her isn't going to be enough.
The hard part is finding a way to keep her.

COURTESY WARNING

This book may contain triggers for some. Triggers include
but not limited to: light BDSM

Mohd Akmal Bin Alqi
Veronica "Vero" Hernandez
Nora - Akmal's mom
Rafil - Akmal's dad
Hasanah
Sakinah
Hidaya

Auntie Irina
Uncle Tuah
Cousin Ismail
Cousin Aryani

Auntie Adila
Uncle Zaka
Cousin Umar
Cousin Nosiah

Fabian Hernandez

Maria Hernandez
Alejandro Hernandez

Matunaagd Big Crow
Atsuko Kobayashi

Bisaam

TRANSLATIONS

MALAY

Makan, Makan - Eat, Eat
Don't be perasan la - don't flatter yourself (la is sometimes
added at the end of sentences)
Ibu, don't kacau him - mom, don't disturb him
Walao eh - Oh my god/oh shit
Can hah - Are you sure?
Bapa - dad
Ibu - mom
Cantik - beautiful/pretty

~

SPANISH

¿Mira, mira quien viene? - Look, look who's coming

Milagro que se acuerda que tiene familia - It's a miracle that she remembers she has family.

La bendición - asking for blessing, typical greeting

Que Dios te bendiga - God bless you, reply to La bendición

Comida - food

¿Quién es tu amigo? - Who is your friend?

¿Porque? - Why

por una semana - for one week

Tu papá estaba preocupado - your dad was worried

Mira tu boca! - Watch your mouth

¿Quién es tu novio? - who is your boyfriend?

ven a hablar conmigo por favor - come talk to me please

Siéntate por favor - sit please

Esposo - husband

Explícamelo - explain it to me

Es un buen chico - He's a good boy

un buen chico puertorriqueño - a good Puerto Rican boy

Hija - daughter

¿Estás embarazada? - you're pregnant?

Vamos, antes tu papá y hermano… - Come on, before your dad and your brother…

Seria/serio - serious

Silencio - be quiet

Dramatica - dramatic

Buen provecho - enjoy your meal

Mira mi culo - Look at my ass

Pero - but

Pinche - fucking..

Dios Mio - My god

Tree & Kylie, this one's for you gals.

1

———————

VERO

*A*kmal is driving us home and I'm still thinking about the plan I concocted at Atsuko's place. I need to get his inhibitions down so that I can convince him to let me touch him. He's so hands-off that it drives me nuts. I'm not used to working this hard, but it brings out my competitiveness. Does that make me a bad person? I don't think so since I've been trying to be good since I met the bastard.

Okay, he's really not a bastard but I'm so damn horny I can't think straight right now. His culture is making it difficult for me to get close to him. He's mentioned that they do date but I can't even touch the guy without him backing away from me. I'm going to have to take this into my own hands or else I'll die from sexual frustration.

Akmal walks us towards *our* door. Can you believe it? I felt like I deserved a gold medal for somehow convincing the guy to let me in his damn door. It's dark out and my mind comes up with a plan before he can escape me and retreat back to his room like he always does.

"Akmal, do you want to watch a movie with me?" Uh-oh, he looks unsure. I cant my hips a little to the side as I cross my arms over my chest, pushing the girls up a bit. His eyes flick quickly there and away. *Sneaky, sneaky boy.*

"Yeah, what do you feel like watching?"

"Whatever you want. I'll go grab us some drinks." *Come on baby, trust me. I'll take care of you tonight. You won't regret it.*

I don't know what Akmal is putting on the big screen in the living room and I really don't care. At this point, my mind is on the mission. Shooting lots of smiles his way, I pass him bottle after bottle. I can see after two, he's getting a little tipsy. *This is going to be fun. I knew Akmal was a lightweight.*

We start watching Star Wars Episode 1, and three quarters into the movie, my mouth is watering at the sight of his crotch. *I'm finally going to meet you today, baby. You and I are going to kiss and make up for the time lost.*

Akmal's eyes are slowly drifting closed and I stare at his gorgeous face. He's so different from any of the men I've been with. My thumb caresses his cheekbones as the palm of my hands cradles his face. How can this man make me lose myself when I've barely even gotten anything in return?

I feel like any scrap of attention he gives me makes my damn world shine brighter and I've already become addicted to it. Addicted to him. Addicted to the one person I can't seem to catch and I am too much of a selfish ho to let anyone else have what I've claimed as mine. Climbing over him, my determination burns inside of me as my breasts rub against his shirt.

There's always something between us. Why is that? And

what is holding him back from me? Am I not good enough to love? I mean, plenty of men come up to me and proposition me, so how can that be? Sure, they're probably all in it for their benefit but I'm not that bad, right? After meeting Akmal that day at the car show, I couldn't put myself out there for a quick fix anymore. Not when there's a prize dangling in front of me in challenge.

I've broken at least two vibrators already and I'm too damn stubborn to get another one. I've been borrowing Atsuko's dildo. I'm sure she doesn't mind since she gets to jump on Mat's cock whenever she likes now.

But how about me? I want a cock to call my own. I mean, I never thought I'd see the day but after witnessing what Atsuko has with Mat, I can't help but feel a pang of emptiness in my gut. Was that what I've always been missing and just didn't know it?

My hand slides down Akmal's warm chest as I watch his breathing slow. The gentle rise and fall creates a soothing lullaby to my senses. He's always had a calming presence about him and it's heady. It makes me want to soak it all up, crawl into him, and just let all my fears go.

My fear is that a man as perfect as Akmal would never want a girl like me. I'm probably not good enough but it doesn't stop me from wanting him all the same.

Determination spurring me on again, my hands deftly start to undo the obstacle before me. My mouth is watering again. I just want to make him feel good, show him I can make it all about him and that I'm not as selfish as I might seem before his eyes. I can be good.

Gosh, just his thigh between my legs is stoking the fire that's already going. A moan slips out of my lips. That damn dildo didn't help one bit.

"Vero?" His voice is doing something to me. Would this

be what he sounds like waking up? The hole in my gut is turning into feelings of yearning. The last guy I woke up to was my high school sweetheart. The day he threw my heart away after he got what he wanted from me.

"Shh...let me take care of you." He doesn't notice me caressing his cock in my hand as I take it out of his pants. He's circumcised and the head is staring at me and winking. I think it wants to come out and play. "It looks angry."

Letting out a breath across his tip, I can feel his dick getting harder in my hand. *My god, Akmal.* How has he been hiding this? I take that back. He needs to be hiding this because I'm about to swallow it fucking whole.

When his taste hits my tongue, my mind gets lost in lust. Has anything felt so good in my mouth before? Akmal feels so forbidden that my pussy is clenching at the fact that I've finally caught him in my clutches. Shit, I want to worship this cock, he tastes so good. My tongue swirls around the head of his cock like it's a dessert I can't get enough of.

His moans do something to me. He's still trying to hold it back but the booze is making his inhibitions go down. No time feeling bad about that right now when I'm grinding my pussy onto his lower leg.

He moans again louder and I feel proud, I feel like I'm in competition with myself as my tongue continues to explore and dance across his slit. Baby boy precums again and now it's my turn to moan with his cock in my mouth. When I lift my sights to him, he's staring right back at me with hooded eyes. *That's it, I want you to let go and let me take care of you.*

I'm hot. I'm horny. I want this man to cum in my mouth and give me all he's got. I suck harder as my hands drift down to fondle his sack and that must have been the magic touch because Akmal starts to pulsate into my mouth, inadvertently making me take him in deeper, almost gagging.

My god.

That is so sexy.

Yes. Give it all to me.

After swallowing every last drop, I moan again, giving him one last lick across the top.

The serene look on his face makes me smile as I climb over him, making sure to drag my pussy along for some friction. Can anyone blame a girl? Look at this man.

Akmal slowly reaches out to me and it makes me fucking shine. *He's finally reaching for me.* When he cradles my face, I feel like offering my heart to him on a silver platter. The way his eyes bore into mine like I'm the only one he sees. Has any man ever looked at me this way? My heart secretly breaks a little when my mind mentally answers me with a solid no.

Putting on a good front, I give Akmal a smile because he genuinely does make me happy. I wake up thinking about him and go to sleep thinking about him.

"Hi." He looks vulnerable. I wonder what he's thinking. I wonder what he thinks of me now?

"Will you be my wife?" Holy shit, I did not see that coming. The butterflies are having riots in my stomach. I'm not one to be held down because I don't want my heart to be trampled on by fuckboys. But Akmal...*Oh, Akmal.* Fuck it, if I don't scoop him up some other ho will, I just know it. That thought makes me want to shank a ho. Hells no. This fool is *my prize.*

"Damn, if all it took was a blowjob to make you see me, I would have done it sooner. Fuck it. Why not? Hell yeah, I'll be your wife."

His eyes are so open, so vulnerable. I feel my heart swell and seal the potential for hurt with a kiss. Akmal is too good of a man to hurt me, right? You only live once and if this is where I had to choose, I'd choose him every time.

He doesn't seem like he knows what he's doing, but that's okay. He better strap up because I plan to give him the ride of his life.

2

———

*T*he booze made Akmal more open to persuasion but I didn't want to scare him off. Our kisses became hot, heavy and really wet. I must have been tired too because I wake up on top of a pretty lumpy bed.

When the bed lets out a masculine groan, my girl parts wake up with excitement.

"Good morning, Akmal." Giving him a peck on the cheek, I'm taken by surprise when he startles, jumps and inadvertently throws me off the couch onto the floor.

Oomph.

At least I landed on my ass, and good thing I got some junk in my trunk to soften the fall. Damn that kind of hurt.

There's the sound of scrambling and suddenly Akmal falls right on top of me, knocking my head back onto the floor. *Ahh fuck it.* I'm just going to lay here for a second as the little birdies fly around my head.

"Shit, I'm so sorry, Vero. Y-y-you surprised me." He's scrambling to remove his body from laying on top of mine but is only succeeding in pushing my tits every now and again before his hands find solid ground.

I laugh, because what the hell am I supposed to do? The morning wood pressed against my core is making me a little light-headed too.

"Akmal, if you wanted to grope me, all you had to do was ask. I love tit play." My hands reach out to grab the front of his shirt to bring him a little closer to me.

"Shit." He jumps off me like I got the plague and plants his ass on the couch while rubbing his hands down his face.

By the time I bring myself up to sit next to him, he's leaning forward with his head in his hands and his elbows on his knees. The groan he lets out makes me wince a little. Poor guy must have a hangover. Sorry, not sorry.

Rubbing the back of his shoulder, Akmal almost stumbles off the couch again when he jumps to the far end of the couch. What is up with this guy? I'm starting to get a little grumpy with how he's treating me right now. Rude.

He rubs his face with his hand one more time and pulls his hair a bit.

"Vero, we-we can't touch like that before marriage. My culture doesn't allow it. Fuck, my culture doesn't allow drinking, and last night was a lapse in judgment." Oh, hell no. I'm about to fucking leave this damn apartment when his hand shoots out to tentatively touch the top of mine.

"Vero, please listen to me. I meant what I said last night. I want to be with you. You don't know how bad I want to be with you. You drive me crazy. The only way I *can* be with you, is this way. Please understand." The tension in my body leaves me at that admission.

There are those vulnerable eyes again. I never realized his

culture was that restrictive. Now I feel a little worse for what I did to him last night. But if I didn't do that, would we really be here right now talking about finally being together? Am I really fucking doing this?

My eyes sweep over Akmal's tousled hair, sincere face, and apprehensive eyes. Is he...is he scared of me changing my mind about last night? My goodness, *this poor baby.*

I must come off like that kind of girl. What a slap in the face that thought is, a slap I probably needed.

"If that's the way it has to be, I'll try it. I don't know what I'm up against here, Akmal. You're going to have to hold my hand the whole way, okay? You can trust me. I'm going to do my best. For you."

It's at that very moment that Akmal's eyes shift to my lips. What the hell, man? You can't tell a girl she needs to put on a damn chastity belt and then look at me like you want another taste. *Naughty, naughty Akmal.*

AKMAL

My palms are sweating. I've dropped my phone three times already and Vero isn't helping. At least she finally stopped walking in front of me, but now she's sitting there in the smallest shorts known to man and a tank top. Her nipples are popping out against her shirt and it's making me sweat. How am I supposed to concentrate on what I need to do?

Maybe this is a bad -

The ringing against my ear stops.

"Hello? Akmal? Are you calling because you want to bring a girl home? Do I need to get things ready?"

"Ibu, geez. I'm just calling to let you know I'll be dropping by tomorrow."

"That's it? Aye, okay but are you bringing Mat? Bring Mat. I'll let Hasanah know he's coming. There will be plenty to eat. See you tomorrow, eh?"

She hangs up on me and I let out a long breath. Damn, that was nerve wracking. It shouldn't be, since I'll actually be bringing someone this time.

"You're leaving me tomorrow, Akmal?" She has an accusing tone and it's making me feel guilty.

"What? No!"

"You didn't tell your mom I was coming. Won't she be upset?"

How do I explain to this beautiful woman that my mother would have probably prepared the wedding before she even knew her correct dress size? I want Vero to have a chance, a chance to make sure she's making the right decision. I really hope she still wants to marry me after meeting the family. I'm cringing on the inside at the thought of tomorrow.

"Vero, it's - it's complicated. My mother can be a bit over-bearing. I wanted you to get a chance to get to know what you're walking into before … before…"

"Before what? Is there something I need to know about? Do you have a girlfriend in the wing or something? A lover waiting for you?"

"What? No! No, no - nothing like that. Sheesh, Vero. I'm not that kind of guy."

"Then tell me, what are you afraid of? What are you afraid of me finding out about?" She shifts her legs and my mind goes blank for a second. My goodness, her legs. Now I'm getting lightheaded since all my blood has rushed down between my legs.

I let out an exasperated breath because this is exactly why

I've been single for twenty-eight years. How do people even deal with this kind of pressure? My head is about to explode. From my mother and now Vero.

Running my hands down my face, I try to find the right words to let her know what I'm thinking.

"I-I'm not good at this. Vero, please believe me. I just don't want you to have any doubts about what you're walking into. My culture is - is different. I don't want you to feel tied down because of me and I'm really hoping you'll still want me by the end of tomorrow." She's nodding slowly at my admission but also looks somewhat skeptical about what I'm saying.

Did that sound as pathetic coming out of my mouth as I feel right about now? But dammit, I want her to see me, all of me, and still want *me*. I sneak a glance at her again while my chin is in my hands and my chest constricts. She's so fucking beautiful and perfect, how could she want someone like me? Someone with no experience in anything woman related. I'm praying tomorrow doesn't end in a disaster. I already feel the heartburn from the thought of her rejection after my mom bombards her with whatever she might have planned.

Leaning forward to rub my hair again, my heart continues to burn beyond comfortable levels. This is going to be a disaster, I just know it.

3

———

AKMAL

I think my cock is going to fall off with how hard it's been since that night. The moment that changed my life forever.

Today is the day. The day I finally bring a woman home to my family. Standing under the showerhead, letting the water spray down my hair, I'm staring at my angry cock. How am I going to get through a meeting with my family like this? The warm water on my skin reminds me of her mouth on my cock and I groan. Washing my body quickly under cold water this time, I step out of the shower stall and almost slip, if it wasn't for my arms grabbing onto something solid.

Vero is standing there with a towel wrapped around her body and my cock is stirring to life again. Shit. I stumble as I grab the towel off the rack and cover my crotch. I can feel my face heat up despite just having a cold shower as Vero sends a smile my way.

"Wh-wh-what are you doing here?"

"Am I not allowed to shower to get ready? I want to smell my best when seeing your family Akmal." Shit, she's right. Okay. I'm overthinking things. She was just waiting for me to be done.

Sidestepping while holding the towel over my crotch, my hip runs into the side of the door as I try to open it without dropping the towel. Is it the steam in the room that's making me sweat? My mind tells me there's a tattoo on Vero's right arm that I never noticed before. Chancing a glance back before exiting completely I get a sight of her luscious ass - her very naked, luscious ass as she steps into the shower.

Tripping out the door, I slam it shut and run to my room to get dressed. I need to survive today and hopefully marry this woman ASAP because I don't know how much longer I can hold out like this, living with a siren.

Standing up after I finish tying my last shoe, my heart stutters at the sight before me. Vero is leaning against the doorframe of my room only wrapped in a towel once again, hair dripping wet. This must be the smallest towel I own because it is giving me a glimpse of heaven right now and my mouth feels dry.

"Akmal, you're going to have to help me with a dress selection because I don't want to offend your parents." Oh right. She's right. Yeah, that makes sense. I don't understand the smile she gives me before she turns and sashays towards the guest room. Shit, I need to tell her not to mention her staying here to my parents.

I'm jogging to catch up with her, speaking as I turn the corner out of my doorway. "Vero, I need to talk to you about something. When we get there don't tell anyone we -" A groan escapes my lips when she bends over to inspect some dresses laying on the bed.

The angle she's bending from where I'm standing gives me the barest of hints to a treasure I'm too damn curious to uncover. I need to fucking marry this woman quickly, before I go out of my damn mind. All my blood has rushed to my cock even more and I have to take a deep breath in and out before speaking.

Will it always be like this between us?

I don't know when I closed my eyes, but when they open back up I see Vero's face turned to look at me over her shoulder, still bent over. *My god.*

Clearing my throat, I close my eyes and try to remember what I wanted to say.

"V-Vero. When we see my family, p-please don't mention us living together. I wasn't supposed to have a woman under the same roof but you were a special circumstance."

"A special circumstance? What is that supposed to mean?" Crap, why does she sound like that? I didn't say anything wrong, did I? Opening my eyes, I see her standing there like a vixen with her hands on her hips. That shouldn't look so sexy. She's mad, right? When girls put their hands on their hips they're usually mad. I think?

"I'm not a damn charity case, Akmal." Shit. Shit shit shit.

"No! N-n-no, that's not what I meant! Please. Crap. Let me rephrase that." One of her eyebrows lifts up but her hands haven't gone down yet. Shit.

Running a hand down my face, I take another deep breath. I need to fix this. It can't fail before it even starts.

"Vero, please. I don't regret anything. You're not a charity case, that's not what I meant. If I could do it over again, I'd do everything in the exact same way. You belong here, Vero, with me. Just the thought of you next to those animals makes my chest burn." Shit, I didn't mean to say that much, but I was on a roll. It sounded right in my head.

Her arm slowly lowers and I let out another breath only for it to hitch again when she starts walking towards me. My palms are sweaty but I don't want to rub them on my pants. When her chest is pressed up against me, Vero lifts her gaze to mine and wears an expression I can't decipher.

"Akmal, you know just what to say to make a girl feel good." My god, her voice is purring and I'm losing brain cells by the minute as my blood rushes to my cock yet again. My eyes flick to the clock on the wall. Do I have enough time for another cold shower?

Her warm hands grab my face and pull me down. We shouldn't do this. I shouldn't be this close to her when I can barely contain myself around her. I need this wedding to happen soon. I need my family to not mess anything up. My mind is racing with conversations I need to have with family members, when her lips brush mine without actually pressing them to mine.

When she speaks, her lips only whisper against my own, sending tremors down my body. How does she affect me like this? She's bringing me to my damn knees and we haven't done anything more than what's already been done.

"Akmal, breathe. Everything will be okay." Closing my eyes, I do as she says. I can feel her rub the tip of her nose against mine and my mind starts to calm. She's right. Everything will be okay. She agreed to marry me. That means she feels enough for me to go through it. It's a good start. I need to just make sure it keeps going well to keep her by my side.

When her hands leave my face, I almost protest the loss of her warmth. Shit, Akmal, keep it together man. You need to make sure she marries you. Keep to the plan.

"So what dress should I wear? I pulled out my most...conservative choices." It's almost a crime to have to cover up all that beauty, but she's right. Best to cover up a bit on a first impression.

"Um, whichever covers you up the most."

"Are you saying you don't like the way I look?" Shit.

"No! No, that's not what I meant." My hands are getting clammy again as Vero chuckles. Where am I going wrong here? Is she playing with me?

"Akmal, you are too cute. I'm only kidding. I understand. I'll make sure to make myself presentable for your family. You can trust me." Her fingertips skate across mine only for a second before she turns and bends over to choose an outfit.

I inwardly groan again before quickly turning, exiting the room to wait for her in the living room.

4

VERO

The drive over to his parent's house is tense. It's Saturday, it should be a relaxing day. I'm getting a little nervous feeding off Akmal's nervousness. *Eesh.* Is his family that bad? Am I missing something?

"You need to relax, Akmal. You're killing me. I'm getting your nervous vibes all over me."

We pull up to a large one-story home with a fairly large front yard. Once the car is in park, Akmal looks over at me from head to toe and takes a big gulp. What is up with him? I can't stand this nervous energy.

"Spit it out. What? Why are you looking at me like that? Is there something wrong with what I'm wearing?" I do a double take at my outfit while I'm sitting here. I think I look alright. My pencil skirt is down to my calf, my cardigan sweater is buttoned up all the way. Well, the top few look like they're about to cry, but they're holding on. I haven't dressed this covered in a while. I look like a damn librarian for crying out loud.

Akmal lets out a deep breath beside me and I can feel my face scowling at him. *What?*

"You look fucking beautiful, Vero. It's just…" I'm internally preening and cringing at the same time. Spit it out!

"The women of my culture dress a little more…more…"

"Just say it already! You're killing me here."

"I-I'm just a man, Vero. I don't claim to be an expert on women whatsoever. But please excuse anything that might make you uncomfortable from this point forward and do not hesitate to ask me anything, okay? We can do this." He lets out a long breath before repeating his last sentence. Maybe more for himself than me. "We can do this."

Akmal gets out the driver's side and runs around the car to open the passenger door for me. My heart pitter patters just a little bit at that, but I'm still not sure where I went wrong and he wasn't being very clear in the car about it. Feeling a little self-conscious now, I make sure to pull my skirt down as far as it will go before following his lead towards the house.

It's a beautiful and fairly large one-story home with a terracotta roof. I assume his sisters live here too. He had three from what I remember when they came by and helped clean Mat's apartment. The windows in the front look like they're covered by white lace curtains on the inside, but you can't see through it, much to my dismay. So I can't tell if we're being watched while we're walking up the path towards the front door or not. Not sure if I should be grateful or more nervous about that fact.

We reached the door and the moment Akmal knocks once, it swings open pulling my hair in front of my face. I guess they were waiting for us after all.

"Akmal! You made it." Her eyes go to me. "The day I've prayed-"

"Ibu!" Akmal's reflexes catch his mother right before she hits the ground. I can hear the feminine screams coming from inside the home and a man, who I assume to be Akmal's father, comes rushing out.

Did she just faint? What happened? We haven't even made it through the door yet.

"Aye! Ling! Are you okay? What happened?" His father has taken his mother from his embrace and is rocking her. A groan escapes her lips as she comes to and I let out a breath. My heart almost stopped when I saw her go down. *My god.*

I put a hand on Akmal's arm in reassurance and it is like time stops. His mother, who just opened her eyes, turns her sight to where I am touching Akmal. Everyone's eyes are zoned in on where I'm touching Akmal. You can hear a damn pin drop.

Removing my hand like I just got burned, I fold them together in front of me to prevent myself from touching him any further. My cheeks are burning from their scrutiny and I can't tell if they're happy or mad about it.

"The day I've prayed for has finally been answered! Come, come." Like it never happened, this small woman who looks like she's wrapped from head to toe in fabric, gets up and hugs her son then turns to look at me.

Her smile is still bright as she pulls me in for a hug too. "Come, come! There is plenty of food. Everyone has been waiting for you."

She's pulling me inside before I can even say my own hellos. It's a good thing I wore flats today or I'd be falling flat on my face right now.

"Vero!" Akmal's harsh whisper makes me whip my face around. "Take off your shoes!"

It's then I notice the pile of shoes outside the front door and everyone inside barefoot. Quickly toeing them off without tripping, I let Akmal's mother drag me further inside.

"Ayah!! Akmal is here and he brought home a woman, huh! Tell your aunties! Hasanah! There is no Mat today. Aye, it's okay. I need you to start making the wedding list la."

I turn to look at Akmal, and all he does is shrug his shoulders with a sheepish smile. What am I missing here?

We reach what looks like the living room and there is a large spread of food and multiple dishes on the floor. In fact, after glancing around a few times, I don't see a dining room table in sight. Do they eat on the floor?

His mother is ushering me near the oldest daughter and comes to sit down between Akmal and me. It's a good thing my skirt has some stretch to it because I'm forced to sit with my legs to the side.

"Hi, I'm Hasanah."

"Vero." I smile at Akmal's sister. She looks to be the oldest of the three. Is this the one his mother wanted to set up with Mat? I need to tell Atsuko the next time I see her. I wonder if she knows.

There's an array of food and the house smells great. I'm reaching out to grab some of the food when Akmal's mom halts my hand. Looking up, I see everyone looking towards his father as he says a small prayer with his hands out like he's about to cup some water. *Oops.*

"Bismillah."

Suddenly everyone around me is murmuring the same word. Oh dear, I'm going to have to spank Akmal for not telling me all these important details. I'm getting kind of embarrassed.

I'm handed a bowl of food but now I'm scared to ask

where the utensils are. I hear a masculine throat clearing and my eyes shoot to Akmal's automatically to see him signaling something to me with his eyes.

I watch as he eats with his hands. *His hands!* Shit, but this girl isn't a quitter. When in Rome and all that. Plus, Akmal's mother is staring at me with a large smile on her face like she's waiting for me to taste her food.

Monkey see, monkey do. I bring the food to my mouth and taste the different flavors. I accidentally bite my tongue and a "shit" comes out of my mouth. I hear feminine gasps from my right and see Akmal's mother with her hand over her heart to my right. I'm shooting apologetic looks at everyone but stare daggers at Akmal. He should have warned me! Too many years in the hood, cussing is almost part of my life blood. I'm going to have to make an effort to rein it in around his family who are probably starting to get scandalized by my uncouth behavior.

The pain from the bite dulls down and I continue to eat. It really is good and I'm still chewing when Akmal's mother leans into me and says, "It's good huh? Makan, makan." She says this right before she adds even more food onto my plate.

My eyes widen but I try my best to act natural. I mean, it's no different than my mother trying to stuff my face when I come over, right? Abuela is even worse than this. With that thought, I relax a little. Akmal's family is kind of endearing, actually.

Once our faces are stuffed and everyone starts slowing down, I figured I'd stop too. Bending over, I reach to put my dish down when it happens.

The two buttons on top that were crying pop off, and my ample cleavage starts peeking out through my cardigan. I hear gasps and someone is choking on their food when I hear Akmal clearing his throat a few times.

A hand touches my right arm and I turn to see Hasanah tilt her head to indicate I should follow her.

How fucking embarrassing. I mean, I'm never embarrassed of the girls, they're one of my pride and joys, but the current moment and mood is making me feel like I should go hide under a damn rock with my figure.

Hasanah takes my hand and leads me to a bedroom. It must be hers.

"Here, take this." It looks like a scarf. Wrapping it around my neck, I tuck the ends under the scoop of my cardigan and flatten the fabric out. Now I look like a fifties librarian who just came back from an episode of Outlander. Good grief. Standing in front of her full-length mirror, I make sure the girls are tucked safely away from innocent eyes.

Now that the problem has been fixed, Hasanah and I walk out of the bedroom only to hear her mother dramatically cry, "Haiyo, my son. She is not what I expected. Akmal, you need to buy her new clothes. Aye, that's okay. Once you are married there will be plenty of time. Make sure you take care of that."

Take care of 'that', 'not what she expected'? I'm not liking the sound of how she's describing my choice of attire as well as how she's talking about me. What's wrong with *me*? I mean, I'm not a skinny woman, and my curves usually come out to play. I've been more than good this whole time, haven't I? I usually never restrain myself back like this.

I need to make a good impression though. Hasanah and I look at each other. Hasanah has a sheepish look on her face that tells me this isn't the first time her mother has expressed opinions like this.

"Does your mother hate me?"

"Ah, it's not that. I mean, it's complicated. Sometimes, Malaysian elders like for their children to... You know?"

I'm in over my head because I damn well *don't know* what the hell is going on. "No, I don't. You're going to have to dumb it down for me."

Hasanah has a sheepish look on her face again. What's going on?

"Sometimes Malaysian parents like for their children to marry... nice girls like Malaysian girls." My eyes widen at that statement and my heart starts to beat a little harder. I don't know if I'm upset, mad or sad.

Hasanah puts her hands out and tries to put on a smile when she says, "No! I mean, it's not you. Really. It's just, culture sometimes runs deep, you know? But I'm sure my mother is already dying to set up the wedding, she probably doesn't care about that. She's waited a long time for this moment for Akmal."

We're halfway back to the living room when I hear Akmal's voice.

"Ibu, don't talk about her like that. I'm going to marry her, she's the only one I've ever wanted. Please respect her, even if she's not in the same room."

"Ah Akmal, Ibu didn't mean anything by it, you know. She is just worried about you and wants you to make good decisions. You could have found a good Malaysian girl any time. We didn't want you to be single this long." His dad wanted him to find a good Malaysian girl, huh?

"Bapa, I don't want a good Malaysian girl. I want the woman I'm going to marry, and she is here today. So please, hold back your comments. This is exactly why I couldn't live here anymore."

"Akmal, I didn't mean it like that. Malaysian or not, it is fine whoever you choose. But you must buy her some modest clothes la."

"Aye, tsk tsk tsk. Relax. We make the wedding arrangements and invite everyone. It will be fine. I already told your sisters to tell your aunts so they can spread the invitations. You need to marry her soon. We should have the wedding-"

Hasanah and I step into the living room and the conversation quiets. I don't know how I feel about all this. Does Akmal's mother hate me or not? Sounds like she's more excited about the wedding than who's getting married.

I'm not sure if we should overstay our welcome. I mean, that's how I'm feeling right now.

"Akmal, I think we should go, if that's okay?"

5

AKMAL

*M*y mother is acting like Vero is unsophisticated when it's far from the truth. "Ibu, don't talk about her like that. I'm going to marry her, she's the only one I've ever wanted. Please respect her, even if she's not in the same room." I feel possessive over her even if she probably won't agree to continue with the marriage after what's happened. Who could blame her? Her breasts are fucking beautiful and just can't be contained.

"Ah Akmal, Ibu didn't mean anything by it, you know. She is just worried about you and wants you to make good decisions. You could have found a good Malaysian girl any time. We didn't want you to be single this long." All these 'good Malaysian' girls are not Vero. She's the only one I've ever wanted so none of this matters.

"Bapa, I don't want a good Malaysian girl. I want the woman I'm going to marry, and she is here today. So please, hold back your comments. This is exactly why I couldn't live here anymore."

"Akmal, I didn't mean it like that. Malaysian or not, it is fine whoever you choose. But you must buy her some modest clothes." *It's a crime to cover all that beauty up. But I understand that my parents are traditional and conservative when it comes to clothing. I'm going to have to find a middle ground on this. I need to show Vero I can take care of her, make her comfortable.*

"Aye, tsk tsk tsk. Relax. We make the wedding arrangements and invite everyone. It will be fine. I already told your sisters to tell your aunts so they can spread the invitations. You need to marry her soon. We should have the wedding-"

The sound of someone entering the living room makes me turn. *Damn, she's beautiful.* From the top of her beautiful dark hair to her voluptuous body down to her little toes. She was carved by the heavens and she's all fucking mine. I need to make sure nothing happens from this point forward to make her want to break off this engagement.

Vero steps out with my sister and I can't take my eyes off the way she moves. My hands itch to touch her, to hold her and make sure she's real.

Her eyes lock on mine and they look unsure. My gut churns at how she's probably feeling right now. My family can be a bit overwhelming.

"Akmal, I think we should go, if that's okay?" *Her wish is my command.* I'm already ushering her towards the front door with my palm at the small of her back when it bursts open. *Dammit, I'm too late.*

"Aye! Akmal, you brought home a woman!"

"Akmal! Finally, the day has come! Let me measure her la!"

"Oh my. I need more fabric huh! Adila! Where is the measuring tape?"

"Ayo Akmal, she is so pretty. Irina, the tape is right here. I said I was going to measure her. Listen aye. Go, move her to the living room so we can get started."

I don't even know when I started holding Vero's hand but she's giving me a death grip. My aunties are coming through the door in a flurry with bolts of fabric in their arms and who knows what else. How did they get here that fast?

"Aye, you finally made it. Come, come. Let's get her to the living room. Hidaya! Sakinah! Start on the list and invitations. Don't forget my friends and Ayah's friends! I need to see the list before it's done."

I run my hand down my face because I knew it would be this way. Shit. Looking over to Vero, she looks like a deer caught in headlights. I've never seen her so quiet.

Squeezing her hand, she looks up at me and I just want to kiss the look away. I'm surprised she hasn't broken off the engagement yet.

"It will be okay. They've been waiting for the day to put a wedding together. That's my Auntie Irina and Adila." I indicate Auntie Irina in the red and Auntie Adila in the purple. I highly doubt Vero is going to remember everyone's names by the time it's all said and done.

"Tsk tsk tsk." My mother is doing her signature head shake. "Akmal, what kind of son are you? You never even told me my daughter-in-law's name. How am I supposed to speak with her huh?"

She slaps me upside the head and I send a sheepish glance to Vero. Ibu is right, I never did introduce her correctly.

"Sorry Ibu. Ibu, Bapa, Auntie Irina, Auntie Adila, this is Vero..."

"Veronica Hernandez, but you can call me Vero." I never

knew her real name, I've always just called her Vero. The thought sobers me and reminds me of the situation I'm in. Trying to convince the woman of my dreams to go through with a Malaysian wedding.

"Akmal! Have you been hiding her from us huh? My goodness, why do you worry us like that?"

"Akmal! Walao eh. My god. You're finally getting married. I thought you were going to die alone."

"What are you talking about dying alone huh? You took longer than Akmal before Adila agreed to marry your sorry self."

I internally groan because it's never going to end. The whole family is coming. Hidaya and Sakinah are probably calling everyone in the vicinity as we speak at my mother's behest.

"This is my Uncle Tuah and Uncle Zaka. Married to Irina and Adila."

"I don't think I'm going to remember everyone's name."

My poor Vero. "It's okay, you'll remember them later." I almost don't even get to finish my sentence before my aunties pull her away from me and start restraining her with a measuring tape.

"Akmal!" Vero is whisper-yelling at me and I'm about to whisk her away when my uncles pull me farther from her in the opposite direction.

"Akmal, we need to celebrate this day! I didn't think it would come. I was placing a bet with Zaka to see if you would end up a bachelor. Zaka, now you have to clean my garage!"

"Let the women do what they need to do, they're going to pull you next for measurements. Come, come. Tell us how you met this cantik woman. Tuah! Look at her. Who knew a woman like her would go for our Akmal, huh?"

"Akmal! You did good. Marry her quickly before she realizes what she's gotten herself into."

Internally groaning, I rub my hand down my face as my uncles continue to talk about how unworthy I am of a woman like Vero.

I already know I am.

~

VERO

Akmal's aunts are putting me through the wringer. I don't know what's happening but suddenly they have my measurements, placing fabrics against my skin and have already picked out the wedding decor with Akmal's mother.

My eyes are searching him out for a rescue but his uncles must have taken him to another room. I miss him. I miss his calm. I'm getting kind of antsy and I don't like it but I'm putting on a smile for the sake of his family. Damn, even Vegas is easier than this. We should just elope and call it a day.

The aunties are shaking their heads when they measure my breasts and hips making me feel self-conscious again.

"Hidaya! Call Akmal in here so we can measure him!"

"Sakinah, did you get the family list yet? Let me see."

"Hasanah! Did Mat ask you to marry him yet? If you wait too long you are going to die alone huh."

Oh, I need to nip this one in the butt because I can just see Atsuko throwing punches where she doesn't need to be.

"Mat is already engaged."

The entire living room goes silent and I think I hear Hasanah clearing her throat.

"What?! Mat is already engaged? How? Hasanah! I told

you that you needed to grab him while he was still single, aye!"

"Ibu! I always knew Mat wasn't into me. It was you who kept pushing him. Leave him alone. Let him be happy."

"Hasanah! I want *you* to be happy, that is why I need you to get married. Haiyah!" Her mother is muttering something Malaysian under her breath that I can't understand. Or do they call it Malay? But it sounds like she's going off on Hasanah judging by the frustrated look on her face.

I have to be in the twilight zone right now. Akmal and I cross paths for a second before his aunts are measuring him in the same fabrics in a flurry of movements.

I can still hear Akmal's mother and sister bickering, but the moment his aunts let him out of their grasp is the moment I grab onto his hand. I need some air. I can only take so much. Begging him with my eyes, Akmal's expression softens before he announces our exit.

When we get back into the car and shut the door, I let out an exasperated breath. *Holy hell, what just happened in there?*

We end up driving home in complete silence. We're both probably exhausted from the day's events and it was just lunch with the family. Am I going to be able to handle this? They say you don't just marry the person, you marry the family as well.

Akmal puts the car in park when we reach the apartment. Turning my head to look at him, my heart skips a beat and my brain tells me that yes, I'm going through with this because Akmal is worth it.

I guess I need to tell my parents about my impromptu engagement, huh? Akmal opens the passenger door for me with a soft smile and grabs my hand before leading us to our apartment. Wow, this is new. I kind of like it. His hand in mine makes me feel things. Good things.

We walk into the front door and he lets go of my hand. I already feel the loss of his warmth but I take a deep breath in and out to suck in the warmth of our home. *Our* home. My old apartment with Atsuko still has a week to go before the lease is up, but I can't find it in myself to care. Not when Akmal has that look in his eyes where it seems like he is fighting an internal battle about what to do with me.

"I need to tell my parents about our engagement." His expression doesn't change.

"Yes, you should."

The tension builds between us as the silence grows louder with each moment that passes by. I don't know what I'm allowed to do now that we're engaged. My pussy is telling me to go to town, but my mind is telling me that I need to see Akmal's culture through. To make sure I make it right in the eyes of his family. I need to be a good girl right now. A good girl that waits for her prize.

I'm not even controlling my legs when they walk towards him. His eyes shine with desire as we're standing face to face with only millimeters to separate us. Running my hands along his arms, I take a deep breath and close my eyes to just soak in the peace our home brings us. The masculine smell of my man.

I'm only about five-feet-five in height to Akmal's five-feet-seven but I love it. Grabbing the front of his shirt, I bring his face down to mine but stop when our lips are only a breath apart. Rubbing my nose against his, I soak in his warmth. My inner ho is crying, crying for something more between us but I need to resist.

This has to be the hardest thing I've ever done.

I let him go and turn to walk away.

6

VERO

I haven't visited my parents in a couple of weeks but I feel good about this, about us. Akmal is all nerves as we pull into my childhood neighborhood. Yards get smaller and bars on the windows start becoming rampant as we drive deeper into the neighborhood. To the untrained eye, it looks like you need to start locking your car doors. To the eyes of those who grew up in these streets, this is home.

Pulling up into the driveway behind the 1970 Chevelle SS, I put the car in park as we step out. My mother is already opening up the screen door with her other hand on her hip. My heart warms as I watch my mother stand there with a smile on her face.

"¿Mira, mira quien viene? Milagro que se acuerda que tiene familia." She always gives me sass if I don't come by every damn day. I'm here now, aren't I?

"Mamá. Don't be like that. You know I would never

forget my family. La bendición." She's right. I haven't asked for blessing in a while. I probably should visit more often.

"Que Dios te bendiga. Hija! You finally decide to stop by and didn't even tell me you were bringing a boy home. It's okay, I made enough for everyone. Come in, come in."

"Mamá, you always have plenty of comida, that's why I didn't tell you I was bringing someone over."

She eyes me skeptically and then stares at Akmal. "¿Quién es tu amigo?"

"Esto es Akmal."

"¿Porque you no call me por una semana? How would I know if you're alive? Tu papá estaba preocupado. He thought you died."

We're already walking through the doorway when Akmal bows towards my mother. I give her a kiss on the cheek as I continue to tell her, "You know you don't have to worry about me. I've been living on my own just fine. I'm not starving, mira mi culo." Bumping her hips with said ass, I try to hold back a laugh.

My mother swats my ass as I walk inside to be greeted by my dad who has an unsure look on his face as he sizes up Akmal, especially after his little bow.

"La bendición papá."

"Dios te bendiga…¿Mira, mira quien viene? Vero, ¿Quién es tu amigo?" I swear my mom and dad are really just one person.

"Vero! It's about fucking time you came home to check on Mamá y Papá. Are you too good for us now, or what?"

My older brother, Fabian, wraps his arms around my neck in a headlock like we're seven again. I swear this fucker never grows up. He's gotten a little bigger since the last time I saw him. He must be working out or something. Despite standing almost a head and a half taller than me, I elbow him in the abs hard. He pretends to be hurt and lets go like he's so damn offended at my audacity. At least he didn't mess up my hair.

"Puta, you almost messed up my hair."

My dad slaps Fabian upside the head while my mom slaps me on the ass.

"Mira tu boca! We have company." My dad is still eyeing Akmal warily, who's been standing there quietly watching how my crazy family interacts. I probably should be embarrassed, but this is mi familia. We never hide who we are.

Taking a big whiff of air, it smells like my mom made some empanadillas. I'm suddenly fucking starving. My nose is already leading my legs where they need to go when I hear Fabian's loud-ass voice speaking to me.

"Vero, ¿Quién es tu novio?" Oh shit, that's right. I got a little caught up with being home again and smelling deliciousness that I forgot to introduce my man.

"Familia, esto es Akmal. He's my fiancé. We're getting married!" I grab Akmal's arm and pull him towards me for a semi hug. He looks really nervous if his hand scratching the back of his head is anything to go by. He's so cute.

My face is hurting from how hard I'm smiling up at my man.

"Vero, ven a hablar conmigo por favor. It is very nice to meet you Akmal. Siéntate por favor." My mom is already pulling me away for 'a talk' but not before I point my finger at Fabian.

"Fabian, be good." I'm staring daggers at him as I watch my dad and brother surround poor Akmal. I forgot to tell him I'm the only girl in the family.

We reach the far side of the kitchen when my mom turns to me.

"When did you meet this boy? I've never seen you bring

anyone home and now you tell me tienes esposo. How long have you been hiding him? How come you didn't tell tu familia? You just go off and get married? I don't even know what kind of family he comes from."

"Mamá, please understand. We're not married *yet*. Quit being dramatic." I slap her arm for emphasis since she has both hands on her hips like she's scolding me. I'm not eighteen anymore, I'm thirty-three.

"Akmal is different. He's Malaysian and his culture says he can't date. He needs to get married before he can do anything. Es un buen chico, Mamá. Believe me when I say that, you know me."

My mom stares at me like she's about to cry. I'm still trying to decide if these are happy tears or sad tears.

"What do you mean? Explícamelo." How do I explain to my mother Akmal's strict upbringing and cultural rules? It's so far from what we know.

"Mamá, you wouldn't believe me even if I told you. Pero, trust me on this. I've never been more sure in my life. He's the one Mamá. He's different." My mom watches my face closely.

"How come you couldn't want un buen chico puertorriqueño?" She's always getting on me about finding a good Puerto Rican boy.

"Mamá!" I hit her again before a small smile graces her face. She knows the commitment issues I've had since my high school sweetheart. She was the one who was there for me when my world came crashing down. That boy was hispanic and honestly, I'm not that inclined to visit that again. Akmal is a damn dream come true.

"I've never seen you like this before."

"Like what?"

"Hija, you glow when you talk about him." I feel like I'm

glowing every time I'm around him. I didn't know it was that obvious.

"Mamá, he's different. I-I didn't think the day would come for me. I didn't think a man like him would be in my life." I sigh and feel myself smiling once more just thinking about him. "He's one in a million."

"¿Estás embarazada?"

"What? No, I'm not pregnant! I just told you Akmal's culture doesn't even let us touch when we date." She narrows her eyes at me like she's got x-ray vision and can see the truth through my stomach.

"Mamá!"

"I just want you to be happy, Hija." She stares at me again but her hard expression finally begins to crack. Her hands caress my face in a really tender gesture that makes my heart feel like it's going to overflow. I love my mom. I'm sticking to my guns, Akmal is the man for me. Just thinking about him makes my cheeks widen again.

"If he can make you happy like this already, I'm happy for you." Dammit, I didn't wear any waterproof mascara and I can feel my damn eyes watering. Was I really miserable that long for her to see the difference so clearly?

She pulls me into a firm hug and I breathe in my mom's scent deeply, trying to stave away the tears before it makes me look like a hot mess.

"Vamos, antes tu papá y hermano says something stupid and chases your man away. Pero if he was un buen chico puertorriqueño, he wouldn't be scared off."

"Mamá!"

She's right. My dad can be overprotective sometimes because I'm his little girl. Fabian can be overprotective sometimes because of what happened with my last serious boyfriend. I never did find out if Fabian did anything to

Roman after he found out what he did to me. But Fabian came home late that night and was drinking and smashing things before he left again. Despite being older than me by three years, at thirty-six, Fabian and I are still close.

"What the hell are you guys doing to my man?"

Both my dad and Fabian are standing in front of Akmal who is sitting in the chair looking like he's being interrogated for country secrets. My dad's got his arms crossed looking like a damn cholo about to bust a cap.

"We're just getting to know each other, aren't we Akmal. That's your real name, right?" I elbow Fabian in the ribs again before sitting my ass right onto Akmal's lap to ward away the guard dogs.

"Why did you keep this from me, Hija? It breaks my heart. You know I love you and you're my favorite daughter."

"Pfft. I'm your only daughter Papá. I'm not hiding anything. It all happened really fast. But he's the one, so be nice." My dad literally looks like his world is shattering. I'm his baby girl and he's probably afraid I'll never come back home to visit again. Everyone in this house is so damn dramatico.

"Papá, don't be dramatic. You know you're my number one man. I'll always come back to visit, I won't forget you."

"Vero, how about me huh? You going to leave me behind? You're my favorite sister."

"Puta, I'm your only sister."

"Exactly!"

"What is that supposed to mean, exactly?"

"Aye, silencio. Everybody sit down so we can eat. The food is getting cold while you guys are acting like babies."

"You can't be seria, Maria. This is the first time Vero is even bringing the guy around and suddenly mi hija is getting married?" Dammit, now my dad is staring at my stomach too. "¿Estás embarazada?"

"No! I'm not pregnant! Stop asking me!"

"What the hell Vero, you didn't tell me you were pregnant!"

"Shut up, Fabian. I just said I wasn't pregnant. Open your damn ears!"

My mom shoots a glare at my dad as she raises a wooden spatula to his face. *Uh-oh.*

"Don't forget how you stole me away from mi familia. You came into mi casa and told my dad you were going to marry me. I was sixteen, Alejandro. He thought I was pregnant too." My dad shut up then. I've never seen his face so red. You go, Mamá. Damn, I almost forgot this story. Sixteen, *eesh.*

"Maria, don't be like that. You were the only one for me."

"Alejandro, Vero says Akmal is the only one for her. Deal with it! Even though he's not un buen chico puertorriqueño." Ugh! Can she just not let that go!? I know he's not a damn Puerto Rican boy.

"Akmal, what are you? Are you Asian or something?" I slap Fabian up the back of his head. How rude! "Vero, I'm just asking. Damn. How am I supposed to know if I don't ask? Dramatica."

"Akmal is Malaysian." Both my dad and brother have the most confused look on their faces. It makes me want to laugh. "Yes, you can say he's Asian."

My dad and brother start nodding their heads.

"So he's the one huh. Vero, you sure? I know my buddy at work is still trying to get you to notice him. He's a nice guy, I trust him. You want his number?"

"Fucker, listen!" I point my finger right at his face even though he's sitting across from me and shoot him a look.

"Akmal is the only one! I don't want any of your buddies hitting me up. I know the crowd you hang out with, Fabian!"

"What is that supposed to mean? I'm a good guy, I only surround myself with good guys." This fool right here. Fabian has been in and out of trouble ever since I can remember. Looking back, I'm honestly surprised Roman is still alive. My brother is known in the hood for his temper and reputation.

But at home, he's just Fabian. Overprotective big brother with a big-ass mouth that doesn't know when to shut up. That's why I fucking love him.

My mom shuts everyone up when she places the food on the table. I grab Akmal's hand and squeeze it for reassurance. He probably thinks we're a bunch of heathens.

"Are you alright?" Akmal gives me a small smile in response to my question and my heart settles a little. Good, the Hernandez family didn't send him running for the hills.

"Yeah, I'm just not used to...your family. But I'm good." Sending an air kiss his way, I let go of his hand as we prepare to eat the delicious meal my mom made for us all. Damn, look at this spread. My stomach is growling with all these smells.

My mom slaps my hand as she walks towards her chair. I'm starving. How can she put this all in front of me and expect me to wait?

Once my mom is seated and comfortable, my dad says 'Buen provecho' and we're digging in. Akmal looks a little lost, so I take it upon myself to fill his plate with some arroz con pollo and whatever else I think he would like. Chicken and rice isn't too far off from what I had at his parents' house. He sends me an appreciative glance before we start eating. The thing about my family is that we take our sweet time to eat and enjoy the tastes we're putting into our mouths.

I miss this sometimes, sitting together like this. But that was when I was single, now I'm not. I can't wait to see what kind of traditions Akmal and I will make together. I can start inviting mi familia over to our place. The thought sends warm tingles to my belly. I really am excited about this marriage. That and I don't know how long I can restrain myself from jumping his damn bones.

Now that I'm thinking of him, my hand runs across his thigh under the table and Akmal chokes on his food.

Rubbing his back, I pretend I'm surprised. "Baby, are you okay?"

"Is there something wrong con mi comida?"

"Mamá, you know your food is the best. Stop thinking like that. It probably just went down the wrong pipe." I'm still rubbing his back when Akmal sends me a sheepish look. Poor thing. I better get him out of here soon before it gets too weird for him.

Lunch was a nice affair. Everyone starts asking Akmal about his culture and religion. When it comes to the wedding, he can't answer much since his mother has taken over all the duties.

"At least we're getting invited to the wedding. Pinche Vero."

"Of course mi familia is going to the wedding. What kind of person do you think I am?"

"I don't know, Vero, I leave work to visit mi familia and all of a sudden my sister is basically already married."

"I'm not married *yet*, Fabian."

"Almost!"

"You two quit fighting. Let's finish this meal in some peace huh?"

"Si, Mamá."

"Si, Mamá."

"So Akmal, when can we meet your family?"

I can see Akmal's hands shaking on his thigh. Placing mine over his, I give him an encouraging smile.

He clears his throat a few times before he answers my dad. "Whenever you'd like, sir. I mean, my mother is probably setting up the wedding for the coming weekend as we speak."

"We come over on Tuesday then." My mom nods her head like she has the right to have the final say. I tell ya. That at least gives us one day to be alone together before the clash of the titans.

7

———

AKMAL

I don't know how this meeting of the families will go and it makes me nervous. Vero's been telling me to relax but I just can't. It's still early and I'm sitting at the breakfast table with my mind running through the many possible disasters that might happen tomorrow.

It also doesn't help that Vero is walking about in a damn tank top and thong. She's going to kill me, I just know it.

She bends over to get something out of the fridge and I groan, rubbing my hand down my face, wishing I could be rubbing something else. If not her, at least my dick that's crying behind my shorts. But I can't.

"Vero…"

When I open my eyes, she's a breath away from my face with a seductive smile that pulls me in like a fish on a hook. She's so fucking beautiful in her confidence. But this angle doesn't help my situation one bit because she's bent over just enough to make it look like her breasts are about to fall out of her thin tank top. I should be used to this by now, right? She's like this around me every damn day since she's been here. Is she doing this to me on purpose?

"Yes, Akmal."

"...You're killing me."

"How so?" Her finger starts trailing down her cleavage and I almost cum right there. Dammit, she *is* doing this on purpose. I love it and I hate it.

The next thing I know, she sits on my lap facing me and I feel like I'm stuck between a rock and a hard place. Or in this case, my rock hard cock stuck between our clothing, crying for where it really wants to go.

Vero grinds forward and I hiss. Shit, how can it still feel so good when we're both fully dressed? Well, I'm fully dressed.

"Vero." Her name comes out almost in a growl as I try to tamp down my desires before I embarrass myself. I can't find it in me to push her off. Just the thought of her sliding against my cock again makes it twitch.

Vero gives a little intake of air before she leans forward. I lean my head back as far as I can go in a half-assed attempt to get away and close my eyes. Shit, we shouldn't be doing this.

Her warm breath fans across the side of my face as she whispers into my ear. "Are you happy to see me, Akmal?"

Through gritted teeth, I try to answer her as civil as I can so as to not push her any further. "I'm always happy to see you."

Her low chuckle does something to me. The way her soft breasts push against my chest makes my cock weep in frustration. The warmth of her body on mine makes me think very nasty thoughts. Thoughts a good Malay boy should not be thinking. Opening my eyes, I stare at the ceiling to try and gain some semblance of control.

Think unsexy thoughts. Think unsexy thoughts.

My mother's voice floats through my mind, reminding me I need to buy Vero more appropriate clothing. The thought disappears when I feel her shift on top of me.

I can feel her hard nipples rubbing against my chest when I finally gain the strength to put some space between us with my hands pushing her away. Fuck, her skin is so soft and she smells like a wet dream come true, feminine and enticing.

"Vero, we need to go shopping before we meet my parents again."

"What's wrong with the clothes I have?"

"Nothing's wrong with them. You look absolutely beautiful in them, but my culture tends to lean more towards the … conservative side."

She crosses her arms and it only serves to push her breasts even closer towards me, making me swallow the large lump in my throat. *My god, what would it feel like to rub my face against all that? What would it feel like to taste that…*

"Look, I'm sorry about what happened last time. It wasn't my fault. At least it didn't happen when your uncles were there."

A growl comes out of my throat before I realize it. Just thinking about my uncles looking at her that way makes me irrationally angry.

"No one is allowed to see what's mine."

Vero goes quiet as her eyes widen a fraction. I'm trying to calm my damn nerves when her arms slowly go around my shoulders. How am I supposed to stay away from this for a whole damn week? This wedding needs to hurry the fuck up.

Vero leans in to rub her breasts on me again and it makes me shudder. My strength is shattering by the minute and I am too damn selfish to push her off again. My hands have a mind of their own as they slowly grip her hips, making her grind down on me again in response.

Leaning my head back once more, I groan in this never ending frustration which was my mistake because Vero takes that exact moment of weakness and starts to lick and kiss my neck. Damn this woman!

"Vero… we can't."

"I know, but sometimes I just need to touch you. To make sure you're real and that you're mine. I can't help the way you make me feel, Akmal. It's been hard for me too. Almost as hard as your cock between my legs right now." My fucking god, the mouth on this woman. She makes me want to do nasty things to her, things I've only seen in my fantasies.

I don't know if she's grinding down on me or if I'm grinding up against her, but suddenly there's a steady, slow rhythm forming between us on this kitchen chair.

The temperature in the room is getting hotter, the air is getting thicker and my nerves are fraying, hanging by a thread.

No sane hot-blooded man would be able to deny this goddess right here, not like this. Fuck, there shouldn't be *any* man but me with this goddess right here. Just the thought of another guy touching what's mine makes me grip her hips harder as I continue to grind into her hot center. I can feel her wetness soaking through my thin shorts and my mind starts to slowly enter a lustful haze, making me drunk off this moment between us.

I don't know who went towards who, but our lips start lightly grazing against each other. We're both fighting and giving in at the same time, unsure when to let our primal instincts go. It makes me delirious knowing I can do that to her too, sending her into a lustful haze just like the one I'm currently drowning in. When my hand starts to trail up her sides on its own accord, something snaps and our lips crash together in a forbidden dance.

I've never kissed anyone but Vero before. I should be embarrassed at my lack of experience but the way she moans into my mouth tells me she likes what I'm giving, making me gain more confidence by the second. Making me more selfish with what she's willing to give me.

She must be a goddess with the way she invokes these things from me, creating me into a person I don't recognize. When her breath hitches, I feel powerful; I feel in control even though I know I'm not. I'm the one who's under her spell.

We're grinding so hard together that we're probably wearing the fabric of my shorts thinner. I should stop. We shouldn't do this. But she makes me too weak...and too strong at the same time. I want to be her weakness too. Make her want me the way I want her.

Her fingers thread through my hair as our tongues fight for something we shouldn't have right now. Does it make it even more enticing that we both know we're doing something we shouldn't?

Vero suddenly shudders and cries into my mouth as she grinds down in an erratic rhythm. I feel like I'm on top of the fucking world, a man that's completed his mission with the orgasm I gave her. Me, virgin Akmal, made this woman cry out in ecstasy. She kisses me like she knows this moment between us won't last. The thought alone makes us both frantic in our tangle of limbs.

The moment doesn't last because soon enough, lightning shoots down my spine as my balls tighten and I climax behind my shorts; the wetness pulls me out of this trance we've put ourselves in. The lust fog clears and the guilt starts to press down on me.

"Fuck. Vero, we can't do this anymore. We have to wait."

"Do you regret it?" She sounds so damn hurt it makes my chest ache.

"What? No!" Grabbing her face between my hands, I kiss her again because dammit, I can't help it. Breaking our liplock for much needed air, I press my forehead against hers. *Damn it all.* I just can't stop touching her, not now that I've had a taste.

"I want you so bad, I'm dying a little bit each day I have to wait." I let out a hard breath and close my eyes. It hurts to look at what I can't fucking have, not right now. My chest constricts at what I'm probably doing to her. Does she feel rejected? I don't know what else to do.

"..I know." She slowly removes herself and walks towards the bathroom door, closing it shut without another word.

"Fucking hell. What do I do?" I must be going insane because I'm talking to myself out loud, expecting some higher being to answer. *What do I fucking do?*

Dammit, I can't leave things like this. I'm supposed to be her man. I'm supposed to always make her feel loved like she's the queen of my entire world. Growling, I get up from the chair and walk my way towards the damn bathroom.

The sound of the water and the heat of the steam makes my insides feel something ugly. I don't like feeling like I did her wrong when we were just feeling so damn right together. Stripping out of my clothes quickly, I slide the shower door open and step inside with my back to the sprayer.

"Akmal!"

I love my name on her damn lips. I want to bury it inside of me the only way I can, the only way I know how for the time being. Pushing her up against the back of the shower, my lips come crashing down hard on hers. The feel of her wet body sliding against mine is a new experience, one I'll have to make sure to visit often once we're married and these shackles are taken off us.

We can't go all the way. We need to stay in control between these slips. My hand is itching to do so much more and the only way I know how to stop it is to grab hers and bring them up over her head where I know they can't cause anymore trouble.

Our kisses become frantic, like we're both starving instead of having just been together not ten minutes ago. The rushing of blood down to my groin makes me light-headed, and when my dick comes up to graze against her pussy, I push myself away from her with a growl. Fuck! We need to stop.

Giving her one last chaste kiss on the lips, I try to regain my senses before speaking to her, my voice gravelly from the pain of holding back. "You've buried yourself in me so deeply, don't ever think I don't want you, Vero. This wedding can't come soon enough."

Turning around and quickly scrubbing myself of the evidence of what just happened at the breakfast table, I slide the shower door probably harder than necessary and make my exit, leaving dripping wet before I do anything else I shouldn't.

Grabbing a towel from the linen closet on the way to my room, I dry myself off quickly and get dressed in jerky movements. I'm feeling pissed. Pissed at myself for letting it go so far because now I'm addicted. I need to be strong.

Fully dressed, I sit on the couch in the living room to wait for Vero. I need to stick to the plan, I need to take her shopping to get her clothes. I need to stop thinking about her wet breasts and the way the water slides down her body. Shit, the more I think about it, the more I realize there was something glistening in her belly button. Leaning forward, I put my head in my hands and growl at my situation. I'm dying to find out if I saw what I saw. But if my face is that close to her, I won't be able to stop myself from smelling her and tasting her. Dammit, now my mouth is watering at the thought of her pussy against my lips and tongue.

"Akmal, I'm ready." Lifting my head, I see Vero in a beautiful dress that hugs her breasts and flares out to her knee. Just thinking about other men looking at how beautiful she is makes me angry again. Fuck, how am I supposed to contain something that just can't be contained? Why am I feeling so damn angry and out of control?

Standing up, I'm not sure what I should do. Do I make her order clothes online? What if she feels like I'm rejecting her company in public? What if other guys try to take what's mine? I can't hide her away forever, can I? I'm starting to go through all the ways I can do just that when Vero clears her throat, taking me out of my thoughts of ways to keep your potential wife captive until the wedding day.

"Akmal, are we going shopping or what? Why are you just standing there frowning?" The frown she throws at me makes me want to kiss her again. But if we do, we might not make it out. Shit, if we stay here even longer, I don't think I can make myself remain celibate. I mean, I'm still a virgin, right? Since I didn't actually stick my dick inside her hot pussy. Fuck, now I'm thinking about how hot her pussy was when my dick tried to say hello in the shower.

"Akmal!"

"Shit, sorry. You're too fucking beautiful and the thought of other guys seeing you shopping in that is making me crazy."

"In what? This? It's just a dress. It's not even hugging my curves."

Growling under my breath as I grab her hand to lead her out the door, I mumble to myself, "Men don't need tight clothes to imagine what's underneath."

8

———

𝒲e're back at our residence and Akmal came home so pissed, he had to go out with Mat to 'let out some steam' as he calls it. I remember Atsuko telling me that Mat goes to an MMA gym to keep a handle on his temper. I didn't think Akmal even had a temper. He's always been such a calm guy. Is it me? The thought makes me feel ugly inside.

Whatever, that means Atsuko is all mine for the time being.

Ding dong.

Speak of the she-devil, there she is! I feel like it's been ages since we've hung out. All this family stuff and tension is getting on my damn nerves. And before that was the whole Alfonso issue. Guess I can see why Akmal's been tense lately.

Opening the door, I can smell my BFF before I even see her.

"Vero!"

"Atsuko!"

We're screaming each other's names and hugging like we're separated twins. Damn, I miss her. Pulling her inside and kicking the door shut, I make sure to lock it before I drag her onto our couch to catch up.

"What have you been up to, chica!?" I'm running to the kitchen to grab us some water before planting my own ass down right next to her.

"Still doing my day job at the makeup counter. Mat keeps me pretty busy at home." Atsuko's face tells me exactly how Mat 'keeps her busy'. I'm so jealous.

"Aye, don't tell me that! I still can't do anything with Akmal even though we're basically engaged now."

"Wait, what?"

"Oh, that's right. It happened so fast, I never got a chance to tell you!"

"Bitch, tell me everything! What the hell?"

"Remember that plan I had?"

"Yeah? I'm guessing it worked, then? But what do you mean you still can't do anything with Akmal? You guys did something that night, right? How the hell did you get engaged so fast?"

Ugh, this thing between Akmal and I is so complicated. But I try my best to tell Atsuko everything from the proposal to meeting the families.

"And now mi familia wants to meet his familia tomorrow. I'm nervous but I'm not. You know how my family can be. What if Fabian can't filter the crap that comes out of his mouth and offends Akmal's family?"

"Yeah, I'd worry about Fabian."

"I'll just have to tear him a new one before we get there so he knows how fucking serious I am." My brother better not do anything to mess this up between the families. "This sexual tension between us is killing me though. I don't know what to do. My pussy says plow forward and take no survivors, but my mind is telling me I need to show Akmal how serious I am by trying to follow his culture. We're scrambling to put out the flames that keep growing between us."

"What happened today? I don't remember ever hearing about Akmal joining Mat at the gym. Is he alright?"

"Ugh, I don't know. I mean, he took me out shopping because apparently I don't dress modest enough for his family. I mean I get it, but how rude, right? So we're shopping and every time I bend over to look at something, Akmal is standing right behind me, almost rubbing his crotch on me. As if my vagina isn't hungry already!"

"Are you serious?" Atsuko is laughing at my misery right now, but I can't help but laugh too now that I'm thinking about it.

"Yes! When this male worker came to ask if I needed any help, you should have seen how Akmal cut him off with a 'we're fine, thank you' and glared at the back of the poor guy's head."

"How cute."

"I guess? But I mean, in the moment I was mad because I really don't know what I'm supposed to be buying and I really did need the help!"

Atsuko is full-on laughing now. "What did you guys do then? Did you get anything at all?"

"Girl, that man kept growling every time I tried to reach for something or get a closer look at something, that I started growling back! Like, what the hell? I need to make sure the fabric works well with my curves, you know? I can't restrict the girls, it's painful."

"They are some nice girls too."

"I know, right? I mean, it wasn't my fault they fell out during his family lunch."

Atsuko was just taking a drink when she starts choking. So dramatic.

"How the hell did your boobs fall out of your shirt? I know every article of clothing you have. What happened?"

"Ugh! I mean, I was trying to be modest. Remember that long sleeve cardigan I have? The one I usually wear open?"

"Oh, no. You didn't button it to the top, did you? Please tell me you didn't. How can you even button it? Why didn't you wear anything underneath?"

"I didn't think I needed to since I was covered like a damn virgin librarian! *Ugh!* For some reason, my hand reached for my light push up bra too, which as you know...pushes them up towards the buttons I had no business buttoning!"

Atsuko is full out laughing and rolling on the couch. This bitch!

"Stop laughing! I'm trying to tell you a damn story! So, we eat on the floor and I bend over to put the plate down when my buttons fly and the girls sigh."

We're both laughing like hyenas now until we finally get it out of our system. Damn, I miss being like this with Atsuko.

"What happened?"

"Akmal's family was scandalized, of course. At least Hasanah helped by giving me a scarf to kind of cover up. OH! I forgot to tell you, did you know Akmal's mother was trying to set up Hasanah with Mat?"

"What? No, Mat's never mentioned it." Atsuko is frowning and I don't want to lead her astray in her thoughts.

"I mean, from their argument during my fitting and measurements, it seemed that Hasanah wasn't interested in

Mat. So don't go crazy on her or anything. She seemed like a nice girl who just so happens to have a mother who wants all her children to be married off quickly."

I'm not sure if it reduces her worries but her frown starts to lighten. Atsuko has become quite possessive of Mat ever since they almost got torn apart by bitches that had no business being in theirs. Now that I think about it, I wonder if there are bitches after my man too. The thought makes me want to scratch some eyes out and shove them down their hypothetical throats. I've worked too damn hard through all this tension to lose my man to some random ho.

"I'm going to tell Fabian to keep an eye out for hoes after my man tomorrow, in case I don't catch everything."

"How the hell is Fabian going to keep an eye out for the hoes? Lifting their skirts?"

We both laugh at that because it sounds like something he would volunteer for.

"No, that wouldn't be good. Malaysians are different, you know? I don't want to cause a huge scandal before I'm even allowed in the family."

"Do you even know the details about the wedding? Every time I even think of wedding details, I get a headache. There's so much that goes into it."

"Shit!" I bounce a little on the couch when an idea comes to my head. Atsuko startles at my little jump and slaps my shoulder.

"What the hell? Don't scare me like that. Why are you yelling?"

"I have an idea! Why don't you and Mat join us tomorrow? I mean, everyone seems to know Mat already. That way I don't need to ask Fabian to look for hoes. You can be my right-hand girl. Plus, you'll get to meet Hasanah and see that she's not after your man. Settle your worries because I know you got them since I've mentioned her. Don't lie!"

Atsuko makes a face, one I know means she agrees but doesn't want to agree. Too bad. She knows I'm right. It will be a win-win for all of us. "Yeah, I guess. When are you going back to work?"

I had called off work for a couple of weeks after the Alfonso incident. Had to make sure he was put away after his attempted rape with Atsuko. I also wanted to be in the right headspace before I go back to bartending. I'm glad I requested the time off too because look where we are now, planning a damn rush wedding.

"I think I have about a week and a half left."

"So you're going through with all this, huh? Damn, Vero. You and your YOLO lifestyle."

"Life is way too damn short, and I ain't letting no ho scoop up Akmal. That boy is mine. After all this sexual tension, I'm not coming up for air after we're married." And that's the damn truth.

"Are you using toys at all?"

"Fuck, I already broke my vibrators before he even asked me to marry him. After seeing his cock, I don't want a damn dildo, I want him."

The door opens halfway through my last sentence, and we both turn our heads to see the boys coming inside.

Akmal doesn't look any happier.

"Uh...we're back." Mat looks a little nervous. I'm trying to think back on what sentence they walked in on to make him look uncomfortable.

"Yeah...um, did you girls have a good time?" Akmal's got his pleasant face on, the one where he's trying to be peaceful and friendly around everyone. I've been around him long enough to finally know the difference now. The thought both warms me and makes me apprehensive because he's hiding his feelings.

"Mat, baby, how do you feel about going over to Akmal's family gathering tomorrow with Vero's family? Akmal, would that be okay?"

I'm still staring at Akmal's face, trying to figure out what's going on in his head when his expression goes from that fake pleasant to actual surprise. His eyes cast to mine and my heart almost explodes when his face softens. There's my baby. I missed him.

"Uh, yeah. I'm okay with that. Akmal, can we tag along?"

"You know you're basically family, Mat. Of course you guys are invited. My mother would be elated to have you over."

Atsuko must feel the same tension in the air that I do because after looking back and forth between Akmal and I, she quickly goes to Mat and grabs his hand.

"Alright! We'll see you guys tomorrow then!" She starts waving goodbye and Mat follows her out the front door, only giving Akmal a head flick as a goodbye.

I start walking towards Akmal as he locks the door behind our guests. When he turns, I bury my face into his chest and hug him. I don't know what's bothering him, and at first I was mad but now I just want him to be happy again.

It probably sounds like a mumble, but I speak into his chest anyway. "Akmal, what's wrong?"

At my question, he finally lets go of some of the tension he's holding and hugs me back. I like this. This feels right.

Lifting my head, I stare at his eyes to see if he still looks upset.

"I'm fine, now that I'm home." He releases me quicker than I'd like and walks towards the fridge to grab a bottle of water. He says he's fine, but why doesn't it feel that way?

"Talk to me. Why does it feel weird? Why have you been acting weird all day? Is it something I did?"

After a few gulps of water, Akmal turns to me and places the bottle on the counter. "What do you mean?" There's that fake smile again.

"Don't lie to me, Akmal. I don't know what's going on with you but you can't fool me with your 'everything's fine' smiles. Talk to me."

Running his hand through his hair, he lets out an exasperated sigh. Damn, what is that about?

"I don't know, Vero. I don't know what I'm doing, I've never been in a relationship. I feel like I'm in over my head with you because I can't get you out of my damn mind and every man that looks your way makes me feel less than a person. You could have any guy out there, *any*...why me, Vero? Am I something you just wanted to conquer? I feel like you're with me because you pity me. I don't know. You're the first girl who's made me feel this way, and I'm so damn confused all the time!"

"Why would you feel less than a person? You're the one I said yes to. We're getting married, doesn't that tell you my level of commitment to this, to us? No, I'm not with you because I pity you. Ain't nobody got time for that mess. I'm with you because I want YOU."

"I just - I just can't wrap my head around someone like you wanting someone like me. Then I come home and you're talking about dildos with Atsuko. I know you have more experience than me, I know you have needs that I just can't fix because of my culture. It frustrates me and at the same time I'm pissed you have to rely on a fake dick to take care of your needs. *I* should be the one to take care of your needs. ME. Just me. Nothing and no one else!"

Woah. I never realized something like a dildo would

make Akmal feel so strongly. I mean, I get what he's saying, but damn.

Taking a tentative step towards him, I feel like I'm approaching a tiger pacing in a cage, ready to snap someone's head off. I've never seen this side of Akmal before. Keeping my voice calm, I try to reassure him again.

"Akmal...I don't want anyone else. If you don't want me to use a dildo, I won't. It's not a big deal."

"Not a big deal? Not a big deal? Vero, how can I even feel like a man when my future wife has to rely on something else to make her happy? It should be my job...no, *my* damn privilege to make my fucking woman happy in all ways. This damn time frame for this wedding is killing me because you're all I ever think about. From the moment I wake up, seeing you walking around this place, smelling your scent that's seeped into my clothes and the furniture. I'm struggling, Vero. I'm fucking struggling and you have no idea."

"Akmal, I don't know what to say. What do you want me to do? What can I do?"

"That's just it! There's nothing we *can* do until we get married and that day seems like a million miles away when my dick and heart is being pulled towards you every waking moment. Seeing guys look at what's mine with desire in their eyes *kills me*. It kills me, knowing that any one of them can give you what you need while I'm restricted! I'm trying damn hard to honor my family and I'm trying *damn hard* to find a middle ground to keep my woman happy. You don't think I see how much you need satisfaction? You don't think I see the need in your eyes when you look at me? I don't know what I'm doing, and it only emphasizes the fact that you probably deserve someone better than me."

What? No! I'm sad, I'm heartbroken, and you know what? I'm kind of pissed.

"Jode esto! No hables mal de ti ni de mi hombre."

"I don't understand what you're saying."

"I fucking said: don't be talking shit about MY man like that."

Akmal leaves the kitchen and walks away from me. Fuck no, we're not done talking. He doesn't get to walk away from me after spewing that kind of shit about the man I'm going to marry.

"Don't fucking walk away from me, Akmal."

He turns in anger and throws his hands out to the side. "This is me, Vero. The insecure virgin who doesn't know what the hell he's doing. You're too much woman for me. There, I admit it. If you want to leave, do it now because what you see is all you're going to get."

What the hell is wrong with him today? He's fucking making me pissed with all this shit spewing out of his beautiful lips.

Now *I'm* feeling irrationally angry because I just told him that I wanted him and yet he continues this self-deprecating behavior. Has someone told him this? Is this something on a deeper level?

He's walking backward as I walk forward. Hell no, he ain't getting away from this conversation that easily. The moment he's in front of the arm of the couch, I shove him, toppling his back onto the cushions. Climbing over him, I grab the front of his shirt and force his lips on mine. Since he's not going to fucking listen to my words, he's going to have to listen to my body. I'm tired of hearing his shit anyway. The time for talking is done.

He doesn't kiss back for a few seconds but after rubbing the palm of my hand against his neck and my fingers up to his hair, Akmal's lips surrender and he's giving it back to me with just as much passion. I lean into him, rubbing my breasts against his warm chest and he growls against me, the vibrations on my lips making my pussy clench. When his hand grips the back of my neck to pull me closer, I whimper into his mouth.

There's a storm of emotions brewing behind this complicated man of mine and it wants to suck me into the chaos. His hips grind up against me as his hands travel down to the small of my back, keeping me firmly against him like he's afraid I'll be the one to pull away. *Not going to happen.* The need surging through him is affecting me, making my own need grow exponentially. We're fighting fire with fire, making this tension between us grow into an inferno.

On one particularly hard grind, I let out a squeak as his hardness presses right against my clit, sending a spike of pleasure through me. This dress is thin and my senses are heightened with how much Akmal is devouring my mouth right now. He's actually the first one to push his tongue past my lips as I gasp on another hard grind. *My god, who is this man?*

My legs resituate themselves over his body to allow me to straddle him more comfortably as our mouths and tongues continue to fight. Fight for what, I don't know. Is it dominance? Is it something else altogether? I nip his bottom lip, making him groan as he kisses across my jaw, sending his own trail of nips down a path towards the crook of my neck. Shit, I'm so hot right now and so damn horny for this man. He's such a fast learner and it makes my pussy weep in anticipation.

My hand slips under the top of his jeans. This shit is fucking too tight for my liking. Without removing my mouth from his, my fingers deftly undo his button and fly to give my hands more freedom to play. Running my palm across his happy trail, I get a firm grip on his cock and start to play.

It's hot, it's hard, and it is fucking weeping. This man is so damn sexy and he doesn't even know it.

Akmal is still kissing me feverishly as his hand comes back up to grip my hair, pulling it back to look me in the eyes with the most intense and vulnerable stare. "We can't do this." The fucker then kisses me again and makes me lose my damn mind with his intensity. "We shouldn't." Lips slamming into mine again, he makes my head spin with this push and pull. He needs to make up his damn mind!

Fuck this, we can find a middle ground. We don't have to stick it in, much to my pussy's dismay. I just need this man to let go of his frustrations. I can do that for him. I can make him feel good.

My hand starts to stroke his cock up and down faster as he groans into the crook of my neck. When his hands tentatively caress the side of my boobs, I almost mewl like a damn cat in heat and arch my body. Yes, I am *that* sex starved, I realize, but Akmal drives me crazy. I love and I hate it. But I love watching Akmal bloom in his confidence, especially after everything that came out of his mouth earlier. I can be that for him. I can lift him up to where he needs to be.

"I love it when you touch me."

"You're so damn soft. Fuck, you're going to kill me." I can feel his cock growing in size and I know he's close, making me even more excited and hot for him.

My kisses travel down his jaw before I whisper in his ear, "Do you want to cum in my mouth, Akmal?"

"Shit" is all I hear before he climaxes into my hand and between us. He crosses his arms over his face and groans again as his hips continue to thrust into my grip, sending spurts of cum between our bodies and clothes. I don't want him to feel bad about what happened or, heaven forbid, guilty. I just wanted to do something for him, to take away the tension of today. He deserves it. I wish I could do more but like he said, we can't.

Pushing his arm away from his face just enough to expose his lips, my mouth finds his once more as we kiss each other slowly, exploring the way our tongues touch and swipe one another without the frenzy of high-tense emotions.

Between our lips sliding against each other, Akmal keeps saying, "We shouldn't have done that." This poor boy and his inner conflict is going to drive me up the wall. I don't know how to respond to these types of statements. Despite his words, his body is telling me something completely opposite. It's relaxed, and his hands are caressing over my ass as we continue to make love with our mouths like we don't have a care in the world.

9

AKMAL

J don't know what happened to me. I was so pissed at all the men checking out Vero that my head wanted to explode. I'm not a violent person, but fuck if I didn't feel like stabbing the eyes out of every man that looked her way, and there were numerous. My emotions are all over the place and it scares me. I didn't know how to handle it, so I called up Mat to see if he could help me.

His solution was to go to the MMA gym with him. I've seen Mat at his lowest, and he was able to get himself out of it. I figured he'd be the best person to go to.

Taking out my frustrations on the heavy bag helped a little, but didn't fix the problem entirely. I was still pissed and I didn't know why. After showering at the gym, we came straight back to my place. The moment I opened the door was the moment the word 'dildo' filtered through, and it felt like my heart was being sliced through by a giant knife and twisted for maximum impact.

These aren't things I ever thought I would feel. The irrational anger and jealousy towards a damn dildo. I didn't even know she had one with the things she brought over, but I should have known. A woman like her needs sex, lots of it. She's walking sex on a stick.

My mind is so overloaded that I barely register Mat and Atsuko saying their goodbyes and leaving. My body was moving on autopilot as it closed and locked the door, only to be shocked back into the present when Vero hugs me. My chest aches like I can still feel the metaphorical knife continually being twisted, twisting my mind into thoughts I shouldn't be having.

It's not her fault she's so damn attractive. It's not her fault she's stuck with a guy like me. I shouldn't be selfish to want to tie her down to a guy like me.

The crap coming out of my mouth, once it started, kept flowing like uncontrollable vomit. It felt both good to get it out and scary because she might just believe the shit I'm saying and leave me high and dry.

Damn, just thinking about her walking out this door to another man's arms makes me boil with rage. Why am I so damn angry all the time?

Vero and I keep having slip ups and I can't say if I'm pleased or upset by the fact. My cock tells me he's more pleased than upset, that's for sure. We can't keep doing this. I need to stay away from her, regain some sort of control.

The living room incident feels like it was hours ago as well as only a few minutes ago. I can still feel the way her soft hands stroked against my erection, bringing me to heights I've never known. Dammit! I need to stop thinking about it.

Night has fallen and the house is dark and quiet. Quiet except for my thoughts as I lay here in the dark staring at nothing and wondering how I got myself into this. I don't regret asking her to marry me at all...but will I be enough for her? For a woman who can command a room by just bending over to look at some dresses. I don't even remember what she ended up buying because I was so preoccupied with rushing her out of that shopping center to bring her back home for safe keeping.

Turning onto my back, I run both of my hands down my face and try to stamp down these self-deprecating thoughts. Vero's right, I shouldn't do this to myself. I shouldn't think these things. The bed suddenly dips, startling me out of my mood. It's still dark in my room but I would recognize her scent anywhere. My cock is already twitching at the thought of her breasts and hands. Damn, will it always be like this between us?

"What are you doing?" Do I really want to know?

"I missed you." Her hand slowly skates across my naked chest and I can feel the goosebumps rising on my skin. "I'm tired of sleeping alone, Akmal. We don't have to do anything. Just...just let me hold you."

Okay, I can do that. That's not so bad.

My hand goes over hers as our fingers interlace. The bed jostles again as she moves her body even closer to my side, laying her head on top of my shoulder. This is new. This is nice. Her warmth suffuses into my skin like a blanket. I can get used to this. Is this what married people do everyday?

"Akmal, tell me your dreams."

"My dreams?"

"Yeah, what do you want to do in life? Was photography always your goal?" The thought of this woman wanting to get to know me, just me, makes my heart swell.

"Yeah, I guess so. It started as a hobby, and it's something I'm good at, I think. IT work forced me into a nine-to-five position and it felt so stifling. Photography lets me be my own man, making my own rules."

"I like that. You are good at what you do."

"Thanks. How about you? What are your dreams?"

"I love photography too, just on the other side of the camera. Atsuko and I both were trying to get modeling to be our full time gig so we wouldn't be restrained to our day jobs as well."

"What is your day job?"

"Oh, I guess it never got brought up, huh? I bartend at a local Cuban restaurant."

"Oh. Do you like it? Bartending, I mean."

"Yeah, I guess? It pays the bills. I guess I'm good at it since they haven't hired anyone else. They're pretty slow in the mornings, which is when I work. I took off after the Alfonso incident, so they're not expecting me back for a while."

"I'm glad you're off."

"Me too."

It becomes quiet after the conversation ends and my mind is going over everything she's told me. I wonder what kind of customers she gets when she's bartending? Are they rowdy? Is she safe? Is anyone there to look out for her?

Soon enough, her breathing starts to even out, lulling me into my own darkness.

I'm coming out of the tail end of a dream and I'm getting frustrated. This is starting to become my constant state of being, it seems. Vero's face of ecstasy as she orgasmed is starting to fade like smoke in the wind the more the fog of sleep dissipates.

Burying my face into the softness in front of me, the scent of my woman takes over my mind. Vero's in my bed...and it feels so damn right, even though she shouldn't be here. I must have slung my arm around her because it's currently holding her like a damn teddy bear with her back pressed to my front. Her dark hair tickles my nose, making me move it towards the soft slope of her shoulder instead.

Some days I still can't believe she's real. I still can't believe she said yes to my stumbling proposal. How did I get so lucky?

My hands pull her in even closer towards my front in case this is all a dream and she really is going to disappear in front of my eyes. The moment my hard cock presses against her ass is the moment Vero starts to sluggishly squirm against me. No, this is not a dream. Not when I can feel the softness of her backside torturing me like that. How am I going to make it through today when we're like this? I can't seem to keep it down around her. I feel high strung from the pressure that's always between my legs, seeking relief where I know I'm forbidden to.

"Mmmm...." Damn, she sounds sexy in the morning. And now I'm thinking back to the tail end of that wet dream. Except she's real, she's here, and I'm holding her against me *right now*.

Would it be so bad? I can give her relief, right? She's always trying to give me relief, reading me like an open book when I'm strung so tight that I don't know what to do with myself. I've been selfish, I realize that now. What kind of husband am I? I need to do better but I don't know what the hell I'm doing half the time.

Trusting my gut, my hand starts to slowly run against her

skin upwards under her top. She's so soft. When my finger-tips graze across the underside of her breasts, my breath hitches. Shit, she's not wearing a bra. I can't stop now, can I? I'm too damn intrigued. We shouldn't. I'm going too far.

The moment my hand moves away is the moment Vero presses her ass against my crotch at the same time as she grabs my wandering hand and presses it fully over the entirety of her breast. *My god.*

Running my nose across her shoulder to the middle of her back, I'm glad she can't see how embarrassed I am with how much I want this.

Mumbling against her skin, I can feel her arch her back in response. "You're so fucking soft. What do you do to me, Vero?"

She forces my hand to squeeze her breast even harder and my hips start to move on their own, slowly thrusting against her. How do we keep finding ourselves in these compromised positions? How can any sane man say no to the temptation of heaven right in front of him?

"The same thing you do to me." The sound of her breathy voice in the morning is going to star in all my fantasies from here on out.

When her other hand guides mine between her legs, I groan against her skin, pressing a kiss to her back. Dammit, I'm so weak. I'm craving everything she's doing to me like my next breath. She pushes my fingers beneath her panties and they glide along the wetness that's already accumulating and soaking through her panties. *Fuck.*

"Tell me your fantasies, Akmal." Fucking hell, I can barely even think straight right now. How the hell am I supposed to answer that? She'll probably think I'm a pervert with every-thing I think about revolving around her.

"You don't want to know..."

I'm not in control of myself anymore as my fingers continue to explore her body, making her squirm and moan. It's just so damn wet and it makes me think of what it would feel like to shove my cock into its heat. Groaning against her back, I lick her skin slowly, just wanting her to be even more wet because of me. I can't believe I'm doing this. I can't believe she's this turned on.

"Tell me, Akmal. I'm so horny right now." I let out a conflicted groan. She can't say these kinds of things to me. Can I really deny such a simple request from my future wife? She just wants to know my mind. I can give her that. She needs to know me, the real me.

Her hands start to guide me higher, towards the top of her pussy where I can't see, but can feel a hood of skin peeking out. Taking her guidance and cues, I follow her silent commands and start to rub where she wants me to. Her moans become louder and it spurs me on. I think we're both chasing something as I continue to grind against her backside while my fingers circle her secret nub.

"I love how wet you are, it makes my dick want to cry with how much it wants to bury itself inside of you. Feel you from the inside."

Her breath hitches before she says, "Tell me more."

The air is starting to feel oppressed again with how hot it's getting. Kicking off the sheets to give us a little reprieve, my hand doesn't let up as it starts to stroke her pussy lips and bring the wetness up to her clit. I think that's what they call it.

"I can't stop thinking about the way your mouth takes my cock. The way it felt when I came and you took every drop. It's been the star of my fantasies every night, torturing me because I can't do a damn thing about it."

Knowing Vero, she never does anything halfway because

she makes my free hand pinch her nipple under her shirt and I almost cum right there with the overload of sensations happening. My mind is stimulated to the point of no return, trying to decide which part of this moment I like the best. Fuck, I want it all. I want it all so bad. This wedding needs to hurry the fuck up.

"I love when you cum in my mouth, Akmal. I've been thinking about it every night too." Shit, she has? Fuck, it's so dirty. I love that she's dirty and is proud of it...and she's all damn mine.

"Are you a dirty girl, Vero?"

Her legs are scissoring at this point, pushing my hand even harder against her center. Damn, how can she get this wet? The thought of my dick plowing into this, sliding in and out and cumming inside of her makes me grit my teeth. I bet she tastes fucking good too. Didn't Mat talk about that? Licking pussy to put his woman into submission? The idea is sounding better by the minute. Fuck! We really shouldn't be doing this.

"I'll be anything you want me to be." God damn. What is she doing to me?

"I want to taste you so bad, but I know if I do, I won't be able to stop."

"Oh my god. I wish I could feel your tongue in my pussy. I'm so fucking wet for you, Akmal." Shit, the way she says my name at this moment, like I'm the most desirable person in existence for her. It makes me feel high, like I'm on top of the damn world.

Feeling braver, my fingers start to swirl against her clit and dip into her channel ever so slightly. Watching her reactions, my hand starts to play her the way her body is telling me to. She starts to pant, but so am I as I watch her body move like a damn siren song, calling me to my death.

"Oh my god, Akmal, don't stop." Hell no I'm not stopping, not when she looks like this. Almost exactly the way I remember from my dream.

Pinching her nipples and tugging, my other hand starts to rub her clit even harder when her body starts to jerk and she cries out in pleasure. Holy fucking shit, just look at her.

Suddenly, her hands seemed to have traveled between her legs to grab my cock from beneath my boxers somehow and she's sliding it against her pussy lips. Fuck!

She presses my shaft against her wetness while gripping the head of my cock, jacking me off between her legs. My breaths grow ragged and I almost see stars when it starts to spurt into her hands when my climax hits. How does it keep getting better with her? How can it possibly even feel better than the last times she's made me cum? Vero must be doing some witchcraft because I'm addicted. She's put a spell on me and I'm forever bound to this vixen who has me by the cock.

Her hand rubs against our combined juices right before she turns her head back to look at me and sticks her coated finger in her mouth.

I can't. I can't look at this and not fuck her right here. Biting her shoulder out of my frustration to make her stop her constant teasing, I jump out of bed right when she lets out a yelp. Serves her right. Damn her.

Jumping into the shower, I make sure to make the water as cold as it can go.

10

VERO

$\mathcal{D}$espite the orgasm this morning, I'm a ball of nerves. I called up my familia and told them to be on time for lunch. Atsuko called me and told me they're already on their way.

Now I'm standing in this kitchen, staring at this chair where Akmal and I were last grinding on each other. How am I supposed to hold myself back at his parents' house? There is no possible way. I don't want to cause a rift between our families. I mean, I can't be all over him in front of my parents either. My mom would have my head while Fabian laughs his ass off.

Okay, I can do this. I need to prove to Akmal and his family that I'm in it to win it. I need to prove to Akmal that I'm committed to see this to the end. Taking a deep breath in and out, I close my eyes and try to find some sort of inner tranquility.

A throat clears behind me before I hear, "Are you ready?" Turning around, my eyes land on the most delectable sight. How can he be sexier every time I look at him? Is it because I'm starting to see him in a new light? Starting to unfold the many layers of Akmal? No matter what we've come across so far, I'm only more intrigued and determined to tie this man to me.

Akmal is standing there in dark dress pants and a very nice light blue button-down top which he has tucked neatly. *My my.* The color compliments his tan skin tone nicely. He almost looks out of my league, and that thought shakes my confidence a little. I watch as his hand starts to roll up his sleeves, one at a time, and I'm in a trance with his movements. What is it about a man with rolled up sleeves? Knowing exactly what those hands are capable of, my legs press together beneath my clothes.

My own hands smooth down the looser dress I'm in. It has a much higher neckline than I'm used to, channelling an Audrey Hepburn look, but at least it's loose-fitting enough to not have any mishaps with the girls. The flare of the skirt will also allow me to sit down easier when we eat on the floor.

"Vero, are you ready?" I was lost staring at the way the dress shirt stretched across his firm chest when his arms were moving around to make sure his shirt was nicely tucked in all the way. This wedding cannot come soon enough.

"Yes, I'm ready."

Leaving the apartment, Akmal opens the passenger door for me and I slide in before he comes around the other side. I'm a little nervous despite having met his parents already. Will they like my family? I really hope mi familia took my advice about dressing modestly. I was able to pre-warn them about eating on the floor and could hear Fabian yelling in the background about it being crazy.

I know. I know. This whole damn thing is crazy, but I wouldn't give up Akmal for anything. YOLO.

"Akmal, what should I be expecting? I'm assuming your mother is taking over all of the wedding planning? Will I be able to invite my relatives?" Last I remember, Akmal's mother already had an entire wedding list in mind.

"I honestly don't know. I mean, I never paid that much attention to it because...I never thought I'd find someone. I'm what Malaysians would consider old in regards to marriage-able age."

"Okay...if you're old...what does that make *me*?" I'm older than he is! Does that make me a spinster?

He pulls up to the front of his parents house, places the car in park and turns to look at me. "It makes you mine."

Oh...be still my heart.

Once we step out of the car, Akmal places a hand behind the small of my back and I'm reminded of the day on the couch. Lord, don't get my lady bits going right before we meet his family. We're halfway up the walkway when I hear the rumble of Fabian's Chevelle pull up next to our vehicle. I can't believe he drove our parents in that thing. They probably all smell like exhaust fumes. Akmal and I have stopped walking to watch as they get out.

My mother is in a long sleeve modest top with pants. My father is in his signature button-down short sleeve top and cotton pants. Fabian...well, good enough. Either his grey t-shirt shrank a little or his body has gotten larger because it's stretching across his pecs, not hiding much of what's underneath. At least his dark pants don't have any holes or stains on them.

"I look fine, quit judging, Vero." Dammit, I have a feeling

something is going to go wrong today. My brother isn't the most well-behaved on good days. He didn't even bother to shave, leaving his five o' clock shadow on like it's a damn signature when in reality, he just doesn't want to be bothered by an extra step.

"Keep your trap filtered today, Fabian, I'm serio. Don't cause any trouble for me. I want this lunch to go well."

Fabian shoots his steel-grey eyes at me and I know there's going to be trouble. These virgin Malaysian girls don't stand a chance against his bad boy looks. His tattoo is peeking out a little from his short sleeve but it can't be helped now.

"What do you take me for? I'm going to be good, trust me." Famous last words coming from his mouth. I love my brother but he throws off an aura of trouble that most women can't say no to.

"I'm serious, Fabian."

Fabian smiles and I can feel my hands starting to get clammy.

"Relájate. Just relax."

"He's right. Relájate, Vero. It will be okay." My dad, always backing up my bro like it's some bro code. Traitor.

"Akmal, good to see you again." At least my dad is being civil this time.

"Yes, it's good to see you again as well. I hope the trip was okay?"

"Fabian was driving, we just sit until we get where we need to go."

"Well, thank you again for joining us. I'm sure my family is excited to meet you."

Akmal hasn't even finished his sentence yet when we hear the sound of his mother's voice. "There you are Akmal! What are you doing keeping everyone outside huh? Come, come! The food is ready. Mat is already here with his wife. Akmal, you didn't tell me he's already engaged! We need to make a double wedding huh."

We make it to the door where Akmal's mother is practically preening at the party coming in. After short greetings and everyone remembering to remove their shoes, we enter the living area where a large spread is already laid out.

"Vero!" Turning towards the sound of my name being called I see Atsuko making her way around the small crowd.

"Atsuko! When did you guys make it here?"

"Oh, only about ten minutes before you guys. Akmal's mother was basically all over Mat and how he didn't mention anything about me. They really do treat him like he's family. It's cute."

"Have you met the sisters yet?"

"I think I see them around the house getting things ready but I haven't talked to any of them yet." My eyes start looking around when I catch Akmal's first sister walking by.

"Hasanah!" Her head is covered in a light purple head-scarf - or hijab, as google has informed me recently - as she turns my way.

"Ah! Sister, so glad to see you!"

I can feel Atsuko tense up next to me a bit. It's so subtle but being her BFF, I can read her really well. Atsuko came to this lunch in something similar to myself, a looser fitting, flared, vintage inspired dress with an appropriately sized cardigan top.

"How are you?"

"I'm good! Have you met Mat's fiancé, Atsuko?"

"Oh! So nice to meet you! I'm so happy for Mat, and for you of course. Now my mother can stop pestering me about marrying him."

"Oh...thank you. Yes, Mat and I are engaged."

"It is good, yes? Mat deserves the best. He is a great guy. He looks very happy with you. Congratulations."

The air between the two starts to thin out to friendlier terms. I knew Hasanah was a nice girl. Just a girl who got caught up with somewhat overbearing parents.

"Hidaya! Sakinah! Come! Meet Mat's wife." The other two sisters come towards us through the crowd and I notice a really big difference between the two. One girl looks to be wearing more modern and form-fitting clothing while the other dons what I assume is more traditional Malaysian clothing.

"This is Sakinah, she is twenty-five. I am the oldest, at twenty-six. Hidaya is twenty-three."

Sakinah does a little bow. Her dress is long sleeved but flows over her small frame nicely like a damn modern day princess while her younger sister wears a more traditional top and bottom skirt that matches in color with embroidery. Sakinah's hijab is a solid black, making it almost look like it's part of her dark hair. Very stylish.

"Nice to meet you. Glad my family didn't scare you off, Vero. Akmal deserves a strong woman to go up against all this." Sakinah and I share a knowing smile because I totally understand what she's saying. The clash of cultures can be a bit much. Overbearing parents, even more so.

"This is Hidaya, my youngest sister." This sister is in a soft pink hijab that makes her look very young.

"Hello, Vero. Nice to see you again."

"Thanks. Nice to see you too. This is my best friend, Atsuko. She is engaged to Mat."

Both the girls look at her with a smile, greeting her with a little bow. No one looks threatening or looks like they have any ulterior motives. Atsuko noticeably relaxes as she greets them back.

"Vero, don't forget about tu hermano. Introduce me." Awww shit. I know that look. Fabian's eyes are practically sparkling as they look at...who was she again? The middle sister, Sakinah.

What is this? It's so subtle but my woman's intuition catches it. Both Atsuko and I look at each other subtly. She catches it too.

"Fabian, these are Akmal's *sisters*. This is Hasanah, Sakinah and Hidaya." Look at this fool right here. He hasn't heard half of the introduction because he only has eyes for the princess in the middle.

Being the freaking Rico Suave he is, he grabs Sakinah's hand and bends down to kiss the back of it. How fucking embarrassing. I can already feel trouble radiating off him.

"Sakinah. What a beautiful name for a beautiful woman. I'm Fabian." Look at this guy right here. Her smile is so coy I want to vomit in my mouth. She's not really falling for this ish, is she? What the hell is happening here? Oh my god. Look at that smile on her face. She *is* falling for his crap. I can't blame her, she's probably never seen the likes of Fabian Hernandez in her life. Lord have mercy on her.

"Fabian. Akmal's sisters are good girls and need to stay that way." Aww crap, the smile that starts creeping up on his face shows his one dimple and I should have known I shouldn't mention the words 'good girls' because a guy like Fabian will take that as a challenge. I try to send Sakinah a look of warning but she only has googly eyes for Fabian since he hasn't let go of her hand yet.

Saving them from a potential scandal, I bump my body between them to break their contact and push Fabian towards my parents.

This fucker is still winking and blowing kisses over my shoulder at Sakinah as she giggles and walks away with her sisters in tow. He needs to rein that junk in before her parents catch him.

Akmal's parents usher us all to the floor to sit down and eat. It seems the parents have their own little circle while the rest of us have ours. The couples are sitting together, not too far from where the parents are, while somehow Fabian and Sakinah are sitting next to each other. What a coincidence, hey?

The food is delicious, as usual. I can hear the parents talking about wedding details while I'm trying to keep an eye on my brother to make sure his hands aren't straying where they shouldn't. Sakinah is just soaking up all the looks he's shooting her way, even if she isn't saying much. There's something about her. I might have to watch out for her too.

Once the meal is done, we all go to stand up while some of us start putting plates away. The front door crashes open and more voices are joining in from outside. I feel like this is deja vu.

"Aye Mat! You finally have a woman too! This is great news! We shall make it a double wedding huh. Tuah, bring the fabric! Zaka, where is Adila? We need to measure Mat's wife."

A whirlwind of people I don't recognize start coming in besides Akmal's aunts and uncles.

"Oye! Akmal, I was in the neighborhood and had to see if it was true. Where is your wife? Finally huh?" Who is this guy? He's got to be related to Akmal somehow. A random stranger or acquaintance wouldn't just waltz in, right?

A few more guys and what looks to be their partners come through the door and I'm feeling overwhelmed again. My parents are speaking to each other in Spanish and I have no idea where Fabian is.

11

FABIAN

A bunch of people are popping in. This place is crazy. That or their family is huge. But you know what? It gives me the perfect opportunity to find out about this middle sister I've been recently introduced to. Maneuvering myself between all the moving parts currently happening around us, I catch sight of her black head wrap. I'm kind of glad she stands out in this sea of jewel-toned colors mingling back and forth.

I watch as she walks back and forth to what I think is the kitchen, putting plates away with the other girls. On one of her walks back into the living room, I whisper her name when she's close enough to hear.

"Sakinah." Her black headwrap whips around and I give her a smile. I watch as her cheeks pinken and I know I got her. She feels it too, this thing between us. Can't say I've ever run across a Malaysian girl, but they can't be that much different than other girls, right?

There's only one way to find out.

"Yes?"

"Can you direct me to your bathroom? I'm a little lost in this place with all these people around." In my periphery, I can see different women gathering together around my sister and her best friend. Bolts of fabric are being held overhead as people start chatting around us, creating a buzz in a sea of voices. I don't know how Vero handles all this shit. I would have been gone by now if it wasn't for this being Vero's day. I wouldn't want to embarrass her like that. I can be good.

"Yes, of course. Follow me." Making my way close behind her, I can see that she really isn't that tall, only standing to my chest. That's alright, I don't mind them being tiny. She smells like something floral, it's light and it's nice. Makes me want to lean in to get a better whiff. Watching the sway of her hips in her dress, I'm mesmerized by the flow of the movement. Why are all these women so covered in seas of fabric? Is this a Malaysian thing?

My mind is now imagining what lies underneath this dress of hers. Is she slender? Just a handful? Would her skin be as soft as silk since it's been kept from the sun, without a blemish in sight? How sensitive would she be to touch? Would she writhe with every breath I blow across her skin? Would she scream in pleasure as I lick her pussy?

My cock is already twitching at the thought of what it would feel like to cover her body with mine when she stops and turns to point at a door in front of me.

Her startled face is getting pink again as I stand in front of her about a couple feet away, staring at her to my heart's content, looking over every detail and memorizing it. I'm sure everyone in the other room is busy with whatever they're doing. They wouldn't notice us missing for a while. Does it make me a bastard for thinking this way?

Her face has the most beautiful even tan coloring and it makes my mouth water for a taste. I wonder if she'd let me?

Vero's words come back to my mind about Akmal's sisters being 'good girls'. *That's what they all say.* I've been with plenty of 'good girls' who ended up being more promiscuous than I am. They were just better at hiding it from their families.

Speaking of sex, I haven't had some for a while with work getting busy. But this little thing in front of me might just be what breaks my fast.

Sakinah's lashes lower and I'm intrigued. Is she shy? What is she hiding? Is she really a 'good girl' as they say? If so, then why was she so willing to lead me to the restroom without anyone else the wiser. I am a man after all, and she's a woman. Is it a subliminal invitation?

I'm a little upset that she doesn't want to look at me right now. There's no one else here but us. I know I'm not bad on the eyes. Grabbing her chin with my fingers, I force her face up to look at me and offer her another smile to calm her nerves. Her brown eyes sparkle with something behind them, but it's when her full lips part that I throw everything out the window and go in for the kill. Who could blame me? She looks like a damn offering.

She tries to escape by walking backward, only succeeding in trapping herself against the wall. *All part of the plan, baby, all part of the plan.* I take it easy on her, since it seems like she's unsure. *Or maybe this is her first time?* That thought does something to me. I've never been with a virgin before, and she sure is acting like what I think one would. Well, this is something new. It's making me even more hungry for her.

Brushing our lips together in the most chaste manner I

can muster, I let my lips linger against hers for just a bit longer than I should without coaxing anything else. Her body tenses up but she doesn't slap me, so this is a good start between us. Her lips are definitely as soft as they look. When I pull back slowly, my eyes scan hers to make sure I didn't traumatize her.

Well look at that. Her eyes can't stay on mine for more than a few seconds since they keep going back to my lips. Things just got much more interesting.

"Why did you do that?" She bites the bottom of her lip and I internal high five myself for being able to bait the little thing so easily.

"Why not?"

"Because we shouldn't." Is that so? Her eyes go a little wild before she shoves me off her and slips away back into the crowd. So she does have a little fire in her after all, not as submissive as I thought. Now I'm hungry to find out more.

Sakinah, Sakinah, Sakinah. She's probably too young for me but fuck it. I'm not stopping until I get this one under me.

I should use the restroom to make it look legit before I rejoin the others as well. Laughing to myself, I open the bathroom door and start planning ways to catch myself a pretty little Malaysian princess.

～

AKMAL

The women are surrounding Vero and Atsuko with all their craziness, leaving the men to the side. Mat is chilling next to me when one of my cousins starts his bullshit that I'm quite frankly tired of hearing after all these years. He needs to find a damn new hobby.

"Took you long enough to find a woman." Uncle Zaka's son, Umar, has been one of the worst ones hounding me about this. Just because he was the first to get married out of our group, he always acts like that makes him a little better than us. Well, mostly better than *me*.

"I never thought you would, you know? I would have introduced you to my wife's friend from the university if you would have just said yes." Cousin Ismail hounds me too, but he's nicer about it. I understand everyone's concern. I shouldn't have stayed single this long.

Glancing over my shoulder, I watch as Vero laughs about something the girls are talking about. The reason I've stayed single this long is because the perfect woman was waiting for me to come into her life. She's the only one I can see myself with. I regret nothing.

"How did you even get a woman like that to want you huh? You don't have much to offer her." He's just lucky we're related. Doesn't he realize I already know all this? I ask myself that every damn day I'm with her.

I'm tired of this conversation already and it's only started.

"Don't let it get to you man." My buddy Mat is mumbling under his breath next to me, and he's right. I can't let all this negativity get to me.

Looking over my shoulder again to make sure Vero is alright, I spot Sakinah coming from the back to join Hidaya in the kitchen. When my eyes catch Fabian coming from the same direction shortly after, my mind is rewinding what Sakinah looked like when she came out. She looked okay, nothing seemed out of place. But why would they both be coming from the same direction around the same time?

I don't have time to ponder the thought when I see something that makes me see red. Umar's brother, Nosiah, is approaching my woman and I have a feeling I won't like what he has to say.

I'm barely registering what Umar or Ismail are talking about, when my ears start to strain to hear what's about to happen.

"Hey beautiful. If you ever get tired of Akmal, just know I'm here to catch you when you fall. I'm Nosiah."

My sisters are laughing but my mind can only see my fist in my cousin's face. My legs have already started walking towards Vero before he even opened his mouth. Lucky for him, my fist was only coming up halfway when my mother slaps him upside the head.

"Be respectful, huh? What are you doing? This is Akmal's wife. Look elsewhere for your own. If I hear something else coming from your mouth like that, you won't have a voice left after I beat you." Nosiah has the decency to look sheepish as he walks away, but not before I snarl at him and hit him upside the head a second time when he's close enough.

I know she's fucking beautiful. It doesn't mean they can try to steal her right from underneath my nose.

Nosiah continues to rub his head as he heads towards the other men. When I turn around to look at Vero, she is staring right at me with an expression I can't read but it makes my chest feel full. The smile she sends my way makes me think of nights holding her as she falls asleep in my arms.

Vero is mine, and I'm going to make sure she doesn't escape before the wedding gets here.

"Akmal, there you are. Give this ring to your wife, huh. That way the other boys will see she is already taken." My mom's got my back. She's right, I need to claim her in front of my cousins before one of the other boys get any ideas.

The second the piece is placed in my hand, I quickly stride the rest of the way towards my future wife. She startles at my arrival but quickly relaxes and her smile widens at me, making her face even more radiant as I grab her right hand and slowly place the engagement ring on her finger.

It doesn't matter what it looks like as time stands still between us. Our eyes make promises to each other as we try to restrain ourselves from public affection in front of our families.

Soon. Very soon, I'll be able to claim her in all ways.

"Daughter, the wedding will be ready by the weekend, huh. So get plenty of sleep so that you can look beautiful on the throne."

The smile that graces both our faces in that moment, tells her that the day cannot come soon enough.

12

VERO

esterday was insane. It went from a casual lunch date to planning two weddings. At least my parents were able to add some input into the guest list. We're probably in the thousands by now and that thought scares me. How can there be that many Malaysian people in this one area? I swear Akmal is the first Malaysian I've ever come across and suddenly they're all coming out of the woodwork.

My fingers start to play with my engagement ring as my thoughts come back to the situation at hand. I need to pick up my paycheck from the restaurant. My boss was kind enough to give me a quick call earlier to let me know it's waiting for me.

"Akmal, can you drive me to my work so I can pick up my paycheck? I want to deposit it today since we're free."

"Yeah, of course."

I watch Akmal walk to the kitchen to pick up his car keys and I'm getting kind of flustered. I love the way his body moves against his t-shirt. The way his forearms look when they flex and grab the keys. When he turns to me, the slight facial hair he has makes me imagine what it would be like to feel it between my legs. He came in and left the shower that one day so quickly, I didn't get a chance to check out his tan body but now I'm so curious. His skin is so damn smooth, now it reminds me of how smoothly his fingers were playing with my pussy the other morning.

And last night…

"Hey, let's go online tonight. Join me?"

"Of course. Do I get to sit on your lap Akmal?" He chokes on his drink and takes a moment to clear his throat. I love doing that to him. He acts like he doesn't like my unfiltered mouth, but he loves that shit.

"Vero…" I pout at him before I let out an exasperated sigh and sit to the side of him rather than on him like I wanted.

We're on the floor with two laptops on the coffee table with our backs to the couch. Akmal is such a nerd with his gaming, but I love it. I've been trying to get into it with him so we can have something else to share together.

The game starts and soon enough, Akmal is so engrossed in what he's doing, he doesn't notice me scooting a little closer.

I'm almost in front of his laptop screen, but he's too lost in his raid. A few more butt scooches and I'm leaning in to breathe against his ear right before I lick his earlobe.

"Shit."

I'm laughing on the inside, but I'm not letting up. Not when he's being so cute.

I can see his character die in my periphery. Poor baby. Placing my palm on his cheek, I force his face towards me and kiss him deeply. My tongue is licking the seam of his lips asking for entry, and Akmal doesn't disappoint when he turns to me completely to devour my mouth. He's gotten too good at this lately, and my pussy is curious to see how well he takes instructions down there.

Pulling him with me as I lay myself down onto my back, Akmal follows without much resistance. Yeah, he feels it too. Our mental walls are getting thinner the more we try to fight this growing need for each other.

I don't know what happens, but suddenly Akmal growls and is kissing the crook of my neck as one of his hands pulls down my off-the-shoulder top, revealing one of my naked breasts to him.

I'm lost in the moment, panting at how worked up he's gotten me, when Akmal's lips go from my neck to swiping his hot and wet tongue over my nipple... and leaves me in a trance on the floor while he goes back to his original position and respawns his character.

"Wha-" I blink a few times, unsure how I got here. My brain is slow in leaving the lust fog. My nipple is getting hard from the chill in the air, reacting to the wetness he left behind.

Seems I'm not the only one who's learned the art of the tease.

I don't know if I'll make it to our wedding day. I'm just going to stop lying to myself. How can he be so strong? I'm so weak, so weak for this man.

"What?"

"You make me so fucking horny."

He groans, turns away from me and runs his hands through his hair in frustration. I'm watching the way his back flexes with the movement, almost panting. I know I don't make it any easier, but dammit it's the truth! Being on the pill should curb your libido but I swear it does *nothing* for me! The last time I picked up my prescription for pills, I was told it got rebranded or something. How long ago was that? I don't remember but shouldn't the pill make your horny-chemical go down? I swear I've been nothing but horny since

Akmal came into my life. I can't even think straight and find the right words in my mind.

Oh my god, what if it's because I haven't been doing it? What if there is some sort of build up inside of me that makes it worse? What should I do? I can't use a dildo after our last argument. I don't want Akmal to feel less than what he is.

Akmal is taking deep breaths before he turns around to look at me with the horniest eyes I've ever seen on him. This fucker isn't helping anything!

"Vero, you can't say that kind of stuff to me. I'm trying really hard here."

"I like you hard." Shit, I swear it just came out of my mouth. Oh my god, I want him to cum in my mouth again.

"Dammit Vero! I'm dying here."

"Maybe..maybe I can help you?" His eyes are intensely staring a hole into me. I'm not sure if I should be scared, but it's pulling me in like a fish hook. My legs are already moving by themselves until I'm standing in front of him. His arms are still up with his fingers threaded through his hair.

Don't make this so easy for me.

Shit, too late.

Taking one more step closer, my hands creep under his shirt and go across his abs as Akmal throws his head back and closes his eyes with a frown.

"You feel so good. I just want to make you feel good."

His voice is so gravelly, my vagina is screaming at me to claim what's rightfully mine.

"Vero...We can't do this. Stop."

I pout. Dammit! I want him!

When he opens his eyes and brings his head down, his frown turns into a delicious masculine chuckle as his warm hands hold my face to bring it in for a soft kiss. A teasing kiss. A kiss that's killing me.

"Akmal, let me suck you. I'll be quick. I just want you in my mouth so bad."

"Dammit Vero. Stop. Let's go get your paycheck, okay? This apartment is nothing but a box of temptation. We need to stop before we can't." Even the way he's saying all this against my lips, as we continue to give each other soft kisses, is killing me from how sexy it is.

My nails start to scrape his sides as they travel to his back, pulling him in closer to me. He growls into my mouth when my nails dig in again but manages to push me away, the bastard!

He's panting as he walks a few steps away from me. I'm panting from the way he's leaving me.

After a few moments of silence and separation, Akmal sighs and turns towards me enough to lace his fingers into mine as he pulls us out the front door to the apartment. The tension between us is palpable. You can almost feel the energy spike when our skin touches.

The drive over to Havana Palace was a quiet one. I still feel a little frustrated with what happened before our exit. Akmal shouldn't look so damn hot in the driver seat, flexing his arms as he works the steering wheel the way he does. Would his arms look like that when he's above me, plowing into my pussy until I cry out in ecstasy?

I'm pulled from my reverie when he puts the car into park and looks at me expectantly. Sighing, I lean my head back and breathe deeply a few times. It's getting harder and harder being around him like this. Wanting yet unable to take.

I still love him being around me despite the torture it brings.

"Akmal, will you come in with me please?"

"Of course, whatever you want." I groan at that statement.

"Akmal you know what I want. But all I can have right now is you beside me."

"Vero, it won't always be like this." He's already exiting the driver side as I answer him anyway.

"...I know..."

Once he opens the door for me, we walk hand in hand to the Cuban restaurant. It's still slow in the morning, so I'm sure the manager doesn't mind me bringing Akmal in with me to pick up this damn paycheck.

Mike, my boss, sees me and gives me a little wave before he heads back to his office. I'm showing Akmal around a bit before leading him to the bar stools to sit while we wait for Mike to get back. The front door of the restaurant opens up, but I don't notice it as I lean in towards Akmal, imagining what it would have been like if we would have met in a place like this.

His chocolate eyes are staring into mine lovingly when I hear my name being called.

"Vero?"

That's not Mike's voice, but it sounds very familiar. Turning, I see a young guy that looks to be in his twenties with wavy brown hair. I know him from somewhere but I can't pinpoint where at the moment.

Giving him what I think is a friendly smile, I respond with a "Hi, do I know you?" Does that make me a bitch? I mean, he knew my name. But he could have just heard my boss calling me when I was behind the bar working some days too.

"You don't remember me? We met right here, in this restaurant." It's honestly still not ringing a bell. If I had a rendezvous with this guy, and by the way he keeps staring at my tits this is probably the case, he must have been a five pump chump. Not really worth me remembering.

Oh shit.

I turn my face to look at Akmal and his eyes are blazing but his face doesn't give anything away. He's so quiet that it kind of scares me.

Turning back quickly, I try to diffuse the situation. "Sorry, I honestly don't remember. But it was nice seeing you...again?"

When I catch his eye stray to my breasts again, it all happens so fast. By the time I realize what's happening, the poor guy is on the ground and Akmal still has his hand in a fist. He didn't even make a sound, how did he move so fast?

"Vero, take this and go. I'll clean this up. Shit, maybe it's good you're still off."

"Thanks Mike." Grabbing the check and sticking it into my purse, it almost doesn't make it all the way in when Akmal silently grabs my hand and pulls me out of the front doors and into the car.

The drive to the bank was silent. Instead of going inside, Akmal took us through the drive through ATM machine to deposit my check. I trust him so I gave him my card and number to put into the machine. He won't look at me the entire time he's performing his duties.

When we make it home, Akmal continues to be a gentleman with opening doors and such but the neverending silent treatment is making my head want to explode. I don't know what to do or say. I mean, that guy was before meeting Akmal. Should I feel sorry about it? But it wasn't like I planned to do the guy right before meeting Akmal. I didn't know I would fall for Akmal so hard.

"Akmal, what's wrong?" We've just come through the front door and he's walking directly to his bedroom.

Not knowing what else to do, I follow behind him … only to see him packing a backpack. What the hell?

"Akmal, what are you doing?" Silence. His movements are jerky. He's pissed at me. I'm getting pissed too because I don't know why. I mean, I kind of do, but it's not my fault. I didn't do it TO him. How can I explain it when he won't even talk to me?

He turns to leave the room and I'm chasing right at his heels. Now I'm getting a little scared.

"Where are you going?"

The sound of the door slamming closed is the last thing I hear as my heart gets shredded into jagged pieces.

13

AKMAL

I'm being irrational, I know it. But that's the thing with irrationality, right? It makes no damn sense. Like how I feel right now. I feel like going back to that stupid restaurant to tear that fucker's head off but I know I shouldn't.

I feel like finding all of Vero's exes and killing them all, but I can't. And because I can't do these things my hands are itching to do, I inadvertently take it out on my wife. Fuck.

I had to leave. I couldn't be there anymore. I don't know what I would have ended up doing. Would I ever hurt Vero? Hell no. But I can't say the same for the shit that might come out of my mouth in the heat of my rolling emotions. I don't even know what I'm feeling, I just know I'm feeling A LOT.

This is all new for me. Apparently, this isn't all new for her and that thought spears me again in the damn chest. Fuck, I'm in over my head with this woman. She probably has a line of men waiting for her to come back to them. Here I am thinking I would be man enough to keep her?

Who thought I'd be this stupid?

I must have been brooding the whole way back to my parent's house. Pulling up to the front, I throw the car in park and get out with the small bag of clothes I packed. Was it immature of me? Probably? But it made sense at the time and I'm already here.

Walking up to the front door, something inside of me niggles at me, telling me I'm overreacting. I just need some time to think. Think about all this without her distracting me, tempting me. My parents still don't know we live together, which is a good thing. They won't know I left my wife alone in my apartment.

Knocking on the door, my mother opens it before I can get the second knock in.

"Eh? Why are you here Akmal? Is everything okay?" I don't think I have it in me to talk sensibly right now, so I slip in and throw my backpack on the ground right before I sit down on the couch with a frustrated groan.

"Akmal, where is your wife huh? Why are you here?" My mom isn't going to let up until I answer her.

"We got into a fight. I need some space to think." I mean, despite not really saying much to each other, it was kind of a fight, right? Ugh, why do I feel like shit just mentally saying that?

Everyone around me doesn't speak another word as they go about the rest of their day.

My mind is in a jumble. Vero has gotten under my skin and into my soul. Even if it was scraped out with serrated knives, she'd still be there. I always knew she was too good for me.

Fuck, is this love? Is this why this shit hurts so bad? I can't think straight. My chest feels constricted, like it's in a damn invisible vice grip. It hurts being away from her and right now, it hurts being next to her. What the hell am I supposed to do in a situation like this? Is there a damn manual to relationships I don't know about? Shit, even if there was, they've never seen the likes of Vero. She's one of a kind.

And now my sorry ass is fucking missing her and it hasn't even been that damn long. I can't go back to her like this though. Not in the state I'm in, like I'm fucking drowning without a life jacket.

The background noise starts to become a low buzz as I lay here on the couch, facing the back cushions.

I think I heard my name called a few times but I'm not sure if it was a dream. It sounds so muffled and my head feels heavy, weighed down by everything that's going on in my mind. Every time I close my eyes I see her face, the way she smiles when I look at her. The way her eyes seek me out in a room, the same way I seek hers, like magnets being pulled together. It makes my chest hurt even more. Fuck.

I must have fallen asleep on the couch because the feeling of someone sitting down next to me, jostling me, wakes me out of this zombified stupor I've found myself in.

"Ibu, don't kacau him. Leave him be."

"Move your legs huh? I want to watch my show and you are in the way." I scrunch up into more of a fetal position as the sound of the TV starts to pull me back into the darkness of my mind.

～

VERO

What just happened? What *just happened*?

He left me. Without a damn word. With a backpack of clothes slung over his shoulder. Is he coming back? Do I wait for him? What do I do?

This is why I was afraid to do this relationship shit! I can't handle this. I don't know the rules to play this damn game. I thought we were doing good. I thought we were making headway with how much we feel about each other.

Why am I feeling so fucking guilty, like my heart is dragging on the floor?

I can't even say sorry for whatever it is he's feeling because he's not even here.

My eyes suddenly feel really hot. I hate this shit. *Hate this shit!*

Flashbacks of my highschool sweetheart leaving me after he got what he wanted flash through my mind. The way I felt like my heart was being eviscerated and stomped on.

Akmal isn't like that though. I know he's not. But why does it hurt so damn much? I don't even know when my hands became fists at my chest until I feel wet drops on them. Fuck, I'm crying. *I hate this shit.* Once it starts, it doesn't stop.

I was fucking trying. I was trying... So. Damn. Hard. To be with him. Can't he see that? Can't he see my devotion? One fuck up. *One* fuck up.

Fuck, who am I kidding? I'm probably always going to fuck up. That fool isn't going to be the last to come out of the woodwork. And when it happens, will Akmal leave me everytime? Will it always be like this?

What if he doesn't even come back *this* time? What if I made the biggest mistake of my life by letting him leave?

I can feel my heart cracking at that thought. No no no no. He's it for me. I can't go back after this. There's not going to be anyone to live up to him. I'm ruined for all men.

The sob that tears from me is ugly and loud. I try to stifle it by covering my face with my hands but it only serves to make me cry harder, my body shaking from the hiccups. Dammit!

I need to move. I need to do something. But what? My feet somehow have led me to Akmal's room and I'm crawling into his bed, grabbing a shirt he left behind and sniffing it while crying on my side.

What the hell am I supposed to do?

14

AKMAL

Someone's pushing me, but my body feels sluggish. Shit, what day is it? I'm so damn tired, just a few more minutes.

This person isn't letting up and I'm starting to get a little pissed. I'm waving my hand outward haphazardly without opening my eyes when I get hit by something hard.

"Wake up! Allah, it's so messy in here. Wake up!" I get hit again and I finally open my eyes to blurrily see my mom with her hijab around her head and a wooden spoon in her hand. Shit.

"You need to wake up Akmal! I'm tired of watching you like a slug in the garden. You don't do anything but sleep. Wake up! Get out of this room!" It almost aches to move. Maybe she's right. I've probably been in one position for so long my body isn't used to moving anymore.

"I cannot even watch my shows when you are like this

next to me on the couch huh! It ruins the mood. I want to enjoy the things I watch, not watch you like this."

My mom leaves my room after she pushes me one more time off the bed. Forcing myself into the restroom the shower helped a bit with getting my muscles warmed up and moving again.

Coming out of my childhood room turned into a guest room, I see everyone working on the wedding and I feel a pang in my chest again. Dammit, it hasn't gone down one bit. What if she doesn't even want me anymore?

"Walao eh. Oh my god, Akmal is still alive."

"Very funny Sakinah."

"Don't be rude la, Sakinah. You keep going to university then you find a good man to marry. Don't find one that makes problems like your brother." Am I the one making problems?

"Are you alright? What happened? Where is Vero?" Hasanah, ever the civil and calm one. How does she do it? This house is already getting to me.

"Hidaya! Make some rice huh!" Just another day for my mother it seems.

"I don't know. I'm sure she's okay." Am I sure?

"Haiyo, my son. You need to go fix this and make sure you marry her huh. We are almost done with the wedding plans already." Can I fix this? What if I messed it all up and the wedding gets canceled?

I can still see her face in my mind, the way her hands feel on my skin. The way she would hold me at night like it's the best thing in the world for her. Her smiles light up my fucking world every time she turns them to me. The way her beautiful lips would tilt up just the slightest when she's thinking of doing something she shouldn't.

How did I survive without those things? I guess the

saying is right, you never know what you have until it's gone. Fuck, did I mess up?

A hand slaps the back of my head hard, knocking me out of my thoughts.

"Ow, what was that for?"

"For you being stupid right now. If you do not fix this you can move home and I will find someone for you to marry so this wedding does not go to waste. Then you can go to work with your bapa huh. I don't want a lazy son la."

"Walao eh." She slaps me upside the head again when she hears me say oh shit. Rubbing the back of my head, I think I just got the kick in the ass I needed to get me out of this stupor. I just got myself out of a constricting nine-to-five job, I don't want to be thrown into another.

And she's right. I am being stupid. I do need to fix this mess I created.

"Aye it's okay huh. Your bapa will not mind having you under his thumb at work. Less work for him." Ah crap. No. No no no no. I can already feel the metaphorical ball and chain being put on me with this conversation.

I fucking miss Vero. She's always been a breath of fresh air. The one to just ask me about me, the things that make me tick. Man, I've been stupid. How long have I been here?

"You've been here two days Akmal. I think it's time for you to go and fix this thing with your wife." Hasanah, reading my mind. Shit, two whole days? Where did the time go? I feel like I just fell asleep.

Rubbing my hand down my face as I sit on my parents' couch, I try to figure out the best way to approach this situation. Will she want me back? Will she be pissed?

...Is she even going to be there when I go back?

Fuck, the thought of her gone has me scrambling to grab my wallet and keys, running out the door.

~

VERO

There's no more ice cream in the house, and now I'm crying all over again. I'm still too embarrassed to call Atsuko and tell her of my failures. It was my fault, my past caught up with me and now I'm not even sure if I'm single or still engaged.

I tried calling Akmal a million times but it just goes straight to voicemail. Am I really that bad of a person, to not want to even talk to me?

I probably shouldn't be here. He probably wants me gone. He hasn't been home for two days and I'm still just as lost.

Do I go home? I don't have an apartment anymore. Where is there for me to go? I can't crash at Atsuko's place, three's a crowd and I don't think I can stand watching them happy together when my world is burned to the ground.

So here I am, crying all over Akmal's pillow again because it smells like him and I'm pathetic and miss the bastard like I've never missed anything before. To be honest, I think this heartbreak is exponentially worse than the one I had at eighteen. Fuck, I feel so low. I'm too much of a hot mess right now to even consider leaving the house.

What's the point of leaving anyway?

Dammit, I feel like I'm going in circles as my mind gets flushed into the realm of negativity. Closing my eyes, I can see Akmal's handsome face and the way he always looks out for me, making sure I'm alright. The way Akmal looks like we're both fighting this thing between us but wanting to give in anyway.

I miss him. It hurts.

It hurts *so fucking bad*. My sobs are getting louder again

and no matter how hard I shove a fist at my chest, it doesn't dull the ache I feel. How can my heart feel like it's getting squeezed when no matter how hard I try, I can't scratch it out of me?

No one told me love was supposed to hurt like this.

The bed is shaking from my wracking sobs and this pillow is getting so damn wet. I should wash it, but then it wouldn't smell like him anymore.

Another loud sob escapes my lips without meaning to and suddenly I feel warm arms wrap around me tightly.

Now my mind is going insane. *It hurts.* Don't do this to me God. Don't play with me. I've lost everything already, don't let me lose my mind too.

When the feeling of facial scruff rubs against my neck, I open my eyes. My mind can't be that good and gone, can it?

Turning and hoping I don't see thin air, I take a harsh intake of breath when Akmal's face is right next to mine. At least I think it's him. My vision is too blurred by my tears.

Letting out another sob, I turn completely to bury my face against his chest and embrace him tightly in case he decides to leave me again. I can't. I just can't. If he leaves me again, I'm going to swear off all men and join a damn convent.

My pussy takes that moment to mentally slap me. Okay, I might be getting a little over dramatic but dammit!

"Ak-Akmal -" *hiccup* "Y-you came back to me. I'm so sorry!" I don't care whose fault it is, I just don't want to be apart anymore. I need him, I feel so lost without him.

"Shhh...shhh...I'm so sorry Vero. I was stupid. I was stupid." His arms band around me tighter at the same time mine does to him.

Look at us. I don't even know what the hell is going on anymore but it feels right to be in his arms again.

His hands cradle my face but I don't want him to see what a hot mess I am, so I bury myself deeper into his chest. Through the snot and the hiccups, I'm still able to take a deep breath in and smell Akmal as it seeps into my very pores.

I showered this morning but I'm sure he doesn't want to see me like this. But his hands are applying more force to bring my head up. Letting out a sigh, I submit to his request and when his eyes land on mine, I can feel fresh tears streaming down my cheeks.

"Vero, I'm sorry. I'm just... not used to feeling all of this."

"I'm sorry for making you feel like you had to leave me. I still want us to be together, Akmal. You're the only one I've ever wanted." I sound like a desperate and pathetic woman but I don't care. I *am* desperate for him. My mind is telling me to just say the words out loud. That it's probably the reason why he hasn't felt my devotion to this, to us.

I'm so scared.

"You didn't do anything wrong. I'm just...I don't know. I just know I can't live without you and the thought of you possibly leaving me for something better makes me want to claw my heart out. I don't think I could ever take it if it were to happen and so I ran, like the coward I am. I just didn't want to see you not wanting me anymore."

My fists are now punching his chest with this ludicrous line of thinking he's spewing at me! *You know why he feels this way, Vero. You never told him. Never reassured him.* I know! I know dammit, but the last time I told someone, it almost ruined me.

But look at me now, I'm already ruined, aren't I? My hands stop punching as I try to blink away the tears so I can see his face clearly. He looks just as vulnerable as I am, lying on his side, watching me with anticipation.

We're two peas in a fucking pod, both afraid the other is going to leave. How did we get here?

When his thumb brushes away my latest tear falling, I finally give myself the kick in the ass I needed.

"Akmal, I love you. You're the only one for me, don't ever think anything else." His thumb stops stroking and I can't read his expression. His breathing is becoming erratic, but so has mine. Please don't leave me hanging like this with my heart on my sleeve. Please don't crush it.

Akmal presses his forehead against mine and I close my eyes and brace myself for the rejection that I know is coming. I should have never pushed him these past few days. I should have never done that because now he's done with the frustration. He's done with me. I'm a hot mess. I'm making his peaceful life a hot mess.

"Vero, you've been the only one for me. I felt so deeply about stupid things and reacted like an idiot because...I'm stupidly in love with you. I can't even control myself around you. I can't even get a handle on my thoughts. My every waking dream is with you in it, don't ever think otherwise."

It takes a moment for his words to sink in, for the walls I've already started to build up to slowly be taken down again.

Did I just hear him correctly?

"You love me?"

When the feel of his lips reaches mine, I open my eyes to see him staring right back at me. It's a chaste kiss, but one that knocks me right in the gut.

"I love you, Vero."

I don't know who this woman is right now but I'm launching myself into Akmal's chest again as a fresh new wave of tears and sobs come out of me like someone fucking died.

I guess someone did die. The old me who would have never taken the chance, the old me who didn't want to put her heart out there anymore.

And you know what, I don't miss the old me because she didn't have Akmal.

~

I was so much of a hot mess, Akmal had ushered me into the shower, telling me that he needed to wash the shirt I had on, the one he left behind on the bed. I didn't smell that bad, I mean… well, I didn't wash the shirt for two days because I wanted it to smell like him.

After a hot shower, I came out to find Akmal had already placed a set of clothing on the restroom sink for me. This is why I'll never find another man like him. He knows just what to do to make me feel better.

It seems he's a fan of my tank tops and panties after all because that's all he left behind. There was no way in hell he was going to leave my side tonight, not after what I've been through.

I come out of the restroom to find Akmal changing the sheets on the bed. I join in and we both perform the simple task in silence. But this isn't like that last time, there isn't the same tension but more of a feeling of relief.

We both climb into bed once we're done and come together like we're two magnets that have found each other again. I lay my head on his naked chest as his arm wraps around me tightly, pulling me against his side. I've missed this.

I must have been exhausted from all the crying jags I've had because the next thing I know my eyes are closing and all I hear is the sounds of his heartbeats beneath me.

Something wakes me up. I'm not sure what it is. Is it the light peeking in through the curtains? Something heavy is on top of me and my body comes to life. It's like it knows just how to respond.

Warm hands are running across my exposed belly. It feels good and it makes me hum in appreciation. A body is being pressed up against my side and I can feel he's happy to see me. I don't know if Akmal is asleep and dreaming but I'm afraid to break the spell. I kind of feel like we're still on fragile glass around each other despite having made up from our fight. Was it a fight? I don't even know. I'm just glad it's over now.

I've missed him so much.

I'm still drowsy and languidly enjoying any of the touches he gives me when I feel his body cover mine a little more. I like this, this is nice. I feel like a cat that wants to force their body against someone for more touches.

When his hand pulls my tank top down my legs start to scissor. Oh my. I think Akmal is being naughty and I'm too afraid to push anything in case he decides it's too much and makes us stop.

His hand starts to slowly caress the side of my exposed boob and it makes me melt. It feels so good. I feel like I haven't had sex in a million years and everything is overly sensitive now. Is this the stopped-up horny-chemical's fault? Is it going to make all his touches extra explosive?

When he climbs on top of me fully, I open my eyes in surprise only to see his head go down and take my nipple in his mouth. Holy shit. It's so warm.

I moan when he gives me a particularly hard suck and my hands automatically thread in his hair to keep him there in case he plans to stop before I'm ready. His other hand is already pulling down my other strap, exposing my breasts completely and the cool air sends goosebumps on my skin, making my nipples hard.

I force his hand to my other breast and make him squeeze it hard. Fuck, the things this man does to me and we haven't even had sex yet.

Akmal seems to be on some sort of roll this morning because after a nip, he removes his mouth with a pop and trails his tongue across my chest to the other nipple. Holy hell on a stick. This mother fucking tease is going to make me internally combust right here between the sheets. Speaking of sheets, it's getting too hot in here. My legs widen to bring him closer to me and my hand tries to push away the sheet covering us, resulting in me getting side tracked when my fingers skim over his ass that's currently flexing against me.

"Shit, bite me Akmal." And he does. Damn, this boy can take direction. Where have you been all my life?

His cock is still covered by his boxers but he's pushing against me like it's going to catch on fire anyway. The fabric brings a whole other level of friction against my lady bits as my hips start to thrust against his. His mouth doesn't let up, and soon I feel like my nipples are getting chapped from how much he's sucking, licking, biting and playing with them. The tinge of pain with the pleasure he's giving me is taking me to another level because I feel like I'm getting close to exploding.

I've been letting him lead, afraid to scare him off but I'm too lost in the moment. Both my hands travel down the dip of his back and grab his ass, forcing him to thrust against me harder as I thrust against him.

It hits me like a freight train, making my body shudder and my head push back against the pillow in ecstasy.

"Oh my god." It comes out as whisper and plea all at once. He's got the magic touch. I've never been this easy before.

My hips are still thrusting against him, riding the waves when I feel his cock getting even harder as he continues to rub against me. His mouth pops off my nipple and he buries his face in between my breasts right as he lets out a sexy groan. The warmth that spreads between our clothes tells me he found his release as well.

Cradling him to me, I don't want this moment to end. My hand slowly pets his back up and down as we descend from our mutual high.

What a way to start the day.

15

"**W**hat the hell? Why didn't you call me Vero? I could have been there with you!"

"I know, it's just. I was processing, okay. Plus, everything is okay now." Akmal leans over to kiss me on the shoulder from behind and my heart melts into a puddle of goo. He's been more touchy since our little mishap and morning make up session.

I'm finding I really like this side of him.

"Well, as long as you're okay...are you? You know I'm always here for you girl."

"I know, it's just - it was something we both needed to handle. But thank you, Atsuko. I know you're always here for me. That's why I love you." With the word still floating around, I turn my head to watch Akmal open the fridge, shirtless, and look for breakfast. He really is quite a specimen. His smooth tan skin does things to me, reminding me what it felt like this morning when he covered my body with his.

I barely register what Atsuko is talking about when I catch his eye as he straightens back up. We're always like this, searching for each other even when we're in the same room. He gives me a tender expression before he smiles at me and I mouth 'I love you' to him.

His smile gets even wider as he takes steps towards me and pushes the phone out of my hand to give me a scorching kiss on the lips.

"Vero! Vero! Are you listening to me? This bitch right here." Atsuko's voice sounds tiny and far away on the phone's speaker while Akmal continues to move his soft lips against me, dominating my mouth with his wicked tongue, until I'm breathless. He gives me a peck at the end and whispers 'I love you' against my lips before going back to make his breakfast with the items he took out.

Fanning myself a bit, I take a deep breath before bringing the phone back to my ear. "What? What did I miss? And fuck you too bitch, I heard that."

Atsuko is laughing her ass off because she's been the same since meeting Mat. All lovey dovey and shit around me. Well, now I have my own man to be lovey dovey around. The thought makes me want to giggle like a damn school girl even though I'm way past the age.

"Alright you lovebirds. I forgive you. Are you ready for tomorrow? I cannot believe Akmal's family is deciding to make it a double wedding. I mean, it takes a lot of pressure off my back but it's kind of weird, you know?"

"Is it? From what it looks like to me, Mat is like a son to them. I'd be surprised if they didn't offer to make it a double."

"You're right. But still weird. I'm just happy to be able to spend the day with you. Our special day, together. Who would have thought?"

"I know exactly what you mean."

"Alright, this is our last day being single. I say we go shopping and get some hot and sexy lingerie to blow the boys' minds. Maybe throw in a garter belt and stockings while we're at it. You know, make them work for it."

I laugh at that. "That sounds like a wonderful plan. When do you want to leave?"

"I'll be ready in thirty minutes. Meet you at your place?"

"Sounds good. We'll let the boys get their bromance on while we're out shopping."

"Haha, perfect. See you then."

"Bye, Atsuko." Ending the call, I scan the room looking for Akmal. He's walking around the living room looking for something.

"What are you looking for?"

"I don't remember where I put my phone."

"Did you leave it somewhere?" His eyes have a faraway look and suddenly he snaps his fingers.

"Yeah, I did. Are you going somewhere with Atsuko?"

"Yup. Girl stuff. Shopping."

"Okay, well have fun."

"You and Mat should hang out, it might take a while."

"Oh, alright. But I don't have my phone. Can you call him for me?"

"Oh right." Calling Atsuko back, I tell her what's going on and hand the phone to Akmal as Mat comes on the line.

"Yeah, I probably left it at my parents' house. Can you swing by and pick it up for me? Sweet. I guess we're hanging out since the girl's got the day planned. Sounds good. See you soon." He hands me the phone and gives me a peck on the lips while I turn to go towards the bathroom to get ready.

The slap on the ass makes me squeal and turn to find Akmal giving me a boyish grin. *Just you wait, baby boy. I'm going to blow your mind tomorrow.*

~

"Oh my god, the boys are going to die when they see these."

"That's the plan, Atsuko. At least you can jump on your man whenever you want. I've been dying a little each day with how much we keep trying to hold ourselves back. I cannot wait for tomorrow."

Slipping in the key to unlock the door, we come in to find the boys on the floor in front of their laptops with headsets on.

"Shit, watch out behind you."

"Damn, he almost got me. Thanks bro."

Atsuko and I look at each other with a smile. They can be so cute sometimes.

"Boys, we're home!" Akmal is the first to look our way. How he can hear me with that headset on, I have no idea. But the moment he sees me is the moment he takes it off and disengages himself from whatever he was doing. My heart swells at the full attention he always gives me. It makes me preen like a little bird.

Mat watches as Akmal leaves and sees Atsuko waiting. He does the same and comes to her side.

"What did you get?" Mat and his naughty hands are already trying to peek in Atsuko's bag when she slaps his hand away.

"No peeking! Come on, let's go home so these two can get ready for the big day tomorrow. We have to get ready too."

Mat throws Atsuko a sheepish smile and turns towards Akmal to do his bromance hug for a goodbye.

"I'll see you two tomorrow! Rest up!"

Atsuko looks at Mat over her shoulder and giggles as they leave. I have a feeling they won't be getting that much rest whatsoever.

Once Akmal closes the front door, I walk to our bedroom to put away my shopping bag. Yup, *our room* because he can't kick me out now. I'm too addicted and too clingy. One room away is just too damn far. Plus we'll be married tomorrow anyway.

Akmal is following me around trying to get a peek in the bag when I turn to shove his shoulder and laugh. I swear, these guys can be so naughty.

"Hang out with me?"

"Where else am I going to be? I'm at home with my man. You're not escaping my company that easily." Akmal hugs me from behind and nuzzles my neck. He's so damn sweet.

"I like it when you call me your man."

"Yeah?"

"But I think I'd love it even more when you get to call me your husband." He nips my neck and slaps my ass before walking out to the living room. My god. Who is this man?

"Oh and Vero?"

Once the shopping bag is hidden away deep inside his closet, behind some other things, I answer. "Yeah?"

"Make sure you pack a bag."

"Why? What for?"

"I just have a feeling. Trust me." Huh, okay then.

16

VERO

What the hell is going on? There are so many moving parts, I'm lost in the sauce, caught in the tornado of Akmal's family and relatives. Akmal told me to send Atsuko the message last night that Saturday, today, will be an early day. We were both so excited we woke up before our alarms anyway. We got here basically at the buttcrack of dawn.

The moment I stepped into his parents house was the moment I realized that a Malaysian wedding is much much different from what I'm used to seeing. Clothes of various colors everywhere and a whirlwind of women all over the place getting things ready. I swear I hear someone mention something about thrones. The house has been converted to a place of ceremony.

The girls are all over Atsuko and I, hands every which way and the next thing you know, we're both dressed in layers and layers of fabric that covers us from head to toe, a soft and flowy hijab accompanied by a small crown on our heads. *Wow.* I kind of feel like a princess from far away lands. I'm not even sure about the actual color of the outfit but there is a mix of soft peach and pinks on me. The embroidery I do see, adds another layer of elegance that makes my heart skip a beat.

This is really happening.

I turn to look at Atsuko and she is in something of a berry red color. It looks amazing against her skin. Atsuko and I were able to do our own wedding makeup and the outfits just took it to another level. I'm impressed with what Akmal's aunts were able to make in such a short period of time.

"Sakinah! Take the girls to do berinai. Your cousin Aryani is already set up."

Atsuko and I look at each other. What in the world is berinai?

"Come on, let's go before my mother remembers something else to put you through. The quicker we get through it, the quicker we get to the actual wedding ceremony." Sakinah is ushering us with quick steps despite her five-foot-three frame.

"Sakinah, what is berinai? Should we be scared?"

She laughs as we continue to weave through all the people here. She brings us to a table with a very friendly Malay woman sitting there ready for us. She has this fat looking pen in her hand. At least, I think it's a pen.

"Berinai is henna. Your continued beautification for your wedding day. You'll love it." Oh, henna. Wow, okay, I'm down with that.

Atsuko goes first and I'm mesmerized by the talent this girl has with her henna pen. Beautiful black swirls and decorations of floral arrangements adorn Atsuko's hands and wrist by the time she's done. Her fingertips are coated with solid black, giving it a slightly gothic feel. It is so beyond beautiful and elegant that my heart wants to burst for her. I'm so happy we were able to do this together.

When it's my turn, I notice the girl change out her pen.

"Why do I need a different pen?"

"Oh, because red will be more beautiful on you and go better with your dress." *Oh.*

The feel of the pen on me and the way her wrist movements flow is mesmerizing. She has a talent that makes it look effortless, and floral designs start to grow along the back of my hand and wrist almost as if by magic. When she starts to color my fingertips in solid red, my heart begins to beat a little harder thinking of what Akmal would say about the way I look in my wedding attire.

Thoughts of Akmal and all the days we've spent together come back to my mind.

"You look beautiful in anything you wear, Vero."

I'm so excited to get this day over with so that I can finally show Akmal how much he means to me. He's seen me at my highest when we first met: my allure, my sensuality, and my confidence. He's seen me at my lowest, when I thought we were going to end. The man I gave my heart to gave me his heart and enough love to put my broken pieces back together.

"I'm stupidly in love with you. I can't even control myself around you. I can't even get a handle on my thoughts. My every waking dream is with you in it, don't ever think otherwise."

How did I get so lucky?

When Akmal's cousin is done, I bring my hands up to admire her handiwork. My gosh. It's the most beautiful thing I've ever seen.

I don't even remember what else happens in the preparation process until the moment my eyes land on Akmal. He's in what I assume to be Malaysian groom attire, a high collared long sleeve top in colors that match my own, with a black hat on top of his head. It's his face that keeps me transfixed as I walk into the room with what looks like a throne waiting for me. *So this is what the girls were talking about.* The flowers and decorations that surround us make everything seem surreal.

But it's the tender expression and one of awe that graces his face that makes me blush, and I can't recall a time that I've been like this. At thirty-three years old, I'm beyond these types of embarrassments, but it seems Akmal has the power to bring them out of me again.

The ceremony goes by in a chaotic blur for me as two weddings are happening at the same time. I can't even hold Akmal's hand for comfort as he sits to my right on the throne. My eyes cast to my BFF's side. Mat's Malaysian attire matches Atsuko's berry red, contrasting his skin tone nicely. They look happy and overly in love. I wonder if Akmal and I look like that?

My heart is still beating erratically from the moment I placed the wedding band on his hand and the moment he places the band on mine. This is it. We're legit. Akmal is finally my husband.

I never realized how tiring sitting around can be until what feels like the hundredth visitor taking pictures with us. Thank goodness for low heels, but my ass is starting to get sore and I'm really starting to get exhausted. I wonder if we get some sort of break time between these visits with the guests? I don't even know ninety percent of the people here. I think I see my family lost in the sea of Asian faces. A few of my relatives too.

Akmal tells me that we *do* indeed get a break and that we're allowed a private bedroom somewhere in the back. Oh, thank heavens. I don't know how long I can sit like a statue up here on this throne. When we reach the back room, I finally let myself relax and let out an exasperated sigh. Damn, who knew Malaysian weddings took this long?

I think Atsuko and Mat were ushered to a different room but I'm glad to get any sort of reprieve from these wedding etiquettes I have to keep up. I'm laying back here on the bed with my eyes closed when I feel warm hands bringing my skirt up.

What is my naughty boy up to now?

"Let me help you relax." *Oh my god*. Is he serious right now? What if someone hears us?

His warm hands push my skirt up over my hips and suddenly a very hot and wet mouth is hovering near my inner thigh. It's such a contrast to the cool air across the rest of my exposed skin. A shiver runs down my spine at the way Akmal has started to come out of his shy shell. *Who is this man right here?*

I'm thinking he's probably just going to tease me when I feel his fingers push my panties aside and a tongue enters my center. *Holy shit*. A whimper escapes me and Akmal nips my inner thigh again to remind me that we're still at the wedding with thousands of people around us outside this little private room. Having to force my lips closed as his mouth tentatively explores my folds and clit makes the moment even more erotic than it already is.

"Vero, you taste so good."

That mouth of his. I can't control my body's reactions when he starts to cover the hood of my clit with his mouth. My hips are already undulating towards his face, silently asking for more as my hands creep to the back of his neck to try and not mess up his hair while still pulling him closer to me. The way his hands start to push my legs apart makes me gasp at his small show of dominance.

"Oh my god."

"Shhh…" That wicked tongue of his is still going to town as he whispers against my pussy to be quiet.

Akmal starts to really pay attention to my responses because soon his mouth and tongue are concentrating on my clit like a champ while his thumb is grazing against my very wet and probably swollen pussy lips. I can feel the tension start to build up, my movements are losing any sort of rhythm it initially had.

Akmal surprises me when he silently crawls up my body to cover my mouth with one of his hands while his other takes over where his mouth left off. The little intermission in his movement didn't stop my internal climb as my body shudders when his thumb does something wicked down there and my cries are muffled behind his hand. Akmal's eyes are sparkling as they watch me enraptured in the climax high, still riding the waves as his thumb continues it's torturous swirl around my sensitive areas. The grin spreading across his face makes me want to fuck his brains out but we still have to wait until the wedding is over.

This bastard is trying to kill me, trying to drown me in a pool of want and need.

And it's working too.

17

VERO

 $\mathcal{I}$ didn't realize there would be a second half to this wedding. Good lord. After some more sitting around and taking pictures with random folks, the wedding party had to get changed again. Now we're in something white with beautiful embroidered embellishments.

As I sit here on the throne with Akmal, I keep catching him peek at me.

After a few pictures and smiles, I turn to my right and mouth 'what?'

Who are these people and why does it seem like we can never get to the end of these damn pictures?

"Nothing." Is that so?

I look to the other throne and can practically see Atsuko internally groaning as well with all these guests.

When Akmal tells me we're allowed another break, I almost run for it but stop myself because I don't want to embarrass him. That would look really bad, right? Girl in white, running for her life away from a wedding crowd.

We're back in the same room and I do let out a groan then. "Akmal, this is crazy. I love you and all, but man, there is *a lot* of Malaysian folks out there. How many more pictures do we need to take?"

He lets out a masculine chuckle and goes to stand by the bed. I need a distraction. I don't want to think about the rest of the night sitting on that damn throne like a princess statue.

Before he can make up his mind, I walk up to Akmal and get on my knees before him. His eyes widen and I can see his hands wanting to push me away but he's not going to, not after I get my mouth on him. My hands go under his top to find...*nice*, an elastic waistband to his pants. In one swoop, I have his pants down to his ankles and am face to face with an already semi-hard cock.

He wanted this too. The sneaky bastard.

Gripping his cock in my hand, I'm entranced by the henna at the back of my hand against the tan skin of his cock. But time is of the essence and I have a mission to make this man fall to his knees.

With a lick up the slit of his opening, I can hear him groan under his breath as his cock starts to become much harder, and much, much bigger. Teasing the head with the tip of my tongue, I flatten it under his shaft right before taking him into my mouth. I love the way he tastes. Like a damn forbidden fruit because we shouldn't be doing this right now but hell if we're going to stop.

Giving him a low hum so as to not expose us, Akmal's dick twitches in my mouth. I guess he likes that. Shit, I like it too. I love the way he responds to my mouth taking him in deeper and deeper.

When my mouth reaches the end of his shaft in a slow glide, I swallow and preen at the fact that there's some lipstick stains against his skin. When I swallow again, Akmal groans a little too loudly. Pulling back, I whisper 'shhhh' to the head of his cock before taking him in again and again.

I can taste the precum on the next glide, letting my tongue play with his slit one more time before going in for the kill. Taking him as deep as I can, my other hand plays with his balls as I make my throat swallow. He starts growing in girth and I think I can feel his hand softly behind my hijab as his hips twitch and his cock spurts jets of cum down my throat, which I eagerly take in. Can't leave any evidence now, can we?

When his dick slows down in his climax, I start bobbing my head again to make sure I clean him up before putting him back in his pants. Nothing can be done about the ring of red lipstick against his skin now. Oh well. Sorry not sorry.

When I stand back up, Akmal grabs me and nuzzles against the layers of fabric at my neck. I love it when he's like this.

"Good lord, I can't wait until this day is over. I can't even touch or kiss you in case your makeup gets messed up and people start to question what's going on." His hands are roaming the back of my neck and my ass, only serving to make me hotter than I already am. These layers of fabrics aren't helping either.

When our break is up, I quickly find Atsuko to see where I can find lipstick to reapply. She gives me the look, telling me she knows exactly what we've been doing and we both giggle together under our breath as we try to fix the issue before anyone else notices.

Once we're back at our thrones, I'm trying hard not to rub my legs together. I'm so worked up. Fanning myself between taking pictures, I look around to see if my family is having a good time. My parents are talking to Akmal's parents and no one's yelling, so that's good. Some of my aunts and uncles are mingling well, lots of smiles.

Scanning the room a few more times, I notice I can't find my damn brother anywhere. Where the hell could he be?

SAKINAH

After the stress of this morning, I'm very glad this wedding is going well. Everyone looks happy, especially my brother. I've never seen him so happy like this. I wonder what my wedding would be like? Would I find a man that looks at me the way Akmal looks at Vero? Like she is his world. Just the thought of all the Malay boys I've been around has my stomach turning. Ugh. Just no. Sometimes I fear that anyone I might be interested in would be related to me somehow, someway.

The guests are finishing up their meal and so that gives me a break from the rush. Walking outside, I take a deep breath of much needed air, closing my eyes and just letting the cool breeze blow against my skin. It feels wonderful and refreshing after being in that hot kitchen.

"Sakinah."

I startle at the sound of my name in such a deep voice, a voice I've been trying to avoid all day. Turning around, I see Fabian looking at me with something devilish in his eyes. There's no other way to describe it, with the aura he always gives off. He's trouble on two legs, I know it, but it doesn't stop my feminine fantasies from coming to life, though I don't let it show on my face. Guys like him don't need any more of an ego boost, he has plenty of it with the way he swaggers.

"Fabian."

"That's it? Just Fabian? No - where have you been? Hey, sorry I didn't get to come by and say hello?" I give him a small smile. He's fishing. No, I'm not sorry I didn't go by to look for him. I wouldn't want anything to happen that might embarrass my family or my brother on his big day.

He chuckles at my silence. "Like that huh? I thought we were past this 'strangers' stage Sakinah."

"So you say. What are you doing out here? Wouldn't your family be looking for you? You should be mingling with the crowd."

"I am mingling. With the only girl I've been looking for all day." My heart skips a beat. Is he serious? He's been looking for *me* all day? I can't let him see me weak. Guys like him would pounce on that and use it to their advantage. My mouth still tingles at the thought of his kiss - my first kiss.

"Well you've found me. Did you need something?"

"Well, for one, since we're basically family now, how about we exchange numbers in case of emergencies." Emergencies, my ass. The only emergency I see happening is this guy getting himself into some sort of trouble. Do I really want to be involved in that?

Watching the way his biceps flex against his button-down long sleeve top that looks too small for his large frame as he reaches the back of his pants to grab his phone, my body's saying yes, yes I would. But my mind is telling me to stay away from Fabian Hernandez and his steel grey eyes with lips that are much too soft to be true.

I don't have my phone with me, so I just put my number into his when he passes it to me. Once I'm done, I leave him there, standing without another word.

"Okay, be like that. What can I do to make you give me a genuine smile my way?" He's sending me a cocky grin that would make any woman's panty melt. He really shouldn't be that good looking.

"How many times has that line worked on the other girls?" Fabian puts his hand over his heart like I've wounded him and I laugh at how ridiculous he looks. This shouldn't make me like him more than I already do.

"Come on, don't be like that Sakinah."

"Like what, Fabian? Like a girl who wants to make sure you have the best of intentions? Don't be perasan la."

"I do have the best of intentions. And what does that mean?"

"Don't flatter yourself." He chuckles and it's the most masculine sound.

Looking him up and down, the man is walking sin. And now he's a liar.

"No, you don't."

"Alright, alright." His masculine chuckle sends shivers down my body. It's a good thing I have so many layers on, he probably didn't notice. "I may not be the perfect guy but I can be good. How about friends then, hmm? Surely we can be friends?"

Is he really asking me this? Especially after stealing that kiss from me in my own home. Now I'm kind of upset with how easily he gave up on chasing me. Am I just a passing game for him? Well, you know what? Screw him. I knew I shouldn't leave my guard down around a bad boy like Fabian.

"Yeah, we can be friends." No, I really don't want to be friends.

He smiles even wider, causing cute wrinkles to show up at the corner of his eyes, transforming his face into something that would stop any woman's heart. I can't do this. Turning abruptly without a goodbye, I leave him there as I walk back into the mingling wedding crowd.

Some of my brother's university friends are standing around and chatting. Walking by I make sure to give them my greetings and show a friendly face to the crowd.

"Sakinah, is that you? Wow, you've changed since the last time I saw you. You've grown into a beautiful woman. Is that why Akmal doesn't talk much about his -" I'm blushing at the compliment and turned confused at why his sentence got cut off. His eyes are looking over my shoulder and so I do the same.

Fabian is standing behind me, grey eyes blazing down at Bisaam. What is wrong with him? I give him a frown but he's still not looking at me.

I can hear Bisaam clearing his throat, so I turn and give him and the guys around him what I hope is an apologetic expression.

Slapping Fabian's chest with the back of my hand, I clear my throat as well to get his attention. Once his eyes are on me, I mumble, "Can I speak with you outside?"

His eyes give Bisaam one more glare before he follows me back out the way we came. Rude, much? How embarrassing.

When the door closes, I twirl around and give it to him. "What is wrong with you?"

"What do you mean what is wrong with me?"

"You're supposed to be acting like a friend, isn't that what we agreed upon?" We're alone out here, letting me raise my voice a little more than I would if we were inside.

"I am. I just wasn't liking the way that guy was staring at *my friend.*"

"Who does that? Look, if you can't control this -" My

hands are waving in front of him to indicate all of him. "-friendship, then maybe we shouldn't be friends."

"Don't be like that Sakinah."

"Like what?"

"Nobody should be looking at you like that."

"Why not? What if I like the way they look at me? What if I'm looking for a husband huh? Why are you blocking my chances at finding someone?"

Fabian growls and it does something to me. I feel a little excited, my face flaming a little but I'm not going to show him that I'm affected. Not with the way he's acting like I'm not worth the chase and yet I can't get compliments either? He can't have it both ways.

"Don't say that shit to me Sakinah." What is wrong with this guy?

"I don't even know what you're talking about. I'm twenty-five and my mother has already been hounding me about finding someone so I can make babies for her before I'm past my prime. Might as well get started. Plenty of men around at this wedding. It's the perfect opportunity." Am I fishing and being petty? Maybe.

We've been turned away from each other slightly during this entire ridiculous conversation. What is up his ass? He's the one that basically told me he wasn't interested.

Chancing a glance at him, I see Fabian turn his blazing molten gaze at me right before he pushes me up against the wall, grabs my face in his hands and kisses me. Oh, this kiss is nothing like the one he stole the other day, not at all. This one is dominant, and quite frankly a little scary. His lips and mouth are coaxing something from me and I don't know how to respond. This is not like the movies where you think you want it. This is so much more *intense*. I open my mouth to try and tell him to stop when his tongue takes the opportunity to invade. The moment our tongues touch is the moment his hard grip on my face softens and one of his hands travels down to rest at my neck, encasing it in its warmth. I shouldn't like how this feels. I shouldn't like how his tongue expertly glides against mine, making me curious where this can lead.

I should be scared. I shouldn't let him put me in this position. *I'm being too easy.* He just told me he wanted to be friends. What the hell? Is this how he treats all his female friends? The thought kind of pisses me off and sobers me enough to allow me to shove at his shoulders and give him a slap on the face before turning to go back inside.

18

VERO

I've been told that Akmal's family has paid for a hotel stay for both wedding couples. How very kind of them. Knowing that fact, now I'm even more antsy to get away from the formalities of this wedding. How long does a Malay wedding go for? Please tell me it's only one day and not multiple.

"Akmal, I'm getting kind of tired."

Akmal gives me a sympathetic look and calls his mother over. He speaks something in Malay and she is nodding her head with a smile towards me. "That is fine, you guys go find your bapa and he will drive you to your hotel room huh. The guests can leave whenever they want, do not worry. We will handle everything."

Oh thank heavens.

Soon both wedding couples are packed into Akmal's

father's vehicle with our bags. I guess Atsuko and I will be in the same hotel.

He drops us off with a smile and says something to Akmal about making lots of babies before leaving. *Geez.* At least you never have to wonder what they're really thinking.

I give Atsuko a hug as we go our separate ways down the hallway. I can already hear Atsuko squealing on the way to her room and it makes me smile. Akmal sticks the key card in the door and once it opens, we're greeted by conditioned air and silence. Perfect.

My husband brings our bags in and is already falling back on the bed with a sigh of relief. I take it upon myself to grab my necessary items before heading to the restroom to change. I'm excited, the day is finally here. All this pent up energy is giving me a second wind as I strip quickly and grab the stuff I bought with Atsuko.

The lace is so beautiful and soft. I really hope he doesn't rip it.

Once my stockings are firmly attached to my garter belt, I take a step back and look at myself in the mirror. Not too shabby. I like it. It looks hot. He better not fucking rip this shit. Well, unless he makes it worth it.

Turning the doorknob, I let the restroom door open by itself to its full extent as I stand there canting my hips to the side for the full sexy effect. With the hijab off my head, I was able to mess my hair a bit to add to the sexed look factor.

Go broke or go home, right?

Akmal is lying on his back in his boxers, relaxing with his arms behind his head, flexing his biceps in the most delicious of ways. When the restroom door hits the wall with a soft thud, Akmal lifts himself partly on his elbows to look at me.

The way his eyes widen and scan me from head to toe is priceless. A look I'll never forget. *All for you, baby.*

"Holy shit…" It's spoken under his breath but I can hear it from where I'm standing and it makes me feel a sense of pride.

Sashaying towards him, Akmal slowly gets up to a sitting position to see me better. I'm loving the way his eyes keep going to my breasts and they start to feel heavy under the lace. The memories of his mouth over my nipples, sucking and biting, makes my pussy tingle and I haven't even reached him yet.

"Did you buy that for me?"

"Yes." Oh what is this coy smile on his face?

"You look fucking beautiful." Hearing those words on his lips never gets old. I've been told I'm attractive before, but the way Akmal says it is so much different.

Giving him a seductive smile, I start crawling over his lap as he starts to lie back down with his hands behind his head in what looks like a relaxed posture. Is he not as pent up as I am right now? Making sure I keep my ass in the air, I slowly rub my lace covered breasts over his chest and trace his jaw with my fingers. He really is too sexy.

"Well, hello…wife."

"Hello, husband." Crawling a little more, I start with a chaste kiss until we're building up the heat that's been stoked since the pre-wedding days. Akmal and I have been at each other for so long, pushing and pulling, that I was starting to think my pussy would explode from the moment he enters me.

Our kisses are soft and coaxing, but soon become hot and heavy in a matter of minutes. What I thought was me seducing him has now become him dominating my mouth with his. *How the hell did he get so good at this?* My body has become lax on top of his, dropping my weight down entirely, as not only his mouth, but also his hands coax me where he needs me to go. I'm internally purring like a damn kitten with how he's petting me and making me pant for more.

I'm drowning in his kiss when suddenly I feel my boobs fall out of my bra, making me gasp. I didn't even feel him unhook the clasp. Without taking his lips off mine, Akmal removes my straps and tosses the bra to the side. His hands return and are all over my breasts, pinching and pulling at my nipples with just the right amount of pressure to make me feel it in my pussy.

Gasping into his mouth once more, Akmal surprises me by flipping me over and settling himself between my legs. *Holy hell, who is this man?* He's grinding into me slowly with his hard cock and my breath stutters with how hot we both feel down there. The friction between his boxers and my lace panties aren't helping one bit.

"Are you a dirty girl, Vero?" *Oh my god.* Akmal loves to kiss and sneak in statements like that between kisses so I can't think straight or respond. When his lips and teeth start to travel across my jaw and down my neck, my body feels strung tight from the day's anticipation. His warm hands are caressing my lace garter belt and panties all the way down to my stocking-clad legs.

Raising both my legs up, I wrap them around him and start to slide them against his hips. His mouth continues to leave a wet trail as he goes lower and lower. Taking my right nipple into his mouth, his hand starts to play with my left. I've never met a man who sucks like he does. It's hard, it's erotic, it's the thin line between pain and pleasure. His teeth will nip, his lips will suck and his tongue will soothe. It's torturous and I can't get enough of it.

When Akmal's mouth travels to my other nipple, my fingers thread through his hair and cradle him to me. I love how he worships my body, like I'm a damn five course meal to be savored. We've probably learned the art of slow seduction and foreplay from all the edging we've been doing since our engagement.

My eyes are closed and taking in all the sensations when I feel him going lower and pulling down the top of my garter belt.

"Fuck, I knew it." His whisper is so soft, I barely caught it. Opening my eyes, I look down at him as the tip of his tongue plays with my belly button ring. I can feel my skin getting goosebumps from the cooling wetness on my breasts, adding another layer of sensation.

Akmal gets up on his knees and I watch as he stares at my center, legs spread eagle for him. He leans in with an arm on the bed and grabs the front of my panties, dragging it back and forth against my swollen pussy lips, making me squirm.

"You have the prettiest pussy I've ever seen." I'm probably the only pussy he's ever seen but it doesn't prevent me from feeling my heart swell with his praise.

"Are you wet for me, Vero?"

"Yes."

"I bet you are. Just look at you. Fuck, I can't believe this is all for me." He's pulling the panties back and forth even harder and it's starting to hit my clit just the right way, making me whimper.

"Open your legs up for me." Shit, how far does he want them to go?

I must not be opening far enough because he rips the lace panties off me, making me yelp from the pain of the snap, and pushes my legs apart with his strong hands right before he dips his head down to lick my pussy. *Dios Mio.*

"I love the way you taste. Always so wet for me." When he hums into my pussy, the vibrations start a climb I'm desperate to chase. How does his tongue do these wicked things to me? Is it because he's become more comfortable with my body and expressing himself? Fuck, that thought turns me on even more.

His fingers are rubbing over my lower lips as his mouth starts to play my clit the same way he sucked and played with my nipples. Shit, he is aggressive and I love it.

"I want your fingers in me."

"Yeah?"

"Yes, please." He groans and sucks my clit even harder after my plea.

"I love the way you say please."

"Please Akmal!"

"Are you a good girl? You've been so bad this whole time." Oh dear lord.

"I've been good."

One finger slowly enters me and I feel like I'm dying, on the precipice of almost there and not quite.

"That feels so good."

"Shit, I can feel you squeezing me. I can't wait anymore." I'm in such a haze of lust that I growl in frustration when he removes his finger and mouth to step out of his boxers. He chuckles as he climbs back on top of me and kisses me again, the taste of me still lingering on his lips. I'm so damn horny, my hands grab his ass and pull him to me.

His shaft starts to slide against my wetness as he drags it up and down a few times.

I'm groaning in frustration again as I grab his cock, the feel of him like velvet steel, and line it up against my pussy. I need him now!

"Fuck." He impales me on his next stroke and just glides in from how wet I am.

"Oh my fucking god." He leans in and tucks his head into the crook of my neck, bringing his hips back to push in again. Fuck! Either he's bigger than I thought or I've gotten tight from the lack of sex.

Kissing the side of his neck, I whisper into his ear. "You feel so good. I'm so damn full."

"Shit, Vero, I'm not even in all the way yet." Holy mother of …

Bringing his hips back he shoves in one final time and buries himself to the hilt, making me feel even more deliciously full to the brim. It's as if something becomes unleashed because Akmal starts pounding me into the bed with stroke after stroke.

His grunts next to my ear make my pussy clench around him, only serving to make him add groans.

"You feel so fucking good, Vero. Hell, I didn't know it would feel like this." I can't concentrate on how his words make me feel when I'm climbing again, chasing an orgasm with the way his hair is rubbing against my clit with every forceful stroke.

I'm so close, so close. His thrusts are becoming faster and faster as we both chase that proverbial cliff to fall over.

"You feel so good." The moment the words leave my mouth is the moment Akmal bites down on my shoulder, starts to grow in size and thrusts deeply into me a few more times before he cums. The way his hips grind deeper into me like he's afraid of slipping out ignites the fire that sends me over the edge with him. Holy shit.

His continued grinds against my oversensitized clit keeps my climax on a high and sends me through aftershocks that rock my fucking world. This has never happened before. I'm almost glad we've been messing around for the past week since his stamina is better than what one would consider for a guy who's never done it before.

He plants his lips on mine and starts to make love to me

with his mouth as he continues to ride the fall of his release, going from deep thrusts to slow and leisurely ones. This man continues to amaze me. How did I get so lucky? This is a first - I feel like my heart is going to burst. My eyes are getting warmer as if they're about to cry.

"I love you, Akmal."

"I love you too." We're kissing like we have all the time in the world when he abruptly pulls his face back, confusing me by his change in demeanor.

"Shit, I didn't pull out. Did you want me to finish in you?" This cute baby right here is looking so sheepish it makes me want to laugh. But I hold it in because I don't want him to feel worse.

Pulling him back towards me for another kiss, I whisper against his lips, "I'm on the pill. I want to feel my husband cum in me."

He groans and whispers back against my lips, "You're such a fucking dirty girl, Vero."

When his cock slips out, I can feel his cum leaking out of me, making me squirm again. Watching the way Akmal stares at how his release is coming out of my pussy is starting to rev me up again. He looks so damn possessive at this moment. When his fingers trail up the mess and shoves back in me, I whimper from the fact that I'm still oversensitized by the recent climax he's given me.

"So fucking dirty…" Biting my lip, I'm excited to see what kind of lover Akmal turns out to be. It's been nothing but surprises so far and my pussy is more than willing to go another round.

19

AKMAL

That was the best experience of my life. I never thought it would be that intense. I was trying to tease her, to hold out, to make it good for her. I know she has more experience than me and I wanted to be able to bring something to the table. With the way she grabbed my cock and shoved it into her, I'd say it went as planned.

Holy hell, the feel of her vagina gripping me is like nothing I've ever known. I think I'm addicted. Watching as my cum leaks out of her pussy does something to me, makes me feel something I haven't felt before. Pride and possessiveness. Fuck, that pussy is finally mine and look how she glistens.

I want to touch her again, but I also don't want to make her uncomfortable. How much is too much? All those days I've caught her in the shower are coming back to me and I like where my mind is going.

Grabbing her hand to pull her off the bed in an embrace, I grab her face and kiss her again. This never gets old. I love the way her soft lips feel against mine.

"Let's go shower."

"Oh, let's … together?" Grabbing her hand and pulling her to the restroom, she doesn't ask any more questions. Turning on the shower head to let it warm up, I start pulling at her lacey outfit, impatiently trying to get her naked as fast as I can. She chuckles at me as she starts the slowest undressing known to mankind. Looking over the beautiful creature that is mine, I notice that she has a tattoo on her right shoulder and another one on her left hip. It's cute and very Vero. A little surprise wrapped up in beautiful clothing.

I need to make sure no one ever sees what she has underneath. The thought of other men looking over her smooth skin makes me want to punch something. Damn, I'm starting to understand Mat's obsession with going to the gym. If this keeps continuing, I'm going to need to do something to exorcise these emotions.

When Vero turns around to bend over and take off her stockings, my dick jumps up at the offering. Damn, her ass is the nicest I've ever seen. Her pussy lips are still glistening with the evidence of what happened earlier, reminding me that I need to get her wet under the spray and wash her body.

She's doing this slow tease again, pretending to take her time to remove the stockings entirely. Grabbing her by the hips I bump my hard cock against her ass to hurry her up. She squeals and I give her a good slap, making her straighten her back. Good. Ushering her into the shower, I slide the door close, step in with my back to the spray and grab her face to kiss her again. She can be such a brat. I know she does this on purpose, killing me slowly.

Maybe she wants to be punished. Maybe that's what I've been missing by not reading her clues. Does Vero want me to put her in her place?

Stepping back, I let the water slide down her chest. Grabbing the soap from behind me, I start to lather my hands and slowly rub it all over her body. She's so fucking beautiful, especially the way she looks at me when I take care of her. I love this look on her. I need to make sure to always keep it there. Her breath hitches when I make sure to go over her breasts a few times, pulling and tugging on her nipples. The water drips down and washes away the suds, making my eyes trail down with it. My fingers trail after them, entranced by the way her abs flex and her breath picks up.

Vero leans into me, pressing her breasts against my chest, and slides her hands up my shoulders right before I take her in another kiss. It's slow, it's steady, unrushed. All the pent up frustration has been worked out of us and now it's just time to explore each other.

My cock is rising fully to attention at the way our bodies glide against each other. I need to feel her again. Pushing her around, I bend her forward, letting her hands hold her against the shower wall as I slide my cock between her legs. It's a different kind of wetness, I understand the difference now and the difference makes me impatient to feel how well I can slip into her pussy. Vero arches her back, silently asking for it. I'm learning to read her now, the way her body responds, the way she moves when she's pushing for more.

Grabbing her hips, I stare at my dick as I slowly thrust into her. Fuck, she's beautiful like this. The way her ass moves when I pound into her. Something inside of me makes me feel a need to mark her. To know that I'll be the only one to see what I leave on her skin. Yes, that's exactly what I'll do.

Slapping her ass, I start pounding into her, leaning

forward on top of her to lick the water off her back. She's moaning and it spurs me on, makes me even harder for her. Grabbing her hair, I tilt her head back and kiss her again as I continue to thrust hard and fast, her wetness giving no resistance to the brutal pace I'm setting.

Squeezing her breasts, I lick the shell of her ear and ask her, "Do you like feeling my cock in you, Vero?"

"Yes."

"Fuck, this pussy belongs to me now."

"Oh my god."

"You're not sleeping tonight, not until I've had enough."

Straightening myself back up, I lift one leg onto the ledge of the shower and start drilling into her. I can feel the tension creeping up my abs and my balls start to tighten as I chase my climax. Vero is moaning louder, the sound of the water coming out of the spray no longer being able to drown out her cries. My grip gets tighter as I fall over that cliff I'm getting addicted to, Vero's pussy taking everything I have to give her.

As my thrusts start to slow, my cock slides out and I turn her around for another languid kiss, washing her under the cold water. She squirms when my fingers slide into her, trying to clean her as best as I can while we're both still in here.

I'm getting sidetracked by the way she pushes her breasts against me again every time my fingers graze her clit. Unable to help myself, I forget to wash her altogether and start to swirl my thumb between her legs as my mouth sucks on the crook of her neck.

It doesn't take long for Vero to reach her peak, her body shivering and her legs giving way. My arms go around her as I cradle her in an embrace, my mouth making love to hers again under the water spray.

Sleeping next to my wife is the same but not. There isn't that push and pull anymore. Now, it's just my wife's beautiful warm body, waiting to be taken.

She squirms in her sleep and I pull her in closer, smelling her, memorizing the moment. *My wife, she's finally mine.* We don't have to be anywhere and it's nice having that burden taken away for the day. This photography job came at just the right time as it allows me to make my own hours to be with her.

I kiss the back of her shoulder, dragging my lips along her smooth skin. I didn't let her get dressed last night before we ended up falling asleep making love with our mouths. Her ass presses against my crotch the more I tease her skin and the morning erection I have is starting to twitch in anticipation of what we might get away with.

Slowly gliding my cock between her legs, I can feel her growing wetness. Her legs are scissoring and her thighs are squeezing my cock, making it grow harder with her movements. We're both lying on our sides, snuggled under the sheets but it's starting to get hot, the air getting thick with what's working up between our legs. My hand trails down her shoulder and arms to toss the sheet off us, letting the cool air of the room try to control the blazing inferno happening right now.

"...Akmal..." I love the way her voice is so breathy and low in the morning.

"Shh...go back to sleep." Lifting her leg, I slide my cock inside. The pressure and heat around my shaft is still something that shocks me everytime. But like a damn addict, I can't help but keep coming back for more. Vero has to have the tightest pussy with the way she takes all of me in her.

With a groan, Vero pushes her ass back, letting me trail my hands down her spine, pushing her back forward so that I can see that delectable ass of hers as I thrust inside. Shit, she's so perfect for me.

It's starting to feel too fucking good to be in this position. Pulling out of her, she cries in protest as I get my knees on the bed and lift her ass to follow. Vero doesn't resist and moans when I take both of my hands and spread her ass for my viewing pleasure. She's so damn wet for me all the time, glistening and waiting for me. The cool air of the room is sending goosebumps along her skin and my hands rub it down with its warmth.

But we can't let her get too relaxed. Vero likes to be a little brat sometimes, just like right now with the way she keeps backing her ass up against me, hoping that I'll impale her again. I shouldn't make this easy for her though. She's been playing my body for a damn week with how she's been teasing me, torturing me slowly.

Squeezing her ass and spreading her cheeks again, I tell her, "Vero, turn around."

She follows commands so well, it makes my dick leak. I bet she loves this.

"Open your mouth." There she goes, following without any sort of protest. In fact, her mouth swallows my dick down so far, I almost cum right there. *Shit, she's too good at this.* The taste of herself on her lips doesn't bother her one bit. She continues with her ministrations and swallows every now and again when my dick is all the way inside to the back of her throat. *Fuck.*

"I love your mouth sucking me. I knew you were dirty, Vero." My hands creep to the back of her head tentatively. I'm not sure how much I can push. In my fantasies, I've been doing such dirty and wrong things to her.

She hums and brings her eyes up to mine. I love this look on her with my dick in her mouth. She worships it like she'll die if she can't do it. It makes my heart swell with love at the moment. My fucking wife, goddam.

It starts to feel really damn good and I don't realize I'm gripping her hair and thrusting into her face but Vero continues to hum in pleasure, sending vibrations down my shaft. I can see the saliva dripping down her chin and I know I want to finish in her mouth. That first night with Vero that changed everything will always play in the forefront of my fantasies.

"Are you going to be a good girl for me, Vero?" She doesn't nod her head but speaks with her eyes instead as her mouth continues to work up and down my shaft, sucking harder at the end in tune with my thrusts.

Damn, just look at her. "That's a good girl, fuck yes, just like that."

Who knew praising her would make her double her efforts. If she keeps this up, I won't last much longer. I groan out loud at one particular swallow when she has my dick down her throat despite her nose being up against my body.

"Shit, if you keep doing that, I'm going to cum in your mouth." She sucks me in deep again, almost making my eyes roll back. "You want that don't you? You want me to cum in your mouth."

When I feel my abs tensing, I try to hold back my climax and start to really shove it down her throat hard. Vero has stopped her momentum and let me take the lead. My grip tightens behind her head, trying to hold onto the smooth strands that are trying to run through my fingers. I can hear myself grunting as my hips hit her lips over and over again. She gags a few times and for some reason that shit just spurs me on even more. *Damn, I'm enjoying that way too much.*

When she whimpers it makes me feel powerful. *I love the way I affect her.* Her hands have come up to hold onto my thighs but she never pushes me back, no. In fact, she's encouraging me to fuck her face harder and faster. Who am I to deny her what she's asking for? In and out, in and out. On a particularly hard thrust she gags again but never pushes me away. Her eyes tear up and it turns me on only because I know she wants this as much as I do.

"Shit, baby. That's a good girl. Take my cock in your throat, just like that." She whimpers again and I can feel my balls tighten. I shove my cock down her throat and hold her face there as I feel my dick pulse and cum, watching how she continues to swallow everything I have to give her. *Fuck.*

When my balls start to empty, I rock slowly into her mouth, letting her savor anything I have left to give. *I love having a wife that swallows.* My hand loosens it's hold on her hair and I pet her face as she continues to lick the head of my cock.

"You're so beautiful, and you're so good to me." She removes her mouth from my cock, pushes it up with her hand and licks the underside like it's fucking ice cream.

"You make me so horny, Akmal." She whispers against my dick, while she continues to lick it clean. My hand continues to pet her and caress her face as she looks up at me from where she kneels.

"Yeah?"

"Yes. I'm so horny. Please." Look at how she begs. I think I can get used to this. She begs so prettily.

"Come here." The excitement in her eyes is hard to miss as I lie on my back, coaxing her to sit on my face. She doesn't disappoint, rubbing her pussy right at my mouth wantonly, not waiting for any more commands.

I love the way she tastes. But I love the way she squirms

over me even more, knowing I hold her pleasure in my hands. Sucking and licking her clit with my tongue, I slide two fingers into her, listening to her gasp above me. Thrusting in and out, Vero starts to move her hips with the motion, seeking more friction. Adding another finger, Vero starts to moan. I can feel her pussy occasionally clamping down on me, hoping for something more, something bigger. All these years pent up must have given me more stamina because my dick is rising to her pussy's call.

Her lower lips are swollen and wet. Removing my fingers, they start to trace a pattern on her pussy opening as my mouth plays with her clit and nips at her hood. I can feel her tense up now and again but I'm feeling a little selfish.

With one last hard suck on her nub, I flip her onto her back and shove my hard cock back into her, pounding her like we're both rushing to win the race. She cries and moans but I want to get deeper. I need to feel more of her around me. Grabbing her thighs, I put both of her legs on my shoulders and lean into the bed and her body to pound into her harder. *That's it, yes. This is the angle.* It feels so much fucking better.

When her nails dig into the side of my arms, my hips hit her harder and suddenly Vero is constricting my dick like it's trying to choke it out. The people in the next room can probably hear her cries but I can't stop. Not now. I'm so close.

Vero releases her death grip and covers her face with her forearms. A few more thrusts and I can feel my sack wanting to empty again. One, two, grind. I growl as I climax inside of her pussy that's still pulsating around me. Damn, all those years of virginity are worth it to meet a woman like her.

Her legs slip off my shoulder, letting me press my body against hers as I share a slow and sensual kiss with my wife.

20

I can't take my eyes off him. It's like the floodgates have been opened and I'm not sure I know who this is, this version of Akmal. He's morphed into something that makes me want to beg, makes me perk up and see if he demands something of me with a look or a smile.

We've been at it like rabbits all night and all day, for two damn days. I was almost feeling dehydrated a few times with how many times he's been keeping me up. Thank goodness for room service because we did not leave the room at all during this honeymoon period.

But today is checkout day. I'm ready to go back home. I think Atsuko texted me sometime a while back that they already left for home, only choosing to stay one night and day at the hotel Akmal's parents got for us. They're used to fucking on every surface though. For me and Akmal, we had some build up we needed to get out.

"You ready?" The grin he throws my way makes me rub my legs together a little bit before getting up from sitting on the bed. The drive home was peaceful and quiet. Akmal, being the cheesy guy he is, insisted he perform a proper bridal carry over the threshold of our home. He can be so sweet.

Once we settle back in and unpack our bags, Akmal brings up a conversation I didn't see coming.

"Vero, are you planning to keep working at the bar? I mean, as a bartender at the restaurant."

"Yeah, I guess. I never really had any plans beyond it. Why?" Akmal is quiet for a few moments and I'm unsure of how to feel.

"You know, my photography business is starting to get bigger. You wouldn't have to work at the bar if you don't want to." I never said I didn't want to. But now that he's brought it up, the question is in my mind. Do I want to stay there? When I was single, it was easy to find quickies. But since Akmal came into my life, I found that I couldn't care less about that fact.

Maybe it is something to consider. But what would I do outside of bartending? I was a few credits shy of finishing my associates degree. I still didn't have a particular direction or major I wanted to work towards.

"I don't know, babe. I never really thought about anything outside of it, I guess. What would I do?"

Something crosses his features, like he's been itching to say something this whole time. "You can always come work with me."

I laugh at that. What would I do? I don't know the first thing about taking pictures. Sure, I can pose and look sexy in front of the camera, but that's about it in that regard.

"How is that going to work? I don't know how to work

the camera, not like you. And plus, you have Mat as a partner for that."

"Yeah, but if we pick up more gigs, we won't have much time behind the scenes to work the website, answer emails and respond. By the time we finish photoshoots, we both have to come back and still do edits." I guess he makes a point. I start to think about it, really think about it.

His hands cup my face and bring me to his lips for a chaste kiss, stalling whatever thought that was starting to shape in my mind. "Vero, be with me. It makes my damn chest burn knowing that I can't be there with you at work. Knowing that other men are looking at what's mine, planning ways to take you from me."

Well, when he puts it that way…who knew Akmal would be so possessive? I love it.

"What if I want to keep working as a bartender serving other men?" I'm being a brat. I know. Akmal's eyes start to burn into mine.

He grabs my ass and picks me up, making my legs wind around him. Sitting down on the bed, I thought I was going to be in for some sexy times, when his strong arms maneuvers me so that my body is hanging over his thighs instead.

Smack! Smack!

I squeal like a little girl. Where the hell did that come from? My ass is throbbing with phantom pain still left behind until Akmal's warm hand starts to rub at my ass, soothing it away.

"What was that for?" Sometimes, I just can't control my mouth.

Smack! Smack! Smack!

My god. "You know exactly what it's for." He doesn't rub my pain away this time and I pout, but it doesn't change his mind one bit.

He rolls me onto the bed and gets up, continuing on like nothing happened. The audacity -

"You're coming to work with me, Vero. That way I can keep that sassy mouth of yours out of trouble. I don't need you riling up other guys while I'm not around to punch them in the face for even looking at you." My heart wants to burst at that and I'm silently giggling into my forearms as I lie here on my stomach on the bed.

I think I like riling up my husband.

Jumping out of bed, I jog to catch up with him. I find him sitting on the couch with a computer on his lap. Just like that, I feel like being a brat again. He just ups and leaves me in the bedroom and doesn't even give a rat's ass, does he?

My plan was to distract him but instead once I'm close enough, Akmal pushes his laptop to his side. He then pulls me onto his lap sideways, giving me a soft kiss on the neck. "Look at what I have pulled up. This is what I want you to do for me. Then I won't have to think about what your ass is doing in whatever outfit you're wearing and how other guys around you are affected." I'm laughing my ass off. *Who is this man?* I love how much he's coming out of his shell.

Grabbing the laptop with one hand, Akmal brings it to my lap. I love the way his forearm flexes and I start to wiggle my ass a little on top of him. Akmal bites my shoulder, making me gasp.

"Stay still, I'm trying to show you something." He's getting bossier and bossier, isn't he? Makes me just want to go against him to see what my punishment will be.

"I'm going to need you to keep track of the inquiries that come in, organize them and let me know before you schedule them. Can you do that for me?" He's kissing my neck while asking me these things. How the hell am I supposed to think straight?

"Yeah, I think I can do that."

"I might need you to get in front of the camera for me when I get new lenses in, to make sure they're working properly." I can feel his warm breath and wet tongue licking at my skin now. It makes me start to breathe harder. Akmal, the damn tease.

"Okay."

"Maybe I'll need you naked, to make sure the lighting is right against your skin." Oh.

"Is that so?"

He nips my neck, right before saying, "But if anyone looks at you I'll kill 'em. So it's going to have to be a bedroom shoot only."

I think my panties are soaked. Akmal scoots me off his lap and gives me a kiss on the forehead. What just happened?

"I'll give you some time to get used to how the website works. I'm going to call up Mat to check up on him after all the festivities. You should have Atsuko come hang out to keep you company." He's really serious about this. He wants me to quit bartending so I can work with him.

"Okay." My mind is still trying to wrap itself around the concept of being a family-owned business as I start to ring Atsuko.

"Hello?"

"Atsuko! Are you free today to come over?"

"Of course! I took some time off because of the wedding. When do you need me over?"

"Right now would be cool. Akmal is calling -"

"- Mat. So that's who he's talking to. Yeah, of course. Give me thirty minutes and I'll be there. Do you need me to bring anything? I'm surprised you guys came up for air after the honeymoon." We both laugh and it lifts my spirits about this change in my life that's about to happen.

"I'll see you in thirty."

"See you then."

Akmal is already rubbing my shoulders as I end the call.

"I'm going to be out and about with Mat today, maybe see if we can find some more clientele. Will you be okay here?" Placing my hand on top of one of his, I give him a gentle squeeze.

"Yeah, Atsuko's coming over."

"Good. You two stay out of trouble. Especially you." What the hell is that supposed to mean? I never find out because Akmal kisses me senseless, making the computer slip off my lap and onto the couch right before he leaves.

21

VERO

"That's so kind of him! He just wants you with him all the time, afraid some guy is going to sweep you off your feet when he's not looking. How cute is that?" I'm hanging out with Atsuko in one of Akmal's t-shirts since we're not going anywhere.

"I mean, when you put it that way, yeah it's cute as hell." We both laugh because I've been talking to Atsuko about how Akmal is coming out of his shell. She loves it and I do too. It's a nice surprise despite the fact that I was initially attracted to shy and nerdy Akmal. Dominant and commanding Akmal makes me squirm.

"So you're going to be their metaphorical office girl?"

"Yeah, it seems so. What do you think? Should I still try to fit in time bartending?"

"Why? Mat has been talking to me about them getting more inquiries and how he really has a good feeling about the photography business booming. Plus, we know some people from the circles we've hung around to help them build up more clientele." She's right. Together, we would be a powerhouse with a lot of potential growth.

"How about you Atsuko? Are you jumping on this photography bandwagon or are you sticking with the makeup counter?"

"I never really thought about it. I mean, the makeup industry brings in a lot of money and I don't work there full time."

"Aren't you worried about the female clientele that might be a little too interested in your man?" Atsuko's eyes blazed at that mention, her lip curling into a small snarl. I knew she didn't think about that fact. After all the woman drama they've been through. Who am I kidding? I'm being selfish because I want my BFF to work with me.

"Are you still holding onto that makeup job, Atsuko?"

"Ugh, I'm going to have to think about it. The thought of someone touching my man makes me want to kill a ho." Oh, I know. Atsuko and I grew up in a rougher neighborhood. We're not afraid to get our hands dirty.

"Don't think about it too long chica, I can't beat them all off for you. I'm supposed to be working." I can see the cogwheels spinning in her head. Good, she really doesn't need another obstacle in her relationship.

"What are your plans with modeling, Vero? Are we still doing it? I remember us talking about trying to get contracts. Life has really thrown us a curveball, huh?" Yeah, it really has. The days of daydreaming together about getting contracts and living the high life has now been put on the backburner. Or rather, more important things have come up like finding our significant others and getting married. I don't regret it one bit, because YOLO.

"Alright chica, let's get our head into the game. I mean, *I need* to get my head into the game. I do secretly love the fact that Akmal is possessive of me so I need to really make this work so he doesn't fire my ass." Atsuko is laughing her ass off, the bitch. But I love her.

"So, what are you supposed to do? Just emails?"

"I don't know, Akmal just kind of threw the computer at me and told me to get familiar with the website."

"He must have a lot of trust and faith in your abilities then. Alright, let's look at it together."

We both straighten our postures on the couch and scoot close together as we scour the photography website. To be honest, Akmal and Mat have got some mad skills. These photos are amazing. But the amount of unread messages dates back to a couple of weeks ago.

I called Akmal once to ask if he would allow me to start scheduling and he proceeded to link his calendar to mine. How he did that, I have no clue. But he's a brainiac so I just go with it. Both Atsuko and I start to answer emails and write down possible scheduling on paper before committing it on the digital calendar.

As a team, I think we did pretty well. It wasn't as stressful as I thought it would be. Mentioning that fact to Atsuko, she seems to agree. Good. Maybe she'll consider teaming up with me. We're basically family after all.

The boys came back in the late afternoon, Atsuko and Mat not staying long after that. Atsuko had helped me get an early dinner ready while she was here and now I'm sitting on the couch sideways with my legs on Akmal's thighs as we watch some mindless television.

"So, we should be getting more emails for inquiries soon. We ran into some students at the university."

Laying my head back on the arm of the couch, my toes

start gliding under the bottom of his shorts. "Okay, I'll keep an eye out. You have a photoshoot this coming Thursday."

Taking a swig of his beer, Akmal nods his head to let me know he heard me. "Yea, Miss Williams. She had scheduled it a few weeks ago. I think she mentioned needing updated headshots and body shots for her modeling portfolio." Putting the beer on the coffee table, Akmal starts to massage my feet. He's so good to me. "She mentioned that the beautiful girls on my page were what convinced her."

I've seen his page, the only girls he has on there are me and Atsuko. That's flattering.

"So I'm free advertisement hey?"

"Just showing everyone what they can't have." Akmal has gone from massaging my feet to kissing up my calf. I'm getting goosebumps with the way his eyes are smoldering into mine, there's an intensity in them that makes me fill with a sense of anticipation. How did I go from miss confidence around Akmal to this, to always anxiously awaiting to see how he plays my body? I continue to watch him as he slowly moves like a predator on the prowl.

He pushes my shirt up over my breasts and exposes me to his gaze. His groan slash growl makes me clench between my legs. "Vero, you're not wearing any shorts or panties."

"No, I'm not. Why should I?" Akmal, groans again at my response.

"The mouth on you, woman." I was going to give him another retort when he steals my breath away with his tongue diving into my pussy. This is where my confidence has gone, into the man before me devouring me like I'm his dessert he's been waiting for all day.

Opening my legs wider, Akmal situates his shoulders until the back of my thighs are on them. Relaxing my head back against the arm of the couch once more, I take in all of the sensations he's bringing out of me. When his tongue dips in and flicks up at the tip, it makes my body arch with his ministrations. His thumb is staying busy, rubbing my clit in circles and it's driving me mad. It feels like I'm riding a high wave with no reprieve of fluctuation and no end in sight at the same time.

I can feel my abs tensing but not enough to get there. He's killing me. I start to whimper as my body automatically starts to inch away from him but Akmal has other plans. His hands grab my ass and pull me back to his face as his mouth attacks my clit with a different kind of fervor. Sucking and nipping, the tip of his tongue teases the underside of my swollen hood and I can feel myself climbing.

The hands on my ass are gripping hard and the occasional sting of the nails biting into my flesh makes me rock my hips against his face this time instead of away. What is he doing to me?

Right when I'm about to orgasm, Akmal pulls his face away and gives me one slow and savory lick up my pussy and to my clit. He raises his head with a devilish smile while I'm about to throttle him in my mind.

It must show on my face because he chuckles as he climbs over me and flips me over like I weigh nothing. I don't know when he pulled his shorts down but when he covers my body with his warmth, I can feel his cock tapping up against my wet pussy like a tease. It's desperate to get in and I'm desperate for it to be in me. Reaching down to do just that -

Thwack!

My ass still stings as Akmal grabs his cock and starts slapping it even more against my core. A few more dick slaps and Akmal is gliding his cock along the wetness, coating his shaft. Everytime the head of his cock bumps against my clit, I moan to ask him for more. Seems he likes to be in control and any attempts I make to get to my finish gets me punishment. Torturous, slow-teasing punishment.

I love it and hate it.

Preparing to be teased to no end, it catches me by surprise when Akmal sticks the tip inside of me before going back to gliding his cock against my pussy lips again. Dammit!

A small growl must have escaped my lips because his hand starts to pinch and tug at my nipples as he bites down on my shoulder.

It feels so damn good, and I'm already so worked up that I might just cum from this. The sensations are starting to climb again when Akmal leans away, bringing cool air across my back, grabs my hips and shoves his dick right to the hilt. He sets a brutal pace and I fall off the hill I was climbing into an almost painful climax that doesn't slow him down one bit. Shit shit shit. This is too much. Too much.

"Shit, I can't take it. It's too much."

"You're going to take it." One of his legs goes to the floor for more leverage and I almost feel like he's pounding my face into the arm of the couch every time his hips hit my ass. I fucking love this side of him.

"You feel so fucking good Vero, taking it like a good girl." Oh my god. My climax was just starting to plateau when his words stir something in me.

"You like this don't you? Bent over and taking my dick like this."

"Yes." I can barely get the words out with the way my face is getting smushed into the cushions of the couch arm.

"Damn, I can feel your pussy gripping me. I'm going to cum. Shit."

"Yes, cum in me. I want it, Akmal. You make me feel so good." He really fucking does. Has sex ever felt like this? No one has ever read my body and my mind like he does with the stuff that comes out of his mouth for my ears alone.

A few more thrusts and Akmal is groaning as he leans back over me, nuzzling against the crook of my neck. I can feel his hot breaths tickling my skin, making my hair move when he whispers, "That's a good girl. Make sure you keep that mouth of yours out of trouble."

"...what if I like trouble?"

He bites my ear as his hips continue a slow rock until his cock slides out. The feeling of our combined wetness dripping down my thighs makes me want to go another round. Maybe I'll be a brat again, just so he can punish me.

"Don't be a brat, Vero. I know you're thinking about it right now. Just be a good girl."

Damn, he's good.

22

The Thursday appointment wanted to do a photoshoot at a parking garage another town over. Apparently this one is hardly used, giving it an abandoned vibe. The model is a gorgeous African American woman with legs for days. Her beautiful curly hair only adds to the whole package.

Akmal is too busy adjusting the settings on his lense to notice the girl looking at him with hunger in her eyes. I'm a little ticked but I get it. He's hot. He's even hotter when he doesn't notice you. There's just something about that. I know, because that's how he got me.

Once he's ready, the model starts posing over the outer edge railing, simulating overlooking the city. Her profile is gorgeous and she knows it. There's a confidence in her swagger, the way her hips move, the way her eyes look like they're enticing the man behind the camera - my man. I'm rationalizing in my mind that this is what models do after all, I've been in front of the camera, I've done it myself.

But that was when I was single. Apparently, married Vero is a possessive and jealous bitch. The more the model sticks out her chest and her ass, the more I want to punch her in the face.

Akmal isn't helping anything by telling her she's doing a good job, asking her to pose certain ways to help with lighting against her skin tone in this dark garage.

I can't help but feel like all of his praises belong to me. I'm also bristling at the fact that the model, Miss Williams, is obviously preening every time she hears a praise out of his mouth. *He is mine.*

A few hundred shots and clicks later or whatever it is, Akmal gives his little talk about how he will get back to her as soon as possible after edits. The same talk he gave Atsuko after our photoshoot at the car show. He's showing her some of the raw images through the viewscreen at the back of his DSLR camera and I can feel irrational fury growing within me with how close Miss Williams is standing next to him.

Breathing in and out slowly, I try to calm my thoughts. This is his job, this is what he does. Get it together.

Time fucking slows as I watch Miss Williams put her hand gracefully on Akmal's shoulder to lean in a little closer to 'look at the raw images'. Her eyes are really giving him side glances and I swear I can see her nostrils flare from taking him in.

I'm seeing red. The Puerto Rican and Hernandez side of me tells me to take this bitch out. The wife side of me is telling me to calm the fuck down because this is his business that might get affected by my behavior.

I'm warring within myself but I'm still shooting daggers

at this ho in front of me right now. She doesn't see me of course because she's secretly sniffing my man.

My hands are about to involuntarily rip her hair off when Akmal gives her a polite smile and steps away, messing with the buttons near the viewfinder. My man is always so clueless when it comes to flirting, thank God for small blessings.

When her eyes find mine, she gives me a polite smile and proceeds to pretend to adjust her tiny outfit. *Bitch, don't act like you don't know what you just did.* Or maybe she doesn't know. Maybe she thinks Akmal is single. It's not like she was looking at his finger.

Walking towards Akmal, I lean my body right up against his, sliding one of my hands on his opposite shoulder, my finger starts playing with his ear. Leaning in to look at the viewfinder too, I kiss his neck.

"Those look great, baby. Good work."

"Yeah, I think we'll be able to turn over edits quickly with this set." My oblivious husband.

Oh, but Miss Williams isn't oblivious. Her eyes are watching our interaction carefully. I know this look. This is the look of a woman still waiting to see if she can squeeze herself in between despite the fact that I just laid claim to my man.

I got my eye on you chica.

Narrowing my gaze at her, we both communicate mentally. Whether she takes my warning to heart or not, we have yet to see. It's a good thing that I'm pretty confident Akmal is going to make her edits look amazing so there wouldn't be a reason for her to come back for another photoshoot.

Akmal being the kind and clueless man he is, tells her he will take a few more shots just to make sure he can find the best photos to help build her portfolio. This time around, she's sticking her ass out even more provocatively, sending bedroom gazes his way and through the camera lense. I'm getting pissed again but she hasn't backed off one bit. No, in fact, she's issuing me a damn challenge.

The hood bitch in me is already clawing her eyes out. I'm trying damn hard to be the bigger person here. Staring at the back of Akmal's head, he's still clueless as ever. I know I shouldn't be pissed at him, but the more he angles his camera and the more he leans in for a 'better shot', I'm about to blow a gasket.

The rest of the session ends in a fog because my mind is just constantly repeating the crap I saw that woman pull off in front of my husband. Being a photographer, I can't ask him to look away. It's his damn job. *Fuck, get it together Vero!*

But he's my fucking man and I worked hard to get him and keep him. I'm like a boiling volcano with how much I'm trying to keep this shit inside. A girl can only do so much as tears start leaking out on the drive home.

Holding back any sniffles, I turn my face to look out the window and just breathe slowly. I shouldn't be this mad, I shouldn't.

Pulling up at our apartment, Akmal only notices something wrong when he opens the passenger door for me. Squatting down, Akmal cradles my face in his hands and has the most concerned look on his.

"What's wrong, Vero? Why are you crying?" Because women are trying to take him away from me and he's so damn nice and innocent that he wouldn't even know what's happening until it's too late. Then where does that leave me?

I don't know what's come over me but I storm out of the car and into our apartment, straight into the damn kitchen to find something to stuff my face with so I can concentrate on something else.

The sound of the door closing and locking tells me Akmal is trying to walk on eggshells around me. Good! He should with how unstable I'm feeling right now. Dammit! We didn't buy any more ice cream.

Slamming the freezer shut, I remove my shoes and layers of clothes until I'm just in my bra and undies before crawling into bed and letting my frustrations get smothered by his pillow. The warmth of his arms around me only serves to make me feel worse, I don't know why.

"Vero, talk to me."

"I don mmf wanno." The pillow is muffling my face, but I don't care.

"What happened? We were having a good day today. It made me happy that you were with me while I worked." I know. I know it does. I could see it in his eyes when he would sometimes steal glances at me. I'm being stupid. But that bitch was throwing it in my face and I couldn't do a damn thing about it.

Akmal, the perfect husband he is, rubs my back to try to soothe whatever is happening in my mind right now. Chaos. It's utter chaos in here. How do I explain that to him? He'll probably think I'm nuts.

He's calling my name I think, but I'm lost in thoughts of all the other women out there who schedule to get photo's done by my sexy as sin husband. What if I'm not there every-time to make sure to stake my claim? What if girls start to do more than just a touch? Is he even going to know how to fight off their advances? He doesn't even know how to read advances.

"Tell me what you need."

Lifting my head off his pillow I mumble, "Ice cream."

"Got it. I'll be right back." And off he goes. This is exactly why women are all over him. Why can't he just be perfect for me at home and a jerk everywhere else? I take that back. Girls like that shit too.

I managed to calm myself down by the time Akmal comes back with ice cream, mostly because of the ice cream. Akmal sits on the couch next to me with his arm slung behind me. I'm feeling good, until he starts talking about her.

"That was a good set, she looked really good with the shadow and the way the sunlight filtered through. I think this is going to be an easy set to edit." She looked good. No… he said she looked *really* good. The fuck?

My spoon is stopped midway to my mouth and I shove it back into the container. Placing it slowly onto the coffee table before us, Akmal still looks like he's off in photographer land while he thinks about this woman's curves.

I mean, I could castrate him but that wouldn't benefit me when I get horny.

"Akmal…"

He's lost staring into nothingness, having to shake his head a little to give me his attention.

"Yes?"

"Please don't tell me how good another woman looks."

"What? I didn't say that. What are you talking about?"

"You just told me she did."

"I was talking about how the photo session went well with the lighting and such."

"You didn't notice her touching you?"

"When did she do that? I don't remember this." Figures.

"She was touching your damn shoulder when you guys were looking at the viewfinder on the camera."

"Vero, I don't even remember any of that. I mean, I remember showing her the raw images so she can get a feel for what to expect. It's how I do things so the client feels confident in the final product. Why are you getting on me like this?"

"What do you mean why am I getting on you like this? I'm your fucking wife and I don't like other women touching what's mine." When did I become this person? And I can't seem to stop once it starts.

Akmal is sitting up straight by now, his hands in a placating gesture and even that makes me pissed. I'm not a rabid dog, even if I feel like tearing that woman's throat out.

"I didn't let her touch me, I'm telling you Vero. I don't remember any of what you're saying. Just calm down for a sec -" Oh hell no. Calm down? CALM DOWN?

"What the hell do I need to calm down for Akmal? Are you saying I'm making shit up right now? Because I saw what I saw and a woman knows when another is sniffing around her territory. I don't like that shit. I'm from the hood. We handle that shit quick, fast and in a hurry before it can grow into anything else. I was being the bigger person by holding myself back while you worked." Shit, am I breathing hard? My head feels tight, like more word vomit is about to come out of me without my permission.

"Vero, Vero… stop. Just relax, nothing happened between me and her."

"Fucking hell! I know nothing happened between you and her, I was there remember? It's just you're so...you're so..." I growl in frustration at my lack of ability to form a cohesive sentence despite there being a million words in my mind right now.

Getting up, I throw the carton of ice cream in the trash since there were only two or three bites left anyway. I'm sure I'm stomping like a petulant child as I go to the bedroom and start getting dressed to go out.

I must have left Akmal in a stupor from my womanly

hissy fit because he's still there staring at the wall trying to process everything. The moment my keys jingle from the hook in the kitchen is the moment Akmal jumps up and turns around to look at me.

"Where are you going?"

"I need to calm the fuck down like you told me to Akmal. Isn't that what you said? I need to *calm down*? Well let me go and do just that." I'm riding the high of my anger. Nothing makes sense and everything makes sense. My mouth and body is telling me what to do but my mind is telling me that I'm overreacting because he's right, nothing happened.

I just need to get away from Akmal's cute face and his stupid hot body that's walking towards me, making me feel weak. Rushing out, I slam the door in his face and run to my car that hasn't been used in the past few weeks. I'm backing out and driving like a bat out of hades and I don't know why I feel so rushed. Not until I pull up to mi Mamá's house.

23

VERO

"Oye. ¿Que pasa? ¿Por que tu está aqui? ¿Está todo bien?" My mom is always able to read my moods like the back of her hand. No, things are not alright. I should feel bad for worrying her like this, but my mind is all over the place.

"I'm fine, Mamá. I just had a fight with mi esposo." She's giving me a look that says 'so what?'. Now I really feel stupid about how I acted. I've seen my parents argue all the time but they're still just as tight together as I remember too. Nothing can break them apart. How do I become like that? Am I being petty?

Once I'm in the door, I can hear my dad's voice talking to Fabian about something. Fabian is always over here despite having an apartment somewhere. What a waste of money. But with his seasonal construction job and carpentry on the side, he's got money to spare.

"Alejandro, tu hija is home!" I can hear the sound of heavy footsteps leaving the carpeted area and coming onto the hard floor of the kitchen.

My dad has always been my main man growing up. He used to feel like such a big presence to me. Once I became an adult, I realized despite him just being a five-foot-seven average Puerto Rican male, he's still my safe space when I feel needy.

Like right now.

"Vero! That was a beautiful wedding." He stops when he sees me and then takes the last few steps to give me a hug. "What is wrong, Vero? Dónde está tu esposo?"

I left him at home because I can't trust myself to not explode and mess things up. I don't tell my dad that though, he doesn't need to worry about my marital issues.

"Vero, what happened? Who's ass do I need to kick?" Fabian, despite being a jerk sometimes, is also my other safe space.

"It's nothing guys. I just… I just need to clear my head a bit."

"Clear your head? What did Akmal do? Why are you guys fighting already?" Fabian can be astute when he wants to be.

"Come on, let's go watch some TV." My dad is still holding me as he escorts me to our outdated floral couch. My mom follows behind. I don't know where Fabian is.

Lying down on my side I put my head on my Papá's lap and just let my mind drift as we watch one of my Mamá's telenovelas.

～

FABIAN

Whatever this fucker did to my sister, I'm going to find out. But the only number I have is Sakinah's. As my fingers scroll through my contacts, I quit lying to myself. It's just an excuse, I wanted to find a reason to call her anyway. Well, good, now I have one.

It takes almost five rings before she decides to pick up. This girl, she likes to leave me hanging. She's probably doing this on purpose because she knows it's me. I can't help but like the annoyance she brings out of me.

"Hello?" The breathy sound of her voice makes my cock twitch. I miss the taste of her lips.

"Sakinah."

"What do you want, Fabian?" Sassy little shit, isn't she? I wonder if she throws this sass to her parents or is it just me? I'm probably just special. At least that means she thinks about me. Hopefully in the ways I've been thinking about her. Does she get wet? Is she waiting for me to come back around? She seems a little too old to still be living with her parents. But look at my ass, I'm here all the time.

"Hurry up, I got things I need to do." Fucking hell. I bet that pretty little mouth of hers would look good around my -

Get your head in the game Fabian.

"Vero came home upset and shit. What did your brother do?" I can't let her see how much she affects me anyway, that'll give her the upper hand. There's a pause before she responds. If I was standing next to her, I'd make her talk in the best of ways.

"I don't know. He's not here with me, he's probably still at his apartment. Why don't you call him?" The mouth on this girl.

"Because I only have your number, or did you forget

when you slapped me and walked away?" I can hear her intake of air on the other side. Yeah, I didn't forget that and I know she hasn't either. I also didn't forget the fact that she didn't complain about it when I brought it up. She probably thinks about it just as much as I do.

"I'll call him and let him know where she is. Bye Fabian." Fuck. Just like that she hangs up on me. What is it with this woman? Good girl, my ass…

Walking back into the house through the backdoor, I find my sister laying solemnly on my dad's lap. What happened?

"Vero." She jumps at my voice, not even seeing me standing here for at least a minute or two.

"What happened? Tell me."

"It's stupid."

"Tell me anyway."

I watch as she takes a big sigh and sits up with my parents on either side of her for emotional support.

"He wants me to work for him."

"Okay…"

"…and we had this photoshoot with this girl who was beautiful. She kept flirting with him. I couldn't stand the way she was trying to homewreck me. She had that look, you know? It's the same way Juana looks when you know she's about to cause trouble."

Well shit, Juana is our local desperate housewife. I mean, she's single but she wants to be someone's housewife, even if that means it's with your husband.

I can see why Vero would be cautious about this.

"But why are you here then? Shouldn't you be over there making sure that shit doesn't happen?"

"I was! I mean, I was trying to tell him that but I'm no good with words when I'm pissed. It all comes out jumbled and then he tells me to calm the fuck down and -" I can already hear my dad choking and my mother cursing under her breath.

Every man should know this rule. Never - and I mean never - tell a woman to calm down. Especially a Puerto Rican Hernandez woman.

24

AKMAL

*W*hat the hell is going on? I must be losing my mind because I swear I don't know what happened or why it ended up this way. I've been driving around town for a good thirty minutes when my sister Sakinah calls me.

"Hello?"

"Akmal, Vero is at her parents house."

"How did you know she even left? Can hah? Are you sure?" That's a bit strange. Did Vero call her? Why would she do that? Wouldn't she call Atsuko first?

"Fabian told me. He was worried about her. Fix this, I don't want to lose my sister-in-law already. I like her." Shit, I'm not about to lose her. I love that woman too damn much to let her get away from me.

"Alright, thanks for letting me know. I'm going to fix this. Thanks Sakinah."

"You're welcome." She hangs up and I look at my mirrors before swinging the car around in a u-turn.

I should have checked her parents' house instead of driving around. Well, we found her now. It takes me a good thirty minutes more from where I started to reach Vero's old neighborhood. I can see her car parked out in front and Fabian's car in the driveway.

Pulling up the vehicle right behind Fabian's, I throw it in park and quickly run up to the front door. I didn't realize I was banging the screen door so hard until it started rattling. I'm kind of pissed and kind of worried about my wife. Worried she's really upset and pissed because I didn't do anything wrong.

Fabian opens the door with a glare. Reminding myself of my last thought, I cross my arms and stand up straighter.

"I'm here for my wife." We're staring each other down for a few moments before he stretches out his hand for a hand-shake. I don't know what is going on but if it gets me closer to my woman, I'll do it.

"I'm glad you are, I'm tired of her mopey ass attitude." Did she really take it that badly? Walking into the front door, I turn to ask Fabian what I'll be walking into when he says under his breath, "A word of advice my man, never tell a Hernandez woman to calm down, bro."

Shit. Duly noted. Nodding my head I start walking past the kitchen to the living room. Vero has her back turned to me as she stands there staring at the small box television sitting on a stand in front of the couch.

"Vero, it's time to come back home." At the sound of my voice, Vero whips around and my heart tightens a little at her look. She looks like she's fighting something on the inside and I'm not sure if I should be worried.

Not letting her get any time to think she can run away

from me again, I grab her arm and pull her in for an embrace. Kissing the top of her head, I just hold her until I can feel her body relax.

"Thank you Mr. and Mrs. Hernandez for taking care of my wife. We'll see you guys later."

I can see Fabian nod his head at my actions over his father's head and I turn towards the front door with Vero still in my arms.

"Are you alright?"

"Yeah."

"Alright, let's go home."

"Okay." She sounds so small and vulnerable that it makes me want to punch something for her.

The drive home is quiet and Vero doesn't look my way, choosing instead to stare out the side window of the car.

The moment we step inside our home, I lock the door and turn to settle whatever it is that's going on. I don't even get a chance to gather my thoughts when Vero lays it on me.

"Why did you have to tell me how beautiful she is, huh? And then when I try to tell you as your wife that she was being a snake, you have to take her side...over me? How do you think that makes me feel?"

What the hell? I'm getting kind of pissed again because we're going around in circles here, wasting time fighting over nothing. She turns away from me but at least she's staying inside this time.

"How the hell am I supposed to keep working with you when I know for a fact all these beautiful model women are going to be all over you during these shoots? Makes me want to fucking pull my hair out when you're all nice and shit to these girls. Makes me want to pull my hair out because I know you have to be for your job."

She's rambling, continuing to walk away from me and

frankly, I'm tired of this attitude she's giving me when - again - I didn't do a damn thing wrong. When we pass the bedroom doorway, I grab her arm and spin her towards me, slamming my mouth on hers just to make her shut up for a moment.

She's being difficult as she starts punching my chest like I'm not her damn husband demanding my right. Winding my arms around her tightly, I squeeze her until her breasts are rubbing against my chest, preventing her arms from making any more impact.

Coaxing her lips to open up for me, she continues to refuse in her stubbornness until I move my lips to her chin and nip at her skin. She tastes good, even in her fury. She tastes like my wife who's being a damn brat about this whole thing that has been blown way out of proportion.

Sucking at the skin at her neck, I can hear her start panting, her arms loosening their tension, no longer trying to push me away. Taking this exact window of opportunity, my lips find hers again, my tongue spearing inside to convince her to submit to me.

She fights, of course she does. Because this is Vero, she's always been that spitfire that ignites my hunger even when it was from afar. To know that she's just as possessive over me as I am over her makes me feel good. Damn good. I must be doing something right then.

Our lips and tongues continue to fight it out as I start stepping us closer and closer to the bed. Ripping at her top without stopping our kiss, Vero gasps into my mouth which only makes me more determined to get where we need to be.

The fabric falls to the floor leaving her breasts only restrained in a bra. Too many obstacles. Too many damn obstacles. She does this on purpose, I just know it. Challenges me to see how far I'll go for her.

When I end the kiss, she whimpers in protest until she feels my hand jerk the cup of her bra down and take her nipple into my mouth. The room is getting hotter by the minute as she buckles and falls back onto the bed, me landing right on top of her. She's not getting away that easily, oh no.

"Akmal…"

I bite on her nipple before moving to the other. I'm going to have to make a no bra rule when in the house. I hate this shit. I need to feel more of her. The tension I felt earlier from my initial fight is coming back to me in full force.

Popping my mouth off her other nipple, I start to quickly strip her out of her pants. She pretends she's fighting when in reality she lifts her hips here and there to help me remove them.

Dammit, panties. She needs to be naked and available to me at all times. Tired of fighting scraps of fabric, I lift her leg to slap her ass before turning her over with her legs hanging off the bed. Perfect.

Vero is already glistening as I lick up her pussy. When she starts to shift and wriggle, my hands find her backside a few more times, watching my handprint disappear. Her skin was made for that, made to be punished.

"Vero, get on your knees."

"No, I'm still mad at you." I laugh out loud as I lean over, grab a fistful of hair, pulling her back for another kiss. This woman kills me. When her body starts to soften from our tongues dancing, I pull her off the bed and down on her knees.

Her eyes are blazing as they look up at me while I undo the button and zipper, freeing my hard cock in front of her face.

"You keep looking at me like that wife, I like punishing

you." The flames spark into something else and I know she wants this just as bad as I do. Vero loves to be put in her place.

"Be a good girl and open up." And she does, letting me shove my dick right down her throat. She gags and tears up but her hands also come up to start stroking me in tune with her sucks.

"That's it. You're always being a brat because you want this, don't you? You just want to be forced to be a good girl on your knees."

Her eyes sparkle and she starts to bob her head and suck harder. Fuck, I can't last when she's enthusiastic like this.

She moans and the vibrations go up my shaft, making my gut tighten at the sensation.

"Fuck Vero, do you want me to cum down your throat?"

She pops her lips off the tip, licking my slit right before she whispers, "yes."

I want to cum down her throat. But she's been bad and she shouldn't get what she's asking for. That's like rewarding bad behavior.

Pulling my dick out her mouth, I grab her and throw her on the bed face down. Lining up my cock to her entrance, I impale her and start pounding my frustrations out. Leaning over her, my hands find her clit, wet from our friction, and start circling and pinching. Her back bows and I know she's found her chase. My thrusts slow down as my fingers pick up speed and soon enough Vero is screaming my name, the feeling of her pussy convulsing around me making me want to let go too.

But I can't. No, not yet. It's not that easy after what she put me through walking out that door.

I push her onto her stomach, releasing my dick from her pussy and turn her around. She doesn't need any direction when her mouth finds my cock again, one of her hands still playing with herself to prolong whatever it is she's feeling. Do girls cum back to back? From the way Vero's eyes flutter, it must be so. The little cheat, finding her pleasure when she's supposed to be getting punished right now. I give her a soft slap on her face to take her out of the moment and concentrate on the task at hand. My little dirty girl gets back into the moment and starts sucking like her life depends on it. I can feel my balls wanting to tighten but I'm holding back. I want to make her work for it, work for it harder.

My fingers slide under her hair and grip it hard to slow her tempo, my hips thrusting into her face instead. Shit, this shouldn't be so hot. Vero at this point has fully submitted, letting me do whatever I want without complaint. In fact, she's moaning and loving this shit.

I want to cum in her, but not like this.

Pulling her head off my cock, I let it fall back on the bed as I lift her legs up and cross them, making her pussy tighter for me right before I shove it back in. It doesn't take me long in this position, Vero bent almost in half, for me to find my release. And when it arrives, I feel like I'm seeing stars from how long I've been holding myself back, the shock of the orgasm going down my damn spine.

Vero moans even louder as jets of my cum shoot into her. Fuck, it feels good. I continue to thrust into her slowly, making sure to bury myself as deep as I can go. I bet she would look beautiful carrying my child. In fact, I need to fuck her brains out and keep her pregnant so she never leaves me again. The thought makes me pound into her some more before my cock finally shrinks and slips out.

25

VERO

*A*kmal didn't let me rest at all for the past week. I don't know what's gotten into him but I secretly love it, even though I tell him he's pissing me off. The expression that darkens his face makes my pussy clench because that's when he gives it to me the hardest, when my mouth gets the best of me.

From the kitchen table, to the floor, to up the wall. Akmal has been insatiable. I'm hanging out with Atsuko today, so Akmal is just going to have to hold himself back before he makes me late. Once I finish up my wiggle dress with some heels, I walk to the kitchen and grab my keys. The jingle makes Akmal come up behind me with a hug, his kisses going down my neck. Shit, I need to leave before I don't want to leave.

"Baby, I gotta go. I don't want to make Atsuko wait by herself by not showing up on time."

"I like it when you call me baby."

"Yeah?"

"Yeah, it makes my cock hard." God dammit Akmal. Turning quickly, I give him a peck on the lips and run out the door before he can pull me back.

I can hear his chuckle right before the door fully closes. Letting out a long breath, I fan myself as I walk to my car. Atsuko wanted to meet up at Sammi's, the sandwich shop we met the boys at on that fateful day. The day I started injecting myself into Akmal's life until there was no one else around him but me.

The drive was short, the cool breeze outside making it fresh when I let the windows down. Christina Aguilera's Nasty Naughty Boy makes me think of Akmal when I know I shouldn't be.

By the time I walk up to the metal table outside, I see Atsuko sitting there with her legs crossed in her pencil skirt and heels. Gorgeous as always my BFF is. Her siren red lipstick stands out against her light complexion. In fact, we must be in tune with each other because I think we're wearing the same lip shade.

"Hey! Vero, you made it."

"Of course, were you waiting here long?"

"Nah, just about five minutes or so. You're good."

"Did you order yet?"

"No, the waitress told me she'd give me time so that she can wait for both of us to order at the same time."

That's exactly what we do when Atsuko starts bringing up the real reason for this meeting.

"I was thinking about what you said, about us working together with the boys' business venture. The other day he went on a photoshoot and was telling me about the model. I almost went to her house and gutted her, I was so mad on the inside. Of course, Mat is oblivious to that shit." She must be reading my damn mind or we have to have been twins in another lifetime.

"Girl, I just went through the same damn thing with Akmal. Had a fight over it too."

"Yeah? How did you handle it? At least you were there! I was at work thinking of all the worst case scenarios."

"Yeah, that would be worse. You need to come work with us. It's the best way to keep an eye out for homewreckers."

"You're right." We've been chatting and eating our sandwiches, just about finishing up when I think I hear my name being called, by a male. It can't be Akmal. He's not that paranoid when I'm out with Atsuko.

Turning around my heart drops to my stomach, making it churn into something nasty feeling.

There standing a few feet away from me is my ex - my high school sweetheart, Roman fucking Guzmán. High school bad boy who played in a rock band. He looks older of course, gained some mass on him and maybe some height. His dark features are still as cocky as I remember too. The waitress comes out to take our empty plates away and she lingers a little longer than she should, probably checking this fucker out. *Yeah, I know, tall, dark and handsome.* But the way he left road marks on my heart makes bile want to rise up my throat.

"Roman."

"Vero!" He's shooting his signature panty melting grin at me and I almost do puke. Is he serious? Is he fucking serious right now? The bastard that played me for a whole damn school year just so he could take my virginity and fucking run?

"You've got the fucking nerve talking to me right now Roman."

"Aww, don't be like that. You know how high school is. We're beyond that now. I saw your face -" As he proceeds to look at my body up and down. And yes, I did grow even more into myself after high school. "- and just wanted to say hello to an old friend."

I turn my face towards Atsuko, who's been quietly shooting serrated knives with her eyes at this fucker, and lift my lip in a snarl. This asshole. Oh yes, I've told her all about this fucker.

We both look at each other for a second and get up, bending over a little to smooth down our outfits. We're both in something skin tight and Roman doesn't limit his perusal to just me. Once a snake, always a snake.

We're just about to walk past him when he has the audacity to grab my arm to stop me.

"Vero, if you ever want to hook up again, I'll make it up to you." I see red.

The punch that lands on his face, knocks him into one of the metal chairs behind him. My knuckles hurt but the adrenaline is dulling the feeling. Atsuko and I walk back to our cars arm in arm and in silence.

Atsuko follows me back to my place, walking me inside the front door. Akmal stands up from the couch when he sees me, and then looks at Atsuko with a questioning expression.

"I'll see you later, okay?" Atsuko's soft whisper against my ear only puts Akmal on high alert at something being wrong. When she exits, I shut the door quietly and lock it behind her.

Akmal turns me around, gently but firmly grabs my right hand and brings it up to his face. "What happened?" His eyes are boring into my knuckles as they start to redden up.

"It wasn't anything important."

"It was important enough for you to throw a fucking punch."

Sighing and leaning into his chest, Akmal embraces me tightly, rubbing my back in soothing circles. I love this. I love his calm energy, especially when I don't feel calm on the inside. My gut is still churning at meeting Roman randomly after over a decade apart.

"Tell me what's wrong." Akmal's whisper makes me hold him tighter.

"I ran into one of my exes -" Akmal's body tenses up and it feels like he's trying to break our embrace but I only hold him tighter. "-but I handled it. I didn't want to see that fucker's face. I'm sure he'll be hiding out for a while until he's healed up, he's always been vain like that."

With a sigh, Akmal continues to hold me until my heart settles back into something warm, happy and content.

26

———

We visited Akmal's parents today for lunch. It was nice and hectic as usual. I swear they are the hub for all Malaysians in the area. I don't know if it's something I ate but I don't feel so good.

"We're almost home, hold on for me okay?"

We make it back without any incident and after a good nap, I feel a whole lot better. I'm going to have to remember what I ate to make sure I avoid it the next time I'm over there.

Akmal must have finished up his edits during my nap because I find him sitting on the floor with his laptop on the coffee table and a game on the screen.

"Hey, baby."

"Hey! Are you feeling any better?"

"Yeah, that nap helped a lot. I must have eaten something that didn't agree with me. Can you help me keep an eye out the next time we have lunch with your parents? I'm not sure which plate it was."

"Yeah, yeah, of course. I'll call them and let them know." Plopping down next to him, I snuggle his arm and watch him play. He has his headset on and I think I can hear Mat's voice.

Giving my husband a peck on the cheek, I get up to go call Atsuko since the boys are busy. It rings twice before she picks up.

"I'm so glad you called. I was starting to get a little bored watching Mat talk to your man on that game. They're really into it today."

"What are you up to, chica?"

"Nothing much, Mat and I had the conversation about me helping out with the business. I think … I think I'm just going to go for it. I'm going to put in my two weeks at the makeup counter soon."

Walking back into the bedroom, I lie on my back and just stare at the picture sitting on our night stand. The luncheon with the in-laws was also for them to give us the wedding pictures and holy hell there were a lot of them. Figures since it felt like we sat on that throne all damn day.

"I'm so glad you're coming on. I need you to help calm me down if I'm about to get on some of the female clients when they're acting the way they shouldn't."

"Pfft. You and I both. Make sure you keep me in check because sometimes my fist speaks first and I ask questions later." We both laugh because it's so damn true. You can take the girl out of the hood, but you can't take the hood out of the girl.

"What are you doing tomorrow?"

"Nothing I guess. Hmm, maybe I should turn in my two weeks tomorrow?"

"Yeah, why not? The sooner the better. There's really no difference in waiting."

"You're right."

"Hey, you want to hang at Big Burger like old times?" That sounds like a damn excellent plan. I love the retro feel of that place. Atsuko and I used to hang out there at least every other week when we still lived together. Has it really been that long?

"Hell yeah! Type up that notice girl, we'll drop that shit off then head over to Big Burger."

"Sounds good. See you then."

"See you then." We hang up and I'm feeling really good. I'm excited to have another girl date with Atsuko. I mean, I love hanging out with Akmal, getting bent into a pretzel and pounded into, but girl time is important too. Keeps my mind on the straight and narrow when my thoughts about stupid stuff get chaotic.

Tossing my phone onto the mattress, I get up from the bed and start walking towards the kitchen. Might as well find a snack to eat if I'm going to sit and watch Akmal play video games. He's so cute though, I have no reason to complain. Other women would kill to keep their men home. I really am lucky in that sense.

When the coolness of the fridge hits me, I take in a deep breath. That feels good. But what doesn't feel good is the fact that the fridge is almost empty. Do two people really go through food that quickly?

"Hey babe, I'm going to go grocery shopping before it gets dark. We're low on food."

"Alright, just grab my credit card from my wallet." A man after my own heart. I love this guy.

A quick shower, getting redressed into comfy clothes and

a hair bun later I'm giving Akmal a kiss on the cheek before heading out.

~

AKMAL

After helping Vero put away the groceries, we join each other on the floor. I could game on the kitchen table, but I find the couch makes a nicer backrest. Plus the coffee table is the perfect height. Vero went through a good handful of snacks she brought home and is now dozing off with her head on my lap as I carefully lean into the game with Mat.

"Someone behind you."

"Shit, I see him."

"How are you and Vero doing?"

"Good, real good. I would say I should have married earlier if I knew it would be like this but then it wouldn't have been with Vero."

"Yeah, I feel the same way. Had to snatch her up before someone else did."

"I feel you. Vero is it for me. Just seeing some guy come in at her work looking at her tits made me want to start going on a killing spree." Mat laughs as we continue to shoot the enemy and creep along the trees to find a new hiding spot.

The sound of characters dying makes me do a quick check on the mini map. Mat's still in.

"I understand man. That's why the gym is good for me. It gets out my rage, you know? You're always welcome to join me."

"That's cool, I might. But I've also found better ways to take my frustrations out."

"Yeah?" I take down three guys and start changing out my

long range weapons for short ones as I take my character into an abandoned house. My mind floats back to the other day...

I need to knock my wife up. Taking her pills away is too much, maybe crossing the line. We're too early in our relationship for that. She'll kill me.

My fingers glide across the phone's keyboard as I start researching the rate of failure for oral contraceptives. I don't like what I'm reading and pulling up, but a line catches my eye.

"Oral contraceptive pills on the other hand have a failure rate of 0.1%, this means that 1 woman out of 1000..." Shit, I can do this.

I've watched Vero and her routines closely but I've never paid attention to the time she takes her pill. That's going to change. That's going to change right the fuck now.

Maybe if I keep her busy, it will throw her schedule off and increase the probability rate. Yes. Sounds like the perfect plan.

The sound of gunshots nearby brings me back to the present, my eyes scanning the screen for any potential threats near me.

"Yeah." I've been fucking her every chance I get, which is never a hardship to begin with. Her pussy just greedily takes everything I give her.

"Care to share, my friend?" Hiding my character behind a dark wall, I take a peek down to make sure my wife is sleeping. She is judging by the slow breathing and feeling of deadweight on my legs right now.

"So, you see, Vero likes to be a brat sometimes." Lately, it seems like all the time. I glance back down at her again. Still asleep.

"What do you mean?"

"Something about her man. She riles me up and I think she does it on purpose. Once I caught on, I started testing my theory by making her take small punishments."

I can hear gunshots from Mat's side.

"What do you mean punishments? Like you're spanking her or something?"

"Among other things." We both laugh and continue to take down a few on the other team. Somehow I run into Mat's character and we start to buddy up on the screen.

He whistles into the mic and I'm glad I'm on a headset. That shit would have woken Vero up.

"She like it?"

"Shit, more than like it man. That girl almost begs for it. She keeps trying to make me cum in her mouth but I've been trying my damndest to put a baby in her."

"Yeah? Already?"

"Fuck yes. I'm going to keep her pregnant. Makes me fucking hot just thinking about it."

"Fuck, maybe I should knock up Atsuko too." This statement is said in a whisper, she must not be too far away. He clears his throat. She must have just walked by. I'm laughing as light as I can so I don't jostle my sleeping beauty that much.

"Damn, now you got me thinking Akmal. My dick is hard. Last game."

"You got it bro. Last game."

27

VERO

*A*tsuko and I carpooled in her vehicle to make it easier on our girl date. I went in with her to drop off her notice. They didn't even give a rat's ass since the new girl apparently is monopolizing everyone's hours anyway. She's young and she's ambitious. It's good that Atsuko is leaving this junk for the new generation. You don't want to compete with that.

Pulling up on Big Burger, it's just how I remembered. Like a flash to the fifties when you open the doors. Atsuko and I sit at our usual table and some of the waitresses still remember us.

"I feel like it was just yesterday when Mat brought me here."

"I know what you mean. Feels like just yesterday I was trying to get the attention of your photographer at the car show. The fool wouldn't even give me a sideways glance no matter how much I tried to push the girls into his face."

We laugh and relax with each other, ordering our usual. Well, maybe a little extra for me. I haven't had a shake in a while and it's sounding real good today.

"Something is up with Mat this morning."

"Yeah?"

"I mean, we always fuck like rabbits, but it's just something extra. I can't put my finger on it."

"If he's not holding out, then you have nothing to worry about. Maybe he's just feeling for a little extra. Guys are like that."

"Is your guy like that?"

"I mean, I'm Akmal's first so it's not like I have anything else to compare to in regards to him but yeah, we're fucking like the world's ending."

The waitress is laughing as she puts our food on the table. They know how we are, we have no filters and we can get a little loud when the conversation gets rolling.

"That's good right? He was such a shy guy to begin with."

"Yeah, it's like something snapped. Well, I take that back, we were teasing a whole lot before the wedding so maybe something happened along the way." We giggle at that because we both know how bad I can get when I want some.

Atsuko throws a fry at me, the bitch. "You're so bad! That poor boy never stood a chance and now you've turned him into a nympho."

Opening my milkshake, I dip the fries in and take a bite. "No no no. Let's not get carried away. Nymphos will bang anything on two legs. Akmal just wants to bang *this* cooch." I smile as I take another bite of fries dipped in milkshake.

"You're right. Akmal is loyal. You got yourself a good one babe. Keep him."

Opening my burger wrapper, I dip the burger into my shake and take a bite out of that too. This shit is so good, who knew? I'm halfway through my burger when I notice Atsuko staring at me with a fry halfway to her mouth.

Making sure to chew what I have in my mouth, I wipe my lips before asking, "What?"

"When the hell did you start eating like that?"

"Like what?"

"I mean, you've always dunked your fries, but your burger?" Taking another large bite, I chew and think over what she said. Have I ever dipped my burger before?

Swallowing, I take a huge gulp of my shake before answering. "I guess you're right. Tastes fucking good though, you should try it."

"Nah, I'm good."

We eat in silence for a few moments and I realize I already polished off my burger. Has it always been that small? Grabbing a few fries at once, I shove it into my mouth and savor the salty flavor.

"Vero." Damn, I'm halfway through my fries. Maybe the shake will fill me up.

"Huh?" Dusting my fingers off with my napkin as I finish my last fry, I look up at Atsuko. She's only halfway through her meal. When did she get so slow?

"Babe...are you-"

Sucking on my shake, the sweetness is such a nice contrast to the salty flavor of the fries. Good thing I ate that last. Yum.

"Vero, are you pregnant?"

"Pfft, not possible. I'm still on the pill. Akmal hasn't mentioned wanting to start so I just kept taking it."

"I guess you're right. You want to drive by and get a test

just in case?" Finishing my shake, I nod my head as I wipe the sweetness from my lips.

"Sure, but it will probably just be a waste of time and money. Why not though?"

Atsuko finishes off her meal as I hit up the restroom. We exit Big Burger and drive by a nearby drug store to pick up some pregnancy tests.

"Oh my god, there are so many." Atsuko and I are just standing in the aisle like a bunch of fools staring at these different boxes. Why do you need so many different kinds if they're all doing the same damn thing?

"Shit, this is harder than I thought. Oh! But look at this one, it's cheaper because it's a box of two. What am I going to do with the other one though?"

Atsuko looks at the box in my hand and shrugs. "I can take one with you if you want. That way we use up the sticks and we're both doing it together."

I laugh because that's just like Atsuko. Why the hell not? YOLO. It's not like the stick is going to change anything. We ring up the box together and split the cost. Supposedly this one will actually have words that show up instead of lines. Good, that way it's super clear and no one can be confused about what they're reading.

We head back to Atsuko's place because my car is parked there. Mat and Akmal went to the gym and were planning on doing whatever guy stuff they do while Atsuko and I had our girl time so the place is empty when we arrive. Perfect for the shit we're about to do. Don't want to freak the guys out or anything over a silly test.

Dropping off our purses on the kitchen table, we grab the box and both head to the restroom. Atsuko opens her medicine cabinet to make more counter space around the sink. It wasn't like it was that full to begin with, but whatever floats her boat.

"Alright, so the directions say that we're literally going to pee on this thing." Atsuko is opening the folded pamphlet and looking at it front and back. There sure are a lot of words for such a 'simple' test.

"Okay, I can do that." Atsuko's restroom smells nice, like something floral. I'm going to have to ask her what she uses so I can use it in our restroom too.

"It says the best pee is probably in the morning but whatever. Let's do this." She hands me one stick while she takes the other. We both look at each other and laugh while we get out of our bottoms.

Both half naked we take turns squatting over the toilet and peeing on the stupid thing. We're laughing after we're done when we realized we didn't have to remove our bottoms completely. This shit is way out of our league.

Resituating our clothing and washing our hands, we leave the sticks on the sink counter - Atsuko's on the left, mine on the right - before we go chill on the couch and watch some TV. The pamphlet said to give it a few minutes but we gave it about ten just in case. There wasn't anything else we really needed to know, so the paper got tossed in the trash right before we left the restroom.

When the alarm goes off on my phone, we both get up and go look at our sticks. Laughing when we get there, we make sure to remind each other which belongs to whom.

Looking at each other, trying to smother a grin at the craziness of it all, we both pick it up at the same time and try to read the little writing that shows up in the little window.

"Well..."

"Yeah."

We both look at each other before putting the sticks back down.

28

I'm kind of scared, I'm not going to lie. Atsuko and I were sitting around trying to figure out what happened. Leaving her house before Mat gets there, I'm trying to take my time in getting home myself.

I stopped at a random parking lot to look this shit up on my phone. I'm probably worrying about nothing because that junk gets wrong all the time, right? I've heard the stories.

Bringing up my phone's browser, I start typing in the failure rate of birth control pills. It doesn't seem too bad. 0.1% chance. I keep scrolling and start to give up because all the information is about the same.

Staring out my front windshield, I watch as people walk by trying to find their cars. I'm getting kind of hungry. I wonder if this store sells food too? But cold food would probably go bad by the time I get done shopping and looking up this shit. Ain't nobody got time for that.

Bringing my phone back up, I start to look up my specific brand of oral contraceptives. I remember it changing recently, I think. Would this have anything to do with it? Eh, it's a long shot, but I'll check it out anyway while I'm here.

Different news feeds start popping up on the search and I start browsing through some of them. Huh, it seems like the formula was different from the other brand it replaced. I don't know if this is good or bad, I mean, I don't feel any different.

The more I read, the more I'm finding that there has been an increase in failure rate among this specific brand. Going back to the previous few articles I've read, I'm noticing a trend I didn't see the first time around.

They all date a few months back.

Turning my phone off, I let all I've learned soak in before starting the car back up and driving home.

When I walk through the front door, I can hear the sound of the shower going. Akmal must be in there. Dropping my purse off and hanging my keys up, I open the freezer and let the cool air hit my face. Opening my eyes, I see rows of ice cream tubs and I want to squeal. Akmal really is the best husband ever.

Grabbing one, and a spoon out of the kitchen drawer, I plant my ass on the couch and turn on some TV. The first bite of ice cream hits me in the right place. Holy hell, what flavor is this? Lifting the carton up, it says Rocky Road. I've had this before but it never tasted like this. Why does it taste so damn good?

I must be moaning too loudly because I didn't even hear Akmal get out of the shower and walk into the room. He leans over the back of the couch and gives me a kiss on the cheek. Sweet, sweet man.

"Hey, did you have fun with Atsuko?" He smells so clean, so masculine. He may even smell more delicious than this damn ice cream I'm shoveling into my mouth right now. My eyes track his movements and muscles as he parades himself to the refrigerator. He's only in shorts and that delectable ass of his is bending over for my viewing pleasure.

"Mmmhmmm."

I'm licking the spoon more than I should as I watch him grab a bottle of water and lift it up to drink. The way his Adam's apple bobs and the way his biceps flex makes me kind of needy. But when am I ever *not* needy around this man? I am one lucky son of a -

The couch jostles a little as Akmal sits down right next to me, placing the bottle onto the coffee table and throwing his arm over the back of the couch. The way his hair kind of falls over his eyes is sexy as hell, I never noticed it before. Akmal pushes his hair back before we hear his phone ring from somewhere in the back.

I watch as he gets up and round the couch while shoveling another mouthful of rocky road in. My body is missing his warmth already. I shouldn't eat this all too quickly. Ice cream will start becoming scarce before I want it to. Akmal doesn't really eat any I've noticed, so I've just been spooning it to my heart's content rather than putting scoops of it in a bowl.

Getting up, I toss the spoon into the sink and close the carton back up before placing it back into the freezer. I need to text Atsuko my findings about that birth control pill. We used to be on the same brand, I wonder if her doctor changed hers too?

Doing just that, I lean over the arm of the couch to grab

my phone, staying in that position as I quickly forward her the links to the articles I read.

Vero: Hey check this shit out.

    Atsuko: Okay, what's up?

    Vero: My birth control brand got changed a while back, did yours?

    Atsuko: You know, I never really paid attention. I have no fucking clue.

    Vero: Well, check this shit out because the brand I got changed to has some issues. It's not working for some women.

    Atsuko: Yeah? I better look.

I can hear Akmal's voice getting closer and closer by the increase in sound.

"Yeah, she got home not too long ago." Akmal walks by and slaps my ass since it's still hanging over the arm of the couch. Good thing he didn't look over my shoulder as I discreetly and nonchalantly try to talk to my BFF about the issue on hand.

Vero: Hey did you get rid of the tests?

    Atsuko: Yeah, I put some toilet paper over it too.

    Vero: Okay, good. The boys don't need to know yet until we know what the hell is going on.

    Atsuko: You got that right.

    Atsuko: Are you scared, Vero?

    Vero: I don't know if I should be yet. I mean, that shit gets wrong all the time right?

    Atsuko: Yeah, I guess...

"Wait, what? Say that one more time, I don't think I heard

you right the first time." I black out my screen when I hear Akmal right next to me. I'm not ready to talk about this yet. I need to find out more information first before I start throwing around false information. Plus there's no point in worrying about something you're not sure of yet.

Straightening up, I smooth down my clothes and look at Akmal who hasn't moved an inch from where he's standing - a foot away from me.

"Yeah, I'll call you back." He's staring at me and I don't know why. I try to give him a smile.

"Is everything okay?"

"Yeah, everything's fine. Did you have a good time with Atsuko today? Do anything interesting?"

"I always have fun with my BFF. We didn't do much, just went to eat at Big Burgers and hung out."

He's staring at me and I'm starting to feel like a mouse under a microscope. What was he and Mat talking about? It had to be Mat, no one else really calls him. All his photography stuff is handled via emails and messenger online.

"Hmmm. You guys eat a good meal then?"

"Yes, it was absolutely delicious as usual. The food went way too fast, they need to make bigger sizes for their combos."

"Is that right?"

Akmal's phone rings again and I watch as he connects it without taking his eyes off me. My hands are starting to get clammy from the tension in this room. Is it getting hot in here?

"Yeah." His eyes are scanning my face, but his expression is still so blank. I'm on pins and needles now. What is going on?

"Thanks for letting me know. I'll call you back." Akmal

hangs up and tosses his cell phone onto the couch behind me, the move startling me with how abrupt it is.

"So, nothing else happened today on your date with Atsuko?"

"Not really, we just kind of hung out at her place for a little."

He stares at me, I stare at him. The tension in the room amps up tenfold but I'm not one to back down from a challenge or break first. No no no. We were being good girls. Yup. Mmmhmm.

"Vero."

"Akmal."

"Fucking hell." Wait, what? "Vero, do you need to tell me something?"

"Nooo. Why would I?" Dammit, why am I like this?

"No?"

"Nope." I make the 'p' pop for emphasis because I'm feeling a little extra right now. He needs to get off my back.

"No." He's repeating me but it's coming out like a low whisper. I can tell he's trying to suppress a grin and it's making me try to suppress my grin. Challenge accepted fucker.

But when he takes the last couple of steps towards me with dark hunger in his eyes, I gulp and start to feel like a little chicken. When his scent surrounds me, my eyes flutter a bit and I have to mentally slap myself to stand strong against his sexy ass ways.

What do they say about facing a predator? Don't look away. *Alright Vero, come on girl, don't look away.*

We're basically toe to toe. He leans in a little and I inadvertently lean back a little, my ass on the arm of the couch.

His hand shoots out and grabs the back of my neck as he leans in, putting his cheek against mine. "Are you lying to me, Vero?" The octaves of his voice have gone so low I can feel the timber of it down to my core. Oh my god. *Stand your ground!*

"N-no."

He starts kissing the crook of my neck, his facial hair scraping my skin and making it prickle. When his tongue starts to lick and his lips start to suck and nip, my legs get a little weak. He's sucking hard now and it makes my nipples perk up, rubbing against the lace of my bra. The room is getting hotter because I swear I'm sweating between my tits right now from how he has me cornered.

He gives me another hard suck to the point of teetering on pain then proceeds to lave at the spot with the flat of his tongue, soothing it away and making me sigh. "Did you go to the store with Atsuko today?" His tongue is trailing up my jaw until he captures my mouth in his, invading it, owning it. He's making my brain foggy. He's playing me like a damn fiddle.

"What does that matter?" I manage to say between our lips colliding. Oh dear lord, Akmal growls into my mouth and starts plundering it with full force, dominating my movements with his. I can only go along for the ride as I find myself lost in what he's doing to me. Our eyes are still open as we stare at each other, the tension in the room so thick you can cut it with a knife.

His hands are moving in quick succession while his mouth continues to ravish mine. Our teeth hitting each other at times from how rough our movements have become. My body is being forced into different positions and the cool air coming between us now and again tells me he's been stripping me like a damn magician.

How he got me naked except for my bra this fast, I have no idea. This man is far from the virgin I remember. He pulls the soft lace cup of my bra down and fists my hair, tilting my head back and taking my nipple into his mouth.

Oh, but he's not in a playing mood today, no. A suck, a lick and a nip later, he grabs my ass and hefts me up. My legs automatically wrap around him to prevent me from falling, trapping his hard cock between us. His head comes forward to take my other nipple in his mouth as he walks us somewhere. With my arms wrapped around his shoulders and my fingers threading through his hair, my mouth is gaping open from how hard he's attacking it. With each step he takes, the hard tip of his cock behind his clothes rubs against my clit and wet pussy lips, making us glide against each other, wetting the fabric between us.

My back hits a wall and it almost knocks the air out of me. Akmal quickly pulls his shorts down and shoves his cock all the way in with one hard stroke.

"Vero -" *Thrust* "Did you" *Thrust* "go to the store today?" *Thrust thrust.*

I'm speechless with how hard he's pounding into me. He's hitting things he hasn't hit before with his enthusiasm. I open my mouth to say something but I can't do anything else but gasp and moan like a wanton ho.

His hands grip my ass even harder with my non-answer and Akmal starts to force my hips against him every time he pounds into me.

"You're such a little liar, Vero." My pussy is already fluttering with everything that's happened. "Why do you need to be brat all the time?"

Oh my god. Am I expected to answer that right now? How fucking rude of him to ask! Oh shit, I can feel my body tensing, the sensations are getting higher.

"Is it because you want me to fuck you? Is that it?" Oh

fuck, what is he doing with his hips? He's twisting it somehow. *Oh dear god.*

"Is it because you like to get punished for being a bad little girl?" Yes! Hell yes! But I can't tell him that because...because -

I cry out as one of his twisted grinds hits me in the right spot and I'm seeing fucking stars as my body tightens and almost wants to convulse. My pussy is clenching around his cock and a few more thrusts later - banging my head against the damn wall - Akmal is groaning into my chest, biting me right under my collarbone.

The feeling of his cock spurting cum inside me makes me ride waves after falling off the climax cliff. It's glorious and I'm panting. Akmal pulls us away from the wall and lowers us ungracefully onto the carpeted floor when he just lies on top of me, trying to catch his breath.

My hands are petting him and rubbing his back, the dampness of his skin making my hands stick a bit. Akmal is nuzzling my breasts and kissing them as he sneaks in, "I know what you did, Vero."

29

AKMAL

I'm flabbergasted at the fact that she continues to deny it. Or at least deny that it's a plausibility. She is so damn stubborn sometimes. We've been insatiable with each other, how can it not be a possibility. I punished her again last night in our bedroom, restraining her when she started fighting against me thinking it would make me stop. I would never stop, not with my wife. She gets like this when conversations are about to escalate into unnecessary arguments. I don't know if she gets a kick out of it or what but I'm starting to read her better and better.

She slept so soundly, not noticing the way I caressed her skin under the moonlight that spilled into the bedroom window. She fought so hard and so long that by the time I was able to get her little spitfire rage out of her system, she fell asleep with my cum leaking out of her - butt naked. That's alright, I love her like this. She's so damn soft and I can't stop myself from rubbing against her from behind as we lie together in bed. She didn't even wake up when I entered her again, only squirming and moaning in her sleep. It was hard going slow when all we seem to be used to these days is fast and hard.

The morning light woke me early. There's a lot on my mind and things need to get done. I wasn't able to rouse Vero until almost noon. We don't have anything booked for the next couple of days so I head to the kitchen to make her breakfast when I hear her stirring in bed. The pan is sizzling with the ingredients I prepared beforehand.

"Good morning, baby." There she is. Even like this, she's the most beautiful woman I've ever seen. The bruises and hickies on her body fill me with a sense of pride. She smells like she's been having sex all night - which is the damn truth, I made sure of it.

"Eat, get dressed. We're heading out today."

She blinks a few times but is still too groggy to argue. Good. I planned it that way. Heading to the bedroom, I grab some of her looser clothes and place them on the bed for her. When I enter the kitchen again, she's just finishing up her small omelette.

"Drink some water." She does as she's told with wide eyes.

The moment she puts the cup down is the moment I grab her and carry her bridal style, depositing her into the restroom and tapping her ass to hurry up. I'm already dressed and waiting by the time she's done with her shower.

She eyes the clothes skeptically, giving me a sideways glance. I'm not playing today and my face surely shows it because she doesn't say a word as she puts them on.

The drive to our destination is quiet, but without the tension that was around us yesterday. Vero is easy to sidetrack when she gets fired up, I've been using it to my advantage and now it's time to get this done right.

Putting the car in park, I quickly get out and open her passenger door. Gripping her hand tightly, I drag her through the double glass doors and straight to the front desk.

"Do you have an appointment?"

"Yes, with Doctor Garcia at 1:30pm."

"Ah, the OBGYN." The receptionist types into her computer for a good second before turning back to us and telling us to have a seat.

Sitting down, I pull Vero onto my lap.

"Akmal!"

"Shh. This is a doctor's office."

"I can't believe you."

"You should. We're here."

"We don't need to -"

"Akmal! Good to see you! How is your family? This must be your wife, congratulations. Your mother has been spreading the news about your nuptials. She's very proud."

"You know how she is. This is Vero. Vero, this is Doctor Garcia, a family friend who was kind enough to give us an appointment quickly."

I can see my wife side eyeing me but it makes no difference. We're already here. Leading us to the back, my wife grips my arm firmly.

Once we're in the designated private room, Doctor Garcia hands Vero a urine cup and proceeds to tell her to take her clothes off for a pap smear right after. It was a bit difficult once the good doctor left the room, but I was able to convince her to do what she needed to do. Vero can be strong willed but yields with the right methods.

Vero comes back into the room without the urine cup

and is avoiding my eyes as I stare at her movements. It's a good thing she didn't wear her signature red lipstick today. My eyes blaze with the puffy way her lips are looking right now, the evidence of what I had to do. When her eyes find mine, they're filled with fire and it makes my cock twitch.

The doctor comes in before we can settle our silent dispute and tells me what I already know.

"Congratulations! You're pregnant!"

Vero is looking at me with a shocked expression and I feel my smile start to creep up my lips.

VERO

"Vero! It was so sad!" Atsuko's voice is getting emotionally high, I wish I could give her a hug right now.

"I mean, what did he do when he found the sticks in the trash can?" It's been a couple of days before I could find some private time to call my BFF about my news.

"He confronted me and asked me if I was pregnant. You should have seen him Vero. The hopeful look on his face." Atsuko's stick was negative while mine was positive that fateful day. When she told me she got rid of the evidence, I didn't think she'd do such a bad job at it. I can't believe she just threw that shit in the trash can. She could have dumped the evidence in a dumpster or something. But I love her and I really feel for her right now.

"I told him it wasn't mine and it almost broke my heart seeing his face crumple. I didn't even know he was wanting to try for a baby, or else I wouldn't have been taking the pills." I can hear Atsuko sniffing on the phone. It must have hit Mat pretty hard for her to react like this.

"Well, you know men. They're not that great in communication. Especially our guys, seeing as how we're their first real relationship."

"I know, I know. But I felt like my heart was caving in with how much it hurt him. I heard him on the phone with someone while we were giving each other space. I didn't know what else to do or say to him." The sound of Atsuko blowing her nose comes clearly over the phone.

"So that's how Akmal knew…"

"Sorry, but I can't lie to Mat. Not when he looked like that. I held him for the rest of the night after we made love. He didn't talk much."

"No need to apologize, I mean it was going to come to light anyway right?" Akmal, caveman he is, made sure it came out to light with a second opinion via an OBGYN. I should be mad with how he dragged me there without my permission, but he's been on cloud nine since the news. He even started rummaging through my things and chucking out all my birth control pills. It's not like they worked anyway.

Wait a minute.

"Atsuko."

"Yeah?"

"Do me a favor and don't ask questions okay?"

"Alright."

"I'll pick you up in thirty minutes." The boys have a small photoshoot today, so they'll be out for a little bit. We can sneak this in.

By the time I drive up to Atsuko's place, she's already walked out to the parking lot to meet me.

"What's happening?"

"You'll find out in a bit." Tires squealing, we head to the last place Akmal took me. Doctor Garcia really is a family friend and was kind enough to sneak Atsuko in for a quick appointment.

"This might be a waste of time, Vero. The stick gave me a negative." My best friend's eyes are still a little pink from the crying jag she had earlier with our phone conversation.

"Then what would it hurt? It won't change a thing. But I mean, I just remembered the fact that you're using the same damn brand of birth control as me right? I saw it at your house the last time I was there. Just do it girl. Do it for Mat." Her eyes tear up a little again at the mention of his name as she nods her head.

Once she's done peeing in the cup, we wait together in the private room, holding hands. Atsuko is nervous and I'm nervous for her. When the door opens up, we both hold our breaths.

"Congratulations! You are going to be a mother!" Atsuko breaks down and cries openly and loudly while I pet her back. "It's okay, sometimes it depends on your levels of hCG and the time of day you pee on the stick. But your levels must be high enough now for it to be detected. Congratulations again."

Atsuko is almost ugly crying at this point against my shoulder. I thank Doctor Garcia who exits the room with a sympathetic smile.

EPILOGUE

$\mathcal{A}$kmal was adamant that we have a whole damn family luncheon for this thing. I'm nervous as hell, but excited at the same time. My mother, being the nosey woman she is, kept asking what this was about when I called her the other day to invite her. It took a lot of persuading but she finally agreed to bring everyone over. Stubborn woman.

Akmal was so excited about this whole thing, he invited Mat and Atsuko too since they're basically family. I haven't talked to Atsuko since the last time; Akmal has been so busy going over things we need to rearrange and such to make room for the baby. He's more into this than I am and I'm pretty into it since I'm the damn mother.

Placing my hand over my flat stomach, I smile at the thought of a life growing in there. It's so surreal. Akmal pulls up in front of his parents' house and is smiling at me from the driver's side. He's so damn happy that I can't help but be overly happy with him. Reading up on first time pregnancies, I did get nervous when google kept telling me that I'm an older mother and at higher risk for issues. Akmal kept reassuring me and went out to get all the prenatal vitamins and healthy food I would need for a balanced meal. I still sneak in ice cream, he's not taking that shit away from me.

Helping me out of the passenger side, we walk hand and hand to the front door where Akmal's mother is already waiting with her hands on her hips. Looking at her hijab, I'm reminded of our wedding day. It feels like it's been a million years ago and only yesterday. Is it always going to feel like this with Akmal? I wouldn't have it any other way. He's filled my life in ways I never could have imagined. Who knew Vero Hernandez was made for the married life?

"Akmal! You need to visit more huh. Why are you hiding away my daughter-in-law?"

"Ibu, I'm not hiding away your daughter-in-law."

"I know you are lying, but it's okay. You're here now. I called Hasanah and Sakinah, they are already here. Come come."

We haven't even greeted everyone yet when I hear my parents and Fabian not far behind us. I'm surprised I didn't hear his car. They must have taken my parent's vehicle. Mat and Atsuko follow a few minutes shortly after and that makes the whole gang.

"Sit down, sit down. Makan, Makan. We can eat while Akmal tells us what he needs to tell us. There is enough food for everyone!" Akmal's mother is admirable with her hospitality. I'm going to have to start picking up some tips and tricks since Akmal literally told me he's going to keep me knocked up, the brute.

The seating arrangement is similar to the last time we had a family luncheon, the parents in one circle and everyone else in another but the two main couples close enough to each other. As we start eating, a weird tension is shimmering between Fabian and Sakinah. I can't put my finger on whether it is from annoyance or hate. But the looks Sakinah shoots his way is scary. The lip curl doesn't help either, she hides it quickly before anyone else around her notices. Fabian being Fabian gives her a grin but there's something else there in his eyes that I can't read from this angle. What happened between those two?

Once most of us are done eating and some plates are down, Akmal clears his throat to get everyone's attention. "Everyone!" The room goes quiet and my cheeks feel flushed from the attention. I don't even know why I'm embarrassed, I shouldn't be.

"Vero is pregnant!" The roar that goes up is almost deafening, most of it coming from the mothers. Congratulations go around and everyone is in a light mood. Backs are being slapped and everyone's getting side hugs.

It takes a good while before everyone settles down but they do quickly when Atsuko's soft voice floats in the air. "Um, I have something to say too." Everyone still has smiles on their faces as they all turn to give her their attention. I smile at her encouragingly when she casts her gaze to me, nervousness in her eyes. *Come on girl, you got this.*

"I'm pregnant too." Mat almost topples her over when he slams himself into her in an embrace and the living room goes into another uproar that will probably have the neighbors calling the cops.

SAKINAH

Everyone is excited over the news of Atsuko and Vero's pregnancies. I am too but my family can be a bit much, so I slip away out the back to get a little bit of fresh air. My parents had called me in for this luncheon, but I need to head back to the university after this.

The crisp air outside always lightens the load I feel on my mind. I'm taking on a lot but I can do it. I need to do it. I want to start becoming independent as soon as I can and start living life. At twenty-five, my mother has been pushing me to get married but I think I need to find myself first.

Malaysian culture can feel so oppressive sometimes. I wonder what it would be like to be like the other westernized girls out there. Girls like Vero are comfortable in their own skin and own themselves, moving with an air of confidence.

Who am I?

"Sakinah." I internally groan when I hear his voice. He couldn't just give me a minute alone, could he? I thought we already established that this friendship thing isn't going to work out.

"Fabian."

"What are you doing out here? Were you waiting for me?" This guy.

"Don't be perasan la. Don't flatter yourself, Fabian. Can't a girl just come out for some fresh air? Not everything revolves around you." I can see him grinning to the side of me but I refuse to give him my full attention. That's exactly what he wants. Fabian is a man who looks like he always gets what he wants. Well, tough luck.

I decide to turn a little bit more away from him, hinting to him that I really don't want to put up with his shit right now when his tall, hard body moves me towards the side of the house farther away from the backdoor.

His front is to my back and my hands become locked in his grip as he brings them up to either side of my face, our fingers intertwined likc the lovers *we are not.*

"What are you doing?" I don't mean to sound like I have an attitude but I am not feeling this crap right now.

"Sakinah. I can't stop thinking about you."

"You mean about that fucking slap to your face. It's supposed to tell you to leave me the hell alone." The masculine chuckle by my ear makes me internally shiver, but I try to remain stoic. That's just what he wants from me, a reaction. He can't stand the fact that I'm not throwing myself all over him.

The thought of other girls doing this with him amps up my anger again, overshadowing whatever feelings he was starting to evoke in me while we're in this compromised position.

"So you think about it too, huh? I have to say, my cock hasn't gotten that hard in a while, Sakinah."

"Walao eh, oh my god." This guy. I'm disgusted and turned on at the same time. What is wrong with me?

I try to buck my body to get him off me but it only makes him grind his crotch against my ass. My face is flaming and now I'm glad I'm facing the wall, so he can't see the effect he really does have on me. It's starting to get hot underneath my clothes with the way his body heat is consuming me like a damn inferno. A dangerous inferno.

"Get off me Fabian."

"Go out with me Sakinah."

"I thought we were trying to be friends."

"Friends can still go out. Come on."

"Get off me." He spins me around and my mind is still

trying to catch up with the movement when his mouth lands on mine again. Fuck. This guy keeps stealing kisses from me and I hate the fact that I love it. The forbidden nature of it all only serves to make it hotter than it should be. Our lips glide for a few seconds and I come to my senses, biting his bottom lip, making him hiss and step away.

I quickly escape the sexual tension by slipping back through the back door and into the living room where everyone is still abuzz about whether the women will have boy or girl babies.

AUTHOR'S NOTE

Why is Fabian and Sakinah's potential relationship forbidden when they're technically not related? Well, an alpha reader [for the Malaysian side] has informed me that once you are married into the family, you are not allowed to have any sort of relations of that kind. It is not allowed and it is very much frowned upon.

What does this mean for our couple? It could mean many things. Middle sister Sakinah is the most rebellious of the girls in Akmal's family. She wishes to be more independent and westernized like Vero, as you see in this epilogue.

But you know what they say: be careful what you ask for because you just might get it.

This will lead to dramatic changes, ones she will have to learn to accept or she will have to learn to deny the love that grows between herself and Fabian.

Who would you choose? Family or love?

PLAYLIST

Christina Aguilera - Lord Have Mercy on Me
Postmodern Jukebox - All About That Bass
Etta James - At Last
NOTD, Shy Martin - Keep You Mine (Acoustic)
Christina Aguilera - Nasty Naughty Boy
John Legend - All of Me
Beyonce - Halo
Nina Simone - I Put a Spell on You
Luis Fonsi - Despacito ft. Daddy Yankee
Christina Aguilera - Save Me From Myself
Imelda May - It's Good To Be Alive
Jencarlos Canela - Bajito ft. Kymani Marley

THE REVELATION OF US

LABELS & LACE

THE REVELATION OF US

LABELS & LACE

YD LA MAR

BLURB

Fabian Hernandez: The man who stole my first kiss.
My recently acquired brother in law.
From the moment he came into my life, he turned everything upside down.
There's a magnetism that keeps drawing us back together.
But we can't.
It isn't allowed.
It would bring shame.
It shouldn't have to be this hard, this complicated.
Maybe if I were someone else.
Someone without a controlling mother, a conservative culture.
A family and culture that sees this man as immediate family.
This is so difficult.
My hijab is getting too tight, everything around me is becoming too constricting.
Why must he drive me to the brink of madness with every touch, every kiss?

When things start to unravel, will I be strong enough to make the hardest decision of my life?

COURTESY WARNING

This book may contain triggers for some. Triggers include but not limited to: violence, familial violence/abuse, subject matters that may be sensitive to some readers.

*** This book may contain authentic speech used by the different nationalities/ethnicities represented in this book. Some grammar usage was purposely done with broken English to continue to allow the story to flow authentically. ***

NAMES

Fabian Hernandez
Nur Sakinah Binti Alqi

Hasanah
Hidaya

Mohd Akmal Bin Alqi
Veronica "Vero" Hernandez

Matunaagd Big Crow
Atsuko Kobayashi

Mohd Bisaam
Mohd Amir Bin Hafiz
Aunti Zunai (Amir's mother)
Jason Trafford

Omar Cortes

TRANSLATIONS

MALAY

Makan, Makan - Eat, Eat

Don't be perasan la - don't flatter yourself (la is sometimes added at the end of sentences)

Ibu, don't kacau him - mom, don't disturb him

Walao eh - Oh my god/oh shit

Can hah - Are you sure?

Bapa - dad

Ibu - mom

Cantik - beautiful/pretty

Anjing - dog

Jahanam - shit (distressful)

Aku sepak - I'll kick you

Apa kabar - how are you?

Nak pergi mana ke? - Where are you going?

SANISH

¿Mira, mira quien viene? - Look, look who's coming
La bendición - asking for blessing, typical greeting
Que Dios te bendiga - God bless you, *reply* to La bendición
¿Tienes hambre? - are you hungry?
Comida - food
Cabrón - fucker
¿Quién es tu amigo/a? - Who is your friend?
¿Porque? - Why?
Mira tu boca! - Watch your mouth
¿Quién es tu novio/a? - who is your boyfriend/girlfriend?
Siéntate por favor - sit please
Esposo/esposa - husband/wife
Explícamelo - explain it to me
Hija/o - daughter/son
No te preocupes - don't you worry
¿Está embarazada? - is she pregnant?
Seria/serio - serious
Silencio - be quiet
Relájate - Relax
Dramatica - dramatic
Buen provecho - enjoy your meal
Mi cojones - my balls
una mujer - a woman
Ella es su novia - she's his girlfriend
Sin respeto - no respect

1

____

FABIAN

"**H**ey, what's up Omar."

This fucker and I have been working together at this construction site for the past five years. When we're on an off-season, we also do carpentry work as private contractors as well.

"Alrighty boys, let's get this shit done today." The boss is rounding up the guys now. It's been good working under Francisco. He's been fair and keeps it real.

We've been working on this building project for ages and can finally see the light at the end of the tunnel. It has been good and hard while it lasted, waking up at the crack of dawn consecutively. I'm actually looking forward to the little reprieve I'll be getting, to actually sleeping in. Shit, my dick is getting hard just thinking about it.

...the same way it does when...

The day goes by quickly. I almost made a few mistakes

because of a certain Malaysian princess who seems to be taking over my mind these days.

Sakinah. The little minx that sasses as good as she slaps. For the life of me, I don't fucking understand why I'm so damn attracted to her. At thirty-six, I've been jumping from tail to tail. They come in droves when the boys and I are working the job. It also helps when the day's labor makes us hot, most of us start taking off our shirts to wipe the sweat off our faces.

Yet this girl, who's covered from damn head to toe in fabric, makes my blood boil hotter than a stripper on a pole. Shit, I need to get my head back into the game before I get myself killed on this construction site.

Yeah, I'm going to miss these days, but it's also good to take a break from this backbreaking shit. I'm probably aging faster by the second with how much I put my body through with these damn building projects in the city.

"Yo, Omar, where you headed after work?"

"Shit, this crap's got me so tired, I'm just going to go straight home, shower and crash. It's been a fucking week since I started getting a little pain in my knee."

"Yeah? You see a doctor for that shit?" Pot meet kettle. My body's been aching and creaking in new places too. I feel it more on cold mornings.

"I am now since the project is done." Fuck, the life of a construction worker. He's got that right. I wouldn't want a doctor's note to tell me I can't finish projects. That's too much money to pass up.

When the boss calls it for the day to end, the boys and I cheer.

"Job well done guys. Keep an ear out, I'll be calling everyone back in when we get a new contract." Everyone nods and starts to disperse, kicking up dust in their wake.

Half the boys say they're going to hit up the bar after work, the other half are going wherever they usually go at the end of a work day. I usually hit up mi Mamá's casa for some homemade food since I'm too fucking tired after work to do any sort of cooking for myself.

Tossing my hard hat into the back of my 1970 Chevelle SS, I wipe my sweaty face one more time. I usually keep a few clean shirts in the back as well for hot days like this. I probably smell like a pig's balls, but at least a clean shirt will get me back home so I can take a cold shower. Moving the driver's seat forward to make room for my shoulders, I lean in and start rummaging through the shit in the back.

The sound of feminine giggles and gasps has me grabbing my shirt quickly and righting myself back up.

Standing about five feet away from me are some young ladies who look to be just coming back from the library downtown with how they're holding books in their hands.

"Ladies." It wouldn't do to be rude despite how they're checking out my naked torso. Scrunching up the grey T-shirt in my hand, I don't miss the gasps when I start putting it over my head.

"Hi." The brave one on the left says. They still haven't left despite not saying any more. Once I'm able to straighten out the shirt situation, I give them a smile and wink and push the driver's seat back to its original position and get in.

The Chevelle purrs before I throw it in gear and pull out of the parking structure. Rolling my windows down, the cool breeze refreshes me. My muscles are aching but it's a good ache. One that tells me I'll be getting a fat paycheck by the end of the week.

My mother still lives in our old dilapidated neighborhood and refuses to move despite the money I give her. Old habits I guess. It does get nostalgic every time I drive back home.

The apartment I have closer to the city is probably collecting dust at this point since I barely go there. I should get rid of it and just save the damn cash. Maybe I should find something closer to mi Mamá's casa. She'd love that shit.

...Maybe I should find something near Sakinah. She'd hate that shit.

Throwing my car in park, I step out and start towards my mother's front door. Of course, she's been listening for my car's roar with her hands on her hips in her signature apron.

"La bendición." Girls might tell me I'm a bad boy but I'm really not. I know my manners and shit and never forget to ask my mother for blessings when I come home.

"Que Dios te bendiga. ¿Tienes hambre? I made a lot of comida because I know you eat like un caballo." Do I eat like a horse? I guess I do. I'm probably eating her out of house and home but she never tells me to leave, she just keeps feeding me more.

That's why I love mi Mamá. She takes care of me like that. I wonder if Sakinah would take care of me like that. I'm a simple guy, one that enjoys eating. Judging by the way Akmal's family serves food, I bet Sakinah can cook like a beast. Shit, thinking about her cooking for me makes my dick twitch.

The good thing about my mother's house is that she's never gotten rid of any of my stuff. Walking towards my old room, I grab a change of clothes before I hit up the modest single bathroom, leaving the door open in case anyone needs it while I'm in here.

The moment the cold water hits me, a shiver goes down my spine. It reminds me of Sakinah and how soft her damn lips are. The energy between us sizzles even though she refuses to acknowledge it. I've driven by her house a few times and notice that she doesn't always stay home. I wonder where she goes or if she lives somewhere else.

An image of that fucker at the wedding telling her how beautiful she is comes to mind and I want to punch the damn tiles. But I wouldn't do my parent's house like that, so I put an effort into holding myself back. Soaping myself up, I make sure to go over everything twice to get rid of all the sweat and dust I've attracted from the worksite. The sound of muffled footsteps makes me stop.

"Oye, Fabian, is that you?" My father always makes sure to use a louder voice when I'm in here.

"Si Papá. I'll be done in a minute." I don't hear what he says, but a few more swipes of soap all over my chest and between my legs, and I'm rinsing under the cold water. Sliding the glass door over I'm hit with the smell of…

"Papá, you need to warn me before you just up and take a shit while I'm in here!"

"A man can only do so much to control his bowels. What the hell am I supposed to do? Wait for you to get done washing tu culo? What if you take too long?"

My god, he knows I only take ten-minute showers. Wrapping my waist with a towel and grabbing another to cover my nose, I high tail it out of this confined room making sure to shut the door to have mercy on everyone else. He can kill someone with that smell. What the hell has he been eating?

Quickly getting dressed, I head into the kitchen to greet my mother again. Damn, at least the smell of her food is overpowering that shit I just walked through.

"Did you talk to tu hermana?" Vero's a married woman now, why would I be calling her? She's probably busy fucking her husband.

"No, she's probably making babies. I don't want to hear

that shit." Grabbing a plate, something hits me in the back of my head hard. "Ow! Mamá!"

"Oi! Mira tu boca!" Turning my head, I see my mother putting her shoe back on. How does she do that shit so fast? Hispanic mothers must take some sort of class to master the chancla throw.

"You need to be making grandbabies for me. When are you going to find un mujer to bring home, huh? You're getting old."

"That's just mean, Mamá. I'm not that old."

"Too old." Am I? I don't feel like I am. Grabbing some tacos, I head to the table. Shit, if my mother thinks I'm old, what does Sakinah think of me?

Well, it fucking doesn't matter because it wouldn't stop me anyway.

Finishing up and putting the plate in the sink, I walk to the back to see if I need to grab any more spare shirts to keep in the car. I need to toss the dirty clothes into the laundry too while I'm here.

"Fabian, how's work going?"

"We just finished up our project. I'll be off for a good while until we get another contract."

"Yeah? Do you have any side jobs lined up?"

"Not yet. Omar is getting his knees checked out at the doctor's today. He said it's been acting up."

"Oh, that's too bad. If you guys need an extra hand, let me know hijo."

The sound of the front door opening makes us both turn.

"Alejandro, tu hija is home!" My mother's voice carries over into the laundry area. Vero's back? I wonder why.

"Vero! That was a beautiful wedding." I'm walking right behind my father when he suddenly stops in front of Vero. "What is wrong, Vero? Dónde está tu esposo?"

What the hell? Why does he sound so concerned like that? I can't see Vero's face too well since it's buried in my dad's chest in a bear hug. The hairs on the back of my neck are starting to rise. What the fuck did he do to her?

"Vero, what happened? Whose ass do I need to kick?" My eyes quickly dart to my mother in case a shoe comes flying but her expression tells me she's just as worried about Vero right now. I stand behind my dad just in case she changes her mind though.

"It's nothing guys. I just… I just need to clear my head a bit."

"Clear your head? What did Akmal do? Why are you guys fighting already?" Since when the fuck does my level headed sister need to clear her head? She's usually jumping into things head first but not without forethought. Well, I'm about to fucking find out for myself if I need to kick his ass or not.

My dad is taking Vero into the living room but I don't follow. Walking back into the laundry area for some privacy, I scroll through my phone for the only contact I have that's close enough to Akmal.

Bringing the phone to my ear, my mind starts to playback our last encounter at the wedding. It takes almost five rings before she decides to pick up. This girl and her ways of stringing me along. I've never been one to fall for that hard to get shit, but there's just something about Sakinah that tells me she doesn't play.

When she finally picks up, I'm annoyed the fuck out. How does this girl get the one up on me like this? I'm usually the one dragging women along.

"Hello?" The breathy sound of her voice makes my cock twitch. I miss the taste of her lips.

"Sakinah." All the shit I should say to her in my anger

dissipates as thoughts of her body against mine start to take over. I'm an old horny bastard that probably should not be thinking of Akmal's sister this way. But how can I not with a voice like that?

My hand starts to rub over the jeans between my legs. She shouldn't affect me this way and not even physically be here to do anything about it.

"Hurry up, I got things I need to do." Fucking hell. I bet that pretty little mouth of hers would look good around my -

"Vero came home upset and shit. What did your brother do?"

"I don't know. He's not here with me, he's probably still at his apartment. Why don't you call him?"

"Because I only have your number, or did you forget when you slapped me and walked away?"

She doesn't say much else right before she fucking hangs up on me. I should leave a sassy little piece like that alone but damn if it doesn't make me want to find her and show her what she can do with that mouth of hers.

Leaving the laundry area in a slight daze I grill my sister about what's up. Sounds to me like a misunderstanding but the moment she tells me that Akmal told her to calm down… that boy just dug his own grave.

Every man should know this rule. Never - and I mean *never* - tell a woman to calm down. Especially a Puerto Rican Hernandez woman.

Sakinah was good on her word because not too long after Vero's dramatic entrance and moping around, I find Akmal coming up the front yard to fix the mess he made.

Giving him the advice he needs to hear, I watch as he mans up and takes his wife home. Watching them get into the car, something inside of me starts to feel funny. Though the screen door is closed, I wait and watch as Akmal takes my sister safely out of the neighborhood and back home where they belong. A breeze comes in bringing the smells of different types of food being made in this small neighborhood where houses are sometimes too close for comfort.

Where would I take Sakinah back to? My empty bachelor apartment near the city? Shit, I probably have bachelor written all over my face. It's no wonder she pushes me away and wants nothing to do with me. What can I do to convince her to give me a second look? Pressing my lips together, the memory of our kiss at the wedding comes back to me. She didn't seem that resistant to the idea of me then. It was actually getting pretty hot up until that slap.

Maybe I need a woman like her to keep me on my toes. All the women I've gone through are all the same. One and done, sometimes coming for seconds. But besides telling me how hot I am, they never want to stick around to even get to know me. And I never want them to stick around to show them who I am.

But Sakinah is basically family now. We'll be running into each other more often than not, right? Shit, maybe I should be running into her more to check up on her. Make sure that guy from the wedding isn't all up in her face while I'm over here eating tacos and watching my sister patch up her marriage.

At least she has something to patch up. What the fuck do I have?

2

---

*C*lasses have been long and drawn out today. The thirteen credits I'm taking this semester aren't too bad. I'm usually going through things in a breeze. What is different this time?

Fabian.

Okay, you need to shut up brain. Fabian has nothing to do with anything. It probably has to do with the news about Vero and Atsuko's dual pregnancy. Yeah, that's got to be it. Walking to my last class of the day, Physics, my mind starts to wander towards the way Fabian pressed his lips to mine. He keeps stealing what doesn't belong to him...yet it was what every fantasy was made of.

I can't believe the asshole called me today saying we need to talk about what happened at the family lunch. It was going so well without thinking about him at all but the moment I heard his voice, my mind has been a jumbled mess.

We've been called back over to my parents house about something. I'm scared because I know Fabian's going to be there. How am I supposed to act around him? We're basically...kissing family members at this point.

My westernized brain is shouting that we're not blood related, but the Malaysian part of me is telling me we're committing the worst kind of taboo. If my parents ever found out...

Shaking my head, I continue to help Hasanah and Hidaya in the kitchen with the food.

About ten minutes afterwards, everyone starts coming in, but my eyes are already searching him out. Everyone does their greetings and Fabian is able to slip by unnoticed. My head is turned down as we walk a little away from the main crowd.

"Sakinah, I've missed you."

"You shouldn't say these things."

"Why?" I'm ticked he's putting me in this predicament, making my feelings bubble up again at the most inappropriate time.

"Fabian! We can't do this here!" I'm hissing under my breath as my eyes dart left and right in case anyone sees us talking a foot away from each other, pretending to mill about like everyone else.

"I can't stop thinking about you. About us."

"You need to!"

"Sakinah." When his hand tries to grab mine, I panic and jerk it away, turning and walking off towards the kitchen. He knows better than to follow me alone in this house. There are too many eyes looking. Too many eyes that might catch us.

"Aye, makan makan! Let's sit and eat. There is plenty of food!" My mother's voice carries all the way to where I'm hiding. Coming back into the living room, it seems there's already a pattern to the seating arrangement as we find our spots on the floor. Of course I have to be sitting next to Fabian. No matter how hard I try, it seems the universe keeps pushing us closer and closer together.

Fabian gives me a look and I shoot him a glare to tell him to behave. This can get ugly fast if any of my sisters catch us.

We're almost done eating in relative peace when my brother clears his throat. This must be what we're all here for.

"Everyone, Vero is pregnant!" Walao eh. Oh my god.

My eyes dart to Fabian's and he's looking at me intensely but not saying a word. Gathering up some of the dishes to put away and try to distract myself, I hear someone else announcing something. It's Atsuko.

"I have something to say too...I'm pregnant t-" I don't even wait for her to finish as I quickly gather plates with my sister and put them away in the kitchen. Hidaya is already starting to wash them, so I excuse myself out the back door.

I need to concentrate on school and head back over there. I'm over halfway through my courses for this engineering major. Soon, soon I'll be able to start living life. My mother's been pushing me to find a husband but no one's been catching my eye.

Except -

I can't. We can't. The more I chant it into my mind the more my chest constricts. It's not fair. Malaysian culture can feel so oppressive sometimes. I wonder what it would be like to be like Vero who's comfortable in her own skin, who takes what she wants and gets her happy ending.

"Sakinah." Groaning, I start to question whether I'm just set up to fail.

"Fabian."

"What are you doing out here? Were you waiting for me?" This guy.

"Don't be perasan la. Don't flatter yourself, Fabian. Can't a girl just come out for some fresh air? Not everything revolves around you." I can't look at him right now. I turn to walk away only to be blocked in by his hard body a little ways away from the back door.

His front is to my back and my hands become locked in his grip as he brings them up to either side of my face, our fingers inter-twined like the lovers we are not.

"What are you doing?" I don't mean to sound like I have an attitude but I am not feeling this crap right now.

"Sakinah. I can't stop thinking about you." My mind goes into a blur as we do this push and pull song and dance again.

When I'm finally able to escape him and the house, I drive myself all the way back to my place without looking in the rearview mirror.

"Ow, watch it." The masculine voice comes above my head as I'm already leaning down from dropping my stack of books. Damn engineering degrees with their ginormous textbooks. I used to wear it in my backpack, but then my back started hurting after a while.

"Oh! I'm so sorry!" Picking up my books from the ground, I stack them back together and start fast walking towards class. My gosh, Fabian needs to get out of my mind.

The roar of a familiar engine goes by but when I turn to look, there's nothing there. Nothing that would match the sound anyway. Ducking my head into the building doors, I make it to Physics with ten minutes to spare. I really should probably start leaving some of these books in my car.

"Hey! Sakinah, what are you going to do for the project?" Jason's turned around from the row below me.

"Oh! I don't know, I haven't thought that far just yet. Maybe something with velocity as a vector quantity."

"Yeah? Man, I don't know what I'm going to do." A cute little wrinkle forms on his forehead as he starts to scratch the back of his head. Jason and I have become a little bit closer than acquaintances since starting physics together. He's a nice white boy who usually greets me when I come in. He greets all the girls around him really, but isn't pushy beyond that.

A loud booming voice comes in and we all straighten in our seats as our professor makes his way towards his table.

"Alright ladies and gents, I've decided to make it a little easier on you guys and let you guys partner up for the project." Hoops and hollers can be heard all around me but I'm not joining in because not only do I have to think of the project details, now I have to find someone who would compliment the way I think. I don't want a partner who makes me do everything.

"Sakinah! Let's partner up! Please! I don't have any good ideas but I'm good at helping an idea that's already there. We'll be good together." Jason has his hands in a prayer position as he turns around to look at me again.

Ugh, I don't know what his work ethic is like, I never cared to know. But since we have to have partners, I might as well pick someone I can at least easily talk to, I guess.

"Yeah, we can partner up."

"Yes!" Jason is literally jumping up and down like a loon but since everyone around us is moving all over the place to look for partners, no one really notices him.

The professor let us use the rest of the time to get together with our groups and lay down ideas for our project that's due in two weeks time. Since Jason already inferred that we'll be using mine, we give ourselves a break today after exchanging necessary information.

"So how about we meet up at the library in two days at ...let's say 3 pm? How's your schedule looking?"

"My Wednesdays are usually short, yeah I can do that."

"Cool, see you then partner."

Waving him off, the professor announces the end of class. I really need to start putting these bricks of a textbook in the car.

Walking out through the front doors of the building, I'm

trying my best to look down so I don't fall over the few steps down. Making it down alive, I almost released the breath I was holding only to run into something hard in front of me. But unlike last time, my books don't fall because the person is holding me by the arms with their strong arms.

"Oh, I'm so sorry! Man, why does this keep hap-" His cocky grin is the first thing I see and I already know who it belongs to. No one has a smile that can make panties melt like that on the science side of this damn campus. I know, I've looked...trying to find eye candy that could replace the image before me.

But no one does dreamy bad boy like Fabian Hernandez.

"What are you doing here Fabian?" Why my voice has so much attitude, I don't know. Just something about him that makes me put my guard up.

"Sakinah, why do you need to be like that? How about 'it's nice seeing you here' or something?" He's kidding right?

"I see you're here. What do you need?" Fabian laughs and my insides glow. It's a good thing my hijab is covering the flush that's probably showing on my skin. Those cute little crinkles by his eyes when he smiles like this makes me want to drop my books and just climb him like a tree.

Instead, I'm frowning at him and waiting for him to stop laughing and attracting all the attention from the females nearby. Ugh. Why does he have to have this kind of energy? Why the hell do I feel like I want to claw all these girls' eyes out? This makes my mood worse.

"Sakinah, you're much more beautiful when you smile, you know that? What's up with the frown? Here, let me help you with those books." What the hell am I supposed to say to that? I want to be mad, but I can't. Yanking my books away from him, I continue like I didn't just act like a petulant brat.

"Fabian, is there a reason why you are here?"

"Well, since you asked so nicely… I just so happened to be in the neighborhood and who do I see? The girl I've been thinking about all day." This asshole probably tells all the girl's this. I can feel my face scrunching at the thought.

"We've already established this Fabian. I don't think this friendship thing is going to work out."

"Sakinah, Sakinah, Sakinah. Why must you give up on us so easily? Come on, we can hang like adults and not make a thing about it, right?" What is he trying to say? That I'm not an adult?

"Look here, old man. I don't know what you're insinuating with your comment."

"Fucking hell, Sakinah. I want to hang out with you. That's what I'm *insinuating*. Can't a guy try his damndest to get a pretty girl by his side?" I can feel the butterflies fluttering inside my stomach, but I can't let it show. How can he just stand there in his stupid boots, form fitted jeans and button down shirt looking like a delicious snack talking about me being pretty? Vero and her brother are two of a kind in their vintage rockabilly looks.

Judging by the lingering females around us, I'm not the only one who thinks this way.

"I'm sure you have plenty of women lined up for the chance. Why don't you choose from your usual pool of females hmm?" I'm fishing, I know it. He better not agree or else I will kick his ass until next Tuesday. I'm staring daggers at him just daring him to say something about another woman.

"Damn Sakinah. There isn't anyone else and even if there was, which there *isn't*, it's not their company I'm seeking alright. I'm here aren't I? Do you see anyone else but us? No." I'm scared. I'm scared to get my hopes up for a man like Fabian.

A man who could very well take my offered heart and stomp all over it if he finds something better along the way. My head starts to feel tight under my hijab and my body is starting to heat up from the embarrassment I feel for something that hasn't even happened yet.

That's the problem though, right? *Yet.*

Turning around without another word, I start walking towards the student parking lot. I need to get out of here. How does Fabian make my emotions feel like I'm freefalling from a rollercoaster just by talking to me?

I can hear his boots following me and I start walking faster. It's juvenile, I know. But I can't help the way this fucker makes me feel like punching him and kissing him all at once! Is this how little boys feel when they're young and on the playground around someone they like?

My car is coming in sight and I'm almost about to sprint but I can't because of the dress I'm in today. My hand is already reaching into my pocket and fishing out the keys but before I can stick it in the door, I'm spun around and trapped by a whole lot of Fabian. Holding my books closer to my chest like it's a shield, my head tilts up to look at him with fire. If I didn't have these books in my arms, I would slap him in the face … again.

Fabian is thinking the same thing because with both arms on either side of me, leaning against my little sedan, he comes closer in with a smirk.

"Sakinah." My eyes narrow.

"Fabian."

"Why are you being like this?"

"Like what?" Ugh, why *am* I like this?

"You should want to be around me. We're family after all."

"Yeah well, family shouldn't be asking each other out on dates then."

"Sakinah, go out with me. You might enjoy it more than you think...if you'd just let yourself."

"I'm busy that day." His laugh booms across the parking lot making even more girls stop. He needs to quit this shit. It's pissing me off.

"I haven't even decided on the date yet!"

"You don't have to. I'm busy."

Quicker than I can react, Fabian grabs my textbooks and puts them on top of the roof of my car right behind me, never letting me out of the cage of his arms.

"Sakinah."

"Fabian."

I'm about to open my mouth to tell him to fuck off somewhere else when his lips crash on mine again. This man…

This man's lips are so damn soft as he uses them expertly against mine and I can't help but fall prey to his wicked ways…

My god, Fabian is sin on a stick and I don't know how my arms ended up winding around his shoulders, pulling him into me even more. When he groans into my mouth as my breasts press against his chest, the spell of the moment gets broken. I nip his lip and push him as hard as my body will allow me.

Like the coward I am once more, I jump and grab my books before getting into the car and slamming the door shut. Letting out a long breath, I close my eyes but not before I lock the damn doors.

A thump startles me and has me looking out the side window to see Fabian rubbing his forehead on my car. This shouldn't look as endearing as it does. What is wrong with him? Why is he like this? His voice floats into the car slightly muffled.

"Sakinah, this isn't over." He straightens up and bores his

eyes into mine, full of promises that make my nipples tighten. His intensity scares me. I don't know how to handle everything that is Fabian Hernandez, not like this. I don't know what I'm feeling, everything is so confusing. Even being the most rebellious sister didn't prepare me for a force of nature like him.

Waiting until he walks back to wherever he came from, I start the car and zoom out of the parking lot as fast as I can, careful not to run any of the other students over in my haste.

3

FABIAN

*T*his girl kills me. Fucking. Kills. Me. Why is it that everything that comes out of her damn mouth just makes my dick harder and harder? Fucking hell. I've run into plenty of sassy brats in my bachelorhood. I usually overlook these girls because life is too damn short to be chained to that kind of headache.

But Sakinah? Damn if my need for her doesn't just burn and come to fucking life when she pushes me away.

Like the pathetic fool I am, I've been following her around. Does that make me an old stalking bastard? So be it. That little spitfire lives in my fucking mind twenty-four-seven and I fucking hate it. I can't even kiss her to get her out of my system because she's slippery as hell.

But each taste she gives me only makes me more addicted - like a damn forbidden fruit. She's right of course, since we're basically family I probably shouldn't be asking her out but what hot blooded male in their right mind would let *that* woman slip through their fingertips without putting forth their best effort?

Shit, she only thinks this is all I got.

I switched out the car at my parent's house the moment I saw her on that damn campus while I was driving around. I'm following her car now because she's never seen me in anything other than my Chevelle. My car's roar is too distinct, she'd spot me a mile away. But with my parent's car, I can be right behind her - like I am right now - and she wouldn't have a clue.

She's been driving around aimlessly for the past thirty minutes. "What are you doing Sakinah?" Look at me, she's got me talking to myself while I'm on a mission to find out everything she does.

This is what happens when I have too much time on my hands. Watching her buy coffee and then drive back to the campus was torturous. She should've been kissing me, letting me touch her, letting me do things that will help keep her awake...then she wouldn't need no damn coffee.

My fingers hit the speed dial on my phone as we get closer and closer to the student parking lot at the side of the university.

"What's up? What do you need?" Damn, am I destined to be surrounded by sassy ass women or what?

"Vero, does Sakinah live on campus or what?"

"Why the hell do you want to know? Leave that girl alone if you're looking for someone to play with, alright? She's Akmal's sister. She's a good girl." Is she fucking hearing herself? Has she met Sakinah? *Good girl my ass.*

"Just answer the damn question."

"Puto, why should I be fucking involved in your shit? You know Akmal's culture doesn't allow for all that public affection and sexy shit before marriage. Sakinah has probably never even kissed before."

"Wait, hold up. Say that again?" This can't be real. I felt the way her lips pressed against mine. That kind of passion is not from a girl who hasn't kissed before. Vero has to be on something today.

"I fucking said what I fucking said. Sakinah and all of Akmal's sisters are innocent. That's why he's been so protective of them, not letting any of his classmates around the house. The girls are pure, Fabian. You probably don't know what that is." This perra right here, she better be fucking glad she's mi hermana. "If you ain't serious, leave her alone."

But that's the problem. All the shit Vero is telling me, just makes me dig my heels in deeper. I guessed Sakinah was inexperienced...but never been kissed? Nah. *No way.*

"You never answered the question Vero. She live on campus or what?" I can hear my sister let out an exasperated sigh. Shit, I probably called her in the middle of fucking her man or something with the attitude she's giving me.

"What the hell do I look like? Google? I don't know Fabian. Stop being weird." The entire time my sister is going off on me, Sakinah's car continues out the other end of the student parking lot and onto one of the smaller neighborhood streets. *Huh, what's this now? Where exactly are we headed?*

"Alright alright. Go back to your husband and tell him to put a leash on you. Sheesh."

"Pinche-" I don't need to hear that shit so I end the call. She can take out her frustrations with her husband. At least she has someone to take her frustrations out on. I haven't had sex in who knows how long with that recent contract taking up all my time and energy.

Well, I would have made time for Sakinah if she'd just let me in. But no...she had to be like *this*. She had to make me follow her ass around so I can get to know her and find better ways of convincing her to give me the time of day.

How did I become this?

When she pulls up into a modest little residence, my interest becomes piqued. Does she live here alone? I mean, it's better than on campus where there's other men around. But what if there are men next door and they take advantage of her because they know she's alone? My hands tighten on the steering wheel as I drive past her house and make another loop around to not look as suspicious.

This is going to have to be something we need to remedy. On my way back around, I pull the car into park right along the sidewalk and jump out. She's had at least five minutes to settle in so she shouldn't suspect me. Standing in front of her door, I try to look into her windows in case she's hiding someone in there. My mind is going a million miles a minute with the possibilities when I hear someone clearing their throat. Turning I see an older woman walking her little yapper dog, staring at me in disapproval.

Giving her a smile and a wave, I try to act like this is normal and knock on Sakinah's front door like I'm supposed to. The old woman needs to mind her own damn business any wa-

"Dammit Fabian! What. Do. You. Want?!" Aw hell, just look at her fire. *Fucking beautiful.* In fact, I'm so fucking turned on right now...

She tries to slam the door in my face but can't since I've already stuck my boot in the doorway. It is a good thing I tend to wear steel toes from working on construction sites. The door bangs loudly and practically vibrates as it jumps back with an equal amount of force.

Her eyes widen in the prettiest of ways and I just then

realize that she doesn't have her headwrap on. *Holy shit.* I can't let this opportunity pass up, no way in hell.

I'm taking steps forward into her home and she starts to take tentative steps back. Closing and locking the door behind me, I turn back around and finally take her all in. *What the hell?* Is *this* how she walks around in her house? What if there are weirdos out there trying to get a good look at what's mine?

Her shorts are hugging her ass deliciously and her tank top? Dios mio, her nipples are about to poke my eyes out with how hard they are. My mouth is fucking watering but I'm trying to stay strong.

Is this what she's been hiding under all that fabric? *Good.* It's what she should be hiding because hell if I'm going to fucking let her walk out in public like this.

"Stop looking at me like that. What the hell is your problem?"

"Look at you like what? Like you're the fucking sexiest woman I've ever seen? Like your body is making it hard for me to keep it in my fucking pants right now? Like I'm going to kill any motherfucker that even looks at you the way I do?"

She gasps and I swear it makes her tits bounce. She's doing this to me on purpose. She's poking the damn beast and right now I can barely walk straight with how hard I am behind my jeans. In fact, it's starting to ache, but seeing Sakinah like this is worth it. It's like being given a glimpse into something I'm not allowed to.

Does that make me a peeping whatever they call it? Nah, because she sees me looking right here and she isn't pushing me away. Oh no, in fact, I think there's desire in her pretty brown eyes right now despite the shit she spews at me.

I can feel my face grinning. I'm loving this game we play

together. I don't even realize that I've been slowly walking towards her this entire time until she starts to bend over the back of her couch from being trapped. Well, I know for a damn fact she's good at slithering away when she wants to...does this mean, she wants this just like I do right now?

We're chest to chest and I can feel every breath she takes as her breasts press against my body, the warmth diffusing into my very senses as I continue to lean in as close as I can. Am I taking advantage of her? Nah, the hate she's throwing at me right now through her eyes tells me she can take care of her fucking self.

And I love that about her.

"Sakinah."

"Fabian." She's putting up a tough front but her voice is coming out breathier than when she answered the damn door earlier.

The sexual tension between us is practically sizzling the longer we both stand here just staring each other down. I know she feels it too even though she likes to deny it.

"How did you find me?"

"I followed you. Had to make sure my girl was alright. Wouldn't want any...predators to be chasing her around without her knowing. What kind of friend would that make me then, hmm?"

"We're not friends."

"Yeah? Then what are we?" My hands have slowly started creeping around her and between her shoulder blades. I can feel the tension radiating off her as my fingers continue to glide up until it threads through her beautiful fucking wavy hair that looks like it was made for a goddess.

Or a Malaysian princess.

Bringing my face closer to her, she shuts her eyes tightly like she's scared of what I'll do next. Haven't I shown her nothing but softness in my touches? Maybe I'm being a little too rough for this… what did my sister say about her?

"Sakinah and all of Akmal's sisters are innocent"

Vero's voice rings in my head but I still don't believe it. Sakinah's eyes are still glued shut like she's waiting for death but all I do is run the tip of my nose over her cheek, inhaling her scent. It's light and feminine, almost hidden just like her.

The longer I trail my nose all over her face, the more she starts to relax. *That's it, just let go.* Her lashes are so long and dark they sweep across her cheeks like the shit you only see in movies. When her eyes flutter open, I softly press my lips to hers so as to not scare her off. She's so skittish around me and thinks her little sassy personality can hide it. But when she's pliant like this in my arms, I know better.

Sakinah is afraid to let go.

I can be a patient man. I can be anything she needs me to be as long as she lets me in.

We both still have our eyes open as I give her another chaste kiss. I'm going to have to play this game differently with her. Find an opening and take it.

She finally turns her head away from me but still doesn't run. I think I'm wearing her down.

"Fabian, you fucking bastard. Why are you always stealing kisses from me?" Her voice has already lost its edge despite the words coming out of her mouth.

"Stealing? I don't know about that, Sakinah. Kind of seems like you welcome me in sometimes."

Her face turns back to me and her eyes are absolutely blazing. I'm about to lean in for another kiss when her hand cockblocks us by covering her mouth. *This girl.* Chuckling against her knuckles, I kiss them anyway.

She shoves me off with a hard push and moves herself quickly on the other side of the couch, creating an even bigger barrier between us. Jokes on her, as I cross my arms over my chest and concentrate my sights on those perky nipples that are still pushing against her tank top with every harsh breath she takes.

"I'll let that slide this time since I'm very much enjoying the view." With a cute shriek, she goes and has to ruin my day by crossing her own arms over her chest. Now we're a mirror image of each other. I wonder who has the ball in their court here?

"Look here..you...anjing! You've already stolen my first kiss. I forbid you from stealing anymore from me!" Holy mother of…

I'm staring at her intently. She's not telling the truth is she? This has to be another one of her games - trying to put me off her trail with shocking statements. Looking her up and down, the girl has to be in her early to mid twenties. First fucking kiss? … and from a bastard like me?

I'd pat myself on the back if I knew it wouldn't piss her off more than she already apparently is. Well now, I think she just upped the stakes and I'm more than happy to take the challenge of being her other firsts.

Shit, did I think my cock was aching behind my pants before? Mi cojones are tightening just thinking about her beneath me, surrendering and moaning in pleasure. Shit, I can make her really happy if she'd let me.

"Well with that kind of information, I'm sure as hell glad it was me instead of some other asshole."

"Did you really just fucking say that?" I'm already starting to stalk her around the couch as she starts to pace around the opposite direction.

"Are you seriously thinking about kissing someone else? Because if you are, they're not going to be alive to find out. Sakinah, let's stop this nonsense. Get over here."

"Why should I? All you ever do is corner me."

"You make me."

"How so?" I jump over the couch and watch as she squeals and tries to run to the front door. The thing with little women is that they think they're going fast when in reality, each of my strides is probably equal to a few of theirs.

Grabbing her from the back, I lift her off her feet as she struggles and wriggles doing nothing but making my cock ache as her ass starts pressing into it. Burying my face into her hair, I groan. Damn this woman. She shouldn't feel this damn good in my arms even when she's fighting me like a she-demon.

Sniffing her again, my brain goes on overload with all this …. *Woman* in front of me.

"Sakinah, you smell so fucking delicio-" The knock on the front door makes us both freeze. "Sakinah, are you expecting company?"

She's panting, rubbing her tits on my arm with each breath as she shakes her head. Well then, it's a good thing I'm here in case this unexpected visit takes a turn. This is exactly why she shouldn't be here alone - this is exactly why I need to be following her around to make sure she's okay.

And now that I know what she wears when she's alone -

Shaking my head to dispel my thoughts, I walk towards the front door with Sakinah still in my arms. She's a small little thing and probably only weighs a bit over a hundred pounds soaking wet.

Shifting her weight to my left arm, I slowly put her feet on the ground without letting her go. She shifts and her ass presses right against my cock again.

"Dammit Sakinah, stop your wriggling. I'm going to end up busting a load right here before I can even open the damn door." Her intake of air is enough to let me know she'll behave for the next five minutes.

Swinging the door open I'm met with someone I don't recognize. Someone male.

"Yes, can I help you?" Luckily my smart brain told me not to open the door all the way but rather hide my delectable little Malaysian princess behind it. No one should be looking at her in what she's wearing or lack of anyway.

"I'm sorry, I thought -"

"You thought what?"

"I think I have the wrong house. Sorry about that." Is that so? This fucker looks Malaysian, so he probably has the right house but I'm not going to tell him that. In fact, once this guy leaves, I'm going to have a talk with my girl about having other men over when I'm not here.

"Tell me who you're looking for and I'll tell you if you got the wrong house. How about that?"

"Ah..she wouldn't be here. But I'm looking for Sakinah?"

"Yeah? That name kind of sounds familiar." Said woman is currently wriggling in my arms but my hand has automatically clasped over her beautiful lips right when this fucker opened his mouth.

He's looking at me funny. Yeah, I know. No normal guy would be struggling to stand just to answer a damn door. Get on with it bro.

"Oh? Do you know where she resides then? I was, uh, in the neighborhood and heard she lived near campus." Is that fucking right? What else does this guy know?

"Yeah? Well, I wouldn't know. My sister is married to her brother though, so you're probably better off asking him." At the suggestion the fucker starts to look a little sheepish. What is this then? I'm smelling something fishy.

"Ah, that's good. Well, if you see Akmal, tell him Amir came by and that we should catch up sometime."

"Sounds good."

"Alright. Thanks and sorry for interrupting anything. You have a good day."

"You too, man." Slamming the door before he could even turn to leave, I drag Sakinah towards the back of the house with my hand still over her mouth. Knowing her sassy ass, she'd probably yell or something just to get on my damn nerves.

Once we make it to what looks like a bedroom, I shut the door and let her go.

"What the hell are you doing!?"

"Why was there a guy looking for you Sakinah? You dating that fucker or something?"

"I have no damn idea what you're talking about. And so what if I am?" My head feels tight and my hands start to fist. Didn't she just fucking tell me I'm her first kiss. She better not be dating anyone. Not after all I've been doing just to get her to give me the damn time of day.

"You're not a cute liar, Sakinah."

"Fuck you. I'm not lying."

"Oh yeah? Guess I should go back out there and let him know you're taken then hmm? My fist is just itching to meet his face." Pretending to turn, Sakinah grabs onto me from behind. Trying to suppress a grin I know she can't see, I keep my body as still as I can. *I kind of like her giving me affection so willingly.*

"Who the hell is Amir and what is he doing here?"

"I don't know. He's one of Akmal's old classmates. My brother never lets any of them come over enough to get to know them."

"Is that right?" Turning around, I bend my knees a little

and lift her by the ass so she can't run away from this conversation we're having so nicely. Sakinah's legs automatically wrap themselves around me as well as her arms to prevent her from feeling like she's falling.

Nuzzling into her neck, I breathe her delicate scent in. "So what is he doing here asking for my girl?"

"I'm not your girl." Her voice has become as soft as a whisper and it does something to me, more so than when she's all fire.

"You're not his either, so he shouldn't be here. He shouldn't know where you live - alone. He shouldn't fucking know where you're going to school either." Her skin is so damn soft and I can't help but run my nose along her collar bone.

"Are you talking about him or are you talking about yourself?"

"Oh, it's too damn late for you and I, Sakinah. You know this. This energy between us can't be ignored, no matter how much you try."

"...We can't" My lips brush over her neck as my tongue starts to lick at her skin, wanting just a taste.

Speaking against the crook of her neck, I'm confused. "Why not?" Oh, the little vixen seems like she's done playing because she's tilting her head back slightly, giving me more access.

Turning us around, I shove her back against the door in case she decides to try and slip away again. My lips are tracing her jaw when she turns her head away in an attempt to stop our connection.

"Fabian, we can't be together. We're family now."

"Not by blood, we're not." She starts to wriggle in earnest. Not wanting her to hurt herself, I let her body slide down against mine but keep her against the door, using my body as a blockade from any potential plans she might have brewing in that pretty head of hers.

She turns her eyes on me and it's a look I haven't seen on her before. It's almost … vulnerable.

"Fabian. It's forbidden."

Lowering my voice to match hers, I ask the question that's burning inside of me. "Why?"

Her face turns into a snarl as she shoves at me passionately and I let her. This is a part of Sakinah I haven't seen before and it's taking me aback.

"Because Fabian! It's the damn same in my culture! It's like I'm telling everyone I've fallen in love with my brother, can't you see that? It's so easy for you to just..to just give into your feelings when I'm trapped! I can't have feelings for you! Not when I know it would just end in heartbreak."

Her voice cracks at the end and I just about tear my heart out of my chest. To see tough as nails Sakinah like this is something I don't want to see again. I'm at a loss for words, I mean, I've never been good with them to begin with - just ask my sister. She's cussing me out more times than not when we talk on the phone.

"I didn't know that."

"Of course you didn't! You're just being...Fabian! Too hot for your fucking self, strutting all over the damn place and making my fucking heart falter when I tell myself to get you the hell away from me!"

Make her heart falter? Does this mean she feels it too? About what we have between us? Life is so damn short, why are we letting this shit get between what's real? This shit. This shit right here, right now, is as real as it gets.

She's practically shaking with passion and rage at everything. Taking my own advice for once, I'm going to just shut up before I dig a bigger hole for myself. Grabbing her gently,

I pull her back as I sit my ass down on the edge of her mattress. She doesn't offer any resistance as her body continues to tremble with everything she's just told me. Finally pulling her in the rest of the way, I let her fall into my arms and just hold her until the moment passes.

4

———

*W*hy must he do this to me? Why must he drive me to the brink of madness and ...and hold me like this when I feel like my world is crashing down around me?

Did I really say all that? It came out like verbal vomit as my emotional threshold hit its maximum capabilities. My head feels hot, like a damn volcano just erupted taking casualties to those around me.

But Fabian - Fabian is still as strong as a rock and steady as the waters as he just holds me, rubbing my back in comfort. My arms are entwined around him, grabbing on like he's a damn life preserver as I drown in my emotions over the situation.

Fabian has come into my life and turned everything upside down. Even with all the rebellion I've thrown at my culture, he's the one I'm the scaredest to gamble on. He has the potential to break my heart and confidence into a million pieces when he leaves. I just can't do that to myself, not when I've been trying so hard to become independent and strong and - be who I've always been meant to be. I don't know exactly what that is yet but it feels so close I can almost touch it.

When Fabian kisses the top of my head, my eyes tear up. My mind is warring with itself and neither side is gaining any momentum. Why must he be like this with me when it's so much easier to hate him when he's just being his cocky self?

"Fabian, please."

"Please what? What am I doing wrong?"

"You're just...too much."

"Sakinah, all I'm doing right now is comforting a friend. Can't we at least just be that right now?" I know I can be difficult. My brain is telling me that I'm leading him on when my heart says it wouldn't be so bad to be with a man who holds you when you can't stand on your own.

"Just friends then?" The cracks in my heart can practically be heard in my mind as I ask him this.

"Is that what you want?" I nod before I can think it through because as much as I push him, I don't want him to go.

He rearranges us until we're face to face, his hand caressing my cheek like I'm the most fragile thing he's ever held and it makes my heart want to burst.

"I'm going to be here for you, the way you want me to be Sakinah. But don't think I'm going to be happy about the fucking fact that other men are knocking on your door asking for you. Don't put me through that shit when I don't even get the fucking chance." It's not fair. It really isn't. Why life decided to throw this wrench at us, I'll never fucking understand it.

I don't regret gaining Vero as a sister, but I do regret making Fabian my family and off limits.

Pressing my forehead against his, I close my eyes because this is fucking heartbreaking. Can a person's heart hurt this bad before they even are allowed to give it away?

"I don't know what to do."

"I don't either. But I'm going to tell you right now, what I feel for you is real. I'mma step back as much as I can but I can't make any damn promises."

"We can't.."

"You said that already." Jumping out of his arms, I stand up and turn in irrational rage.

"It's not easy for me either! Just go, Fabian. I can't do this right now. Just go!" My tears start to fall as the sound of his footsteps and door slamming does exactly what I asked him to do.

It's been two days since Fabian crashed into my house. I'm almost scared to admit that I miss his stupid face.

The first half of the day went by in a blur, my mind still in a whirlwind about how I'm supposed to handle being 'friends' with the man who makes my insides and outsides tingle. This isn't going to work. I just know it. What did I get myself into?

"Sakinah!"

"Huh? Sorry, you were saying something?" Jason smirks my way from the seat in front of me and I realize the whole class is starting to clean up and leave. Damn, I don't remember a thing the professor even said.

"Yeah, I was saying it's Wednesday. Let's walk together to the library and hash this shit out. Get this project out the way quickly."

"Oh! Right, right. Yeah, okay." Bringing a backpack this time and leaving half my books in the car, the walk towards the next building wasn't riddled with me running into people since I can hold my head up.

The glass entrance to the library is wide and inviting. The sea of heads bent down on tables letting us know that there are people at work and to keep the noise level down. Jason picks a table towards the back end of the library and we both put our stuff down onto the chairs. There's only one other person back here so it shouldn't be too bad if our voices carry a little. Once we're seated, we drag the chairs on the carpet towards the round table.

"Okay, so what do you have? You said you already had an idea right? I'll just see where I should insert myself and we can start researching more from there."

"Okay." Having placed my backpack on the back of the chair, I turn around to unzip the compartment only to feel a displacement of cool air around me. Grabbing my folder, I straighten back out only to see another chair, turned backwards, placed between me and Jason. Fabian is sitting there with a smirk as he sticks his hands out towards my Physics partner.

What the hell is happening right now?

"Fabian. I'm Sakinah's friend. Figured I'd stop by and see what she was up to. You don't mind if I hang for a bit right? I was thinking of taking her out to lunch after this."

"Uh...nah, I guess not." Jason's eyes shoot to mine questioningly. I should be pissed at his audacity but in reality, I'm smiling on the inside about the fact that he's still forcefully inserting himself into my life.

I missed him. I shouldn't, but I did.

"Keep your damn voice down Fabian, we're in a library for crying out loud. Fabian, this is Jason. Jason, Fabian."

"Quit getting on me about everything, woman! I know it's a damn library for crying out loud. I have been in a few during my time, you know."

I hold back the laugh that wants to come out and Fabian narrows his eyes at me. Yeah, probably ten years ago.

"So…. You said your project was something on Velocity correct?" Jason's got a good memory.

"Yeah, velocity as a vector quantity." I'm pretty excited about it. Haven't thought of any sort of models to represent it yet though.

"That shit's way over my head Sakinah, maybe we should dumb it down a little."

"...Yeah Sakinah, help a dumb boy out." I elbow Fabian in the ribs even though Jason didn't hear him say it under his breath. How rude!

Opening my folder of notes, I try to find a way to explain it to him to see if he'll understand it better without having to change the whole project itself. Fabian leans into my side, crowding me as he looks over my pages too. This guy.

"Well…." Where do I start?

"It's like a beam moving in the air. If it goes one way and stays there, there's a velocity because it results in a change of position. But if your shit swings back, well … then the motion just results in zero velocity because the thing practically comes back to its original position, that is until it swings back and knocks you off the building. Your shit shouldn't be swinging that hard to begin with."

My eyes widen as Fabian describes the situation to Jason. Jason is nodding his head trying to imagine the picture he just painted. Does Fabian work on building construction then? My eyes zoom in on his biceps flexing as he turns his head towards me and winks. My god, who is this man?

"But if you do need some housework done let me know. I got a few guys that can help out." Just imagining Fabian working with his hands is making me press my legs together.

"Um, thanks but we got it from here. Maybe you should wait for me in the car? We won't be too much longer since we're just laying the ideas out, right Jason?" Jason is looking between us back and forth probably wondering what's really going on but nods his head.

"Yeah, we'll just handle an outline today and meet again to see what kind of model we want to make to represent it."

"I'm sitting my ass right here. I don't mind waiting, Sakinah. Don't fret your pretty head over me for my sake." The stubborn bastard. I'm trying hard to be civil and not rip his head off because we have company and he knows it judging by the smirk he's giving me.

"Well, then scoot over there so I can show Jason my notes."

"Nah, I'm fine right here. Jason can see that shit from where he's sitting, right Jason?"

He's looking between us again, the tension in the room starting to amp up. "Right…"

"In fact, I don't mind passing the notes. How about this, Sakinah will make you a copy and I'll make sure to hand it to ya tomorrow? Sakinah, we don't want to be late for our lunch. She studies too much. Need to keep on her check before she starves herself."

"Yeah? Yeah, of course." Jason gets up and starts packing. My eyes are boring into the back of Fabian's skull but he doesn't notice because he's watching Jason's every move, making sure he really leaves.

Once Jason is halfway towards the front of the library, I

hit Fabian with the back of my hand on his shoulder. "Oi Fabian! You can't just barge in and cut my project meetings short! This is an important assignment."

"Yeah, I figured that, which is why I'm going to hand lover boy over there a copy of your damn notes so he doesn't waste any more of your time pretending to listen while he's really looking at your tits." What the hell?

"What the hell are you talking about?"

"Come on Sakinah, you can't be that dense. As a *friend*, I need to make you aware of how you affect the opposite sex. After all, I would know." Fabian takes that very moment to blatantly stare at my tits and I become self-conscious, covering it up with the backpack I just removed from the back of my chair after packing it back up.

I should have never worn this long sleeve shirt. I thought my hijab was doing a good job covering the neckline. Fabian startles me when he grabs the backpack off my hands and throws it over his shoulder. I'm standing there stunned by his actions when he grabs my hand firmly and starts walking us towards the front of the library, towards the exit.

"You need to know by now that men don't need the hint of actual flesh to visualize what's underneath. He'll probably be jacking off to fantasies of your tits in his face tonight, I guarantee it."

"Fabian!"

"Shhhh! This is a library Miss!"

"Sorry!"

"Yeah Sakinah, keep it down. This is a library for crying out loud." Another round of shushes follow us as we exit out the double doors making me stifle a laugh. This trouble-maker is going to get me kicked out of the damn library, then where would I go for projects?

My short legs are struggling to catch up with him as I

almost trip over nothing. Fabian turns around abruptly and throws me over his damn shoulder, continuing on our course like it's just another day.

"Fabian! Put me down! How fucking embarrassing! I can walk!"

"Yeah, well you're taking too damn long and I'm fucking starving. All that talk of physics and beams knocking you over the side of a building builds an appetite." He slaps my ass after one of my kicks hits him in his hard abs. This guy is like a damn brick house and his muscles don't help my stomach when he's bouncing me over his shoulder.

I almost fall backward when he throws me off his shoulder and back into standing if it wasn't for his arms holding me against his chest. Rubbing my head against him, I try to get my dizziness back in order before glaring at his stupid cocky face.

"Better? Now let's go." The sound of a metal car door opens and he's shoving me into his Chevelle. The only reason I know this is because I was scouring google the moment he left my parent's house after that first meeting. That doesn't make me obsessed though, I was just trying to get information, that's all.

The door slams, reminding me of a damn tin can for some reason as I watch Fabian round the car to the driver's side. "Alright, put on your seat belt, we're going on a friendly lunch." My eyes playfully look at his as I do what he says. Friendly lunch huh, I think he just wrangled himself a date.

Surprisingly for a stick shift, the car ride over was a smooth one. I had to try my best to keep my eyes forward so as to not let him know that I'm checking out the way his forearm flexes every time he shifts. Knowing what I know now - Fabian being a man who works with his body - my mind is now trying to imagine what's under his shirt.

He pulls up into what looks like a taco shop near the campus. How does he even know this is here anyway? Doesn't Fabian live in a whole other town?

"Fabian.."

"I scouted it out. Keep your sassy comments to yourself. Just go in and eat with me, enjoy the damn time. I want to hang out with my friend, is that so bad?"

Blinking a few times, I'm starting to wonder if he can read minds. I'm also starting to look at him from a different light. From his talk of physics to this, Fabian Hernandez is not the stereotypical bad boy I thought he was. I mean, he still reeks of trouble but something about what he's shown me is making my insides melt a little.

Despite the fact that he just kind of admitted to stalking my stomping grounds. *That should be creepy.*

Watching Fabian come around to open the passenger door for me, I can't help but tell my brain to shut up as I place my hand in his so he can help me out of the car. His smile makes me blush but I look down and clear my throat to get his eyes off me.

"So tacos, huh?"

"Best place to take a friend, I say. Plus I'm starving as hell." I laugh as he leads me to the front door and opens it for me. Such a gentleman under his cocky exterior. Guess his mama taught him well.

We sit down and I swear Fabian is ordering half the menu. The server is batting her eyelashes a little too much and smiling a bit too long. It makes me want to sharpen my metaphorical claws. Crossing my arms, I clear my throat to get her attention. I can see Fabian smirking at me from my periphery as I ask her what their specials are.

"Just give her a plate of chicken tacos. She can share some of mine if she wants to try something out. Thanks."

"I could order for myself, you know."

"Yeah, but I ordered for you so I won't starve to fucking death waiting for you to make up your damn mind."

"You're such a…"

"Great guy, that was kind enough to order for you so you don't have to look like you don't know what you're doing? You're welcome. That's what I'm here for." Suppressing a smile, I look down at the table as Fabian's masculine chuckle comes from across the table.

"What do you like to do Sakinah? Being friends, we should be getting to know one another."

"I like..science? And engineering. That's what I'm going for. I'm hoping to be able to break away from the family work and just do something for myself, you know?"

"Yeah? You seem good at it." I automatically beam at his praise. My mother used to complain that I'm taking the long way when I could have majored in something else that would spit me out of school faster so I can find a husband and make a million babies for her.

Looking at Fabian and his free spirit, I find myself a bit envious but I swallow it down as the waitress comes back with a few cups of water for us.

"What do you do Fabian?" After a few large gulps that make my eyes zero in on how his Adam's apple bobs, he set's the cup down.

"I work whatever I can. Usually, when the site has a contract, I'll have work for months on end, maybe even years. But between the contracts, I'm basically a private contractor for myself, selling my skills to whoever needs it." I love the fact that Fabian says everything so confidently like it's just a part of who he is. I want this kind of energy, this kind of confidence.

The food arrives and we eat in relative silence. Well, I eat while I watch Fabian inhale about five plates of food in front of my very eyes. Holy shit. Knowing what I know now about him and manual labor, I can see why he would be so damn hungry - he has to keep his energy up.

The … friendly lunch is over before I know it and we're back in his car, driving around aimlessly. Doesn't this thing burn gas?

"Don't you live another town over?"

"Yeah."

"So why are you all the way over here?"

"Let's not play this game Sakinah. You know I'm over here for you. I'm watching out for you. The moment I found out you're living alone is the moment I started coming by to make sure you're alright. Your parents should have never left you here like this. At least get you a damn roommate. Even that's iffy."

"What the hell do you mean, my parents should have never let me? I'm a fucking adult, why should they dictate where I go? I needed to be near my campus."

Fabian laughs. Fucking laughs! What the hell is so funny right now?

"Keep your claws in, alright? All I'm saying is that a pretty woman shouldn't be left on her own in a neighborhood that might be filled with predators."

"Oh, like you?" We're stopped at a red light and Fabian turns his face to me with a look I can't decipher.

"Yeah, fucking like me. But unlike me, they don't have your best interest at heart, ya feel? Because we're fucking family *as you say*, and I take care of family. I'm not letting other guys come over thinking they can take advantage of you."

I'm pissed but at the same time flattered. He always does this to me, leaving me without a good retort back. By the time I'm about to come up with something to say, the moment's already passed and he's parking in front of my little place behind campus.

"Come on, I'm going to see you inside. That way any neighbor thinking of trying anything will think twice." With the rolled-up sleeves on his t-shirt letting his tattoos peek out to the chain hanging down his front to his back pocket, I don't think any of the students who live near me would dare to do anything.

He walks me up to the front door like a damn proper date and my skin is prickling with awareness. We're both lying to each other right now with this friendship thing, and we both know it. Isn't this where the boy kisses the girls? I'm nervous and I don't know why.

Unlocking the door, I can feel Fabian's body heat right behind me, blocking me from anyone on the street that might walk by. He makes me feel protected but I'm not going to tell him that because it would just solidify everything he's been spewing in the car. Opening the door and stepping through, I turn to find Fabian with both of his arms on each side of the doorway, leaning in.

"Well, thank you. For lunch." Why am I so embarrassed all of a sudden? My face feels like it's flaming and it's getting hot under my long sleeve.

"Of course."

We both stand there awkwardly, unsure of how this friend thing is supposed to work, how far we're allowed to go. *You did this to yourself, you know.*

"Sakinah." When did I start staring at the floor? Lifting my eyes to his, I don't have time to prepare for him to barge in again, grabbing my face and kissing me so softly that I want to cry. Why am I so damn emotional?

He must have kicked the door shut with his boots

because he doesn't take his lips off mine until we're against the back of the couch once more.

Is this Deja vu or what?

His tongue teases the slit between my lips and I'm lost in the moment of wanting something so badly, something I can never have. Inviting him in, our kiss turns passionate and frenzied until I'm left there standing with my lips parted as Fabian sees himself out, slamming the door.

5

Fabian was good on his word and gave Jason a copy of my notes. I'm assuming so anyway since Jason didn't ask me for it when I saw him in class the next day. All we talked about was whether our library meeting was still happening tomorrow.

My mother called me back home for something and since one of my later classes got canceled, I decided to head over there around lunch. I wonder what this is about since Hasanah and Hidaya are still around the house to help out if she needs it.

Pulling up my sedan to the front of the house, Ibu is already standing out there at the doorway. Damn, how long has she been waiting? Getting out of the driver's side, I try to put a polite smile on my face.

"Ibu! I hope you haven't been standing there long."

"Sakinah! Come on, come inside. Your sisters are already in the kitchen." Okay…

Once I make it inside my childhood home, the smells of different food cooking make my stomach growl. I haven't eaten yet so this is perfect. My sisters and I start setting up plates in the living room and I swear it looks like way too much food for just us -

"Ahh, come in, come in. Food is done, there is plenty to eat!" My mother's voice is loud and clear from the front door and my sisters and I look at each other in confusion.

"Who's coming?"

"I don't know." Hidaya just shrugs her shoulders when I look over to her.

When the voices get closer, Hasanah and I look at each other again with knowing glances. *Oh no.* Ibu is trying to set us up again.

"Bisaam, Amir, please sit down."

Hasanah and I nervously say our greetings as we start to sit on the floor. My father isn't home right now so it's just us girls as we all sit in a circle.

"Hasanah! This is Bisaam, he comes from a great family. You remember him huh? He is Akmal's classmate. So is Amir. You remember Aunti Zunai? This is her son."

Hisanah and I are trying not to laugh and groan at the same time. Ibu always does this. I mean she's stopped for a while since I started university but has never stopped hinting at us finding a husband.

"Bisaam! Doesn't Hasanah look beautiful? She helps me around the house the most la. Amir! You asked me about Sakinah at Akmal's wedding. Did you know my daughter studies at the university? Engineering la. Very smart girl, very smart."

"Yes, Ibu." Hasanah and I have been through this before. But Ibu has never been this pushy.

"Bisaam and Amir will make very good husbands, their families have very good business. Hasanah and Sakinah are very good wives too, they learn from the best huh?"

We all laugh nervously together at this makeshift match-making auction. Gosh, Malay culture can be a trip. How do I get myself out of this? Wasn't Amir at my house the other day? How did he even know where I live? My eyes narrow a bit when I look at him. He catches my eye and just gives me a soft smile.

He looks like the typical Malay man. Clean, hair combed back -

"They come from good families. You would be proud to have these men as husbands." Walao eh - Oh my god. Can my mother be any more embarrassing right now? When I look over to Hasanah, I noticed that both she and Bisaam are making googly eyes at each other.

There has to be a story here. They must have already expressed interest in one another. No way, homebody Hasanah, would just quickly like someone on the first day.

Turning my head to look at Amir, I can't find myself feeling the same sentiment. His eyes are soft as they look at mine, the way Fabian sometimes looks when he lets his guard down. But … he's no Fabian. I can't help but compare them even though I know I shouldn't.

"I'm going to go to the kitchen for something huh, you guys talk. Makan, makan. Ooo, Sakinah! You and Amir look so good together! Talk, talk, I'm going to the kitchen huh." My mother is so *not* slick with her blatant interest in us all hooking up like some damn dating show. She's probably going to be peeping from the other room, eavesdropping on everything that's said.

Poor Hidaya looks like a third wheel, just trying to stuff her face so she doesn't feel awkward right now. My mother comes over to me and I'm anticipating something weird, which I should because she starts to fix my hijab like she's prepping a show dog before heading back into the kitchen.

"Sakinah, apa kabar? How are you?" Amir is almost leaning into me as I lean back.

"I'm fine, thanks." My mother flutters back with another plate of something while she takes some of the half-empty plates back into the kitchen. *So freaking weird aye.*

"How's the university? I came by the other day but I think I got the wrong house?" *How does he even know where I live anyway?* I side-eye my mother who's hiding behind one of the pillars in the kitchen, pretending to put some plates back into the cabinet. *I bet she pushed him my way.*

"Oh?"

"Yeah, some Hispanic guy answered the door. I was sure I was at the right house too."

"Oh, yeah. That was just a friend. He was watching my house for me when I was in class. I needed something fixed inside the house." Sounds legit, right?

"Yeah? Hey, look. If you'd like to go out sometime -"

"Sorry, Amir. I don't think so."

"Yeah? But your mother-"

"Yeah, she can be a bit pushy, you know?" My mother's booming laugh comes from the kitchen and I jump from getting startled. I think she's laughing at something Hasanah and Bisaam are talking about. What a creep aye.

"Um, excuse me for a minute…"

"Nak pergi mana ke? Where are you going?" Far away from you and from my Ibu who is scolding me with her hand gestures from the kitchen. Aduh, my god this is too much. My head is practically pounding from this stupid luncheon. I didn't even get to eat everything since my mother practically shoved these guys down our throats wanting to be matchmaker.

My mother grabs me by the arm and literally drags me back into the living room towards our male guests again.

"Haiya Sakinah, why don't you show Amir around the neighborhood, hmm? I'm sure you'll get to know each other better after spending some time together." Ibu claps her hands together in excitement, almost like a little kid. What is going on here? Who is the one getting matched? I swear my mother acts like it's *her* getting a new husband.

"If you like him so much, why don't you marry him huh?" I'm whisper-hissing at my mother and she just shakes me with a stern look. I can't stand this shit. I need to get out of here. I feel stifled, pressed down. This can't be what my life is all about. My mother throwing the 'perfect Malay' guy at me - a guy I'm not even attracted to whatsoever.

"Sakinah, you need to do the right thing and start looking for a husband. You are getting old!" She did not just say that to me. I'm only twenty-five! She's acting like my eggs are drying up before her very eyes.

"I'm getting old la! I need some grandbabies. Akmal is at least working on it. How about you huh? What are you doing? You are watching me get old and die before you even find a man."

"Ibu! Why are you so dramatic!?" She pinches my tummy and dramatically responds like a damn soap opera.

"You are getting old! Then you will not look as pretty anymore to catch a good man. You need a husband now before it's too late!" Her voice raises in octaves towards the end and everyone in the living room shuts up as she screams to the world that I'm going to get too old and decrepit by tomorrow, therefore will not be able to find anyone to take me as a wife.

I want to die. Why is she like this? I'm looking around thinking there has to be some sort of prank cameras set up because this is straight out of the Malaysian soap operas she watches.

"Your aunty is only 45 and she just became a grandma. When is my turn?" *My god.*

"Ibu! You'll have Akmal's baby soon!"

My mother temporarily gives up on me because of my sheer stubbornness in this and starts to flutter around Hasanah who is preening like a damn peacock. Hasanah is older than I am, she's also expressed her hopeless romantic notions of finding love soon. I'm happy for her if she's showing interest in Bisaam. He seems like a nice guy who looks like he's really into her as well.

While my mother is ooh-ing and aah-ing over the potential match, I slip out the backdoor and run to my car to make my escape. I've only just started the car when I hear my Ibu's voice yelling in the wind.

"Sakinah! Where are you going? What are you doing? When are you coming back huh?"

I put the gear in drive and step on the gas like the cops are after me. I guess I'll have to get lunch when I get home.

The drive back to my residence was a calming one. With soothing music in the car, I let the windows down and just take in a breath of fresh air. I don't know how long I'll be able to avoid my mother with her plans on matchmaking.

My neighborhood comes into view and the sight of the campus starts to release some of the tension I've been holding in from my escape. Who knew the sight of the place where professors torture your mind would be relieving?

Pulling up to my tiny one-car garage, I park the car and

my mind drifts to Fabian again. There's no competition. If Amir were to stand side by side with Fabian...

Shaking my head, I tell myself I can't think this way because it'll never happen. Grabbing my bag out of my car, I rip off my hijab and inner cap in frustration and shake my hair out. What would it be like to be a normal westernized girl with no restrictions? To not have the confinements of a culture that literally feels like it's pressing you down into the ground - and then presses you down even more with situations like the one my mother loves to put me in.

Slamming my car door in frustration, I remind myself once more to stop thinking along those lines because this is who I am, this is the family and life I was born into. I can't change a damn thing about it. I'm rummaging through my purse for my keys, walking up my steps when I run into a hard body. Dammit! I'm about to cry with how frustrating this lunch went. I'm so damn *hangry* that I can't think straight but when I lift my head I feel like a weight has been lifted off my shoulders.

Fabian's here with what looks like a bag of food in his hand.

"Fabian." His name on my lips comes out almost like a sigh of relief.

I throw caution into the wind and just hug him. All of the day's activities are catching up to me and I don't know who to talk to. I used to be able to talk to my sisters about it, but with the way Hasanah was looking at Bisaam, I think that boat has sailed for me. I no longer have an ally on my side in these marriage matters. Well, except for Hidaya, but it's not the same - the trio is breaking up.

"What's wrong?"

Burying my face even deeper into his chest, I just shove my keys at him. Fabian didn't need more instruction than that as he unlocks the door and drags us both inside without separating our embrace.

I hear the door shut before I feel him pick me up bridal style while still holding onto the bag of food and sitting us on the couch. He leans over carefully to place the bag on the coffee table before sitting back and just rubbing my back. *How does he always know what I need?*

We're both quiet as Fabian rubs my back until I'm ready to sit up. A few minutes go by and we both start taking food out of the paper bag Fabian brought over and eat in silence. It's a dramatic contrast to what I just left at home, a house full of bickering over when the hypothetical wedding should be - even if my mother didn't say it out loud just yet - and when I'll be making babies.

Fabian brought over some burgers and fries and my chest feels full with what he's done for me in a time of need without having to be told.

"Thank you."

"Of course. I gotta feed my girl. We're friends after all."

The term always stabs me in the chest when I think about it. A double-edged sword that I pointed at myself. When we're done eating, I get up to throw the trash away and Fabian follows me into the kitchen. It's quiet and there's a subtle tension and energy simmering between us but neither of us wants to point it out. I'm backed against the kitchen counter while Fabian cages me in again, but this time...this time it feels comforting rather than intimidating.

We're staring at each other and I swear I can feel the electricity pulsing, pulling us closer. How can we possibly even try this friendship thing when it's always like this between us?

Fabian leans in and I find myself closing my eyes, surrendering to the moment when right before his lips touch mine, there's a knock on the door. Groaning right before he gives me a chaste kiss anyway, Fabian turns to go answer the door like he lives here.

"Yes?"

"I'm looking for Sakinah. I'm guessing she's not home because you're here. She told me that you help watch her house for her."

"Is that right?" I swallow a lump in my throat, afraid of Fabian getting offended because I didn't get to explain to him what happened at my mother's house. *Oh god, I don't even want to see how he would react to that.* My face feels hot from embarrassment and my scalp is getting tingles from what Fabian might do right now. Is he going to tell Amir I'm home?

"Yeah, so when she comes back, will you let her know that uh...I was serious about what we were talking about." Fabian's back tenses up but he doesn't move his position in front of the door - the door that's only opened halfway while I'm hiding in the kitchen once more like a coward.

"I'll make sure to … let her know. Though it'll be hard to tell her a clear message if I don't know what the message actually is. What did you say you guys talked about again?"

"Ah..well, tell her I'll come by tomorrow to pick her up. Say around seven. Alright, thanks for giving her my message man. I'll text her later as well."

Fabian literally slams the door in Amir's face before he turns those blazing orbs at me. I feel like shrinking into myself, my hands are clasped before me.

"I-I"

"Where were you today?"

"I-I was at my mother's house. She asked me to come over and-and-"

"And what Sakinah? Why is this guy here saying he's

coming by tomorrow to pick you up? For fucking what? A date? What the hell is he talking about with this 'what we were talking about' shit? Were you with him today Sakinah?"

"Fabian! It's not like that! My mother was trying to be a matchmaker again!"

"So you're saying you're supposed to marry this fucker?"

"Dammit, Fabian! I'm trying to tell you! Just listen!"

"Did I not just hear that fucker standing at *your* damn door talking about picking *you* up tomorrow for a fucking *date* at seven? I heard every. Damn. Word." I can feel the burn behind my eyes from the tears that want to come out but I'm so pissed I just want to throw something at his stubborn ass head. Why isn't he listening to me?!

"Fabian! I didn't agree to anything! That's why I came home fucking hungry. I left before it could go any further. It's not my fault my mother wants to marry all her daughters off. It's not my damn fault she invited him over to trap me!"

Fabian rubs his hand down his face and is starting to pace around the living room. I don't know what to do, I don't know how to feel. I'm embarrassed, I'm scared, I'm mad - I feel like I'm suffocating right now and I don't even have my hijab on.

After wearing my carpet down with his boots, I watch as Fabian starts running his hands through his hair right before he turns towards me again. The anger in his eyes has lessened but there's still something else there that makes my stomach churn.

"So you were put into a predicament and yet...yet you couldn't even tell him I was a friend? I'm reduced to some guy that what? Watches the house for you? That's pretty fucking messed up Sakinah."

"I-I-I didn't know how to explain what happened last time! It just came out like that."

"Yeah? It just came out like that...like what? Because I'm too beneath you to be called anything else?" Fabian turns again, punches the back of the couch and storms out the front door, slamming it shut as I fall to my knees in this stupid kitchen I thought would protect me from this tornado of emotions.

6

I parked a couple of blocks away because I didn't want her to hear the roar of my engine when I came over. I wanted it to be a surprise because friends do that, right? Just a nice little lunch to help pick up her spirits or whatever.

I'm fucking glad I parked far because I need to cool my head right now with everything that just went down. My head feels tight, like it's about to explode and no matter how many times I run my hand through my hair, it doesn't fucking help to ease the tension that's building.

The cool breeze cools my ardor only a little bit while my mind is still racing with all the information that was just thrown at me like a damn hand grenade. Her mother wants her married and she brought a damn candidate over.

Fucker comes to Sakinah's house and just throws down the gauntlet in front of my damn face with that date shit. I saw the way he was looking at me because I was looking at him in the same damn way.

Walking around the back of my car, I open the driver's side and slide in, slamming the door harder than I should. This neighborhood is quiet. After scouting it out a few times, I haven't seen many troublemakers about. It was another reason why I came by with lunch - I recently ended my lease for my apartment near the city. What better place to look than to be near the woman that haunts me every damn waking moment.

Pulling out onto the street my mind starts to whir with different scenarios between us, none of which involves that fucker at her door. Am I so bad that she couldn't even stand up for me in front of him at her mother's house? I mean, I'm fucking family after all, she could have said *that*.

About halfway out of her neighborhood, I turn around the front of the campus when my mind finally gives me the answers. Well, part of the answers I'm looking for. Sakinah thinks our closeness is a forbidden taboo. Could this be why she couldn't tell anyone why I was there? But if that's the case, what the hell does that make me? A hidden secret? *A dirty secret.* My skin itches with just the thought of that. I don't want to be anyone's fucking dirty secret.

I think it's time for Sakinah to start making up her mind about what she's going to do. With this Amir guy in the picture, it's only going to make her even more confused. Yeah, he'll be there tomorrow at seven alright...and so will I.

With the decision mentally made, my mood starts to lighten now that I have a plan of attack. Pulling around the campus to do another sweep over her street, I noticed a new sign posted in front of a house about five houses down from hers. *Well now, it seems the universe is agreeing.*

Jotting down the number on the sign, I hightail it out of

there and head back to mi Mamá's casa for some planning. It takes about thirty minutes to get back on my side of town. Pulling into my mother's driveway, I jump out and head towards the front door.

"Aye, why are you in such a hurry? What's happening?"

"Nothing Mamá, la bendición." Giving my mother a kiss on the cheek, I start to look for the person I need. "Papá, are you here?"

"Oi, back here!" I find my father sitting in his lazy boy in the living room watching telenovelas.

"Papá, can you come help me get some of my stuff from the apartment. I think I found a new place."

"Si, si Hijo. Let me get on my shoes."

Once my father is ready, we both hop into his old truck he keeps in the back and head towards my old apartment. He turns the radio on and Despacito comes up, lightening up the mood. My dad loves that shit, always trying to be 'with it'. I cut him off when he starts singing though, a man can only take so much.

"So what happened Fabian? You don't like the city no more?"

"I was barely there anyways, I'm always hanging out with you guys. Plus, an apartment is like tossing your money away. I think I'm going to buy a house."

"Yeah? You find one already?"

"Yeah, it's near a nice neighborhood. I think you guys will like it." Plus, I'll be near Sakinah. If all works out, but he doesn't need to know that. My father never asks questions about my relationship affairs anyway.

We made it in good time and with my dad's help, we were able to get my stuff in one load. It's kind of sad when you think about it. I barely had anything in there - shit, I didn't even have a couch, just a bed, and table really. A couple of chairs. Damn, this move was a long time coming. I needed to get out of this depressing place.

My dad was able to rearrange some stuff in the garage to store some of the big stuff. Once we come inside, the smell of food floats in the air and my dad plants his ass right back on the lazy boy.

My fingers are dialing the number I jotted down earlier for the real estate agent. I need to hop on this shit before someone else gets there before I do. I *need* this house. Now.

"Hello, you've reached Ace Reality, how may I help you today?"

"I saw the sign in front of one of the houses behind the university. It just got put up today."

"Ah yes, we did just post one today. Did you want to make an appointment to go look at it?"

"Nah, I already decided I want it. What's the price?"

"Sir, are you sure? We highly recommend one of our agents go with you to check the property out, in case you have any questions or concerns?" This shit is giving me a headache. Can't I just buy it and call it a day? Damn.

"Alright fine, who do you have that will meet me there in thirty minutes?" The sound of shuffling papers and movement comes across the speaker before some sounds of typing.

"Okay, we have agent Ken Scotts. He will meet you there in thirty mi-" Ending the call, I grab my keys and start driving back over to Sakinah's neighborhood. It's a good thing it's far enough away from her where she won't hear the roar of the Chevelle. I'm going to have to remedy that issue too. Can't have her knowing I'm moving in.

I make it there in record time and I'm already walking around the outside of the house. Looks solid enough, any work that needs to be done on the inside, I can do. I'm almost hoping it's a piece of shit inside so I can get a better deal on it.

A nice and shiny sedan pulls up the front and an African American male comes out the driver's side door. He's dressed to impress so it's probably this Ken Scotts guy.

"Ken Scotts?"

"Yeah, that's me. I take it you're the one interested in the house?"

"Yup, let's get this show over with because I already know I'm buying it."

"Well, let me get this door lock for you and we can step inside." All these stupid formalities are killing me. I didn't miss the fact that this Ken Scotts character was looking me up and down with doubt when I said I was going to buy the place.

The house tour was taking too long so instead of waiting for him to shut his trap, I started doing a walk-through. Could use some work here and there, some water stains that are barely noticeable but nothing that can't be handled by hand.

"Alright, I saw the place. So what's the asking price?"

"Oh, uh…" He must have really doubted me because he's finally starting to scramble to take out his paperwork on the place. "$310,000 is the current asking price."

"Knock off twenty Gs and I'll buy it in cash." I should laugh at the way his eyes start to bulge but I'm in a fucking hurry here. All those years working my ass off and just coming back to my mother's house for food has allowed me to pile up shit in savings. What better way to spend it than to invest in property and find a way to keep me close to the woman I'm trying to catch.

"I'm going to need to talk to my supervisor but we'll see what we can do." This guy is sweating like a pig, I know for a damn fact I just offered him a good deal. How often does a real estate agent come across someone offering cash?

Crossing my arms and tapping my shoe on the hardwood floor, I nod my head. Agent man starts to dial whoever he needs to dial and after some mumbles and whispers, he turns back around and gives me the okay for the deal. *Good.*

We both head back to the ACE realty office and fill out all the necessary tons of paperwork for house purchases. Damn, they probably felled an entire tree just for this contract alone. When the final sheet is signed, I'm already standing up and stretching from how long I've had my ass planted in their stupid chair.

"Alright, what's next?"

"Well, we'll need the payment for the property." Checking my phone, the bank is still open. I get my ass in gear and take the Chevelle to the closest one that happens to be a few miles away. I hate standing in these stupid places, you swear everyone's got all day to get shit done.

Once my turn comes up, I tell them what I need and I'm handed a cashier's check made out for the house. This stupid trip and last-minute decision is making me burn gas. Pulling back up to the real estate office, I slap the check onto the table and tell them to finish the damn transaction.

"Congratulations Mister Hernandez, you are now the proud owner of-"

"Yeah, okay. Got it. Make sure to send me a digital copy of this paperwork shit too, yeah?" Heading out the front double doors my mind is already trying to figure out another mode of transportation so Sakinah doesn't get suspicious of her new neighbor down the street.

7

SAKINAH

ow did this happen? Amir went from asking to telling in the blink of an eye. Was it because Fabian was here? I'm so damn depressed, I don't know what to do.

Have I offended him? I mean, the way he says it makes me sound like a real jerk. Is he right? About the fact that I couldn't even recognize him in front of Amir, that I couldn't admit he's more than just 'a guy'. But if I said anything else, my mother would have started asking questions and I'm just not ready for that. Not with the way she was blasting my life of doomed singlehood out loud in the living room.

This is just a big 'ol mess. One I don't know how to get out of.

And I know I should apologize to Fabian, but I'm scared. Scared to see just how mad he is with my fuck up. Dammit! *Maybe my mother was right. Maybe I am doomed to be alone.*

Walking towards the adjoining restroom to my bedroom, I start to strip off everything like a snake shedding skin. I need to just remove these depressing thoughts from my mind. I made sure to make the water cold to knock some sense into myself.

But I can't shake the way Fabian looked right before he left. I messed up. Would he ever forgive me? My eyes are burning again with how shitty I feel. They say relationships are difficult, well...whoever said it has never met a Malay girl stuck in the middle of the road between someone you have feelings for and cultural obligation.

Scrubbing my hair quickly, I get out of the shower and stare at myself in the mirror. Who is Sakinah? Is she the dutiful daughter of a Malay family? Is she the one that Fabian so easily called beautiful? Is she the one that Amir sees as his perfect match? My mind is conflicted in which direction is the right one?

Fabian's face flashes in my mind. Why must the decision between him and I be taken away from me before I can even think about it thoroughly?

Frustrated, I leave the mirror and start rummaging through my closet for something to wear. Stupid Amir and his demand for this date. I hate being rude and leaving someone hanging so of course, I'm going to go. He probably knows this and that's why he issued it that way. Tossing aside the nicer things, my frustration comes back full force and I find myself gripping some of the fabric to the point of creating wrinkles.

Why is this happening to me?

Shoving my face into a dress, I scream, letting the fabric muffle my cries. It doesn't change the fact that I still have to get dressed for this date but it does make me feel a little bit better to be able to let go of the tension building within me.

My head feels hot and my chest hurts in the worst of ways. I fall to my knees and start to sob, truly. I can only do so much to be strong. I miss Fabian. I miss the way he held me while my world was crashing down again.

Why can't we just be together? Why is my life destined to go through this misery of having something I want so bad be taken away from me?

Wiping my eyes with the dress in my hands, I toss it into the laundry hamper and start looking for something to wear in earnest. I need to get this date over with. Then I will no longer have any obligation. I can tell my mother I tried and it didn't work out. I can let Amir know on the date that I'm not feeling it and set him free to pursue someone else.

Alright, now that there's a plan in my mind, my body starts moving in automatic movements. Picking whatever looks casual but not nice, I start to get dressed and tame my hair for my hijab. I've just gone back into the restroom to make sure my hijab looks okay when there's a knock at the door. The clock on my bathroom wall says six forty-five. Amir must really be looking forward to this date. Now I feel bad that I'm about to let him down when clearly he must have more than some sort of interest in me.

Grabbing my bag, I walk towards the front of my home and open the door for him. Amir is standing there in a very nice buttoned shirt and dress pants. He even has flowers in his hand like a damn Hollywood movie. Trying to summon a smile on my face, I take the offered flowers.

"Thank you, Amir." I can't bring myself to look at his face. Not yet. Not when it only reminds me of how Fabian left. "Let me put these in something and we can go."

Without waiting for me to invite him in, I can hear his footsteps following me as I grab one of my bigger cups from the cabinet and put some tap water into it. Rearranging the flowers slowly, I know I'm just delaying the inevitable - This date is happening no matter what.

Internally sighing, I close my eyes and pray for strength. Turning, I plaster a fake smile on and tip my head towards the door.

"You look beautiful Sakinah." Why doesn't it feel the same?

"Thank you."

Once we're both beyond the threshold to the front door, the roar of something comes closer. I haven't heard anything like it in this neighborhood before and it's a whole lot louder than Fabian's Chevelle.

The sound starts to disappear and Amir leads us towards his BMW sedan. I bet my mother would be falling over and fainting if she knew we were going on an actual date. Judging by his car, Amir's family is well off. He opens the passenger door for me and I slip inside, taking a deep breath as he comes around the driver's side.

The seats are soft, much too soft for someone who is currently building mental walls around her. I need to see this plan through. Get through the date, make pleasantries, then tell him I'm not interested.

"Sakinah."

"Huh?"

"Is there anything you'd like to listen to in particular?" He's already pulling off my street going who knows where. I didn't even think to ask since my mind's been so busy with what I need to do.

"Whatever you want, I'm not picky."

The drive is quiet and awkward. Maybe it's just me. Looking out the side window, we pull up to a fancy restaurant I don't recognize. But I mean, I don't usually eat out, choosing instead to cook at home because it gives me more time to study.

Amir escorts me inside and the ambiance of the place is supposed to be romantic, I suppose. I feel far from romantic right now. I'm nervous about how long this date is going to go. The server comes by and I haven't even picked up my menu yet. When Amir orders for me I feel beyond annoyed and want to stab his eyes out with one of the forks before me.

"So what do you do, Sakinah?" Didn't my mother give him all the information he needed already? You'd think she'd compile a file and hand it off to him the way she's trying to hand me off like cattle.

"I'm going to the university nearby, studying engineering." He takes a sip of water from his stemmed glass and never takes his eyes off me. It's unnerving.

"Yeah? Sounds complicated. What's a girl like you trying to do with an engineering degree anyway?" Did he just say that? Did I just fucking hear him correctly? Is he implying that women should do other things? I can feel my face scrunching in a frown and school my features. Good. This makes the 'I don't want to ever see your face here again' easier when the time comes.

"Oh, I don't know. Guess I was just trying to make my mother angry because an engineering degree takes longer than she would like. You know, since my eggs are drying up and all."

He chokes on his water and laughs. *Go ahead, choke some more buddy.* The server chooses that exact moment to bring our meals. What the hell is this? My eyes glance at his plate and he has the same thing.

Are these...snails?

"What the hell is this?"

"Escargot."

"Why would I want to eat snails when I have plenty in the garden?" I'm seriously starting to question this guy's sanity, despite not having a garden but there's plenty of these suckers on my flowers and grass back there.

"Sakinah! Don't be like that. It's a delicacy and really expensive. Just try it."

"No."

"Sakinah, let's try to do this. Come on." The fuck?

"What the hell are we trying to do?"

"We're trying to do this dating thing! Sakinah, I've been trying to get your attention since the wedding and you've had your head up in the clouds."

"What the hell is that supposed to mean?"

"What I mean is that I've seen that guy hang around you, and I had to make sure you knew I was in the running. Your mother approves of me, does she approve of him?"

"Him who?" I know I'm playing dumb and I'm fishing. But the audacity of this fucker, acting like he has anything over me, is making my blood boil.

"You know who I'm talking about Sakinah. Are you sure you wanna go out with him? He's not Malay you know." I'm seeing red. My head feels hot, and this fork in my hand is starting to hurt my palm from how hard I'm gripping it.

"We're not going out." I'm practically vibrating as I grit my teeth and tell him this. How dare he?

"Oh, okay, good. Because I remember him saying that he's your brother-in-law, right? Yeah. I guess I have nothing to worry about since he's practically family." Why does the universe feel the need to rub this fact into my face every waking second? I can't stand Amir right now, but I also can't get up and leave since he's my ride here, wherever here is.

There's some muttering going on around us, making me

shift my attention from the asshole in front of me to the front of the restaurant. Someone is standing there with a motorcycle helmet on and the server is trying to say something to him.

"Sakinah. Here, let me help you with that and show you how to get the meat out."

"I'm not eating this." Placing the fork down, I cross my arms. This is ridiculous. I lost my appetite earlier with how upset I was but now that I can eat, I can't because all I have is this shit in front of me. Even if I did eat it, it would only be like five bites. Who gets full on five damn bites?

"Come on, don't be like that." I watch as Amir gets up and comes over to my side like he has the right to. My eyes dart left and right, feeling embarrassed right now. Who does this? I'm twenty fucking five and he's coming over to show me how to eat?

"Amir. I'm. Not. Eating. *That.*" He chuckles like I'm being funny when I'm really being dead serious. I'm appalled when he actually shucks the thing out of it's swirly shell and starts to bring it towards me.

"Amir, no!" I'm getting scared, I don't want that thing near me. My hands are up like a barricade and I'm starting to scoot my chair back making enough noise for the people around us to start looking.

"It's okay, it's okay. She's just being dramatic." Amir is telling everyone looking that *I'm* being dramatic? He's the one trying to feed me like a child!

Then he has to go a step further and try to lean in for whatever he has planned but I'm already leaning so far away that I'm almost falling off the chair. What is going on?

He chuckles. I'm starting to get tired of the damn sound. "Sakinah, your mom said I can marry you. She knows I'm pursuing you, so you might as well just go with it. You said so yourself, you're twenty-five now huh. I might as well take the thing I want since it's right in front of me."

What? No! I didn't agree to anything! His lips are already coming towards me and I'm seeing everything in slow motion as I try to push off his advances. He's stronger than I am so I push harder and shut my eyes when I do fall forward and off my chair from his weight disappearing.

Scrambling to my feet, I lift my head to find the biker grabbing Amir by the front of his shirt. Oh, thank god. That was so close, my gut was churning. I thought I was going to puke in his face if his lips touched mine.

"I believe the lady said no." *That voice.*

He shoves Amir into his seat across from me, toppling him over backward making the next table jump up in surprise.

"Sir, sir! You can't do that. I'm going to have to ask you to leave."

"Don't want to eat any of your shit anyway." Fabian turns around and grabs my hand, hauling me out towards the front door. What is going on here? I'm still in shock with how this crazy snail date was going, that I didn't even feel it was Fabian who came in earlier.

When we exit the doors, the fresh air outside makes me able to breathe again. *My god, that was so close.* What is wrong with him? What is wrong with my mother? What kind of guy is she trying to set me up with? Why did I even agree?!

"Sakinah, are you okay?" My eyes do tear up then because...because I thought he was still mad at me.

"Fabian-" I don't know what comes over me but I jump into his arms and cry. Why am I always crying around him? Fabian holds me and the warmth of his leather jacket is soft enough to let us hug tightly. "I thought - I thou-"

"Shhh. You don't have to think anymore. Come on, let me

take you home." Nodding my head against his chest, I give him one last squeeze for my own sense of comfort.

We walk side by side down the street a few blocks and turn the corner to find a blacked-out Harley parked in the restaurant's parking lot. How is he going to take me home on *that*? Looking down at my outfit, I'm not sure if this will work. I mean, I'm in cotton pants with a long sleeve top but -

Fabian grabs me and turns me around, putting his leather jacket on me...and his helmet. "But what are you going to wear?"

His smirk brightens up my sour mood as he starts to buckle the helmet under my chin. "I'll be alright, but thanks for worrying. You can make it up to me later." He winks and my heart flutters. Watching Fabian swing his leg over his motorcycle makes me feel things between my legs. How can such a simple act look so damn sexy?

Turning his head, he flicks it to indicate I should get on. *Oh hell.* "Come on Sakinah, just get your ass on so we can go." He turns forward and starts the bike with a roar, the steady vibration can be seen on his handlebars.

Sucking up my fears, the thought of snails and Amir make me place my hand on Fabian's shoulder as I swing my legs over his backseat.

"Hold on tight, okay?"

"Okay." I've never been on the back of a bike before so the momentum from him pulling out of the parking space makes me feel like I'm about to fall off the back. Leaning in, I squeeze his waist tightly as we roar down the street, away from the restaurant - Issac Newton's third law and all that in the back of my mind.

It seems like it took a shorter amount of time to get home than it did to go there. The vibrations of the motorcycle have been doing a number to my lady parts, I've probably wet through my cotton pants from how much it was stimulating me. They never tell you that in the movies. It also doesn't help that every time Fabian shifts or moves, my hands can feel his muscles flex beneath his shirt as the wind whips at us on the ride here.

Fabian pulls up into my driveway right behind my car before kicking the stand down and shutting off his bike. He taps my thigh with his hand and I think he wants me to get off first. Stepping on the peg, I straighten my legs and swing one over. If it wasn't for his other hand holding my thigh and my hand on his shoulder, I probably would have fallen onto the pavement. Fabian swings himself off with ease like he's done it every day of his life even though I don't remember ever seeing him on a bike.

He chuckles as I look up at him through his full-face helmet, his hands delicately unbuckling it for me and pulling it off. It's a good thing I had this hijab on or else, I would have some serious wind-blown hair to tame later.

He smirks again as we both start walking towards my front door. Nothing needs to be said as we both come inside once I get it open. The feeling of relief is immediate and my mind is telling me I should be worried about what he's going to say to my mother. Our families probably run in the same circles after all.

Taking off the leather jacket, I drape it over the arm of the couch as I drop myself down unceremoniously onto the cushions and sigh. How do I get myself into these messes? The sound of metal and something hard taps my kitchen counter and suddenly the couch depresses near me, making me tumble towards his side.

"Well hello there." A cocky smirk is plastered on his face.

Suppressing a smirk of my own, I straighten myself beside him.

"Thank you, for saving me."

"I was going to kick his ass after the date was done anyway." I do laugh then. He can't be serious. "You keep laughing, I'm still thinking about it..once I find out where he lives, that is."

"Fabian! Don't you dare. It was - ugh, it was a disaster waiting to happen. I knew it but I didn't want to stand him up."

"Instead he let you fall down trying to get away from his advances."

"I-"

"Don't. I told you what would happen if someone even so much as tries to kiss my girl. Fucker got lucky he didn't make it all the way. When I heard you crying 'no', I was about to gut him right there in the restaurant and make him the next dinner special."

I should be appalled but my insides are glowing and my cheeks are feeling hot. Turning away from him, I take off my hijab and cap now that I'm home. *What if Amir comes by again? What do I do?*

Fabian pulls me over his lap and I let him. His eyes track over my face and my hair, the longer I look at him the longer I realize that he's not mad anymore from our previous fight. *I'm glad.* It lifts one of the weights off my shoulders. Leaning into him, I rest my head on his chest and wind my arms around his neck.

If I had to be saved, I'm glad it was him. It must be my tumultuous mind that made me do it because I suddenly find myself lifting my head, pulling his towards mine, and pressing my lips against his.

It's the first kiss I've ever given and it's *liberating.*

8

———

FABIAN

I must have won the damn lottery or something because things like this just don't happen. Not with Sakinah. It's the first time she's ever initiated anything with me and I don't know how to take it.

I used to be the kind of man that just jumps in head first, fuck the consequences because there will always be other women out there. But this girl has wrapped me around her finger so damn tight I'm about to bust a nut just from her pressing her lips against me.

Grabbing her waist, I pick her up and make her straddle me as we continue to explore each other with our lips. She's soft, tentative but growing in confidence the more I let her lead. It's heady to watch her slowly unravel and bloom like a damn flower in the sun.

The smell of her surrounds me, making me drunk off the moment more than any drink would ever do, as she starts to press her breasts against my chest. My hands thread into her hair and the strands feel like fucking silk between my fingers. The moan that accompanies the pelvic grind takes me by surprise and my eyes shoot open to make sure I'm not imagining things. Sakinah's eyes are hooded as she stares right back at me, grinding down again.

Who is this woman? Shit, better to not ask any questions because I'm loving everything she's giving me. Her broken voice floats back into my head and I pull her lips off mine. What if she regrets this?

"Sakinah-" She pounces right back at me and I lose my train of thought. My tongue starts to demand entrance and she opens up to me in invitation making me groan in response. This version of Sakinah is going to bury me, I just know it.

Our position changes and I find myself on top of her as she's sandwiched between me and the couch. *This is a bad idea.*

"Fabian, I want you so bad…" What the hell? She can't say that kind of shit to me right now when I'm trying to be good.

"Sakinah, we don't have to-" My lips travel along her jaw and down to her delicate collarbones. *Fuck, she is so soft.*

"Dammit Fabian, we shouldn't but I want you so damn bad it hurts." My god, what those words do to a man.

"I'm dying here Sakinah. Tell me what you want." Her hand pushes me off her before she seductively takes off her long-sleeve top and holy hell I've never seen such an expanse of perfect skin before. Well, I take that back - the last time I caught her with her nipples poking through her tank top was the last time I saw this much perfection.

Unable to help myself, my tongue dips into her belly button as I create a trail up towards her bra. Fuck, I don't want her to regret this but my dick is starting to hurt.

"Dammit, Sakinah."

"Shut up Fabian and kiss me." *Shit, yes, ma'am.*

Biting the top of her breast along the way, I kiss her with all I have. The room starts to become hot and heavy with the sexual tension between us and all we've done is kiss. Our breathing starts to pick up and every time she moans into my mouth, my hips thrust forward against her covered pussy. I'm torn between ripping her pants off and trying to respect what happened before when she broke down in front of me.

Dammit, what am I supposed to do? My dick is telling me I need to bury myself inside of the woman that's been driving me towards the brink of madness, but my mind is still trying to be a good guy here.

There has to be a middle ground.

"Sakinah, tell me what you want me to do. I don't want you to regret this. I fucking want you so bad but -" She kisses me again but this time much more slowly than the erotic rate we've been going. She stops and cradles my face, her eyes look so sad it breaks my damn heart.

"I don't know Fabian. I don't know." The male in me tells me to fix the fucking problem, but my mind is telling me there is no right solution here.

"Is it really that bad? For two people who feel the way we do...to be together?" Shit, she's starting to tear up and I'm about to slap myself upside the head for making it happen.

"Fabian, I don't know! We can't but-"

"But what Sakinah? Tell me." She's holding something back, I can feel it and it only solidifies my resolve.

Removing myself from her, I stand up and bend down to pick her up in my arms. She comes willingly, wrapping her arms around my shoulder as I take her to bed...

...to let her sleep the night off. She needs to clear her

damn head before we make this crap more of a shitshow than what it already is, if what she told me before was correct.

"Fabian-"

"Shh. It's been a long day, you had a lot happen. I'm going to stay here tonight in case you need me." Watching her roll over and cover her face in embarrassment does something to my chest, but I need to be the bigger person here - not the one to drag her into something she shouldn't be involved with.

Forcing myself to turn around, I walk out of her room and lay myself on her couch, staring at her ceiling. My dick is crying for me to take care of it, but right now my mind is cycling through all the possibilities of how we can make this work, without Sakinah getting in deep shit. Because let's be real, I don't give a fuck what it says about me. But Sakinah? I don't want to scar her with my selfish decisions.

Sitting back up, I start to untie my boots and take off my jeans and shirt. Might as well get comfortable if I'm staying the night. My house is down the street but fuck if I'm leaving her alone after that prick tried to kiss her. Just thinking about him makes me want to punch his face in. Good thing I had enough restraint at the restaurant. Vero always told me I had a volatile temper when it gets ignited.

Lying back down on the couch, my hands go behind my head as I listen to Sakinah shuffle around her room getting ready for bed. My thoughts drift back to the way the swell of her breasts rose and fell when things were getting hot and heavy on this very couch I'm laying on.

The sound of the shower comes on and I tell myself, fuck it. I need to get rid of this hard-on so I can at least attempt to sleep tonight.

Bringing one of my hands down under the waistband of

my boxers, I grip my shaft firmly, making me hiss. Stroking it up and down, I can feel my stomach muscles tightening with how hard my cock already is. The way Sakinah feels under me, the way her body was writhing...hell, the way she moaned against me all start to play through my head on repeat, like a fucking porno flick.

With each stroke, I'm gripping harder and harder but the climax feels so damn far. Growling in frustration, I take my hands out of my boxers, get up and start to pace her living room.

"Alright, think Fabian." She tells me we can't do this. She tells me it's forbidden. She fucking kisses me like she's drowning yet...

What the hell am I supposed to do? Do I walk away from this? What happens when we have a family get together? What if this spark between us never dies down? What then? Fuck, what if her mother makes her marry some asshole and I have to watch the way he touches her and kisses her.

I'd fucking kill him.

Amir's face comes into my mind and the rage I felt earlier at the restaurant comes back in full force. Slamming my hands on the back of the couch, I hang my head trying to think of something - anything - that will make this shit work. *It has to work.* There's no way around it - I can't stand the thought of my girl with *anyone else* but me.

I stop pacing her floor and start for her bedroom door. I don't know when the shower ended but I'm barging in like a man on a mission - because I am. This is it for me. I can't see myself with anyone but this fucking woman right here. Just the thought of her with someone else makes me want to choke and go on a killing spree.

"Fabian?"

She's in her fucking tank top and shorts again and my

mind fills with unbridled lust. Grabbing her, I lift her off her feet and kiss her with all the conflicting emotions running through me. She doesn't disappoint as she wraps her legs around me and starts to give it back just as passionately. Walking us towards her bed, I drop her back onto it as my hands go under her tank top and caress the side of her breast.

Moaning against my mouth, Sakinah's hands pull down her tank top straps, exposing both breasts without taking her lips off mine. *Hot damn.* My mouth leaves hers as they take one of her nipples into my mouth while my hand squeezes her other reverently. *So damn soft.* Her body is writhing under me, her hot pussy pushing against my erection behind my boxers and I almost fucking pass out from more blood rushing between my legs.

Popping my mouth off her, I lift her higher into the bed so her head reaches the other end. Ripping off her shorts and panties, I toss it aside as my hands grip her inner thighs to open them up for me. She's glistening like the damn sun shines out of her pussy and it calls to me. Dipping my head down, my tongue licks upwards between her swollen lips, finally tasting the forbidden fruit that's been causing us nothing but heartache the longer we push each other away. *Fuck, this is turning me on.* I moan against her pussy as I continue to lick up the wetness that's already accumulating.

When my tongue touches her clit, my mouth covers it and sucks. Sakinah gets louder in her cries, her body responding to everything deliciously. *Look at how responsive she is.* Damn, the thought of me being the first down here makes me start devouring her like a starving man. Because honestly, I am. This moment has been long coming. My hands go under her ass, forcing her closer to my face the more she tries to squirm away. Her moans drive me more and more into a zone that makes me want to lose my everloving mind. When her legs squeeze my head, I know she's close. Dipping my tongue inside of her, I bring my thumb up to circle her clit and pinch it on and off. A few more thrusts of my tongue and ...

"Oh my god!" The feeling of her pussy pulsating on my mouth makes my pride and ego swell. Continue to lick her through her orgasm, my hands pull off my boxers, letting my dick breathe from its confinement. With one last lick and suck on her clit, my tongue trails up her body towards her other breast and stops for a small detour. Her intake of air and moans tells me she likes what I'm doing, so I keep going, torturing myself in the process.

But little Sakinah has other plans as she grabs my head and brings it up to hers, tasting herself on my lips. Rubbing my dick against her wet pussy, we continue to duel with our tongues, our kisses becoming sloppy and hot.

"Fabian," she whispers my name between kisses and I can barely make a coherent sentence to answer her. My hips continue to thrust against her, the head of my cock hitting her clit on every pass. Sakinah starts to respond to what my body is doing as she begins to grind up against me as well.

My mind takes that very moment to finally come with a damn solution to our little sexual tension problem. I'm just going to have to do everything I can to not penetrate her. With this decision, I start to grind down even harder until the tell-tale signs of my balls tightening tell me I'm close.

"You feel so damn good against me."

"I'm so wet."

"I know, you're about to get wetter because I'm going to fucking cum." And I do - and it's fucking glorious. Growling against her mouth, my hips start to twitch every so often with how intense the orgasm is. She's coated in me and it makes me want to beat my chest, instead I opt for running my nose along her cheek and biting her earlobe before sucking it into my mouth.

"Oh my god."

"Yeah, Dios Mio is right."

My hips are still slowly thrusting against her as she continues to thrust back. This shit shouldn't feel this good. If I just move my dick a little bit, maybe I can just put the tip in-

"We shouldn't have done that." There she goes again. I groan into the crook of her neck and bite her to punish her for killing my afterglow.

"We didn't do anything Sakinah."

"What do you mean?"

"Don't worry your pretty little head so much."

"What if my parents find out?"

"How the hell are they going to find out what happened in your bedroom?"

"I don't know Fabian! I've never done this before!"

"I know you haven't. I'm glad I'm the bastard that gets to introduce you to it." She slaps my chest and I chuckle.

"Be serious Fabian!"

"Fuck Sakinah! I am being serious. Fuck if I'm going to let any other assho-"

"I mean about what just happened!"

"Nothing happened. I didn't even put it in you. Don't worry so much. Though now that I've had a taste of that pussy of yours, I don't think I can ever go back to not having it."

"Fabian!"

"What?"

"I can't stand you sometimes."

"Yeah? Well, the feeling's mutual. But you have to admit,

you feel better don't you?" She giggles. She fucking giggles. Giving her another kiss to shut up her yammering, she melds into me and winds her arms around me tightly.

"For a girl who keeps telling me we shouldn't, you sure arc a tease." Nipping her lip, I get up and go to the bathroom to get a washrag. Wiping myself off, I rinse the rag and come back to wipe off the evidence of my...passion on her stomach. *I should make her sleep like that.*

The daggers she's shooting at me with her eyes tell me to hurry up and clean it up. *Bossy little Malaysian princess.* Once the task is done, I chuck the rag into her dirty hamper and climb back into bed with her.

"We should get dressed."

"I'm done with your 'shoulds' and 'shouldn'ts'. Just go to sleep Sakinah."

"Fabi-"

"Shhh.." Pulling her back closer to my front, I nuzzle the back of her head and let out a sigh.

9

SAKINAH

I don't know what to do. We went from kissing in laws to in laws that mess around in bed. *This is bad.* Yet as I lay here listening to Fabian snore behind me with his arms preventing me from leaving the bed...I can't help but feel like a dam has been opened.

Tapping his hand to wake him up, all he does is grumble into my hair. *It's too damn cute.*

"Fabian, let me up."

"Why?" The way his voice is all gravelly makes me scissor my legs. His arm squeezes me tighter as he starts thrusting behind me.

"Fabian!" He thrusts even more and I can feel just how hard his cock is. I'm getting freaked out because what if he's too sleepy to realize what he's doing? *You didn't seem to mind last night.* Shut up brain! "I need to pee."

"Yeah? I can get into that."

"Oh my god, Fabian! Let me up!" He chuckles as he rolls over, releasing me from his restraint. The asshole. Making sure I slap him with the back of my hand at least once, I roll to get out only to have Fabian pull me back and roll on top of me.

My heart starts picking up in speed as he looks down on me. What is he planning? I follow where his eyes are tracking and he's looking at my -

I squeal as Fabian starts sucking on my neck really hard. It hurts but feels good at the same time when he starts to lick at it and suck it again. Pushing at him with all my might, I try to knee him in his dick but he quickly jerks away, laughing again.

Growling at his antics, I get up from the bed quickly and run to the restroom, slamming the door shut. Staring at the mirror, I can see a huge mark where he was sucking. Ugh! The asshole did it on purpose!

A knock comes at the restroom door, startling me. "I know you're looking at it. Every guy close enough to you will be able to see it too."

"You-you-!"

"Sweet and charming lover who doesn't want any stray guy to sniff around his girl? Yeah, that's me. Get your ass dressed so we can go get some breakfast, I'm starving." *This guy.*

Taking a quick shower, I peek out the restroom door to find the bedroom empty. Quickly throwing something on, I try my best to hide the giant hickey with whatever minuscule makeup I have. It's no use, it's just right there! Giving up, I grab one of my little short sleeve shirts and a pair of shorts.

Walking out of my bedroom I see Fabian standing there in just jeans, his naked back making my mouth water. The tattoos on his right upper arm and shoulder spread over part of his back, some sort of black and grey artwork that only adds to his bad boy look. I know I remember seeing some sort of circular tattoo on his left pec but in the heat of the moment last night, I didn't pay it any more attention.

"Mamá, don't expect me over today. I'm going to grab breakfast somewhere else." He usually eats at home? How sweet.

"No Mamá, I know you're the best at making comida. Don't be like that. I don't want you cooking for me all the time." Suppressing a smile, I walk towards the kitchen and start taking out some pans to get started on food. Fabian must spend a lot of money eating out if his appetite is anything to go by.

Opening the fridge, I start to catalog what I have before deciding on what to make when a warm arm go around my waist. Fabian gives me a kiss on the cheek before turning around to continue with his phone call.

"Mamá, there's nothing going on. No te preocupes. I'm not going to starve, geez. Just relax today or something. I'll talk to you later. Adios." He's so cute. But I'm not going to say anything.

Grabbing some vegetables and eggs, I close the fridge and start on a big omelette. Looking over Fabian's broad back again, I go back into the fridge and look for some beef too. He looks like he needs the protein.

My chopping board is already sitting on the counter as I lean over to my block and grab one of my favorite knives. My mind zones out as my hands start chopping up all my vegetables and setting them aside. Grabbing a plate from the cabinet, I make sure to use another knife and chopping board to cut the meat.

Once everything is set, I start to preheat the pan, standing here patiently with the spatula already in my hand. The eggs sizzle the moment they hit the pan and my hands start to toss in the other ingredients. The heat of the pan is starting to get to me but eggs usually cook quickly.

Sliding the omelette onto a dish I already laid out, I toss in the meat, letting it sizzle and crackle.

"Dios Mio, what are you making in there? My mouth is watering, fuck." Laughing, I turn to glare at him.

"Sit your ass down and wait until I'm done. Don't worry, you'll get fed."

"Why do you have to be like that Sakinah?" Ignoring him, my spatula moves the meat around until there's a brown crisp all over, the aroma filling the house.

"Like what? Like the woman who's making your damn breakfast?"

"You're killing me with that mouth of yours because I don't want to interrupt your cooking and you know it. Feed me woman!"

Sliding the beef on top of the omelette, I grab a fork before heading over to the table where Fabian is seated. Setting it down in front of him, I watch as his eyes go wide with desire. Is this what he looks like when he looks at me? Like I'm something to eat?

"This looks fucking amazing Sakinah. If you didn't already have my heart, I'd rip it out for you right here." Oh…

He grabs me by the waist and pulls me onto his lap, my arms winding around his shoulders. Kissing my neck, I pull away, remembering the hickey from this morning. We don't need any more evidence of what happened between us.

"Oh no, you don't. One hickey is enough." He leans in again and plants a soft kiss on my shoulder.

"It's never enough. I need to let everyone know to leave you alone."

"You're so crazy. Eat your damn food." Growling against me, Fabian chuckles. It's a sound I'm starting to anticipate between us. I love it.

"Yes ma'am. Buen provecho." Fabian practically moans when he places the first forkful into his mouth and I internally preen with delight despite my face not showing it. I've never seen anyone react like *that* before. My goodness.

Getting up, I go make myself a plate of something quick - I guess it will be cereal for today. Fabian's already done with half of this food by the time I come back to sit down next to him.

A few more bites and the plate is practically clean. Where does he put all that? He sits patiently and waits for me to finish my breakfast before grabbing the bowl and the plate to take to the sink. Be still my heart, the man is washing dishes in my damn house. His keen eyes also grab the knives and chopping board.

"What time do you have your first class today?"

"In about an hour."

"Ok good, I'll be back and then I'll take you to school."

"You are?"

"Yeah, why wouldn't I? It's just right there."

"But I usually drive myself."

"The bike uses less gas."

"I can drive myself."

"Yeah, that's cool. But I'm taking you to class."

"Fabian." I watch as he places the clean dishes in the drying rack, wiping his hands on his jeans, and then walking towards me. *He can't take me to school on that thing!*

His damp hands grab my face and gives me a kiss before he says, "Sakinah, I'm taking you to school so everyone can see you're fucking taken."

"But, we're not supposed to-" Another peck on the lips

and he leaves me to grab his shirt and walks out the door with his helmet. "What about your jac-" The slamming of the front door makes me want to throw something at the back of his head. The stubborn ass.

Walking into my bedroom, I change into some jeans and a button down shirt that comes to my forearms. I'm going to have to fix my hijab again once I get off the bike. Grabbing my books to make sure I have the ones I need, I hear the roar of an engine coming closer and closer. Fabian barges into the front door. Did I not lock it? What if it was someone else coming in? Jumping and running to the bedroom door, I let out a sigh when I see that it *is* Fabian.

"Fabian! Lock the door next time!"

"Relájate, I'll lock it now. I was only going a couple blocks anyway. Are you ready?" Turning to grab my backpack, I come back out and nod my head.

"Good. You can use my helmet, I'll get you your own after your classes are done so you can get fitted correctly." Why does it feel like he's giving me a promise ring or something? This is getting serious - my own helmet? What if he doesn't let me ride anymore? What the hell am I going to do with a helmet?

"Quit looking like that. You're always going to be in the backseat." *How does he do that?* Grabbing my hand, he hauls us out the front door and ...locks it. *Wait a minute.*

"How did yo-"

"I just made a key for myself. Here's yours back." He opens my palm and drops the key. What the? When did he?

He smirks and leans in to give me a kiss before pulling us down the front steps and up to his bike. *This guy.* I'm going to have to tell him to cut back on public affection. Someone might see us, someone who might know my mom.

Once my helmet is on and we're settled on the seats,

Fabian brings up the kick stand up and starts the rumble. The vibration can be felt up my spine, I'm not sure I'll ever get used to this.

We make it to the front of the campus in about ten minutes and my legs are still feeling the vibrations even when he turns off the bike. Getting off, I stand there and wait for Fabian to come help me take my helmet off. His fingers deftly move under my chin as he smirks at me.

"What are you smirking about?"

"How cute you look in my helmet." Slapping him on the chest I give him a glare even though I love this between us - the way we're always fighting like we mean it when we really don't.

Once the helmet is off, I try my best to fix my hijab. When Fabian's hand comes up to try and help, I dodge it subtly making him frown.

"Please, we need to cut back on the touching when we're out. Someone might know my family and news might get back to home." His frown doesn't disappear but his hand falls to his side. I feel a pang in my chest at the rejected look that flashed across his eyes but it can't be helped. We shouldn't have done what we did and touching too much in public will just make us look even more guilty.

When my hijab feels like it's back in place, I turn to look at Fabian to see him putting the helmet on his own head. "When does your last class end?"

"I have to meet Jason for the -"

"What time?" His eyes sharpens with the mention of my partner's name and I start to get worried about what will happen this time.

"I'll call you after I'm done."

"No you won't, you little liar. What time are you guys meeting?"

"Fabian, I need to do this project."

"I'm not stopping you."

"But you're making it hard!"

"How so? I recall being helpful last time."

"There's not going to be a next time, that's for sure. I need to get this project done quickly so then I wouldn't have to meet up with him anymore." Fabian narrows his eyes at me and I narrow mine right back.

"Give me your phone."

"Why?"

"Can you just be agreeable for once and hand me your damn phone Sakinah." With my eyes still narrowed in suspicion, I watch as he takes my phone, shoves it back at me to unlock it, then taps something over and over again. What the hell is he-

"There."

"What did you just do?"

"Don't worry about it. I'll pick you up after class."

"Wha-"

The bike starts with a roar and Fabian pulls out onto the road without another comment. Rude much?

Walking towards my classes, I notice all the girls looking after Fabian's bike. My insides feel a little irrationally angry even though I know it's not his fault he's got that bad boy look down pat - especially with this Harley.

I wish my culture would let me show more public affection, then I'd be able to claim him in front of all these girls. But again, I'm stuck between a rock and a hard place.

Each of my classes come and go and I find myself anticipating seeing Fabian again.

"Sakinah!"

"What?"

"Come on, let's go to the library. I've been looking over all your notes for the project and I think I have an idea of what we can do." How long has Jason been trying to get my attention? Shit, I need to get my head into the game before I fail this class.

Jason is rambling on about something physics related but all my mind can think about is the way Fabian's cock felt against my pussy lips. He didn't even try to slip it in when my pussy was all for it. How can he be that strong? I thought men were all slaves to their baser instincts. Fabian has proven time and time again tha-

"So what do you think? Good idea right?" Jason is whispering since we're almost halfway to the back tables in the library. When we *do* make it to the end, my eyes light up when I see the sexiest man already sitting at our old table, waiting for us. My heart starts to pound and I can feel my face smiling before I even tell it to.

Fabian looks so attractive sitting there with his chair turned backward, smirking at me. How can I feel so strongly for this man before me? I shouldn't. We're family...

"Jason, what's up? Sakinah. Good to see you again."

"Fabian."

"Hey what's up, man? Thanks for the notes, it really got me ahead of this shit. I got a really good idea-"

Funny enough, it becomes entertaining to see Jason start gushing over Fabian's example of velocity. We get a lot done through Jason's ramblings and I'm actually sitting back just watching him blossom into the science nerd he is.

Fabian's input every now and again is actually pretty impressive. It makes me see him in a different light. Beneath the bad boy exterior who seems like he doesn't give a shit about anything is a man with a very sexy brain. When Jason would go on his tirades about things, Fabian would pass little winks at me, and touch my thigh under the table away from anyone's prying eyes.

This game of chance we're playing makes me blush and scared at the same time. What if we get caught? But the idea that we're so close to getting caught is making my blood run hot for him.

When his hand almost brushes between my legs, I shoot daggers at him and he just smiles towards Jason, nodding his head like he's talking about the most interesting thing in the world. How does he keep so cool and calm when I'm turning into a slow-growing inferno for him?

"Alright, sounds good. What do you think, Sakinah?"

"Huh? Yeah, it sounds good." *What the hell are we talking about?*

"We'll see you next week man. Get that model going and I'll see if it jives with the notes we got going."

"Sounds good man, thanks for bouncing ideas with me. Shit, it must be so cool to be sitting on those skyscrapers, putting that shit together."

"Yeah, it's an experience. Ain't nothing like the breeze flowing through when you're sitting hundreds of feet up in the air. Living life on the edge, you know what I'm saying?"

"Damn, you got bigger balls than I do. That's for sure." Fabian is suppressing a grin that makes me want to slap him. I know exactly how he feels about Jason.

"Yeah, you can say that. Sakinah, are you ready to go?" Go? Go where?

"Yeah." Nodding my head and smiling, I just play along so Jason can leave us alone.

"We'll see you next week bro." Fabian grabs his helmet and starts ushering me out the front of the library before I can even say goodbye to my physics partner. The sleek black motorcycle comes into view and my lady parts are tingling.

What's going to happen now? Is he going to take me back home and then….then *what*?

Are we going to mess around again? Oh my god. Is he going to ..put it in me? If it feels like I'm falling off a cliff with him just rubbing against me, what would it feel like with him actually inside of me?

My breaths are already starting to come out in small pants when his gaze swings to mine, watching my chest rise and fall. He feels it too because his eyes become hooded when he looks at me. There's electricity crackling between us but we haven't spoken a word. When his hands place the helmet over my head, my breath hitches whenever our skin touches. My eyes are glued to his as he starts to buckle the helmet under my chin. I can feel myself biting my bottom lip in anticipation of what's going to happen - if anything is going to happen at all.

Taking a deep breath in, Fabian smells male - masculine - with a hint of exhaust fumes from his motorcycle. His strong hands flex and I stare at all the veins and tendons working with him as he takes off his leather motorcycle jacket and swings it over me, tucking my arms into the sleeves. There's a smoldering spark starting inside of me as we both stand out here in front of each other. Each touch, each graze is making me burn up, the phantom feelings of his touch lingering long after it's done.

How can these simple movements - that's far from anything sexual - feel so sexy that I'm melting in a metaphorical puddle of goo? I can see his chest rising and falling more than usual as well. When he lets me go to swing his leg over his bike I almost groan with the movement. He has such a nice ass in those jeans of his.

Fabian starts the bike and sticks his right hand out to me. Taking it, I step on the back foot peg and swing myself over the back of him. My arms slither around his abs, sneaking a little touch under his shirt as he pulls away from the front of the campus. Girls milling about are stopping to watch *my man* take me home. It's the only time I really have an excuse to touch him the way I am - I mean, I wouldn't want to fall off the bike, right?

SAKINAH

He parks his bike behind my car and we both get off. It already feels so comfortable and right...like we're both coming home. What would it be like to have him with me every day like this? I need to stop entertaining the idea because it's never going to happen - my family wouldn't allow it.

Once we make it through the front doors, all thoughts of family and potential marital obligations go through the window as we both start stripping off our extra layers. Fabian helps me with the helmet and places it gently onto the kitchen counter, but the moment he takes off his t-shirt is the moment my pussy starts to pulse with need.

Oh my god, he shouldn't look this good. He's a danger to all women, especially to me. Fuck, the thought of other women seeing what's beneath his shirt makes me mad.

Taking off my hijab and the layer underneath, I strip out of my shirt as well, leaving me in just a bralette.

Fabian's eyes are burning as his hands start to untie his bootlaces and unbuckle his jeans. My own hands are struggling to take my jeans off since they're starting to shake, making me have to look down and make sure I don't trip and embarrass myself.

When my eyes come back up, they widen in surprise because - because - Fabian was commando under his jeans this entire damn time and his dick is huge and pointing right at me. My heart starts to race from fear and anticipation. Can I really do this? How the hell can that thing fit inside of me?

Casting my eyes up to his quickly, I'm about to do a chicken move and run but Fabian grabs me from behind after only a few steps.

"Easy, Sakinah. Why are you always running from me?" His warm breath coming from behind me calms my nerves only a little bit.

"That thing between your legs is scary as hell, Fabian." He laughs as he lifts my feet off the floor and starts walking towards the bedroom.

"Yeah? Maybe it just wants to get to know you?"

"It already got to know me."

"Maybe it misses you."

"I don't know about that."

"Sakinah, Sakinah, Sakinah. Why are you always like this?"

"Like what?" I squeal as he tosses me onto the bed, landing me in a cloud of comforters and pillows.

"Like a little brat that wants it but just can't admit it."

"I don't know what the hell you're talk-" He climbs over me like a panther on the hunt and I'm caught by surprise -

though I shouldn't be - as he covers his mouth with mine. It's always been the way he subdues me. Maybe he's right. Maybe I *am* always running, but I can't help it. The unknown is too scary.

But when his hands caress my face, and his soft lips coax mine...he always makes it a little less scary resulting in my surrender.

The feel of his warm skin under my hands, the way his muscles flex as he brings us closer together - it's all just so much stimulation for me. My mind isn't sure what it wants to concentrate on. When our tongues start to tangle and dance, I'm lost in a sea of overflowing emotions and thoughts that I didn't realize he was trying to remove my panties. After a few moments, there's the sound of a snap and a sting on my skin making my eyes shoot open.

"Fabian!"

"You can buy more." Did he..did he just rip my damn panties off? I can't keep buyi-

His lips are suckling on my neck again and the pain and pleasure he's eliciting from me is making my toes curl. When I feel his teeth graze across my skin, my heart picks up speed but Fabian knows just how to make me relax again when the flat of his tongue starts to go over my pulse.

"Are you hot for me Sakinah?" How the hell do I answer that? I'm nervous again - he's so much more experienced than I am.

"Maybe." He chuckles and starts to move lower and lower - I can't keep my eyes off him, curious about what he's going to do to me. His hands come up and pull down the cup of my bralette and my eyes widen when he literally tugs at my nipple ... with his damn teeth. He pulls it back into his mouth and the feeling of his tongue swirling around it makes me want to squeeze my legs shut but I can't because his large body is blocking me.

The light kisses he plants down my torso makes the butterflies in my stomach start fluttering in utter chaos until he dips his tongue into my navel and bites the skin right beside it. My body starts to squirm and my head falls back the moment I feel his lips start to suck again, knowing he's going to leave another mark on me. At least it will be where no one can see it.

I don't know what comes over me but my hand starts to push him lower, where I really want him to be. It felt so good to have his mouth on my pussy that I crave it again but I'm too embarrassed to ask.

I guess I don't have to since Fabian starts to chuckle against the inside of my thighs as his fingers glide between my folds that's already so wet down there. The sensation is so teasing it makes my stomach muscles tighten in anticipation.

"Fabian, please…"

"Please what?" His fingers rub up and down some more. It's too much and it's too little.

Biting my bottom lip, my pride doesn't want to admit that I want his mouth on me. Can't he just..just feel my need?

"You want me to lick your pussy, Sakinah?" I gasp at his crude language during the moment. Why does it make me so hot?

"You want me to eat you like a damn buffet? Because I'm a hungry man and I do like to eat." His tongue teases my folds but it doesn't go where I want it to go. Would I be too greedy to ask for more?

"Are you going to feed me Sakinah? I love a woman that can feed my appetite." I'm turned on and pissed off at the same time. I should be the only woman who feeds Fabian's appetites. Grabbing his head, I pull him right up to where I need him because he does this shit on purpose to piss me off.

"Yes, Fabian. I'm going to feed you right now..I need you to eat my pussy." He groans right into me as his mouth covers my pussy. The feeling of his tongue dipping inside of me makes my hips thrust forward, wanting him deeper.

Fabian Hernandez has made me a greedy woman. My hands thread through his hair as my body starts to react to every single little thing he does down there. Why does this feel so damn good? When his warm mouth covers my clit and his tongue starts to flick the hood, my body bows off the bed, my legs spreading wider for his assault. I feel so wanton...but at the same time I feel so free - free to just feel and enjoy this moment between us behind closed doors.

All the teasing today and the bike has made my lady parts sensitive, it seems, because I can already feel myself climbing, the sensation wanting me to chase the finish that feels so far but so close.

"That feels so good." He groans again into my pussy and the vibrations almost tip me over the edge. I'm just about to fall off that cliff, my legs squeezing him between me, my stomach muscles tightening when..

He pulls his mouth off me and starts to climb my body. I'm so mad!

"Fabian!" His chuckle and smile soothes my soul as he starts to kiss me, making me taste myself on his lips. I greedily do so as my tongue starts to lick across his top then bottom lip before dipping inside to entwine in his.

Wrapping my arms around him to bring him closer to me, I don't feel his hand creeping down my body. Not until a hard slap jolts me.

His mouth starts to increase in passion, preventing me from getting a damn word out as he slaps my pussy again.

This asshole! Some of his slaps are hard, some are soft and each time the palm of his hand rubs against my clit to soothe the sting I feel myself loving every moment of it. He slaps hard a few more times and I cry out between our lips - that is until his fingers start to stroke my clit with vigor, sliding down my wetness and back.

Fabian tilts his head and bites my neck again just as his fingers hit that perfect spot and suddenly my body is twitching and writhing in ecstasy as my fingernails grip onto his shoulders for dear life. The harder I grip him the more he growls into the crook of my neck, telling me how much he likes me being rough.

Naughty Fabian isn't done with me yet though as he brings his hand up and sticks his wet fingers in my mouth. His eyes blaze as he watches me suck them, his hips thrusting against me. Is he going to put it in me this time? This is so bad - I shouldn't want it so much. The feeling of his hot and hard cock rubbing against me makes my legs open wider in invitation. I know I shouldn't but...

Fabian pulls his wet fingers out of my mouth, trailing it along my cheek before covering my neck with his hand. I should be scared, he could easily choke me if he wanted to, I'm at his mercy and drunk on everything he's doing to me. But my heart tells me that I know the real Fabian, not the bad boy everyone thinks he is - but the man that holds me when I need it most, the man that continues to come back no matter how much of a brat I become out of my fears. This is the man I'm staring at right now.

Our eyes lock on each other as his hand gently squeezes, making my legs wrap around his body in response. His hand pushes up against my chin, forces my head to tilt back as he starts to suck and nip my shoulder all the way to my collarbone. His dick continues to slide against me but never in me and I start to become frustrated with need as my pussy starts to grip onto nothingness - wanting him inside of me so badly.

On a particular thrust, I swear I can feel the tip of this cock almost going inside of my core but he pulls his hips back, making me want to cry.

"Fabian, I need you so bad."

"I know baby, but we can't." Dammit! Is this how he feels when I tell him we can't? Because it's already killing me! "Goddamn you're so fucking wet for me."

"I need you inside of me."

"Shit, don't tempt me."

"Fabian, please!"

It seems like every other stroke, the tip of his head butts up against my opening and when I try to wrap my legs around his tighter to bring him inside of me, Fabian pulls out like the tease he is. This push and pull continue on for what feels like an eternity of torture when all of the sudden his hips falter and he cums onto my lower abdomen. I want to scream at him but I also want to kiss him because he's so much stronger than I am.

I've noticed that even when Fabian climaxes, he still continues to thrust. When the tip of his cock hits my clit, I hold my breath wondering if he's going to put it in me now that his hot pulses are starting to die down.

But much to my frustration, he doesn't. Instead, he just chuckles, covering my mouth with his, removing his hand from my neck to grab onto his cock and rub the head of it all over my clit just to tease me even more. This asshole.

"You're so dirty Sakinah. We're supposed to be good."

"What the hell about what we just did qualifies as being good."

"You're still a virgin. Don't worry so much."

"Shut up Fabian! I'm not worried, I'm just so fucking horny and want you inside of me!"

"Dammit Sakinah, don't do this to me. I'm trying really hard here."

"I love it when you're hard."

"Dios Mio."

"Fabian…"

"Sakinah, stop. You know we can't. You've said so yourself." Pulling his forehead against mine, I close my eyes in frustration once more because he's fucking right. We shouldn't even be letting it go this far, yet…it feels so right to be this way with the person you l-

"Fabian." My eyes start to tear up again at the messed up position we find ourselves in. It shouldn't have to be this hard, this complicated. Two people should be allowed to feel deeply for each other and just…be.

"I know." He kisses my eyelids before wiping away my tears with his thumb and getting up to go to the bathroom to clean up.

Sweet Fabian always comes back to take care of me, cleaning me, wiping away anything that might make my mind break down to tears. When he climbs back into bed to hold me - he doesn't realize that he's already broken me in the best of ways.

11

Sakinah and I have developed a new pattern to our ...so called non-relationship. We wake up together, I take her to school, then go back to move my shit into the house down the street. Sometimes when I'm done early or just want to take a break, I bust out my phone and watch it track all her movements as she walks all over campus.

She probably doesn't realize I'm doing it, but what she doesn't know won't hurt her. I mean, it's good to know where your loved ones are, right? In case she needs me, I'll know the exact location she needs me to be. That's another good thing about getting this bike, I can weave in and out of traffic faster to get to her.

I think Jason and I have established an understanding. He knows she's off-limits, so I don't worry too much about it. It doesn't mean I'll let him sit next to her alone though. I'm not stupid.

After returning my dad's truck from the last load, I take the bike and bring it around the student parking lot of the university. Was it really just the other day that Sakinah was running away from me, making me chase her ass here just to get a kiss from her? How times have changed.

I regret nothing. It was all worth it to get to where we are now.

Turning off my bike, I swing my legs off and grab my phone out of my jacket. There she is, sitting in class. The dot hasn't moved for a while but I know her class is about to end. Taking off my helmet and hanging it on the handlebar, I walk towards her last class of the day - Statistics.

I've studied the layout of this campus and have found every nook and cranny near every single class she has. Why? Well..

"See you later Sakinah!"

"Sakinah! There's a party that's coming up tonight to celebrate the end of the semester. You should join us!"

"I'll think about it." Her head is still turned towards the sea of students spreading out as they start walking towards all the different classes they have. Grabbing Sakinah, she gasps as I pull her into a dark corner and into one of the unlocked closets nearby. She doesn't scream because we play this game daily. Me finding her and hiding her so we can stave each other off until we can finally be together at home.

The closet is dark enough with a privacy glass that no one would be able to see us even if they walked by, but light enough for us to see each other as we both start to kiss each other desperately, aware that time is of the essence until one of us gets caught. Sakinah has become bolder and bolder as time goes on, expertly kissing me back and making me want to fall to my knees and worship her right here. But she always has to wear so many damn layers, frustrating the hell out of me, teasing me to no end. My hands grab her ass as she moans into my mouth, tempting me to just say fuck it and take off her pants right here, right now.

But like every time we do this, she pushes me away with a sultry look, fixing her hijab and blanking her face right before she leaves me and joins into the sea of students walking about in the hallways.

Slamming my head against the wall, I give myself a little time for my dick to die down. What am I doing right now? What is my thirty-something-year-old ass doing sneaking around with a student? If the shit between our families doesn't make this forbidden, hiding our sexual misdeeds in closets surely does. But fuck if it doesn't drive me to want her even more.

Once my breathing calms down, I open the door slightly ajar to make sure there aren't too many witnesses as I walk out casually like nothing ever happened. Of course, my leather jacket stands out in a building full of nerds but I can't do anything about that. The breeze that greets me once I make it outside makes me take in a few lungs full of air as I walk towards my bike to wait for Sakinah.

The sound of feminine giggles following my wake starts to annoy me because I know damn well Sakinah doesn't do that. My head is about to burst with how much I just want to stick my dick in her and just claim her as mine for everyone to see - but I can't. I should. But then she'd kill me. If not her, then her family would kill her - then she'd be pissed at me. And I don't want Sakinah pissed at me - I love it more when she loves me. At least I think she does, if the way her body responds to me is anything to go by.

What if she's only using me to explore her sexuality? The thought pisses me off to no end but I tell myself that I'll just have to try harder to make her want to stay. Leaning against my bike, I find my mind brooding again over the possibility of Sakinah and I being together. How can we make it work?

Do I just take her to Vegas and marry her ass so she can't go anywhere? Would she even want to? Fuck, I've never had to plan this far before with anyone I've ever been with. To be honest, I've never felt this much before for anyone I've ever been with. She's different. She's under my skin and I feel like it's hard to breathe when I'm not around her. I need her scent around me all the time which is why I had to keep calling my mother to tell her I'll be eating elsewhere...and also why I haven't slept a day in the new house I bought.

"Hey." My eyes snap up like an automatic response to the voice that's continued to haunt my days and nights despite hearing it in person just as much. I can already feel my face muscles stretching into a smile when I see her standing before me in the sun, looking as stunning as the first day I saw her.

"Hey, are you ready to go home?" Her smile lights up my fucking life everytime I see it. Is this what love is like? Looking forward to the little things like a damn smile, like you need it to keep you living. I've never felt like this before, so I wouldn't know.

The ride home makes my heart feel full and tight. *Home.* We've kind of made it that way, haven't we? I already have a couple of pairs of clothes at her place to change into. I don't think she noticed me slipping it in, if she has she hasn't said anything about it.

Parking the bike behind her car, I swear I see a BMW drive by. It's noticeable in this neighborhood full of students who can't afford anything that shiny with their student budgets.

Walking into the front door, Sakinah drops off her backpack and veers towards the kitchen to start on food. This woman is amazing, just watching how she flutters around the kitchen so expertly makes my dick come back to life. I've had to stop wearing boxers because too many layers were becoming restricting with the constant hard on I have around her. Jeans over my dick aren't any better but I need some sort of protection when riding the bike to and from her school.

"What are you making me today?"

"Who said I'm making you anything?"

"Sakinah."

"I'm making myself a plate of something. You're welcome to make your own."

"Aww don't be like that. I love your cooking!"

"Yeah? Well, what if I decide not to cook? Are you going to starve to death?"

Growling, I get up from the chair and start walking towards her. Her eyes get wide but I can still feel the brattiness coming off her as she stares at me like a kitten with her claws out. Caging her against the kitchen counter, we stare at each other some more. This stubborn woman…

"Are you going to let me starve Sakinah? Is this how you feel about me?"

"Food has nothing to do with how I feel about you Fabian."

"Yeah? So how *do* you feel about me?" I'm fishing, but can you blame me? My mind has been in circles about this non-relationship we have going. I don't know where I stand with her and I've admitted to myself that it kind of scares me a bit. I don't like feeling this way.

Her hand cradles my face, but her eyes tell me she's going to spew something that makes me pissed.

"Well…"

"Well what?"

"For one, you're a pain in my ass."

"Yeah? The feeling's mutual."

"You're lucky you're hot and I keep you around for decoration."

"That's cold Sakinah." She giggles at my face as she pulls me down for a kiss. This girl right here drives me nuts. She pulls away from me but keeps her lips just a breath away.

"Fabian, the way I feel about you...it's too much. It overwhelms me and sometimes scares me. I don't know and yet I feel that deep down inside I do. But I'm scared, Fabian. What are we doing?" We stand here in silence for a few moments as I let her words soak into me. I'm scared too but my mind is telling me to just fuck it and take her. Take all this shit as it is, fuck everyone else. How can something so damn perfect - so damn right - be wrong?

Sakinah places a gentle kiss against my lips once more before she winds her arms around me in a warm embrace and we just hold each other, trying to comfort each other in this shit we're in. We're not going to be able to hide this much longer, not with my growing feelings for her. I can't always be a dirty little secret she keeps behind closed doors.

But today is not the day to decide on it just yet. No, today we can just be Sakinah and Fabian in the kitchen, about to eat a nice meal together while the world goes on outside without us - without bursting our bubble we have going on in here.

Sakina breaks the embrace and shoves me out of the kitchen. "Go sit down Fabian, I'll make you something to eat." At the mention of food, my stomach growls and she laughs. It's the lightest sound but also raw. I haven't heard her laugh like this until a few weeks ago when we've finally started to let our true personalities free, getting to know each other.

Whatever Sakinah is making is causing the house to smell damn good. When she places the plate piled high with whatever it is, I impatiently wait for her to sit down with her own plate so we can say Bismillah.

"Buen provecho." I start to dig in and almost cum right there. How can this little woman cook like this? Does she not taste her own damn cooking?

"I got invited to a party with some of my classmates." I'm barely hearing it as I continue to shove mouthfuls of this amazing meal into me.

"I think it will be fun. I've never been invited before. I should make an appearance right?"

My plate is almost finished when she kicks me under the table, almost making me drop a spoonful. What the hell?

Wiping my mouth with the napkin she has on the table, I glare at her. "What the hell was that for? I was trying to enjoy my meal."

"I was trying to talk to you about something! Listen!"

"Alright, alright. I'm listening. Tell me again." She lets out an exasperated sigh and it's the cutest thing.

"I said I'm going to a party tonight. I got invited today. It'll be fun. I need to go out and mingle and all that. It's college, this is what college people should do right?"

Flashes of my own years of partying play before my mind - images of girls all over guys and guys all over girls, drinks overflowing cups and a whole lot more I don't wish to remember. I don't think I like the idea of sweet little Sakinah around that kind of shit.

"No."

"No, what?"

"I don't want you to go."

"Why?"

"Because they'll be guys there. They'll be all over you trying to get into your panties. No, I don't like it. No."

"Who the hell made you my dad anyway? You can't tell me I can't go."

"I just did."

"Fabian! I'm going. I want to go. I finally got invited to something. I don't want to be an outcast."

"Who said you're going to be an outcast? Parties happen all the time. I'll take you to some."

"No! It's not the same as you dragging me somewhere. *I* got invited, I'm going."

"Why are you like this Sakinah?"

"Like what? Why are *you* like this?"

"I'm like this because I know damn well guys only go to these kinds of parties to fuck all the drunk girls."

"Is that what *you* do at all these parties?"

"Yes! That's why I know you shouldn't go." Her eyes sharpen and I think I just stuck my foot in my mouth. She looks pissed and there's practically steam coming out of her ears. Trying to rewind our conversation in my mind, I'm barely even able to comprehend what just happened when she starts to yell.

"Get out!"

"Wait, what?"

"I said. Get. The. Fuck. Out!"

"Sakinah, let's talk about this. I wasn't trying to make you ma-"

"Fabian! Get the fuck out of my house!"

Shit.

12

SAKINAH

That asshole! He tells me he goes to parties to fuck girls yet I can't go to the one party I'm finally invited to? The thought of him fucking other girls when he hasn't even stuck it in me makes me want to scream. In fact, I walk to my bedroom, pull out his clothes he's been hiding in my damn dresser and scream into it to muffle the sound.

He drives me insane! I'm so damn mad I want to cry but I'm too pissed to cry. Nothing fucking makes sense and it makes me angrier.

Oh, I'm going to this damn party especially since he doesn't want me to. Stripping out of my clothes, I turn the shower on cold to try and cool my temper. Fabian always does this to me, either he drives me up the wall or drives me crazy with lust. I can't control myself around him. Scrubbing my hair a little extra hard, I rinse myself and everything off and get out still pissed at what just happened.

"This asshole thinks he can tell me what to do." I mumble to myself as I start drying myself aggressively with the towel in my hand, wringing out my hair.

"Tells me he can take me parties like he's fucking still going every damn week or something." Tossing the towel towards the hamper so hard, I miss it but leave it there anyway.

"Says guys only go to parties to fuck drunk girls. I don't even drink!" Grabbing a more form fitting outfit off my hanger aggressively, the hanger flies off and falls to the floor making me even more pissed since I have to pick it up.

"I'm going to show him and his stupid pretty face that I can handle myself just fine at a party. I'm twenty fucking something years old. Where does he get off telling me what to do?" Bringing the dress I'm gripping to death towards the restroom, I hang it on the doorknob while I start to lotion my body up with something that smells nice. Forgetting to grab a bra and panties, I take the dress off the doorknob and toss it onto the bed.

When I put the dress on, I try to smooth out the wrinkles I made. It's form fitting - more than usual - the neckline a little lower than my others but my hijab should cover it. The fabric drapes nicely, showing off my curves without showing off too much skin. The fact that the sleeves only go to my elbows makes me feel risque already. Good. I need this. I need this party to lift my mood.

Letting my hair dry before wrapping my head, I look in the mirror one more time. Being around Fabian has made me more confident in myself. Every time he touches me and tells me how beautiful I am and how smart I am. I can already hear my mother's voice in my mind yelling at me about what I'm wearing. But I need this. I need these small little victories for myself, to break free from the restraint I keep feeling.

Grabbing my bag with my necessary items, I head out the door and make sure to lock it securely. When I turn around I swear the back end of the car that just drove by looks familiar. Shaking my head, I think about the party and start walking towards my car. I haven't driven in a while and it almost feels weird. Fabian's been taking me to and back from school practically every day since this thing between us started.

Ugh! Why can't I stop thinking about that asshole? *Okay, party. I'm going to a party. Let's do this.*

Pulling out my phone, I input the GPS to the location where I was told the party was being held. My eyes glance at the clock on the dash - the party's been going on for about an hour now. That's alright, I shouldn't come in that early anyway. It looks like the house is not too far from the campus, kind of like mine but on the opposite side.

Pulling out of my driveway, I turn on the radio to drown out any more thoughts of Fabian. The trip only took about fifteen minutes and the street is already starting to fill up with parked cars. Finding a spot a few blocks off, I pull the car next to the curb and put it in park. Using the car's mirror to check my hijab again, I let out a breath and gather my courage to enter this party like I know what I'm doing.

My dress flows with the breeze as I walk towards the music that's starting to blast through the front door of the house party. This really is just like the American movies I watch, my goodness. Friendly faces hanging outside wave at me, some with plastic cups in their hands.

Entering the house, the air is thick and warm from all the bodies everywhere milling about in different groups. Some are on the couch hanging out, some are standing to the side. My eyes dart around trying to find a familiar face as I continue to walk deeper and deeper into the house.

"Sakinah!" Turning towards the voice, I see Jason shoving people aside to get to me. He looks different, looser, calmer. My eyes shoot to his cup and assume he's already been drinking. I'm going to have to be careful.

Fabian's words echo in my head but I try to not let it get to me. I'm going to enjoy myself at the party.

Some of the other girls from class find me and I hang out with them in their little group. Everyone's excited about the semester ending, getting closer to our goals and our different degrees.

One of the girls hands me a cup and I become leery. "I don't drink."

"Oh don't worry, this is just punch." Sniffing it, it does just smell like some sort of fruit punch. When I taste the first sip, it's cool against my lips and I don't taste anything funny so I keep drinking as the girls and I talk about things from our projects to cute guys they've been trying to hit on.

A few hours later and a few cups later, my head is starting to feel funny. I'm also starting to feel really warm but every-thing around me is starting to go in slow motion. Am I just tired? Maybe I should leave the party soon before I fall asleep behind the wheel. I want to take this hijab off and feel the air against my head to cool down. It's a good thing this place is only about fifteen minutes away. The girls and I have taken over the couch and when I go to stand up the world starts to spin sideways a little, freaking me out.

What's happening to me? How am I supposed to drive home when the world can't even stay still? Stumbling a little bit, I make my way out of the living room towards..towards somewhere away from the partygoers.

"Sakinah, are you okay?" It's Jason's voice but I don't know which direction it's coming from. Not until his hand touches my arm to steady me. I'm glad he's here, maybe he can tell me where the restroom is so I can pee and then go home.

"J-Jason, do you know where the restroom is?"

"Yeah, come on, I'll help you." We're walking towards the stairway, having to go around so many people hanging out in random places, everywhere. How can this many people fit into one house, I wonder?

"Hey, I'll take it from here. Our families know each other."

"Yeah?" Jason sends me a look but I didn't even catch everything the voice was saying. Something about family. Damn, if my family saw me like this right now I'd be in so much trouble. They sent me to school to get a degree, not to party. It's a good thing I'm already doing well in all my classes.

"Sakinah." When did I start sliding down? Or is it forward?

"Sakinah. Come on, I'll help you." His voice is different. This isn't Jason. When I turn my head, the room spins a little but when it stops, Amir's face is right next to me. What the hell?

"Amir? What are you doing here?"

"Keeping an eye out for you. You shouldn't be here. You're lucky it's me who found you and not someone else. I won't tell your mom, but you can't do this anymore." What is up with these guys who think they can keep acting like my dad?

"I need to pee."

"Alright, let me see if I can find the restroom. I think it's upstairs." Upstairs is right because it feels like I'm tasked to climb a damn mountain with how many steps there are. Why are there so many steps? My bladder is about to explode from the amount of punch I've been drinking.

"Alright, I think this is it. Go in and hurry up so I can take you home." Whatever. I knock on the door first in case there's someone in there. No response. Opening the door I step inside and make sure to lock it - well it took a few tries, but I locked it. The feeling of peeing is almost orgasmic as my bladder finally finds relief.

Getting up, I wash my hands and look at myself in the mirror. I don't look any different. Maybe my eyes? Why do I feel like this? Was there something slipped into my drink? My heart starts to beat harder at the thought and Fabian's words come back to me. Maybe he's right. But, it was the girls who kept bringing me drinks. This doesn't make any sense.

The knock on the door makes me almost jump out of my skin. "Sakinah, are you alright? Hurry up. Do I need to go in there?" Come in here? For what? To help me pee?

"Why the hell do you need to come in here?"

"What are you doing in there?"

"I was peeing, what do you think I was doing? It's what I said. I needed to pee." Unlocking the door, I'm thrown back a little bit as Amir barges inside and then shuts the door behind him. What the hell?

"You have a fucking mouth on you, Sakinah. I don't like that shit. When we get married, you're going to have to learn to respect me as a husband."

"Who said I'm marrying you?"

"Your mother. You think she's going to be happy to hear her daughter is hanging out behind closed doors with her brother-in-law, hmm?"

"What the hell are you talking about?" Why is he so close to me all of a sudden?

"Every time I come by, his motorcycle is there. Every time I come by to see you in class, he's picking you up. I can't get any time with my fucking future wife when there's someone blocking me. Is that why he came to get you at the restaurant? Were you already fucking him by then?" Future wife?

"I'm not your damn wife." The sting on my face starts to bloom into something. I didn't even see him raise his hand but my face is telling me he just damn well did.

"Did you just fucking slap me? You asshole!"

"You need to know your place, Sakinah. I can't have that fucking mouth of yours spew shit like that when we go out as a couple." The audacity of this fucker right here.

Whatever is happening to me right now must make my inhibitions go down because I'm screaming at his face.

"Get the fuck away from me! I'm not your damn wife!" Amir has a look of distaste on his face but the knock on the door stops him from doing whatever he's about to do.

"Sakinah! Are you alright?"

"Jason!" Amir covers my mouth with his hand as he answers.

"We're fine! I'm going to take her home. She's not feeling too good."

"She was fucking fine when I left her." The doorknob jiggles and I'm praying Jason gets in here so he can get Amir away from me.

"I said she was fine!"

"Then why the fuck don't you let her answer?" Jason busts in with his shoulder to the door, slamming it back and Amir lets my mouth go. My mind is still working slowly, trying to figure out what's happening.

I think Jason and Amir are yelling at each other but my hands are grabbing my phone in my purse as my fingers fumble on the screen. Please please please, come on! Fabian must have put his number on my speed dial, because there's his face right there under favorites. Hitting the button, I hear the phone ring just as my eyes shoot back to the guys who are starting to shove each other.

"Sakinah. I'm on my way."

"Fabian, I'm so scared."

"Shit, I'm halfway there. Hold on." My mind is trying to comprehend how he even knows where I am but I'm just glad he's coming. I don't know what Amir is going to do if he takes me home. The boys are still yelling and staring each other down blocking the doorway. I can't get out of this damn restroom.

The music is too loud to know if anyone is hearing us and this fight that's about to break out, but suddenly a hand pulls Jason back and punches Amir in the face, making me scream. Amir gets up and grabs Fabian before he can get to me, but Fabian must have been anticipating it because he turns quickly and grabs Amir by the throat and slams him down in the hallway.

Oh my god. What the hell is happening? Scrambling to get out of this damn restroom prison since the boys have created an opening, I make it to the doorway when I hear Fabian growl.

"Stay the fuck away from my girl. The next time I see you anywhere near her, I'm going to kill you, you feel me?"

Amir is choking out his answer but I'm stunned with his response as I stand behind Fabian.

"You mean my fucking wife? Yeah, her mother has already given me the okay. She's already mine. You're the one that needs to fucking stay away from his sister-in-law." I just about die right there when the tail end of his response echoes into the hallway making those who are left around us staring at the show before them. I can feel my cheeks getting hot, I'm so embarrassed. Of all the ways for our secret relationship to get exposed...a party was not what I envisioned.

Fabian's back tenses as he lifts Amir up by the neck and slams him into the wall. He looks so enraged and I don't know how to stop him. No one else does either because everyone starts to go down the stairs or back away. Jason is standing a few feet away but he's not saying anything. What *can* you say?

Watching Fabian bring his elbow back stuns me as he lands two more fists into Amir's face before letting him drop to the floor. Blood is starting to ooze out his nose but he's not moving. Is he dead?

Fabian turns his face to me and I can see the storm of emotions raging behind his eyes as he comes towards me and lifts me bridal style, making the room spin. Wrapping my arms around him, I bury my face into his chest and close my eyes to stop all the motion from making me want to get sick. He continues to descend the steps as the music continues to blast in the background. No one says anything, not that I can hear anyway. I know we make it outside when the air changes, becoming cooler from the sun having gone down.

The sound of a metal door opening tells me Fabian came over with his Chevelle. He tries to put me into the passenger seat but it's just too much of a change in position, so I latch on even tighter.

"Sakinah, I need to take you home. We have to put your seatbelt on okay?" *I'm scared. What if the world spins again?*

His warm hands rubbing my back make me feel a little bit

better. Relaxing some of my tension, I open my eyes slowly to make sure the word still looks the same. Fabian kisses me on the cheek before pulling the seat belt around me and shutting the door. The air that whooshes in from him opening the driver's side feels good on my skin. It is definitely time to go home.

13

FABIAN

I knew she shouldn't have gone to that shit. I knew it! But I'm not stupid enough to bring it up right now. No, instead I'm going to stay the night and take care of my girl.

That fucker Amir is lucky I didn't kill him. There were too many people watching us. But when he called her his wife… all my insecurities and fears about my relationship with Sakinah came bubbling out, like a volcanic eruption of emotion.

Carrying her into her house, I place her gently on the couch as I go to the fridge to find some water for her. She needs to sober up. I just bet someone gave her spiked punch because she'd fall for that - she's too innocent for that party scene.

Coming back, I sit her up slowly and keep her right

beside me so she doesn't topple over. Twisting the cap off the bottle, I hand it to her.

"Sakinah, you need to drink some water. Come on, it'll make you feel better."

"Okay." Watching her closely, I make sure she doesn't spill it all over the place - and she doesn't. *Good.*

"I'm staying the night. Someone's got to make sure you're okay." She drinks almost half the bottle in one go and hands it back to me. Putting the cap back on, I place it on the little coffee table she has in her living room.

"Okay." Her body slowly starts to fall towards me and I lay us both down on the couch. She's too drunk to even keep a sitting position. My adrenaline is still dying down so we might as we both relax for a minute.

"Thank you for coming."

"Sakinah, I was coming for you anyway."

"I'm glad." Her face nuzzles my chest and my hands wrap around her tighter. That fucker's words still make me want to break something but I can't move right now. When Sakinah's breathing starts to slow down, I carefully straighten her up and carry her into the bedroom. Removing her shoes and hijab - or whatever it's called - was easy, but this dress? Where the hell is the zipper? Does it have a zipper? How the hell did she even get it on?

I feel like I'm flopping her around like a ragdoll by the time I figured out that it's a pullover type outfit. Holy hell, who makes this shit? It's a good thing she's pretty much passed out at this point because she doesn't rouse with all this movement at all. Taking off my own shoes and shirt, I head out to the living room to bring back her bottle of water and another one just in case and place it on her nightstand.

Taking off my jeans, I start to rummage through her dresser only to find my clothes missing. *What the hell?*

Looking around the floor I see a bunch of stuff strewn around haphazardly, some of which are my damn clothes. She must have been really pissed at me today. Well, she can stay pissed because I said what I said.

If I had left the house any later -

Shit, I don't even want to think about it. Grabbing my boxers off the floor, I slip it on and get into bed behind her. She's still in her bra and panties so she can't be too mad at me when she finally wakes up.

SAKINAH

I'm laying down somewhere. Opening my eyes, it looks like my room. There's water on the nightstand and suddenly my throat is so dry. Grabbing it, I finish off the one that's half full and put the empty bottle back on the nightstand. Closing my eyes, I turn over and am met with a lot of flesh - very masculine smelling flesh. *Fabian.*

He rescued me again. Snuggling into his side my mind starts to drift off but not before Amir's voice starts echoing quietly into my ear.

Something jostles me awake. Fabian starts to move an arm behind his head and my head lands on the mattress. How long was I asleep? I woke up last night, didn't I? I think I drank some water. Blinking a few times, I stare at Fabian's sleeping form. He really is a beautiful specimen of a male. Studying the planes of his abs and biceps, my body starts to respond. He's so hot, and he's always lying next to me practically naked.

Looking down at myself, it seems he's stripped me to my underwear. It's making my resolve melt more and more. This relationship of ours should have never grown into what it is but after Amir blasted the fact out there...what the hell do I have to lose now? Everyone already knows.

Lifting my head, I scoot closer to his side and place my chin on his chest, staring at his jaw. He hasn't shaved in a while and it shows. He's looking even more gruff than usual, the motorcycle doesn't help either. I didn't miss the fact that early on at the party some of the girls nearby were talking about the hottie on the bike that comes by.

My fingers trace each of his abs one at a time. The dip on his hip leads my fingers down towards the boxers he has on. He must have found it on the floor since I remember getting pissed and throwing it down there. That's another thing about Fabian, he's so good at rolling with the punches.

Oh god. The way he punched Amir and stopped him...it shouldn't be hot, but it is. It makes me want to .. oh I don't know.. I'm not good at this relationship stuff.

Running my hand softly down and around his waistband again my mind goes to all the times he's put his mouth on me. It feels so good. I wonder if I can make him feel good too. My heart starts to pound a little harder in my chest. What if I do it wrong? I mean, all you do is suck...right?

My face gets hotter just thinking about putting him into my mouth. I bet Fabian never gets embarrassed about putting his mouth on me. My legs start to scissor as I climb over him even more. Pulling his boxers down that's starting to tent anyway, his dick pops out and almost slaps me in the face. Holy shit he's big. I've never seen a dick this up close before. Shit, he's the only dick I've ever seen...or felt.

His dick is bouncing a little and it's scary. Does it have a mind of its own? How am I supposed to put it in my mouth if it moves like that? Blame it on the residual liquid courage because my hand grasps his shaft and Fabian moves a little bit but still doesn't wake up. His skin is so soft and his dick is so hard at the same time. Moving my hand up and down, I start to build a steady rhythm and feel a little braver. Pulling his dick towards me, my tongue licks the top. That wasn't so bad, but now I'm really damn horny. Just knowing he's still asleep makes me want to swallow him whole. *Maybe I should try.*

Putting my entire mouth on him, I suck him down between my lips until it feels really far inside. Is it? What do girls talk about at school? Deep-throating? What does that mean? Does that mean I shove him all the way down my throat? My god, he's way too big for that.

Pulling my mouth off him, I lick the top and swirl my tongue around the crown of his dick. This shouldn't be so sexy. Sucking him down again, I hear Fabian groan in his sleep. On the next pass up, my tongue tastes something different. *Oh my god.* I'm so hot right now. I need more of this - I love seeing his reaction to me. It makes me feel powerful and sexy.

Rearranging my body over him so I'm straddling his legs, I start to suck him up and down in earnest, learning to relax my jaw to try and take in more of him. There's no way this man will fit down my throat. The farther I take him the more I start to occasionally hit my gag reflex, and every time I do, he moans. My eyes glance towards him now and again but Fabian is still sleeping, the only change being his change in arm position from behind his head to the side of him.

Fabian has some big hands. Thinking about the way he slapped my pussy makes me squirm on top of him. On an upward pass, I feel hands threading through my hair and when I swing my gaze to his, I see that he's looking at me through half-lidded eyes. *He's so fucking hot.*

When my mouth takes him in again, Fabian tilts his head

back, thrusting his hip towards me to take him in even deeper. My mouth starts moving faster and his hand starts to grip my hair harder and his hips slowly start to fuck my face.

"Fuck."

I like the way that sounds. I really do want to fuck him because it's getting really hot and really wet between my legs. My panties are soaked and the friction is killing me.

"Get up here." Giving his dick one last suck and lick at the tip, I crawl up his body. He growls when I take too long and pulls me up until his lips crash against mine.

"You're so fucking bad Sakinah."

"I know."

"That's what I fucking love about you." My heart stops at the mention of the L word and suddenly I want it all. *I want all of Fabian.*

"I need you inside of me."

"We can't, remember?"

"I'm so horny."

"Come here."

He grabs two handfuls of my ass and pulls me down onto him to grind. But it's not enough. These damn panties are going to give me a burn between my wet lips.

"My panties."

"Don't worry about it." Fabian's finger roughly pulls the crotch of my panties aside as he starts to slide his dick against me. It only does so much when my panties keep getting in the way.

"Fuck, stop wearing panties to bed." Fabian rips off another pair, snapping the elastic against my hip causing a burn against my hips but I'm too lost in lust to care.

Sitting up straight, my hands go behind me to unhook my bra as Fabian kicks off his boxers. We come back together, flesh against flesh, my nipples rubbing against his chest in the most agonizing way. Fabian has sucked on my nipples so much, they've started to become chapped. But right now they're crying to be sucked on again for some relief.

"Fabian, I want you to suck me." He groans and pulls me up until my nipples are right above his mouth. The head of his cock is right at my entrance with this change of angle and I'm feeling brazen. Moving my hips over him, I can feel his head dipping in and out ever so slightly. What would it feel like if he went all the way in? He's so big, would he even fit?

"Stop grinding on me like that Sakinah, it's going to slip in."

"Then let it."

"Dammit woman."

"I want you Fabian."

"Fuck." His mouth moves to my other breast and I can feel that shit down to my pussy. Shoving my hands between us, I grab his dick and squeeze, making him groan and suck my nipple harder.

Rubbing the head of his very hard cock against my clit, my body starts to move to a sultry dance even I'm unaware of. It's like it knows what it wants and it's trying to convince him to come inside.

"Sakinah." His voice comes out like a plea as he starts to lick the top of my breasts and try to push me down lower. Scooting back, we both slip a little, the head of his dick sliding in and stretching me. *Oh my god.*

"Shit, you're too big."

"Dammit, Sakinah." Fabian's arms go around me and he flips us over and onto my back.

"Fuck, you feel so good."

"I want you so bad."

"Shh, shh. I got you."

Fabian starts a slow and shallow thrust, dipping the head

of his cock inside my wet pussy and I want to cry from how good it feels. *I need more!* My legs wind around him, trying to pull him into me and he thrusts in what feels like another inch making me frustrated.

"Shit, you're so fucking tight. Are you sure?" After what happened at the party, I've never been more sure about anything.

"Yes, Fabian! Please!"

When he pulls his hips back slowly, the feeling of his dick leaving me makes me want to whimper in protest until he thrusts back into me, filling me up and stretching me in the most delicious and painful of ways.

"Oh my god. I feel so full."

"Dios Mio Sakinah, I'm not all the way in yet." *Shit.*

Fabian kisses me and distracts me as he continues a slow thrusting motion. I'm so damn wet he's literally gliding in and out of me with little resistance - until he gives me one hard thrust and fills me to the hilt, making my mouth open in a hard gasp.

"Let me take care of you." Once the feeling of being impaled starts to slowly dissipate, my mouth starts to respond to his kisses.

A few thrusts in and the sensations inside of me starts to lean more towards pleasure instead of awkwardness. It helps that Fabian's been rubbing his thumb on my clit during his slow thrusts because now I need more. *Is this hungry feeling ever going to end?*

"More." He chuckles against my lips as his hips start to move faster. "It feels so good."

"Yeah? You like that?"

"Fuck yes."

Fabian grabs the back of one of my legs and throws it over his shoulder before he starts pounding into me, making my breasts bounce and making me feel like I'm about to be pounded right off this bed. *Holy crap.*

"Shit, you feel so fucking good around my dick."

I can barely breathe right now with how hard he's ramming that monster between his legs into me. The sound of wet flesh on flesh fills the room accompanying the smell of sex. It's getting so hot, I feel like I might internally combust any moment. The sensations he's drawing from within me is starting to feel like a chase.

Fabian twists his hips somehow and I almost squeal. *What the hell?* He keeps changing his pace while his hand continues to pinch and roll my clit in the most delicious of ways. When he forces my body sideways and pushes my lifted leg farther back, I feel like a damn acrobat. But whatever he's doing is making me feel so damn close to the finish line that I want to cry.

Watching the way his dick slams into me must be what it feels like to watch porn because I'm getting even more aroused from the sight. The way his shaft glistens each time he pulls out of me only to ram it back in just as hard - The way his abs flex with his hip thrust forward.

I must be going out of my mind because I'm starting to feel even more full, like he's getting bigger. His hip thrusts falter a little bit and I think I feel it throbbing inside of me as I watch him pull his dick out, cumming on my pussy lips and all over my clit. His free hand is gripping the head of his cock and rubbing it hard against me that it pushes me over the edge.

"Oh my god."

"Fuck yes. Cum for me Sakinah." He rubs the head of his dick against me even harder, still pulsing cum all over and between us as I try to suppress my cry of pleasure, my body tumbling over the precipice as I watch Fabian rub his cum everywhere between my legs. How can a man produce so much? It's so erotic it makes my mouth water.

Letting my leg go, Fabian falls forward and kisses me as he continues to slowly thrust his shaft between us. It's not as hard anymore but still feels just as sexy as when we started this whole situation.

The situation being...I just gave my virginity to Fabian Hernandez, *my brother-in-law*. Once our breaths calm down and our heart rates start to slow, Fabian rubs his face against my breasts, making me laugh.

"Stop."

"Why?"

"You're being weird."

"No, I'm not." His lips pull one of my nipples into his mouth again as he starts to suck and nip.

"Fabian! Stop."

"You didn't tell me to stop before."

"Asshole."

"I know." He turns me and slaps me hard on the ass right before he gets up and gives me a smirk. He stands at the edge of the bed with his hand out towards me. "Let's go shower."

His dick is still glistening from everything that's happened and I think I will. In fact, I feel like a fully glazed donut.

"Okay."

14

———————

FABIAN

Showering with Sakinah is a new experience. In fact, she's the only girl I've ever showered with because most of the girls in my past left before I could even wake up. This..this is nice.

Well, it would be nicer if it wasn't so fucking small in this stupid shower. Damn, how the hell is a man like me supposed to even scrub himself?

"Quit squirming around."

"I'm not squirming, this shit is too small."

"Well, that's not my fault."

"Are you saying it's mine?"

She splashes the loofah over my chest and starts to scrub again, pressing her body even closer to me as the loofah travels down to my dick. Seems she likes to pay close attention to it as it starts to become semi from her ministrations.

"I think it's pretty clean by now." Lifting an eyebrow I watch as her lips tip up into a sly smile.

"I'm not sure. Maybe I should take a look."

"Why would you need to take a look?" Grabbing her hand, I force it around my dick that's now rock hard with thoughts of her on her knees in here. As nice as it would be, this shower doesn't have enough room for that. I'd be fucking her head against the damn tiles giving her a concussion.

Turning us so the water is hitting my back, I push Sakinah against the tiles in front of me. "Wrap your leg around me." She has her moments when she does what she's told because she likes what I give her.

Grabbing my dick, I start rubbing it against her hot center. Watching as the water droplets run down between her breasts, my eyes go over the curve of her body. She's so damn soft and feminine - it makes me hot knowing I'm the *only* man allowed to touch her like I do.

Leaning my arm against the tile, I slip my dick slowly inside of her, watching it disappear. It's the most erotic sight, the way her chest starts to heave up and down - the way she tries to get away from me only succeeding in pressing herself against the tile even more. Before my dick can make it all the way in, my hips are pulling it out just as slow and Sakinah whimpers. She acts like she doesn't want it but every time I'm about to pull out, she looks like she's going to kick my ass for even trying.

I do love her fire.

Pulling out all the way, I rub my dick against her wet folds again and kiss her so she can't say anything sassy. Thrusting back into her, she gasps into my mouth and my tongue dives in, simulating the motion my dick is working. Her hands have come up to my chest, running her nails down, making me want to thrust my dick harder. It's her little play, but I got her number. She's not winning this.

On a particularly hard scratch, my hips thrust forward until I'm all the way to the hilt, jostling her enough to break our kiss when her head falls back.

"Hold onto me." She does as I lift her ass up to wind her other leg around me, letting me pound into her the way she wants it. I'm going to have to be careful here because Sakinah's pussy feels too damn good. I think I pulled out in time when we were in the bedroom. The memory of her pussy covered in everything I gave her makes my abs and balls start to tighten. I'm close already. Shit. Pulling out of her, I drop her legs down and cum over her mound again, just watching as jets and jets of it keep coming out like it knows she needs to be claimed this way.

Sakinah's mouth is biting the top of my pecs making me hiss and my dick throb even more. She drives me fucking nuts.

When it's all said and done, we wash ourselves one more time under the cold water and finally get out of the smallest shower known to man.

It takes Sakinah a few good days before the light bruising on her face disappears. I had to take her to the drugstore to get some makeup. It did a pretty decent job but it doesn't hide the fact that I know how it came to be. It burns me up every time I see it, my mind working different ways I can kill the fucker and not get thrown in prison. Maybe if I get Omar to call his b-

"Fabian, are you listening?"

"No. I'm thinking of ways to kill Amir."

"Fabian!"

"Are you serious right now, Sakinah? That fucker hit you! He needs to be buried six feet under."

"Fabian, you can't."

"Just you watch me -"

"No! What if you get put in prison? Then who am I going to have to protect me huh?" Fucking smart ass sexy woman. She's right. Now I have to think of other ways -

"Fabian! Stop thinking about it!"

"I'm not."

"You're lying! I can see it in your face!"

"What kind of face is that?"

She plants her ass on my lap as I sit at the kitchen table, winding her arms around me and rubbing her little nose against mine.

"It's the same face you made when you came to save me." Tilting my head, my lips brush hers and she melds into me. Our kiss is soft and slow, a constraint on the emotions brought up by the memory of that stupid party. Our tongues start to dance when there's the sound of someone slamming on the window, breaking us apart.

Turning our heads to the side we see...her mother staring at us both, pointing her fingers and yelling something in Malay. *Oh shit.*

There's someone standing behind her - someone male - and my hackles rise because I already fucking know. Amir leans down and smiles his shit-eating grin as Sakinah's mother starts towards the front door, pounding on it.

Sakinah jumps off me and covers her mouth, her eyes wide, not able to say a damn thing because we're caught red handed..by her mother of all people. Fuck!

"Sakinah!! Open the door!"

"Jahanam! Shit! Fabian, what do we do?"

"What can we do? She already saw us. We're just going to have to suck it up and deal."

"She'll kill me!"

"No she won't. It was going to happen sooner or later, you know that."

"But not like this!"

"We can't control everything." More knocking comes through, much more aggressively than before.

"Sakinah! I know you're inside huh! Open the door!"

"Fabian!" She wants me to rescue her but this is the only way. We have to come clean, I'm tired of hiding us anyway. Tired of having to hold back my feelings for her in public when all I want to do is shout that she's mine at the rooftops to every fucking male that looks at her.

Taking one for the team, I go to open the door. Sakinah's mother doesn't even look my way as she barges in right for her daughter. Amir, though, he doesn't dare to step over the threshold because I'm already killing him twenty different ways with my eyes.

Lifting my lips in disgust, I shove the fucker farther out and shut the door in his face. I hear Sakinah in distress and her mother yell, *"Aku sepak!"* I turn to find her mother grabbing onto her arm and kicking her while Sakinah yelps and tries to run away. *What the everloving hell?*

Grabbing her mother by the arm, I pull her off my girl. Mother or not, that shit is just too far. "You need to stop."

"What will everyone think? Auntie Zunai sure will embarrass me for this! Allah, how embarrassing!" She throws her hands in the air before she starts wringing her hand like a damn witch about to cast a fucking spell or something, eyes darting from her daughter to me. I'm so confused.

"You two will bring shame to my family! Sakinah! You need to marry Amir so no one hears about this! You cannot marry your brother in law, no!" The tiny woman is walking around the house looking for something. My face scrunches in confusion as I watch Sakinah's face morph into pure fear.

Her mother comes back with a damn broom of all things - didn't I say she was a witch? - and starts to chase Sakinah who escapes to hide behind me. *What the hell am I supposed to do right now?*

"Ibu! I don't want to marry Amir!" Her mother lunges like a little jackrabbit and starts to pinch Sakinah in the arm, making her cry out, while trying to whack her ass with the broom. Pulling it out of her arm, I keep it over her head so she can't get to it again.

"People will be talking behind our backs! How could you do this? You need to marry Amir!"

"No!" Sakinah is shoving her mother off her as much as she can but her mother latches on like a damn leech on a mission to suck the life out of her.

"Sakinah! You need to not shame the family! You cannot do this to us!"

"Ibu! I love him!" Her mother shoots daggers at me right before she ignores me again and proceeds to kick Sakinah in the shin, hitting mine in the damn process.

My temper starts to rise as I toss the damn witches broom aside, grab Sakinah's mother and lift her up kicking and screaming something I can't understand, taking her towards the front door. My hand struggles to grab the damn doorknob but I get it to open and shove her outside with a still smirking Amir.

Shutting the door on both their faces, the pounding starts up again. Sakinah runs into my arms, crying her heart out as her mother says something that makes my girl shake even more.

I don't know what the hell is going on, but I know it isn't

good. How are little Asian women so damn vicious? Flash-backs of my own mother with her wooden spoon and chan-clas come to mind and I retract the thought. Mothers are *all* vicious, especially when they're pissed to that degree.

But hell, Sakinah is a twenty-something-year-old woman. She should get more respect than that. No wonder this rela-tionship's been confusing her and making her mentally break down.

Some more yelling and screaming comes from the other side of the door and I can feel Sakinah gasp and grip me tighter around my middle. *What is going on?*

The sound of footsteps getting farther and farther away releases some of the tension I was holding. Rubbing Saki-nah's back, I kiss the top of her head and hope she can stop crying enough to tell me what her mother said.

"Fabian."

"What is it? What do you need me to do?"

"Fabian she-" This girl is killing me with the suspense.

When Sakinah lifts her head up to look at me, my heart breaks. What is this look? What the hell did her mother say?

"Fabian, she disowned me because I brought shame to the family. I-I can't go back home and - and she's going to take this house away from me."

Well damn.

"What do I do? Fabian, I'm so scared! Where do I go?"

Holding her tighter, I shush her and rock her. We can work this out. It's not so bad. "Sakinah, it will be okay."

"How can you say that? I don't have anywhere to go. I can't go back home!"

"Sakinah."

"My family, my sisters-"

"Sakinah."

"Fabian, my-" I kiss her on the lips to stop her damn talking. The tactic works because she deflates a little, letting go of some of the anxiety she's holding onto.

Putting my head against hers, I breathe slowly in and out to make her follow suit and she does.

"Baby, you're my girl. Why would you need to go anywhere other than with me? If you say no, I'm taking your ass there anyway because I can't wake up without you."

It gets her to laugh a little as she deflates even more. "Fabian...how did we get to this?"

"To what? Listening to my girl breathe fire and yell at her mother that she fucking loves me?"

"Dammit Fabian, you know what I'm talking about." She's getting shy, hiding her face from me but now that I know the truth, I can take this crap shot in stride.

"I do. We can finally just be together, Sakinah. I can finally kiss you-" pressing my lips to hers, she looks at me adoringly and it makes my heart want to burst. "-in fucking public and tell all those fucking guys around you that you're taken."

She playfully slaps my chest and gives me an honest laugh. *Good.*

"You drive me nuts."

"You do me too, but I can't live without you. Move in with me?" She gives me a soft smile and nods. "Come on, let's get your shit and go."

15

Fabian drove to his mother's house and switched out his bike for his dad's truck, bringing it back to the front of the house. The only big items we took with us were the couch and the nightstand. According to my *boyfriend*, the couch held too much sentimental value to leave behind. My clothes and books didn't take up too much room and we decided to leave the sedan behind since my parents had provided that for me as well.

During my mother's spiel on the other side of the door, she told me that I wasn't allowed to live in the house or be provided for anymore. It was heartbreaking knowing your own mother can so easily say those things to you.

But it is the way of our culture. I *knew* this relationship was going to put me in the hot spot, I just didn't know it would get *this* hot - boiling and scarring my heart. But I wouldn't change my choice for anything. I don't want to marry a potential wife beater - not that my mother even has a clue about that. I bet Amir conveniently never mentioned anything about it, for her to be pushing me his way.

Fabian would always be my first and final choice. We were always meant to be together. No matter how hard we tried to stay away, the universe kept throwing us right back to where we started with the fire between us stoked even higher.

Getting into the passenger side, Fabian walks around and slams the driver's side door shut. His father's truck sounds as much of a tin can as his damn Chevelle; All these old cars are full of metal. Hopefully, no one runs into us, and does it even have airbags?

"Don't give me that look."

"What look?"

"You're offending the old clunker. He runs just fine."

"Clunker indeed…"

"Now, now Sakinah. What are you trying to say? You're hanging out with my rusty ass too. I'm probably classified as vintage."

Laughing my ass off, I shake my head. Fabian is just too much.

"Yeah, well, you're stuck with me now, old man."

"Good. I was going to kidnap you soon anyway." I stare at him in disbelief as he gives me his signature smirk and wink.

Pulling out from the sidewalk, he drives what feels like half a block and pulls to the side to park. I'm sitting here baffled, wondering if we forgot something when he says, "We're here."

How did I not know this asshole lives about five houses down from me. Looking out the window in skepticism, I see his Chevelle sitting in the driveway. *No wonder I haven't been hearing it drive by. He's been keeping it here the whole time.*

"Fabian…"

"Yup! I knew you'd like it. Now get your ass out and help me bring this couch inside."

"Fabian! How long have you been living here?"

"Long enough to fix all the shithole up on the inside, waiting for you to come to this moment." This asshole *boyfriend* of mine always has a way with his words that make you want to strangle him and kiss him senseless at the same time.

No wonder he's been staying at my place, it's no different than staying over here.

After maneuvering the couch through the door and placing it down, I straighten up and look around. It's sparse and very Fabian - always looking like he's gone with the wind wherever the wind takes him because he just doesn't care.

The layout inside the home is actually not that far off from what my old house looks like. Pushing Fabian's handful of clothes aside, I start hanging my dresses in neat and tidy order. Sometimes when my life feels out of control…I find myself starting to control what I can - in this case, the closet.

"Hey, are you hungry? I can eat a damn horse."

"You're always hungry."

"I don't have jack shit in this fridge. What do you feel like eating?"

"Whatever you want. Just don't get any pork for me."

"Got it."

His phone rings right at the very moment and my ears perk up when I hear him answer.

"What do you want? Fuck, stop yelling at me, I can't understand a damn thi-" A knock comes at the door and I drop the dress I'm holding. It can't be my mother right? She doesn't even know I'm staying with Fabian.

"What's up, man." The sound of flesh on flesh hitting each other makes me run out the bedroom to find Akmal shaking his hand and Fabian rubbing his chin while his head is turned to the side.

"Akmal!"

"That's for my sister."

"Alright, alright. I feel you. I wanted to punch you too when my sister brought you home."

"That's the thing Fabian, you never brought her around at all. She's not your fucking dirty little secret."

Fabian lets out a booming laugh and I'm wincing because isn't that exactly what Fabian's been telling me about how he felt the whole time we were hiding our relationship?

"Akmal, it isn't like that." How can this crap blow up so damn much in such a short period of time?

"Are you pregnant?"

"What? No!" Akmal turns his glare back to Fabian and I'm getting offended on his behalf.

"Did you fucking knock her up and get her kicked out of the family? Hasanah called me and told me what happened. What the fuck do you think you're doing with my sister, you asshole?"

"What I'm doing with Sakin- cabrón what the fuck do you think I'm doing with her?" Dammit, Fabian!

"It looks to me like you're taking advantage of *my fucking virgin sister.*"

Fabian stops rubbing his chin and starts to lean down towards Akmal, making me scared he's going to knock him out.

"Take advantage? Let me tell you something *brother.* What I'm *doing* with *your* sister is keeping her fucking safe from assholes like Amir who slaps the shit out of her while trying to do what *your mother* wanted and marry her - trapping her in a fucking life of punches and fucking foolery. *What am I fucking doing with your sister?* I fucking *love her* enough to not let her go through that shit!"

My heart stutters. Fabian is fuming, his back tense, his body heaving breaths in and out as his hands fold into fists...but my heart - oh my fucking heart - did not miss the fact that he just yelled out that he loves me.

Akmal's eyes are shooting from Fabian to me and back again. The tension in the room is so damn thick, I'm choking with it. It looks like people outside are starting to slow down when they walk by, trying to see what's happening in this fucking house.

"Then *brother*, I expect you to do the right thing and make this shit *right*."

My brother turns around and storms out. What the hell has my life turned into? A damn soap opera?

Fabian slams the door, locks it and walks to the couch to grab the phone. Was that thing still on this whole time?

"Vero! Your fucking attack dog just came by! Keep your fucking esposo on a damn leash." The sound of Vero's voice yelling from the other end is loud but I can't make out what she's saying. Fabian's eyes lock onto mine as he says, "I fucking love her. Don't worry about it. I know how to take care of what's mine." His hand ends the call and tosses the phone back onto the couch and he continues to stalk towards me. I'm stunned again by how easily he just throws out the L word to anyone who's willing to hear it.

He continues to stalk towards me and I'm captivated by the hunger in his eyes. This is it, isn't it? We've made our stand with our families. We've chosen *us* over obligation and guilt. My eyes are burning again with how momentous this moment really is - from my fight with my mother to Fabian throwing his love for me around for anyone to hear.

We've chosen our path.

We both start stripping where we stand as he continues to stalk towards me like a predator, ready to claim his prize. I'm feeling hot and too constricted anyways, wanting to shed the old me away. Does this mean...does this mean I don't have to wear my hijab anymore? I didn't even remember to put it on after what happened with my mother. I'm down to my bra and panties when Fabian takes off his pants, showing me that he went without boxers, his dick proudly pointing at me, telling me what he wants.

Unhooking and tossing my bra aside, I slide my panties down my legs, bending over the arm of the couch so he can see just how wet I am for him.

Fabian doesn't play this time as he comes up behind me, grabs a fist full of my hair and shoves his dick into me in one go. I feel so full, so overflowing in this position with my legs closed together that when Fabian covers my back and hisses in my ear, I almost combust right there.

He pulls my head back enough to suck and bite on my neck as he pounds my hips into the arm of the couch. He's right, it does hold too much sentimental value to be left behind. My hands are outstretched onto the cushion to prevent me from tipping all the way over. Fabian fucks me like he's trying to make a point and I love every second of every pound that's probably going to leave bruises once we're done.

He's twisting his hips again as he rams it into me and I can feel myself wanting more and more of everything he has to give me.

I can feel the warmth of his chest pressed against my back as he leans over me, removing his hand from my hair and instead holding me across my chest, grinding his dick into me deeper and deeper. The sound of our combined juices squelching loudly in the living room but we both could not care less at this point.

"I love the way your pussy feels, like it wants to swallow me whole. Is your pussy hungry for me Sakinah?"

"Yes." His hips are hitting mine again, harder and without the twist making my breasts swing wildly as I try to hold myself back from toppling over this damn couch. I can feel his arm move as it grips onto one of them, holding me in place as his thrusts start to falter and his dick starts to almost grow bigger inside of me.

When his mouth latches onto the crook of my neck and he growls, I know he's cumming - but this time he doesn't pull out and I can feel the warm jets of his cum shooting inside of me, making me feel so dirty it almost throws me over the edge...almost.

As his thrusts become slower and slower and as his tongue starts licking the wound he probably left behind, Fabian pulls out of me making me cry out with the abrupt change and turns me around. He lifts one of my legs onto the arm of the couch, spreading me wide and open, holding the small of my back preventing me from falling as his fingers start to thrust inside of me like it's another round.

Our kisses become sloppy and hot, passionate and uncaring. His thumb slowly circles my clit as his other two fingers penetrate me and start to curl into a spot I never knew existed. A few more strokes inside like that and I fall over the edge, crying out in ecstasy, trying to hold onto his shoulders for support because my legs have suddenly become weak like jello.

What the hell was that witchcraft? My mind is still in a daze, confused at how fast he made me orgasm.

He kisses my lips and grounds me back into reality, his wet fingers trailing across my hips before his hands grab my ass and pulls me closer to him, pressing our bodies as tightly together as they can go.

"You're fucking mine Sakinah, and I'm going to make sure everyone knows it."

Picking me up, I wrap my legs and arms around him as he walks us both towards *our* bedroom.

16

SAKINAH

*A*fter the confrontation with my mother and my brother, our days have been relatively peaceful. Fabian brought his bike back home and our usual drop offs and pick ups continued. I don't know what he does while I'm in class but he's always on time no matter how early or how late my last class goes.

It's the most curious thing.

Fabian and Jason have a sort of..little agreement going ever since the incident at the party. Jason has been dubbed Fabian's extra eyes. Well, more like Fabian threatened him about watching my back or else he'll be next, but it's close enough I guess.

The project was done when Fabian decided to bring his Chevelle so he can transport the little building model he has made for us. We were the only group to get an A on it.

With classes ending, it leaves me with one last semester in

the university before I don't ever have to return. I'm glad I had a full scholarship since it means I won't have to worry about paying anything back once I'm done - I don't want to add any financial strain to what Fabian and I have going on.

The roar of Fabian's bike in the distance makes me smile and look up as my hair blows into my face. I've slowly started to stop wearing my hijab. It was almost an unconscious decision until Fabian noticed the pattern. I guess my subconscious mind was trying to tell me to shed my old life and the things that used to hold me back.

The smell of exhaust fumes and the heat of the bike as he starts to pull up near the curb is what I notice first. Next is the shiny new helmet strapped to his backseat, the one he recently got for me so he doesn't have to give up his. Lifting his visor up, Fabian turns off the bike as he tries to tell me something.

"I can't understand you." He takes off his helmet and hangs it on his handlebar before pushing his short hair back. Some girls have stopped around us to watch and I take that moment to pull his face towards mine and give him a proper hello kiss. It was beyond liberating the first time I did it and it took Fabian by surprise even though he was the one who brought it up. I love that he continues to respect me no matter what his opinion is on the matter.

With a final chaste kiss on the lips, we pull away and smile at each other.

"I was saying - before you interrupted me - that we should go see my mother. I haven't been over in a while and she's probably worried."

"Oh." This makes me nervous. I've never met anyone's mother like this before. I've never had a boyfriend before. I've only recently had *the* talk with Vero on the phone the other day.

"So you and Fabian huh? What did he do?" She sounds so accusing. I shouldn't be surprised since Fabian is trouble.

"What do you mean?" Best I ask to make sure.

"Did he make you be with him or what? Did he force you? Use his manly charms on you?" Force me? Fabian's not like that.

"No! It wasn't like that. Not at all. It's-It's complicated." How do I even begin to explain our relationship?

I mean, yes? It kind of started that way but our emotions started mirroring each other the more we found ourselves together. It was just me and my own mind warring over something that was meant to happen anyway.

"Girl, I know 'complicated'. Tell me the truth about everything so I don't have to go over there and kick his ass." A laugh bubbles out of me because Vero's personality is just as intense as her brother's. Some days I wonder if Vero is just a female version of my man.

"That won't be necessary. I can handle him just fine."

"Yeah? Are you sure about that? He has that Hernandez temper. I should know, I have it too." My mind goes back to the day of the party and my heart wants to spill over with emotion - Fabian has always been there for me in his way.

"Yeah..I've seen it."

"Pinche- Look, if he ever does anything to scare you, dial me. I will string his balls up to a tree, hermano or not." Her voice takes on a whole different octave, sounding like she's about to jump through the speaker.

Vero can be kind of scary. Images of her chasing her brother around with a knife held in the air float in my mind and I have to shake my head to get rid of it. She wouldn't, would she?

"No! He was - he was protecting me from someone. I love Fabian, I truly do. He's been there for me through ...everything. I don't know what I would do without him. I can't - I can't imagine life without him."

"Chica, you got it bad. How my asshole of a brother got someone like you, I'll never know. But I'm happy for you two. He loves you? He must if he's willing to take punches from mi esposo. Fabian never backs down from a fight. Well, except for that one time - but then the guy didn't show up around the neighborhood for a while. I always wondered about that -"

I have no idea what she's talking about as she continues to go down her own memory lane of her and her brother. Despite her calling him an asshole, I can tell they have a really good relationship together. Where does this leave me and my sisters? Will my mother ever let me talk to them again?

"- But anyway, enough about the past. How are you doing with everything that's happened? Do you need anything? What can I do to help?"

With the thought of not seeing my sisters and Fabian's sister trying to step up to the plate, my eyes start to tear up. I swore I would stop being like this over this situation. It's said and done - life has to move forward.

Wasn't it just the other day I wondered what it would be like to not be oppressed by my culture and religion anymore? I guess what they say is true - be careful what you ask for.

But looking over at Fabian measuring something in the house and jotting down notes on how he's going to fix it...I wouldn't change my decision for anything. I would always choose Fabian.

"Thank you, Vero."

"For what? I didn't even do anything yet."

"Just for being there for me, and for letting me love your brother."

Vero laughs and it almost bursts my eardrums. I can hear my brother in the background asking her what's going on and it kind of makes me want to smile.

"Chica, I don't know what you're smoking but I hope you're ready to be a Hernandez. When it comes to Fabian, I don't 'let' *anything - Fabian is his own man who makes his own decisions. He's a good guy who always takes care of family. Keep him out of trouble and you two will be alright."*

Vero's easy acceptance of me into their family makes my heart hurt and want to burst at the same time. Saying our goodbyes, I end the call and turn to look at Fabian who has now removed his shirt to wipe the sweat off his face.

How did a girl like me get so lucky?

"Sakinah, get your ass on the bike and put on your helmet. My mother is probably already waiting for me at the doorway so she can throw a damn chancla at me for being late." Shaking my head at his dramatics, I shove the helmet on and start to buckle under my chin. Swinging my legs behind him, he starts the engine back up, strapping his own helmet on.

I hope we don't smell like exhaust fumes by the time we get there. His mother's neighborhood takes about a twenty-minute ride on his bike since Fabian is weaving in and out of traffic like a heathen, scaring the crap out of me. At least he has the decency to tap on my hand to let me know to hold on tighter because he's about to speed up.

My eyes start to notice the change in neighborhood scenery the closer we get. The houses become closer together, yards become smaller, the bars on the windows and doors become more prevalent. Fabian pulls up into the driveway of a very modest looking home and just like he said, his mother is already standing at the open screen door in her apron with what looks like a wooden spoon in her hand.

Swinging myself off the bike, I proceed to take off my helmet and leave it on the seat as Fabian does the same.

"¿Mira, mira quien viene? Why did you take so long? I'm here making comida for you and you want to make me wait?

You don't even come over anymore. ¿Porque? ¿Quién es tu amiga? You did not tell me you were bringing una mujer." His mom is kind of scary, she reminds me of Vero when she's on a tirade. She continues to shake her wooden spoon at him but smiles at me. At least that's something.

I try to fix my hair since it's probably messed up from the helmet as Fabian starts responding back.

"Mamá, take it easy. La bendición. I'm here now aren't I? You should be happy I'm bringing someone over to see how good your comida tastes." My eyes widen when it looks like she wants to take her shoe off but thinks better of it since I'm standing right here.

"Que Dios te bendiga. You no answer my question, Hijo. ¿Quién es tu amiga?" Fabian opens his mouth to say something when another vehicle pulls up behind the bike. We all look over to see Vero practically hanging out of the passenger window yelling back.

"Mamá! Ella es su novia!" What?

I can see Akmal in the driver's seat as they pull into park.

"Su novia? Why do my children never tell me these things huh? They just come to mi casa and surprise, they're married? Sin respeto."

"Mamá, don't be like that. We respect you, that's why she's here today. I was going to introduce you to Sakinah."

"Oi, Sakinah? ¿Ella es su hermana, no? Explícamelo." The wooden spatula gets pointed at Akmal who just exited the car and is now leaning back with both hands up, palms out, in case Fabian's mother decides to go through with the threat.

"Mamá, let's all go inside so we can explain everything." She looks skeptical, mostly at Fabian, but allows him to usher her back inside.

"Oi! Fabian. ¿Quién es tu amiga? ¿Ella es tu esposa?" I

didn't even notice Fabian's father standing at the doorway. He must have been watching all the dramatics outside on the front lawn this entire time, judging by the smirk on his face.

Some of the neighbors have conveniently come out to do things in their front yard too. I recognize the gossipers and eavesdroppers. We have them at our house as well - well, my old house.

"La bendición papá."

"Que Dios te bendiga, hija. Welcome back Akmal. You taking care of my daughter?"

"Yes, sir. Always."

"Papá! What kind of question is that?"

"The kind a father asks because he loves his hija." I watch as Vero hugs her father before we all trail behind and enter the home.

Akmal brings himself next to me and whispers, "Apa khabar? How are you? You holding up alright with everything that's happened?"

"Yeah, I guess. Fabian is helping a lot." My brother shoots a glare at Fabian and he smirks right back.

"If you need me for anything, just let me know."

"Thank you."

Once we pass the threshold of the screen door, we enter a cute little kitchen area. The smell of delicious food surrounds us as Fabian's mother starts pushing people to go sit down at the table. My culture being so deeply rooted has me following her into the kitchen to see if she needs any help. Vero is there already.

"Can I help you with anything?" I want to make a good impression and Vero knows it by the way she's trying to suppress a smile.

"Mi Mamá is a control freak. I just hang out to make her

feel less alone. Ow!" Watching Vero get slapped upside the head shouldn't be as funny as it is.

"Mira tu boca! I've been doing this since before you were born. I don't need anyone breathing down my back."

"Mamá, why do you have to be so mean? You know I love you, I just want to hang out with you because I miss you." A wooden spoon gets swatted on her ass and Vero is laughing all the way to the table.

Now I find myself in an awkward position because I don't know what to do. It's the first time meeting her and I'm not sure how to talk to her now that we're alone.

"Are you Fabian's novia?"

"I'm not sure what that means."

"Mi hijo never brings a girl around. You are the first I've seen. But he's never mentioned you. I did not recognize you without that -" She waves her hand around her head to explain what she means. "- around your cabeza, the wrappy thing." My hand automatically goes to my head, wondering if maybe I should have worn it now.

"You look nicer like this. You have very beautiful hair." Feeling my face heat up, I mumble my thanks.

"Mamá! What are you saying to mi mujer? Be nice." Fabian comes up behind me and kisses me on the cheek right in front of his mother. *Oh my god. Is he allowed to do that?* I bury my face in his chest to hide my embarrassment. "What did you do Mamá?" I can feel his arms wrap around me in comfort.

"I did nothing. You're the one who brings home un mujer and don't tell anyone. How long have you two been together? Why don't you come over to mi casa anymore? Is it because of her? Why don't you just bring her here so I can see you too?"

"Relájate. She's here now isn't she?" Peeking sideways, I

watch as his mother puts a hand over her chest as she takes a harsh inhale. What just happened?

"¿Está embarazada? You have un baby? Am I going to be an abuela? Are you married already? Did I miss it? Did you leave your poor Mamá y Papá out of your wedding?"

"Mamá, breathe. Let's just have this lunch and relax. Geez. Let us at least sit down first. So dramática."

"I wouldn't have to be dramática if you tell me these things! Okay, okay. Siéntate por favor. I will bring out the food."

"I can help you, if you want." Now I feel bad. I need to help somehow.

"No, no. Go sit down. I will bring out the food."

"You better just do what she says because she's a control freak." Something flies and hits Fabian. He doesn't even look to see what it is, only laughs and drags me by the hand to go sit down at the table.

Once seated, Fabian's father turns to me and stares at me intently. My hand starts to shake the longer I wait for him to say something.

"Oi, Fabian. ¿Ella es su hermana, no?" His hand points to Akmal on the other side of the table.

"Yes. Sakinah is Akmal's sister. Stop asking." His eyes haven't left mine though and I shoot a look at Akmal for some help. Vero isn't saying anything at all, just watching what's going down like it's her mini entertainment before lunch.

Before his dad can say anything, Fabian's mom starts to pile plates and plates of food on the table. Once everything and everyone is settled, the table says 'Buen provecho' and everyone starts digging in. Both Akmal and I whisper 'Bismillah' and start to do the same.

A few bites in and some of this stuff doesn't seem to agree with my stomach. So I try to find the ones that do.

"You okay?"

"Yeah. I guess I'm just not used to some of these things."

"Don't worry, you come around enough and you'll be eating everything she makes. She won't let you leave otherwise."

"What's wrong with mi comida?"

"Mamá! Nothing. I'm just telling her how good everything is. Geez." She narrows her eyes at him but continues to eat without further comment.

Some of this stuff really isn't agreeing with me, so I slowly stop eating. It feels like I'm just pushing my food around to make it look good but my stomach still says no.

"Fabian, go to the store." His mother's voice makes me snap my head up.

"Why? I'm still eating."

"Listen to your Mamá and go to the store. Su esposa está embarazada." Fabian's dad and Vero drop their utensils and look directly at me.

"I'm sorry?" The screech of Fabian's chair across the floor startles me as he kisses me on the cheek and runs out the door, Vero laughing right behind him.

"You're so dramática, Mamá."

"Oi, I know these things hija." Fabian's mother nods her head like it all makes sense, while I still have no idea what is going on.

"Yeah? Well, Akmal and I have an announcement to make." My brother chokes a little on his food with Vero's sudden change in demeanor. She slaps him on the back but ignores it and continues anyway.

"What is it now? Are you getting a divorce?"

"Papá, stop it. No, we're not getting a divorce. We're having a boy!"

"Dios Mio! I'm so excited for you! I'm going to have to make some blankets for the baby." Her mother literally starts crying and laughing at the same time with her hand over her heart while her dad is still looking at my brother skeptically.

"Papá! Be happy for me. You're going to be an abuelo."

"I am happy. I'm too young to be an abuelo. Fabian was enough." He laughs at that comment just as the roar of his bike comes back to the house.

Fabian comes stomping back into the house like he just ran back from wherever he just went off to. "Okay, Okay. I'm back. Sakinah, go to the bathroom."

"Huh? Why?" I stand up to see what he's talking about when he comes around the table and shoves a plastic bag full of boxes at me. *What is going on?* "What-"

"Go in the bathroom and pee on all of them."

"All of what? I don't even feel like I need to pee." He's pushing me and suddenly I find myself in a cozy little bathroom...with Fabian inside who's now shutting the door behind us.

"I'm not peeing in front of you!"

"I need you to pee on all the sticks. I didn't know which one to get so I got everything I saw."

"Why am I peeing on sticks?"

"Dammit Sakinah! Just do it!"

"Well, I'm not doing anything with you in here! Get out!"

"I need to see it to make sure."

"Make sure about what? What the hell are we talking about? What if I don't want to pee on anything? Fabian, what's going -"

He grabs my face and kisses me hard, passionately. If his plan was to calm me down, it's working because his warm body is pressing up against mine as I'm pushed against the sink of this bathroom.

"Sakinah."

"Yes?"

"I need you to pee on everything." Our warm breaths are caressing our lips with every word we say from how close we still are.

"What if I say no?" The knock on the door startles us both out of our moment together, the sound of Fabian's mother's voice makes me push him towards the door.

"What's going on in there? Fabian! Let her do it and come out here!"

"You're lucky this time. Pee on the sticks." His finger points at my chest where I'm still gripping tightly onto the plastic bag he shoved at me when he got back.

Watching him leave and shut the door, I sigh in relief. Turning, I untie the bag and look at what the boxes are inside, my eyes widening when I start to read the print.

"Tu esposa inside?" Great, now his dad is right outside too.

"Yeah."

"Does she know that?" Vero's laughing and I stop opening the box to listen intently.

"Not yet."

Taking a deep breath, I start to open each box and read the directions. My hands are shaking a little bit and my mind feels lightheaded. I mean, I should have expected it but it never crossed my mind. It was stupid of me. I should have been more careful.

I almost don't have enough pee for all of the damn pregnancy tests Fabian brought back. Why does anyone need this many? Washing up, I wring my hands nervously and start to wonder if I should wait outside instead of staring at the sticks as each second passes.

I should go outside.

Opening the door, all I see is Fabian's back. He turns to look at me with a big 'ol smile on his face.

"Why are you smiling like that?"

"Because I knocked up my wife."

"I'm not your wife."

"You were going to be anyway, so might as well get used to calling me husband, *wife*."

"Oi! Am I going to be an abuela again? You *did* get married?! Why you not invite your Mamá y Papá to your wedding? Fabian!"

"You didn't miss it Mamá, I'm going to marry her as soon as I find out what that stick says. She's already mi esposa anyway."

"We're getting married?"

"Yeah, we are. I'm booking a flight after we go back home."

"Where are you going?" His mother's voice sounds a little frantic. I'm feeling a little frantic too with how fast everything's going - but a little excited as well.

"It's been ten minutes already." Vero's voice brings me back to the present and my heart starts racing as I run back to the restroom to see the results.

There are seven sticks all lined up across the sink and my hands try to match the directions to the brand of each stick. Why can't they all just read the same? Why must it be so damn complicated?

Vero pushes her brother aside as they bicker about who should be in here with me but my mind is concentrating so hard on the fine print of these directions my eyes are about to cross.

"Sakinah."

"I'm not sure which one goes with this one."

"Sakinah."

"Huh?"

"You're pregnant." My hand drops the paper as I stare at Vero through tear blurred eyes.

"Are you sure?"

"Yeah, I've taken a few of these myself." She laughs as she rubs her small growing belly and I'm reminded of the day they made the announcement at home.

No longer my home.

"It's okay, it's okay." She hugs me and my tears fall quickly turning into sobs.

"What did you do to her?"

"I didn't do anything Fabian. Relax. Let her feel whatever she needs to feel right now."

"Sakinah, are you okay?"

Lifting my head from Vero's chest, I turn and throw myself into Fabian's arms.

"What's wrong?" Wiping my eyes against his shirt, I shake my head.

"Nothing's wrong. I'm just...happy and sad."

"She's pregnant." Vero supplies and nods since I seem to have become an emotional mess.

"You're crying because you're pregnant with my baby?"

Lifting my head up, I slap Fabian in the chest to make him shut up.

"Not everything is about you, you asshole. I'm crying because I'm happy that I'm pregnant, but I can't celebrate it with my family because - because -"

Fabian leans down towards my face and gives me a soft smile. "You don't have to worry about that Sakinah. We're a family now. And mi Mamá y Papá, and I guess we'll let Vero come too. Ow! What did you hit me for?"

Vero laughs and walks out the overcrowded bathroom as Fabian continues to rub the back of his head, trying to suppress his own laugh. His attempt to lighten the mood works and I hug him tightly.

I'm pregnant. He's right. We're a family now. What was he saying earlier about booking flights?

Fabian is pulled off me as his mother looks at me with tears in her eyes. "¿Está embarazada? I'm going to be an abuela again, sí? Oi! I'm so feliz!" She hugs me so hard that I can barely breathe.

"Fabian!"

"Sí Papá."

"You bring home your first girl and you're already married and starting a family? How come you don't tell me this when I was helping you move? Is that why you buy the house?"

My mind starts to click things together as Fabian looks over at me with a wink and a smile, his hands doing something on his phone.

"Familia, pack your bags for a few days. Yeah, you too Akmal."

"¿Porque?"

"Why? What's going on?"

"Tu Papá better be your best man." I'm standing here trying to figure out why Fabian's dad is talking about himself in third person when -

"For the wedding. We're going to Vegas."

"Dios Mio. I need to find my nice dress."

"Hermano! That's what I'm talking about! Come on Akmal, we have to go home and pack!"

My eyes tear up again and I'm starting to wonder if it's

from the hormones or if I've always just been a crybaby on the inside.

Fabian comes over and cradles my face in his warm hands, wiping away the tears that have escaped. "You're stuck with me now."

"Asshole, you're stuck with me. Are you sure you want to be?"

"Sakinah, I was sure the moment you slapped my face." A laugh bursts out of me as Fabian wraps his arms around me and lifts me up for a kiss.

17

FABIAN

The flight to Vegas is quick and simple. Vero isn't too far along yet and Sakinah hasn't shown any other signs or symptoms of her pregnancy that would prevent her from sitting on a plane. My parents are a ball of nerves as they haven't traveled much. I figured this little trip would be a nice gift for them as well. They've worked hard taking care of us and bringing us up right; They deserve a little vacation. I called Omar to let him know what's happening and for him to keep in contact with me in case we pick up another contract.

"I'll be right back."

I look at my soon-to-be wife, seeing if anything is wrong but she looks alright. I should ask her anyway. "Do you need me?"

"No, I'm just going to the restroom."

"Maybe I need to make sure my pregnant wife is okay."

"Fabian, you're too much." She says this but I'm already following her out of my seat and she's not even stopping me.

The flight attendants are on the other side of the plane and the plane itself is only half full since we booked a flight on a random weekday.

When Sakinah opens the restroom door, I usher both of us inside, closing and locking it.

"Fabian! What are you doing?"

"Taking care of my pregnant wife, what do you think I'm doing?"

"I just need to check myself a little bit. You didn't have to follow me."

"I'm always going to follow you Sakinah, you're mine and I always take care of what's mine."

"How are you going to take care of me? We're in this small bathroom." This room *is* fucking small.

"Well, my pregnant wife was looking a little stressed. Maybe I can help with that."

"Oh yeah?" Her cute little smile graces her face and I know I got her. Ever since the blow out with her family, Sakinah has been slowly dressing a little differently, not wrapping her head as much. And as beautiful as she is, it just makes me even hornier every time I see her.

Like right now, for instance.

Leaning into her, I start to nip on her earlobe. She loves that shit, always starts to squirm. "Are you wearing any panties, Sakinah?"

"Fabian!" My hands are already going up her skirt and can feel the wetness soaking through the panties that shouldn't be there. I'm going to have to make sure she stops wearing it when we go places together.

Pushing the crotch aside, my fingers start to play with her folds as Sakinah's fingernails start digging into my shoulder and up my neck sending shivers down my spine. She's become a little more aggressive and brazen lately, making me excited to see how far she'll let me push her. Not that she really has much of a choice anyway because my dick is going in her one way or another.

It's a good thing women's panties are thin as hell because I give it a good tug and rip these off her, sticking it into my back pocket as my lips press against hers to distract her from yelling at me.

"Fabian."

"Don't worry, I'll take care of you. Open your legs for me." She wraps one of her legs around me as my hands start to unbuckle my jeans. Unlike some people, I come prepared with no boxers to hold me back. I can feel my dick spring out and slap her in the pussy, making her whimper against my mouth.

Liking the sound, I grab my dick and slap her a few more times, rubbing the head of my cock against her wet opening but not pushing it too far in yet. Sakinah likes it when I tease her despite how hard her nails are digging into me right now, she's just afraid to admit it. It's a good thing her husband is good at reading her body.

I've never had a chance to join the mile high club, I guess today is going to be the day as I slowly shove the head of my dick inside of her tight little pussy. She moans into my mouth and my hands lift her ass to bring her up higher, making her other leg wrap around me for leverage. The sink in this damn plane is tiny as hell but so is Sakinah so I place her on the edge of it as I start to pound into her.

Her moans and whimpers are getting louder. Sticking my tongue inside of her mouth, I try to mask the sound. Wouldn't be good to be caught fucking my wife in public places, not that it would stop me anyway.

When her breaths start to come out in pants, I whisper against her lips. "You're so fucking wet down there. Were you waiting for me to fuck you?"

"Maybe."

"Maybe?" My hips thrust into her even harder for the simple fact that she always makes me chase her, the little brat. "Maybe next time I should just fuck you in front of everyone, so you can remember to tell me instead of making me follow you around and spreading your legs when I catch you."

"I like it when you make me spread my legs." I groan into her neck as my hands start to squeeze between us and play with her pussy. The good thing about everything that's happened is that I don't have to fucking pull out anymore.

She's the only girl I've ever gone bareback with and I don't think I could ever go back. Sakinah is just going to have to stay knocked up.

Thinking about her stomach swollen with my kids makes my balls tighten as I grab her ass even harder, slamming into her while my thumb and forefinger start to pinch her swollen clit. Knowing her body the way I do now, I can tell she's about to cum on my dick when I hear her try to moan my name in that way she does. My mouth covers hers again to stifle the sound before she can cry out as she orgasms and starts milking my dick for all it's worth, making me cum right after her.

Still thrusting into her, making sure none of it comes out, someone knocks on the door ruining our beautiful moment.

"Cabrón! I need to go pee. Hurry up in there and make sure my sister looks good before you let her out."

Sakinah giggles against my lips as I let her legs down, my dick slipping out of her. I can't help but keep touching her as my fingers push my cum back inside her pussy as it tries to go down her legs.

"You're so dirty, Sakinah. You're going to sit next to me and feel this between your legs until we land. When we get to the hotel, I'm going to fill you up some more."

"Fucker! I need to go pee, I'm pregnant and shit!"

I chuckle as Sakinah's eyes widen, moving her off the sink so I can wash my hands. Fixing our clothes, we both exit out the little restroom door as my sister stands there with her arms crossed.

"Relájate, you didn't pee on yourself. You're fine." I dodge Vero's punch as she pushes us out of the way and slams the door shut. *Sheesh*. Hopefully, Sakinah doesn't get like that the further her pregnancy goes.

Then again, I'm usually surrounded by sassy women anyway, I should be used to it by now. The flight goes for another thirty or so minutes before the captain tells us we've reached our destination. We land during the hotter seasons and we're already sweating before we can even leave the damn airport.

I had booked separate rooms for my parents and for Vero and her husband so I can have time to spend with my girl before the wedding.

I'm glad we're doing Vegas. I need her to be my wife like yesterday. Vero and I had a discussion prior to boarding the plane - She's going to go out with Akmal to find the rings once we split up while I help my girl settle in the room.

We have a day to relax before the wedding happens tomorrow. I wonder if we'll get an Elvis impersonator to marry us? Doesn't matter, as long as I tie this woman to my side forever. Who knew Fabian Hernandez would be settling down. I didn't. Not until Sakinah came into my life.

"I've never been to Vegas before."

"Yeah? Well we're here now. Soon you're going to be Mrs. Hernandez. Are you ready for it?" She turns to me once we get inside our hotel room door and gives me the brightest smile I've ever seen on her. It makes my pride glow, knowing I put it there.

"Yeah, I am."

~

"Fabian, stop. It's too much."

"It's not. You can take it."

"Oh my god."

Sakinah is practically bent in two on her back as I fuck her harder and harder like I'm punishing my dick for wanting her so damn much.

"It's not my fault you make me this way."

"What fucking way? You barely let me sleep at all last night."

Slowing my thrusts down, my thumb starts to rub her clit in slow circles, watching her breasts rise and fall with her breathing. Her mouth parts and bring one of my legs up to help me fuck her harder into the mattress. She doesn't disappoint as she cries out while squeezing my dick. Being the bastard I am, I pull out and rub my cum all over her pussy, shooting some on her stomach, watching it glisten in the sunlight that's streaming in from the window as it coats her.

She's so fucking beautiful like this.

Plus, we have to go shower anyway and get ready for this wedding.

Slapping her ass, she tries to kick me but I jump out of the way anticipating it. "Come on, let's go shower and get this day over with so I can bring you back and fuck you again."

"Fabian! I'm going to come back and take a damn nap."

"You can try. You don't have to be awake for me to stick it in you. Just keep sleeping."

She slaps my chest with a cute little snarl as we both get into the biggest shower I've ever been in. *Good, plenty of damn room.* Turning the water on, I watch as Sakinah bends over to look at the little hotel shampoos and my hand grabs her ass from behind. She really does make it too easy.

"Dammit Fabian! We need to get ready!"

"Fine, fine. Relax, don't get so mad. We have plenty of time."

"We do not, you horny asshole. You don't have to wash long hair." Grabbing the little shampoo bottle from her hand, I push her under the water to wet her hair as she continues to cuss at me lovingly the way she always does.

Moving her body out of the water, I squirt some of the girly smelling shit into my hands and lather her hair. She stops squirming and calms down just like I knew she would, letting me wash her hair for her.

Sadly, she didn't let me sneak a quickie in as we both get out of the shower and dry ourselves off. I'm just walking out of the restroom when there's a knock on the door. Opening it I see Vero and Akmal all ready. Damn, what time is it?

"Why aren't you dressed? You're going to be late to your own damn wedding." Vero pushes me aside as she walks towards Sakinah and ushers her to the other side of the room to help her do whatever it is girls do to get ready.

I'm left standing here with Akmal and none of us want to be the first to talk. It's been a little strained between us since the whole 'I fell in love with your sister' thing.

"Look man, I'm not sorry about what happened before."

"I'm not sorry about falling in love with your sister."

"Yeah, I can see that. Just - Just take care of her alright? Make sure she's happy. We're all she's got now."

"Of course. I wouldn't have it any other way. She makes me happy, man. I've made it my mission to keep her as happy as she makes me." Akmal puts his hand on my shoulder and nods. I think we've come to an agreement on this at least.

"Alright, well, unless you're getting married naked, I think you should start getting dressed. You got about fifteen minutes."

"Fabian! Get your ass dressed, I'm not marrying you naked!"

"Ah… my lovely wife calls. Alright, let's do this."

18

———

SAKINAH

*I*s this really happening? I'm walking down this short aisle with Akmal on my arm. I'm sad that the rest of my family can't be here but at least I have support from my new family. The moment I see Fabian standing near the Elvis impersonator, is the moment my eyes start burning with accumulating tears but I try to blink it back so it doesn't streak my mascara down my face. Vero worked her magic on me and I couldn't even recognize myself in the mirror.

Not wanting to choose favorites, Fabian ended up telling both his dad and Akmal that they're his best men. I did the same with Vero and my future mother in law. I don't remember anything the Elvis guy said because he was trying too hard with the accent but time stood still as Fabian put the most beautiful ring on my finger. *When did he even have time to get this?*

We seal our marriage with a kiss and grab the marriage

certificate before we leave the building. The parents tell us they're splitting and going to have fun at the casinos leaving Akmal and Vero the only people left with us.

"You want to hit up the buffet?"

"Didn't I just see you sneak something into your mouth when the Elvis guy was talking?" Vero shoots Fabian a look that would make a normal man cringe.

"I'm pregnant you idiot. I'm fucking hungry. Akmal, take me to a buffet please!"

"Relájate. We'll all go eat, I need to feed my pregnant *wife* anyway."

"How sweet." Vero makes a gagging sound and I laugh my ass off.

Vegas has so many buffets to choose from, I'm surprised Vero can even make a decision. But she does and we all sit down at a booth together once everyone gets their food.

"So, Sakinah, what are you planning to do after you finish school? This is your last semester right?" Vero is making heart eyes at all the plates in front of her as she asks me this.

"Yeah, it is. I haven't thought about it yet."

"You're smart, you'll figure it out." Akmal, always so supportive.

"Why don't you go into structural designs? That project you and Jason were working on was pretty solid."

"But you made that little model."

"Yeah, from *your* notes."

"Fabian made a model of something?"

"Just keep eating, Vero." He flips his sister off and I try not to laugh. Their personalities are contagious.

"I don't know…"

"You know, my buddy Omar and I have talked about starting a business together. Waiting on these contracts can be frustrating because there's never a set period of time that'll be a dry season. That's why we take up private contractor work in the meantime. I've built sheds and extra garages in some of the nicer neighborhoods. Maybe we should start something and you can help us with the design work."

"Really? I don't even know the first thing about that stuff."

"Yes you do. You're smart Sakinah. Don't sell yourself short. I've seen the kind of notes and stuff you write down on your engineering homework. That shit is way out of my league. But together, we might be able to do something good." My cheeks feel hot from all his compliments in front of his sister and my brother. He seems so confident in me. "Plus, I want my wife to be by my side anyway. Can't have other men around her when I'm not there to make my claim, you know?"

"Omar sounds like a guy's name."

"Yeah, but he's an old fucker. We've worked together forever, I trust him. If it makes you feel any better, you can offer something up to that Jason kid, since you guys work well together. He's a good follower and keeps out of trouble."

We continue to eat and talk about random things but my mind is trying to organize everything Fabian is throwing at me. Would it work? Can we start a business together? Me designing blueprints while Fabian puts them together. The thought of Fabian working shirtless around our house gives me tingles. I probably should be there with him so no one tries to take my man from under my nose.

Vero comes back with her fifth plate of food when I finally ask myself: what do I have to lose?

The next day in Vegas was nice, hanging by the pool and walking along the strip. A honeymoon filled with lights and laughter surrounded by great company. I'm almost sad to have to say goodbye to it. But reality calls and time moves forward.

Coming back home as Mrs. Hernandez is weird but exhilarating. My cheesy husband even insisted on carrying me over the threshold, even though we've already been living together for a while.

"Why do you need to carry me over the door? We've been walking over it every damn day."

"Sakinah, quit being a brat and just let me do this."

"Why? I'm not a brat." Standing on the sidewalk in front of our home, I jump when I see Fabian start coming at me from around the driver side of the car, leaving our bags behind. I only make it a few feet when he lifts me up and runs up our stairs, unlocks the door, walks in and drops me unceremoniously onto the couch before heading back outside.

"Asshole."

"I can still hear you!"

"Good!" Getting off the couch, I start to walk towards the door to help grab the bags and bring them into the bedroom to unpack.

Fabian smacks me on the ass when I'm not looking and the sting of the hit still lingers as I stick my tongue out at him.

"You keep that up Sakinah. I know what you want."

"You don't know anything, Mister Hernandez."

"Oh, I believe I do, Mrs. Hernandez."

The asshole didn't let me sleep that night either.

～

Classes started back up quickly, the countdown to graduation getting closer and closer. Jason and I had some classes together and I did in fact bring up the business idea to him.

"Hell yeah! I'd love to work with you guys. Fabian is a genius with his hands. The precision of that model was out of this world. Just tell me when."

"I'll let my husband know you're on board."

"Woah! Your husband? I just saw you guys like a month ago?"

"Yeah... it's a long story."

"Sakinah."

"Huh?"

"Baby, I've been trying to get your attention for the last few minutes. What are you thinking about?" My hand rubs my stomach unconsciously as I look at my husband standing in the kitchen shirtless. I always seem to find myself sitting down somewhere as my thoughts become scattered.

"About graduation and the business."

"Don't worry about it. I'll handle all the details. All you need to bring is your brilliant mind and that puppy that follows you around - what's his face."

"You're such an asshole. You know his name is Jason."

"Yeah, that guy." Throwing a cloth napkin from the table at him, it falls short making me laugh and almost peeing myself. This pregnancy stuff is no joke.

"Sakinah, if you wanted me to bend over for you, all you had to do was ask nicely. Don't go throwing shit in the house."

"I don't think I'm going to walk for graduation."

"Why not?"

"Look at me, I'll be showing even more by then."

"I can barely see anything. Maybe I need to fill you up some more to make sure you're really pregnant."

"Fabian!"

"Damn woman, relájate. It will be fine. Walk up there proudly. I'll be waiting to catch you in case you tumble." How does this man always know the right things to say to make me feel better?

I just kick my feet up on the other chair when there's a knock at the door.

"That must be Omar, I invited him over."

"Why didn't you tell me? I could have at least put something decent on."

"Baby, you look beautiful. Stop. He's just coming in to help me do some stuff in the laundry room I'm setting up. Plus, I haven't seen his ass since the last contract. It'll be good for you to get to know him too since we'll be business partners and all that."

Taking my feet off the chair, I stand up at the exact moment an older middle aged gentleman comes in with a friendly bearded smile.

"Omar! This is my wife, Sakinah."

"I've heard so much about you, glad he wasn't just lying out of his ass." He sticks his hands out to me in greeting. His handshake is firm but kind - and also really dry. *Someone give this man some lotion.*

"Really? What has my beloved *husband* been saying about me exactly?" I side-eye Fabian but all he does is blow a kiss at me.

"It really wasn't what he said, but how he talked about you. I couldn't get him to shut up and get to the damn point of his phone calls. I've never seen Fabian worked up over a girl before."

"Knowing my husband, I'm not sure if I should be flattered or if I should kick his ass." Omar's booming laugh shakes the windows and makes me want to laugh too. His sun weathered face is charming and the way his shoulder shakes is something else.

"Alright. I see why he loves you. You make sure you keep that boy in line."

"You know, I'm standing right fucking here."

"Yeah well what you need to be doing is telling me what the hell you called me over for. What are we doing today?"

"Well, I need to expand this laundry area and add some cabinets on top. I also called you over because we need to follow through on that business venture we've always talked about."

"Yeah, you're down for it? When are we doing this?" Fabian looks at me and then at my stomach and back at Omar.

"Like right fucking now."

19

I was able to convince Sakinah to walk for graduation. No one could even tell she was pregnant under the graduation gown. She cried when she made it back to my arms, I was so proud of her. Hopefully, the baby gets her smarts and my good looks. I bet the baby is going to be a boy, I can feel it. Plus every time she's asleep and I tell him to kick me if he's a boy, he does - so there's that. Already a good kid that listens to his dad.

Omar and I got the business loan and started creating our company: C&H Construction. Some of the guys from the old work site agreed to come on temporarily to help us get a good foothold on our clientele.

Sakinah and Jason work the office we leased, going over ideas on blueprints and whatever else they do in the office. Sakinah is really good with organization, so I leave that shit up to her. Omar's taking a liking to her, always hanging out and dodging work when Sakinah brings food over. Fucker thinks I don't see it. Good thing I'm always hanging out too when she brings food to work.

Sakinah has started to glow even more than she usually does the farther along she gets with this pregnancy. She decided she didn't want to know the gender, so who am I to say anything. I just need the baby to get here so I can put another one in her. I'm excited to be a father. My mother is the most excited of all, coming over and bringing trays and trays of food. You swear she thinks we're both going to starve now that Sakinah is carrying a baby.

"Do I look big in this?" Oh hell no I'm not falling for that shit. Coming up behind her, I hold her and kiss her head.

"You look beautiful, like the woman who's bringing the miracle of life into the world." She looks over her shoulder with a lifted eyebrow. *What?*

"You're just lucky your tongue game is good."

"Yeah? Do you need me to convince you again? You look skeptical. I don't like my wife doubting me."

"Fabian! I mean your way with words."

"I can speak words down there too."

"How can you still love my body when I can barely see my own feet."

"You want me to lick your feet?"

"Dammit, Fabian! Be serious!"

"I am! You look fine. Stop acting like that. I'd love you even if you're spitting out our twentieth kid."

"Twenty kids?!"

The first item off the dresser flies at my head but I managed to duck in time. Damn, it's a good thing I know how to fix drywall because at this rate, there's going to be a million holes.

Atsuko and Vero were kind enough to start buddying up with Sakinah for maternity clothes shopping. I'm glad Sakinah has found new sisters she can hang out with - of course it's not the same as her own but still good.

The boys and I are hanging out at home, checking out the added laundry room Omar and I completed when the sound of the girl's giggles come in through the front door.

"It is so cute! You should just buy everything in neutral colors so you won't have to take anything back!" My sister's voice is, of course, the loudest one.

"That's so smart!"

"Well men, looks like the hens are back in the hen house."

"Cabrón, who are you calling hens? What have you boys been up to since we were out?" Why does she have to be like that? This isn't even her house anyway.

"We painted the damn baby room." The project went fast with two other guys helping me. Sakinah asked me to paint it this weird shade of green and yellow, but what do I know? The baby probably doesn't even care what color the damn room is.

"Oh my god! You did?"

I catch my wife before she can take a tumble and pick her up for a kiss. This pregnancy has made her clumsier but it gives me an excuse to touch her more - and for her to miss when she tries to kick me when she's pissed.

"Of course. Ask and you shall receive. What kind of husband would I be if I didn't do all the hard work?"

"You guys make me sick."

"Vero, be nice." That's right Akmal. You tell her.

"He's mi hermano, I don't need to be nice."

"How you handle her on a daily basis, I will never know, Akmal."

"I don't know either. Ow!" Damn, mi hermana has become even more vicious with this pregnancy.

"You're supposed to back me up."

"Vero, you can be a bit much sometimes." Finally a woman with some sense.

"You too Atsuko?"

"Stop it you two. She's not any better." Damn Mat, you just stuck your foot in your mouth and buried yourself.

"What is that supposed to mean Mat?" Atsuko looks like she's about to withhold sex for the next damn month. I feel sorry for him.

"Nothing!"

I better save these fuckers before they dig their hole any deeper.

"He means that all you hens together start cackling like crazy and it drives the roosters up the wall." Dodging my sister's attempt at throwing a pillow from the couch at my head, I laugh as I go into the kitchen and bring out some snacks.

These crazy pregnant women always calm down when there's snacks.

We all sit down in the living room and start to chat about random things. But the name that comes out of Akmal's mouth makes me tense up.

"What did you just say?"

"That, um, my mother got a recording in the mail and she finally found out the kind of man Amir is." His eyes dart to mine and then to Mat's but the girls don't notice since they're all currently stuffing their faces.

Shit, just hearing that fucker's name makes my blood boil. While the girls were out one day, the boys and I hunted down that asshole. Well, it was more of me hunting his ass down while I dragged Akmal and Mat with me. They didn't believe me when I told them. So what if I have a reputation for being hot tempered? I know what I saw - the way Sakinah looked at me that day will be ingrained into my mind like a damn scar.

"Bisaam was able to set something up for us. He told Amir to meet him up at this place for a get together - like a boys night." It's a good thing Bisaam is a mutual friend or else this wouldn't have worked. Well, I would have made it happen anyway but there's less police involvement this way.

"You think he took the bait?" Mat is already looking through his phone to make sure it goes on record when that fucker gets here.

"Yeah. He likes that kind of uppity shit - going to parties so he can show off something about himself. I never liked him, that's why I never let him come over to my parents' house. But I guess he must have convinced my mother somehow. She invited the whole damn city for our wedding."

"I don't care how that asshole got into the family, he just needs to stay the fuck away because he's not touching another woman in our family like that again." If I had it my way, he would never be allowed to breathe again.

"Shit, I can't believe he hit my sister, man. She's so damn quiet." I chuckle under my breath because he has no idea what Sakinah is like when she lets her filter down.

"Shh.. I think he's coming." We're hiding in the back of an alley by some dumpsters - I know, typical like a bunch of thugs - but we have to get him where no one can see.

His shiny BMW pulls up the back towards us thinking there's a party. It's a deserted building but with enough pedestrian traffic going by with the other buildings that it doesn't rouse that much suspicion.

The moment he opens his door is the moment I come up behind him and use his body to slam the door shut.

"The fuck?" His eyes widen when he sees me and my boys behind me.

"Glad we can meet again, asshole."

"Shit, you already got the bitch, what more do you want?" Punching him in the face, his head whips to the side, blood trailing out the corner of his mouth.

"Excuse me?" I bet my brother-in-law believes me now.

"Fuck, Akmal, I didn't see you there. Nah, I didn't mean anything by it." Yet the words just came out of his damn mouth.

"Like you didn't mean to slap my fucking sister in the face?" Yeah, that's right Amir, look scared because we all know who's the little bitch here. Can't hide behind your lies anymore.

His face goes from pretending to be innocent to something ugly.

"She kept talking back, I was trying to get her to stop. She brought it on to herself." I throw Amir towards Akmal as he lands a punch or two in his gut. I would kill this fucker if I didn't think Sakinah would bury me for getting locked up. Can't leave my pregnant woman alone like that.

Mat's been recording this whole shit, his job is to edit us all out and just get Amir admitting what he did so we can have evidence on him.

I let Akmal get his beating in a few more times before I pull the rich fucker off the ground and slam him onto the hood of his car - It needs a little dent or two anyway, shit has no personality just like its owner.

His head must have been knocked around a little too much because he starts talking right out of his ass the more punches we land in him.

"You can fucking have that whore! I was going to keep her in line and fucking knock her around anyway to get your spawn out of her before I even stick my dick inside that used cunt." Did I think

I was pissed? It was nothing like Mat blowing up and knocking this fucker's teeth out after he pulled me off him.

Both Akmal and I just stepped back as Mat went to town, almost killing the bastard. We were able to pull him off in time, feeling Amir's pulse to make sure he's still breathing. It was later, after we left, that Mat admitted what happened to his parents and the hair trigger he has about guys who beat on women.

Damn, if I ever need some guys to back me up, I'm glad I don't have to look far.

"Yeah? And what did your mom do?" Mat's voice pulls me out of the memory and back into the conversation. The guys are trying to play it cool.

"Well, she was fucking pissed. She started going off on his mother until she found out he was in the hospital. It only toned down her anger a little bit because she felt bad but she's spreading the news about how he tried to trick her into marrying one of her daughters off to him."

"I don't care. I'm glad he got what was coming to him. Fabian is my husband. I would have never chosen Amir even if Fabian wasn't in the picture." Sakinah is pissed as she talks about him.

She stands up and tries to leave the room but I grab her arm and pull her onto my lap and hold her. She doesn't need any more stress, it's not good for the baby.

"Damn fucking straight. My woman is smart, it's what I love about her." Kissing her on the cheek, she calms down a little bit.

My eyes go to Mat and Akmal and they both subtly nod in understanding. What happened that day is a secret that will go to our grave.

EPILOGUE

SAKINAH

"Alex, get away from that!" Oh, the little rascal!

"Alright little man, up you go!" Fabian always amazes me with his timing. It's like he has daddy intuition when his son is up to trouble. I guess the fruit doesn't fall too far from the tree, so he would have a good radar. He lifts our son in his arms and the boy squeals in delight. He loves his daddy. I love his daddy too as I watch him blow on our son's tummy, making him squirm.

At two years old, Fabian's little mini-me, Alejandro, is giving me a run for my money - making me chase him all over the place. Every time it gets quiet, I get scared. Every time I catch him doing something and start to get mad, his little smile and dimples melt my damn heart.

He's got his daddy's smirk too. We named him after his grandfather who started tearing up when we told him the news.

Fabian and Omar built a little playground in the backyard but Alex is still much too small for some of the things. It doesn't stop him from trying. When the girls come over for playdates, Dawn and Yaakob love running around and playing on the swings since they're about four months older than Alex. Who knew that a few months would make such a big difference in kids? But little Alex always tries his best to catch up.

Akmal and Vero decided on a more traditional name for their son, Yaakob while Mat and Atsuko were tired of complicated names and went for something much more simple.

My mother-in-law was so ecstatic about the kids that she started crocheting little baby clothes and blankets all over the place. I'm glad Alex grew up enough to not get his finger stuck between the yarn. His little toddler bed is full of blankets, I can't even keep track of how many since he drags some of his favorites around.

Following the boys inside the backdoor, I waddle myself over the kitchen table and grab a bottle of water.

"Sakinah, baby, sit down. You don't need to be chasing this little guy around. I got him."

"Okay." Finishing the bottle of water, I put it down on the tabletop next to the baby monitor. Little Fernando is still sleeping in his crib soundly - thank goodness he's a deep sleeper.

Rubbing my hand over my belly, I kick my feet up on the other chair to give my ankles some rest. I can hear the boys in the living room playing with toys and so I bring my feet down and stand up to get some food ready. Fabian's sons eat just as much as he does, I don't know how they do it or where they put it. Good thing I love to cook, so I don't mind too much.

Taking out some of the pots and pans, I set the ingredients out for a simple spaghetti meal when the doorbell rings - Fabian had installed one a few years back.

"I got it." Fabian never wants me to do anything but stay barefoot and pregnant.

Continuing what I started, my ears listen intently in case one of the babies needs me. Now that I think of it, I might as well grab the baby monitor and bring it into the kitchen. Walking towards the table to do just that, I hear a voice I never thought I'd hear again.

"Is Sakinah here? Oh-"

"What do you want? You're not going near her."

"She's here to apologize for what she did. Tell him la, I want to see my daughter again." Walao eh - oh my god - Is that my dad?

My eyes start to tear up as I turn off the stove and waddle towards Fabian who is standing at the front door, holding Alex in his arms. My husband does not look happy to see my family and I don't blame him.

"I was trying to bring happiness to my daughter by finding her a husband so she can have her own family. I did not know about Amir and his reputation until later. I did not know."

"That doesn't negate the fact that you - her mother - was abusing my wife when you were trying to get her to marry that good-for-nothing bast -" Fabian stops his tirade just in time as he looks to our son in his arms. It's a heated subject that he never wants to bring up, choosing instead to concentrate on giving his family the best life he can.

"Ibu, bapa." My father's eyes widen and my mother's hand goes to her heart when they see my stomach peeking out from behind my husband. Little Fernando takes that exact moment to start crying and I turn to go to the kid's room to get him. When I return, Fabian still hasn't let my parents through the door yet. I'm not sure what I should do.

"Sakinah. I didn't know." She makes this sniffing noise while crossing her arms almost side-eyeing me. "I made a mistake, Sakinah."

"It doesn't matter, Ibu. Even if you did, I still love Fabian. I do not want anyone else."

"Your Ibu means well. She can get carried away sometimes. I am glad you are doing okay. These are all your babies?"

Rocking Fernando on my hip, he hides his face into my chest, not recognizing them. I can see the hurt in my Bapa's eyes but they did this to themselves. Though my mind tells me this, I don't know why my chest and heart still feels so heavy with guilt.

The sound of another car pulls up and my eyes leave my parents standing there awkwardly when I see Vero, Akmal and Yaakob come out. When my parents turn to look at our new visitors, my eyes go to Fabian, unsure of what I should do.

"You tell me what you want, baby. I'm here for you, not for them." That's the hard part, I don't know what I want - I don't know what to do. Hugging him and squishing our babies in between, I take a deep breath, taking in his comfort and strength.

"Bapa, Ibu, what are you doing here? Don't upset Sakinah, it's not good for the baby." My brave brother gives our mother a stern look as he nudges her with his hand. Vero is curling her lip at Ibu while holding Yaakob on her hip.

"Aiyoh, okay, I made a mistake Sakinah." It doesn't sound like she means it at all. My mother will always be my mother, too prideful to apologize for what she did.

Bapa tries to fix her apology by inserting himself after

her. "Sorry for all the trouble. We won't make the same mistake again." Ibu stares at him like it was his fault to begin with. I just can't with her.

But my deeply ingrained manners refuse to let them stand out there any longer. "Okay, come in and sit down everyone." Poor Akmal and Vero are still staring daggers at Ibu. She has to feel the tension around her.

Leading by example, I turn and put Fernando on the floor as Fabian does the same with Alex. Yaakob is already squealing as he runs past his grandparents to go play with his cousins. My brother ushers our parents towards the kitchen table and Vero comes to help me finish the spaghetti I put on hold. I was going to make extra anyway so there will be plenty for our last minute guests - Fabian will just have to go into the pantry for a snack if he's still hungry.

Awkward silence and small talk ensue as Vero and I start serving up plates and making sure the kids have their share at their little table in the corner next to us.

Murmurs of 'bismillah' and 'buen provecho' go around the table and we all start to eat in awkward silence.

"So you have another baby coming huh? Is it going to be a boy? Or a girl? Is it twins? Triplets?" I choke on my spaghetti as Fabian laughs out loud making the kids laugh and squeal. Vero is slapping my back as Akmal tries to hold back a grin.

My mother continues her interrogation of my life like nothing ever happened.

We continue to eat, the mood lightened by my Ibu's outburst. My gaze sweeps over the table and watch as all of us find ourselves smiling at each other and conversing more easily, the tension from earlier slowly melting away.

My heart feels so full that my eyes start to tear up again. *These damn hormones are going to kill me.* Fabian grabs my hand under the table and gives me a smirk and a wink reminding me that life is what we make of it.

I was always scared to find out what the consequences of our actions held, how it would blow up in our faces. The cultural obligations and fear of the unknown crippling what our future had in store for us. It was Fabian's strength that got me through my toughest times, when my mind was starting to fall into the depression of our consequences. And it was Fabian and the children who kept me going even when my family issues seemed like there was no way of fixing itself.

But here we sit surrounded by loved ones, forgiven and finally...at peace with everything that has come to pass.

When the constrictions of labels limit us. Sometimes it takes the right person to be strong enough to unravel the stereotypes and wrap us in the right kind of lace.

PLAYLIST

Big Bad Voodoo Daddy - Why Me?
Luis Fonsi feat. Daddy Yankee - Despacito
Imelda May - Johnny Got a Boom Boom
Pedro Capó, Farruko - Calma
Jencarlos Canela feat. Kymani Marley - Bajito
Haley Reinhart - Can't Help Falling In Love

If you get your kicks in a magical manner, order toys from websites like bad dragon, and prefer your monsters *in* your bed instead of *under* them, then Y. D. is your girl.

Writing everything from spicy dark fantasy to fluffier-than-a-cool-marshmallow romance, Y.D. La Mar has her fingers in all sorts of man-meat pie, and the sky is the limit. Somehow, this magical mistress manages to balance her spicy author life with her responsibilities as a mom, a wife, and a resident of Sin City—*oh, irony, you've felled me.*

When the world is full of black-and-white, Y.D. plays in the grey zones, spending her time creating new ways to shock and awe her editor, as well as her readers.

Follow Me!

WANT UPDATES AND SNEAK PEEKS?

Sign up for my newsletter!

ALSO BY YD LA MAR

STREET ARRHYTHMIA TRILOGY

The Scent of Jasmine

For The Love of Import & Blood

To The Beat of The Streets

Spinoff

Arachnophilia

REVERSE HAREM

Warring Suns

SCI FI

The Essence of Esme

PARANORMAL

The Hunger of Thieves

Heart of The Reaper

Heart of the Reaper: Tales from the Underworld

Soul of The Reaper

Fate of The Reaper

Bury Me Alive

Lead Me Through The Fire

PSYCHOLOGICAL THRILLER

The Truth Enslaved

CONTEMPORARY

The Formation of Us

The Conception of Us

The Revelation of Us

The House of Eden (cowrite)

When the Bloom Burns (cowrite)

OMEGAVERSE

Gero

Bernhard

Severin

DYSTOPIAN/POST APOCALYPTIC

We Are the Fallen

MONSTER SHORT STORIES

Sinful Attraction

The Sky Below

Maeonia

Between Heaven and Earth

Fantasies Inflamed

Her 13th Hour

Ignus Fatuus

ANTHOLOGIES

Used and Bound

Captured by Darkness

Until the End

After the Rain

Into The Woods

A Foster Fling

Bound by Monsters

Once Upon a Nightmare

Monsters in Love: Lost in the Dark

Monsters in Love: Lost in the Forest

Monsters in Love: Monstrous Ever After

Monsters in Love: Lost in the Deeps

Monsters in Love: Aloha Nui Loa

Pollinators

The Red Key Club: Valentines Day Edition

The Red Key Club: Halloween Edition

Creepy Court

Crimson Vendetta

For the Love of Villains

SHARED WORLDS

Inferno World

Games of the Underworld

Rise of the Dreads

Monsters Ball

Rescue Me: A Hero Romance Collection